HURRAH FOR LIBERTY

To Vicki
Life begins where your comfort zone
ends. Thanks for the push over
the edge. *[signature]*
06-19-2019

ORAN BRUCKS

Tellwell Talent
www.tellwell.ca

ISBN
978-0-2288-1196-1 (Paperback)
978-0-2288-1725-3 (eBook)

To Theresa and our many adventures that still await.

There's a race of men that don't fit in, A race that can't sit still; So, they break the hearts of kith and kin, And they roam the world at will. They range the field and rove the flood, And they climb the mountain's crest; Theirs is the curse of the gypsy blood, And they don't know how to rest.
Robert W. Service

CHAPTER 1

Out across the water, the last waning rays of the full moon shone off the crests of the riffles sparkling above the waves in an effervescent procession of ethereal flashes and crystal sparks as the night began to yield her hold of the land to the approaching dawn. The air, which had sat so patiently still through the night, now stirred, rising and twirling in a translucent mist. First, as if confused in sulky spirals, then, acknowledging the warmth of the rising sun, the air swept forward to meet the morning light. Drawn towards the dawn's early warmth, the air moved in undulating yet steady waves over the river, across the banks to the forest beyond, carrying with it the damp cold of the trout-laden waters, the mustiness of the willows, the pungent aroma of decaying leaves littering the forest floor, and the scent of men.

From all of these familiar smells, the scent of men roused Major from his slumber. Raising one sleep-laden eyelid, then another, Major lifted his keen hound's snout to test the air, searching for and finding the scent. He slowly pushed out his forelegs and hefted his body reluctantly from the warm comfort of the floor while keeping his head lowered to keep the scent in his nostrils lest he loses it by moving. Now it came stronger, the smell of men moving towards him and his home, his master's home. Suddenly, from deep within his great black chest, thrust forth by a primitive protective instinct, he burst into a low snorting growl.

Abe Springer woke with a start. Lying still, he looked quickly about the cabin, darting his eyes left and right, peering about the dark, and gauging the danger. Deftly and quietly, he rolled sideways out of the bed and with the swiftness and stealth of a barnyard cat quietly crossed the cabin floor in three smooth, stealthy paces. With an eye to the cabin door and the potential peril beyond he seized his rifle from its peg on the mantle and in a smooth, practiced motion checked the priming on the flintlock and cleaned the head of the flint with his thumbnail. Throwing his powder horn and bag over his shoulder, he crept cautiously to the firing ports cut into the cabin windows.

Abe was a cautious man. His vigilance had been borne from a lifetime spent on the edge of frontiers where death came in a myriad of ways: slow, cruel, frightening, and sudden, mostly sudden. He did not immediately look through the firing slot but instead held in the shadows behind, well aware that many an unsuspecting settler's life had ended in a fusillade of gunfire aimed at a bright moonlit face peering into the night from a darkened cabin.

"Indians?" Abe wondered to himself in a mutated mumble. "It's the season." The onset of summer was the traditional time for the first war parties to sweep down from the North. The bright moon was called a hunter's moon as this was when men hunted men. Abe watched and waited. Major's growl alerted him to a distant motion. Off in the morning gloom, a barely discernible movement drew his attention. Men were moving towards the ford in the river, just below the cabin.

Abe drew the hammer back slowly, and it cocked with a loud "Snap." Like a slap in the face, the sound woke Marie from her sleep; she whispered sleepily, "Abe?"

Abe silenced her with a low hiss and tensed himself to the rifle. Out past the ford, running along the shore, two men intermittently flitted in and then out of the early morning mist. Ghostlike they appeared and disappeared, shadows more than men, never coming out of the fog long enough at this great distance for a clear look. The men ran in long strides, Indian-fashion, bounding over the scrub willows and cane along the bank. Abe squinted intently into the gloom. Waiting. Anxious. Afraid. Ready.

The sudden "click" of Marie cocking the spare rifle startled him from his thoughts; his eyes remained unwaveringly fixed on the bounding shadows in the mist. Slowly, Abe removed the powder bag and horn from his shoulder without turning and passed them to Marie who was now standing behind him. Their fingers touched ever so briefly; for a short moment each was reassured and calmed by the presence of the other. How many times had they faced peril standing together like this in the darkness? Marie, always trusting in Abe's cool nerves and marksmanship to make every shot count. Abe, trusting in Marie to reload and keep one rifle readily at hand for a second shot. This mutual trust and cooperation had kept the Springers together and alive through all the hard times.

The men cleared the fog. Silhouetted against the gray background, the men's broad-brimmed hats and long rifles carried at arm's length and reaching strides identified them as long hunters. "But, who?" Abe whispered to himself, lifting his rifle to the edge of the window port. He pulled the rear set trigger so that the tender caress of the front trigger would fire the rifle.

The hunters turned towards the ford and, with rifles and powder horns held high over their heads, plunged into the icy river. Their pace slackened as they met the resistance of the current; pressed by it, they pushed slowly through the depths as the water held them in its frigid grasp, swirling and gurgling around their thighs like cherubs in a merry dance.

Soon, Abe thought. Soon I must fire before they leave the river and gain the concealment and shelter of the forest darkness behind. He drew the rifle to his cheek, the front and rear sight searched for each other, and the barrel swung to the chest of the lead man. Abe exhaled slowly; then, holding the last partial breath, he began the final tender squeeze of the trigger.

Suddenly, from behind the front man, a great wolf-dog leapt forward in springy splashy bounds, cleared the water in a flying leap to the shore, and disappeared into the underbrush.

Abe sighed. The tension flowed out of him like whiskey from a mug. He turned to Marie, a small wry smile on his lips, and said calmly, "Tanners."

Springing from the river, Travis cleared the embankment like a deer over a split rail-fence. Tiny spirals of icy droplets spun off the fringes of his leggings and sprayed under his wamus, soaking his back with their frigid embrace. His waterlogged moccasins splashed and squished as he sought a soft footfall amongst the rock-strewn shore, neither lengthening or shortening the mile-consuming pace he had maintained since early evening the night before.

With a quick glance to the darkened cabin, Travis acknowledged the home of Abe and Marie Springer with a wave of his rifle over his head. He smirked grimly at the thought of Abe watching him over the sights of his long rifle. The Springers had lived on this edge of the frontier too many years to be surprised by the racket Squib and he had been making crashing about the river. A cold shiver sliced up his back as he imagined the flash in the dark, the sudden burning impact of a ball punching into his belly, and the ringing, CRACK — POP — in his ears as his legs were knocked from under him by the bullet.

No shot came. Travis passed the shore into the forest trace beyond.

From behind him, Travis could hear the last splash as his brother Squib left the river, and beyond that, the panting crashing of Fidious, their wolf-dog, frolicking in the brush along the shore and searching for rabbits. Once more the gloom of the forest trail, sheltered from the first rays of the dawn by the entanglement of branches and leaves above, wrapped around the runners like a black robe. Neither looking down or around they ran on, trusting to their instincts and a high-stepping lope to prevent them from crashing off the path. Many hours before, a messenger had arrived at their encampment with news that their father Aaron had been critically injured several days before. Leaving the messenger to guard their winter cache of hides, Travis and Squib had immediately set off at a mile-eating pace, pushing themselves to speed their trail home.

Thinking of his father, Travis felt a yearning emptiness. He recalled a hollow memory he had not felt for some time, a grim reminder he had been away on his first long hunt when his mother Rachel had died suddenly of the fever. Squib and he had run through the night then too, only to arrive home where Aaron stood bowed over the freshly dug grave, hands and forehead pressed to the spade, tears coursing down the handle in tiny cascades.

Arriving too late to say goodbye, too late to do anything except feel helpless, Travis had burdened himself with guilt at his mother's death, and now once again he had been away when his father needed him the most. Spurred by his guilt and anxiety, compounded by a fear that he may be too late again, Travis lengthened his stride and quickened his pace. Squib, grunting with exertion, strained to keep up. Fidious, sensing the new urgency, sprang ahead, assuming the vanguard, his great head swinging from side to side as if on a spring, constantly searching the trail ahead for the scent of danger.

Chapter 2

Beth escorted the doctor to the landing. She stood silently, staring pensively at the bottle of laudanum he had placed in her hands while he mumbled some instructions for its use. The doctor continually and apologetically shook his head while he spoke the only words of encouragement he could offer, "It will be painless now." Then, with a tip of his hat he turned, strode to his horse, mounted without looking back, and rode away.

Holding the small brown bottle close to her face, she was barely able to read the worn handwritten label. "For pain" was the only portion she could decipher. "For pain," she said quietly. All the doctor could do was give Aaron some painkiller. No cure, no attempt to repair the massive damage to his chest, no words of reassurance, just that constant clucking and head-shaking like a hen over her broken eggs.

Apprehensively, she looked up over her shoulder. Aaron lay asleep in his bed, covers drawn down to his waist to keep even that small weight off his shattered chest. From the porch, she could hear the rasping scrape of the crushed ribs grinding against each other with his every pained breath. His once barrel-shaped muscular chest was now reduced and distorted to remind her more of a bubbling pot of oatmeal. She had never realized a human body could be so easily crushed. The accident had happened so swiftly she still had difficulty believing it had occurred, even though she had witnessed the entire event. Thinking back to the moment of the accident, she wondered if she could have prevented it somehow. "No," she told herself. Helplessness always breeds guilt. She had no warning; how could anyone know, except there had been that sense of dread whenever Chester McKay was present.

Chester had arrived in the evening, just as the Tanners had sat down to their evening meal. As always, he was too impolite to accept their hospitality and too impatient to wait for them to finish supper, so he stood on the veranda mumbling to himself while the family ate. Annoyed with Chester's continued rudeness, Aaron had gulped down his meal and stomped out of the cabin. With Chester at his heels yapping like a spoiled lap dog, they headed towards the shop.

Aaron and Chester had been at odds ever since McKay had moved into the area some years earlier. Aaron had little use for McKay and his mean mannerisms and whining attitude, but the elder Tanner was the only gunsmith for a hundred miles, the best known in the county, and so professional pride kept him from throwing Chester out of his house. If a man needed a repair, even when it was the result of abuse or poor maintenance (which was always the situation with Chester), then Aaron would do his best to repair the rifle. Chester's complaint today was the usual one of a faulty mainspring. As usual, there was nothing wrong with the spring except that Chester kept his rifle constantly cocked. Eventually it lost its strength and lacked the backbone to strike the flint. But Aaron had long ago given up on trying to convince Chester of the risks of carrying a rifle always cocked.

With his head down and teeth gritted, Aaron walked blindly across the darkened yard and surprised Chester's mule that was tethered to the shop railing. Unexpectedly, the mule kicked out with both hind feet striking Aaron full in the chest. Aaron had been thrown through the air like a circus tumbler. The sickening crunch of hooves crushing bone assaulted Beth's ears as she stood on the veranda. Startled, she felt more than heard Aaron come down hard on the stairs below the cabin threshold. Confused, she stepped into the darkness, down the steps, and bent over Aaron's groaning body.

"John," she cried, "bring the lamp. Aaron's hurt!"

Her husband John, Aaron's eldest son, came running with the candle lantern; the dim light flickered over them as Beth drew back in horror. Aaron lay on his back, his chest laid open through his ripped and torn shirt. Tiny wells of purple-red blood pulsated, swirling and eddying amongst the harsh white shards of splintered bone protruding from the ruptured skin; bubbles frothed and burst along the edges. John bent and lifted his unconscious father gently into his arms. He whispered, "Beth, light the way," and followed her through the house into the back bedroom. He laid Aaron carefully on the bed and gently began to pull the fragments of the torn shirt from the wounds. He worked quickly, pulling at the sticky pieces of gore-soaked cloth. Some pieces stuck to his fingers and he flicked them distastefully away with a snap of his wrist.

"Oh, dear God," Beth moaned as the bloody rags hit the wall and slithered to the floor leaving behind a crimson trail.

"Beth, ask Chester to ride to Doc Hardy's for help," John asked. Beth ran through the house into the yard. The hitching rail was empty. Chester had run off.

Pulling up her skirts as she ran, Beth jumped over the corral fence, seized John's saddle horse by the bridle, and threw herself onto the horse's bare back. Without dismounting, she bent over, opened the gate, and whipping the horse across the yard, she shouted, "John, I'm riding to Hardy's — McKay's run off."

Inwardly Beth shivered as she recalled the frenetic ride to Doc Hardy's. Her fear for Aaron overwhelmed her dread of the dark forest, and she had galloped through the night.

Freezing and sopping wet from the many stream crossings, her arms and face lashed and scratched by unseen branches and thorns, her red hair streaming behind in a fiery mane, she charged across the meadow before the doctor's home, shouting, "Doc Hardy, Doc Hardy!" Dashing to the edge of the landing, she threw herself off the horse and flung herself through the front door, landing in the arms of a very much surprised Dora Hardy.

"Aaron's been kicked — need the doctor — come quick," Beth panted between ragged breaths.

Dora pulled a chair from the table and carefully placed it under Beth before she replied, "He's not here. He went down the river yesterday." Beth sagged in exhaustion and despair.

"Don't worry, dear; I'll send Thomas after him and go back with you myself," Dora added.

Turning to her son who was still tugging on his clothes and rubbing the sleep from his eyes, she said, "Thomas, get in your canoe and get your Pa, quick." Turning back to Beth slumped in the chair, she asked gently, "Are the boys home, or is it just you and John then?"

"Yes," Beth rasped, "Travis and Squib are hunting on Eagle Creek."

Looking for her son just leaving the cabin, Dora called, "Thomas, ask Ben if he could ride north and bring the boys back, and do hurry."

From a milk pail in the corner of the cabin, Dora dipped a ladle and steadied it carefully in Beth's hand. "Drink this while I get some things, then we'll be getting you home."

Dora was no rider. The ride back took much longer than Beth would have wished and she fretted at their slowness. The house was dark when they returned, the silence hanging ominously over them as they entered. Beth followed apprehensively as Dora strode swiftly through to the back bedroom. They entered the room together. Aaron lay on the bed, bare from the waist up. His chest was now grotesquely swollen and misshapen. Horrifically, the splotches of black where John had applied pine tar to staunch the bleeding quivered like a hungry army of huge spiders feasting on the tortured blue-green flesh below. Aaron, now conscious, acknowledged Beth and Dora's arrival with the slightest lift of his eyebrow. A shudder of pain was his reward for even that small movement.

John rose expectantly from the chair beside the bed and silently questioned Dora with his look. "Shh," she whispered, "the good doctor will be here soon."

Now, as Beth looked at the brown bottle in her hand, remembering the anxious wait for the doctor seemed like another world and time. The sleepless night, the helplessness, the waiting, and waiting. The doctor finally came, and all hope left with the terrible truth. Now the wait would begin again, this time the wait for the end.

"God," Beth prayed aloud, "please bring the boys home and speed Aaron from his pain." Hiding her teary eyes, Beth turned away as John stepped onto the porch and placed his arms gently around her. Settling his head on her shoulder, he nodded towards the road and the running figures in the distance. Her tears turned to great ragged sobs as John said, "They are home."

Aaron awoke to the familiar musty smell of oily wood-smoked buckskins which permeated the entire house within minutes of Travis and Squib's return from one of their long hunts. The pungent odor had always produced cries of indignation from Rachel and Beth, followed closely by a flurry of activity as they heated wash tubs of bath water and hurried the boys to undress. Modesty forgotten, in an emotional outpouring of good-natured bantering, hugs, kisses, and the occasional tear, from the wood smoke, they would say, the boys were stripped, bathed, and returned to a civilized state. Aaron welcomed the acrid aroma for the warm glow of wellbeing it produced; the odor was a signal announcing that the boys had returned safely from another hunt. For a few moments, Aaron allowed the warm contentment to flood over him before he slowly opened his eyes. John and Travis were standing at the foot of the bed. John was holding Travis at arm's length, his large hands on his younger brother's shoulders. He was speaking to him in a low whisper. Travis, distraught, struggled against his brother's powerful grip. Aaron watched his sons. How dissimilar they are, he thought. Not so much physically, for they were all tall, well-muscled, and dark-skinned from living in the outdoors. John's brawny blacksmith's chest and thick arms stood in contrast to Travis' wiry almost feline leanness. Squib's towering ursine presence seemed to round out the trio. While their physical appearances were similar, their characters were different. John, the eldest, older by a decade, had already assumed the mantle of leadership in the family. Solid was the only way to describe John. From working side by side in the gun shop these last few years an unusual relationship had evolved; they had become more than master and apprentice or father and son. They had become close friends. Maybe the isolation, absence of neighbors, and the long hours working together had kept them from developing relationships with others. Even John's recent marriage to Beth had not changed their closeness. If anything, Beth's youthful exuberance had infected them all and brought them closer as a family. Aaron felt proud that John would carry on building rifles and, like himself, was known for his skills as a gunsmith. At least John would carry on the family business; his other sons were completely different.

Squib, his adopted son, stood almost a head taller than his brothers. His new beard hid his youth and gave him a dark, brooding look until you looked into his bright blue eyes and saw the mirth that glittered behind all that hair. Sensitive and gentle, usually quiet, when Squib had something to say, he did so with a few well-chosen words. Preferring witticism bordering on humorous, his words were usually spoken in kindness without a trace of pettiness.

Travis, Aaron thought, is everything Squib and John could or would never be. Rash, headstrong, and as unpredictable as a throw of the dice, every cast was different and unknown until the roll stopped. An enigma, Travis somehow never quite fit together with his brothers. Not that he was bad or rude, he was mischievous; he tended to do the right things for the wrong reasons. Travis was mercurial like his mother. But then those Drurys were all like that: stoic and sophisticated till some small thing, a small indiscretion or a veiled threat, and they were at your throat. But the big things, those were thinking problems, and they would sit and think and think. While others were running or hiding, they would be thinking, patiently waiting, before venturing an opinion or giving voice to their decision or thoughts. That was Rachel. During the war with the Shawnee raiding from the North, the countryside around them in flames, Aaron had wanted to abandon the smithy and go down the river to Harrisburg. "No," Rachel said, "we're not leaving our home without some thought first." And think she did. For three days and nights, the terror-stricken and wounded refugees streamed past the cabin in droves, each with a new story of burning and killing, all headed for safety. All the while, Rachel had to think. No amount of arguing or entreating or threats would sway her. Finally, on the third night, she had come to him and said firmly, "This is our home, we built it, and we'll stay." And that was that.

But the little things really set Rachael off, like the first time McKay had come to the house after he built his ramshackle cabin up on Black Creek. Rachel, always so hospitable and friendly, had invited him into the house for tea and biscuits. Chester had no more than sat down when he started to complain, "All Pennsylvania gunsmiths are dishonest, robbing poor settlers with their poor workmanship and haughty German talk." Before he could even finish the sentence, Rachel had cracked him over the head with one of her best tea cups. What a scene that had been, with Chester scrambling across the floor like a hound on all fours while Rachel towered over him, scolding him for his bad manners and worse upbringing. Chester probably still had splinters in his knees from that day.

So much like his mother, Aaron thought, Travis could do much worse. A warm inner glow washed over him at the thought of Rachel. Memories flashed across his mind of their life together. Rachel, her raven hair streaked in later years with silver, dancing dark eyes so bright and vibrant, steadfast and strong through their many hardships. While the war had raged around them, Rachel ministered to the injured, the refugees, and the homeless while he repaired their broken firearms so they could defend themselves. Taking tiny Squib from a settler who found him abandoned at a burnt-out homestead, she had adopted him as her own. So many images and memories ran wildly around Aaron's head; he couldn't focus on any one thought. The more he tried, the harder it was. He concentrated, trying to remember Rachel's face, her laugh, and her smile. How could he ever forget her smile? She stood by his side, smiling quietly down on him. Pain forgotten, Aaron smiled back.

Squib saw his father's smile first. "Travis," he whispered, "look." Travis and John turned and came together to the side of the bed.

"He knows we are here; look at his smile," Squib said.

Taking his father's hand, Travis said, "I'm home, Pa." Aaron couldn't hear him; he had finally rejoined Rachel.

Chapter 3

Great succulent drops of melted butter dripped from the bright yellow cornbread as Squib swirled it about the outer rim of the trencher. Drowned in rich brown gravy, the bread disappeared into his mouth.

"More?" Beth asked, smiling.

"Oh, no," Squib, replied, shaking his head, extending one hand held palm forward while the other patted the hard slabs of his belly.

After a moment's thought, he said, "Well, maybe just a little more. Please." Beth ladled stew onto Squib's trencher for the third time that evening.

Holding a large piece of cornbread, she asked, "Bread?"

"Oh, no. Well. Yes. Thank you." Taking the bread, he buried it into the butter jar and scooped the contents out onto his plate.

"There's a big slice of apple pie left," Beth said.

"Oh, no," Squib replied, giving the pie the hungry eye. "Well. It's very good pie, maybe with some cream on top. Please."

John and Travis shook their heads, puffing out their cheeks and rolling their eyes at each other in wonder and merriment.

"Next time, Beth," John said, "just fill the apple barrel with flour and sugar and bake the whole thing so Squib can eat it all at once."

"No. No," Travis laughed, "just stuff a whole cow with cornbread and apples and roast them together." Squib reddened as his brothers laughed and made grunting noises at him.

"Don't let these hogs bother you," Beth chuckled. "They only wish they could have as a good an appetite as you. And don't you be laughing at Squib, John Tanner. I remember the time when you ate most of the cherries off the cherry tree, and you disappeared into the little house out back for two days."

Gravy and butter dripping down his beard, Squib acknowledged the story with a smile and nodded in agreement with Beth. She smiled and winked. It's so good to hear them all laugh again, she thought. Aaron's death had been such a shock, but now they sounded like their old selves. If we will ever truly be ourselves or the same again. Death had marched through their lives so many times these last few years, Rachel first, struck down so suddenly by the fever. And then when they thought the epidemic had passed, death had countermarched through their ranks again, striking out both her parents in one vicious swipe. God, she wished the boys would stay home a little longer before they left, but John was right, inactivity only left them too much time for mourning. With Aaron's funeral done and the condolences said by the many attendees, it was time for the brothers to return to the forest they loved and let time bury their sorrow in the wilderness.

"With an appetite like that," Travis said, "we'll never be able to carry enough ball and powder to keep us in game for our trip west."

"You'll have to shoot every deer from the Susquehanna through to the Mississippi to do it," John jested.

"When will you be leaving then?" asked Beth, trying to direct the conversation away from Squib. She instantly regretted the reminder since only a week had passed since Aaron's funeral. Folks had attended from miles around, for Aaron was well-known both as a gun builder and as a good man who helped anyone in need, whether with a few coins or by rolling up the sleeves on his muscled arms to help with chores or build homes and barns.

"The day after tomorrow or whenever Squib's done eating — whichever is the soonest," Travis replied.

Pushing away from the table and standing up, John said, "Come to the shop, and we'll see to your gear before Squib rediscovers his appetite."

Leaving the house together, they all walked across the yard to the smithy. The shop had remained closed since Aaron's death. The moment weighed heavily on them all as John opened the large double doors, letting the sunlight shine in. Aaron had built the workshop facing south to allow as much sunshine to light the shop during the day. That was his father, Travis thought, always paying attention to detail. Everything was well-thought-out and carefully planned. The forge was situated along the east wall so that the prevailing winds from the west blew the smoke from the fire that burnt all day long, away from the shop and the house behind it. The workbenches were made of heavy slabs of rough-hewn pine for stability, topped with smoothed hard oak for a work surface. Files, chisels, drills, hammers, augers, saws, gimlets, and mallets were arranged by size or purpose in neat rows on the back of the workbench. Rifles, ready for sale, hung from brass hooks set into the wall along the front of the shop. There were long rifles with brass and silver patch boxes, all oiled and polished; sharp tomahawks of steel and iron; powder horns of assorted sizes, white steer horns, and the larger amber hewed buffalo horns. Under these, in wooden boxes on a shelf lay smaller accessories: vent picks hammered from iron, pan brushes of hog bristle, copper bore brushes, good English musket flints, and brass bottles of sperm whale oil. In the rear, curly maple stock blanks of varying quality were hung and seasoned till judged suitable for carving. Billets of iron and brass stacked in the corners waited to be fashioned into flint pans, gun hammers, trigger guards, toe plates, and rifle barrels.

Here, first John, then later Travis and Squib, had spent many hours a day working with their father. Under Aaron's tutelage, they learned the rudiments of the gunsmith's craft by building rifles from the rough wood blanks and raw iron billets. In teaching his sons, Aaron was the most organized and patient of all. He began the lessons before they ever touched a rifle, and first taught them how to use the tools correctly. Each tool had a specific use and each tool must be constantly maintained in a specified manner. Travis remembered his father, his gray hair encircling growing baldness, his kindly patient manners, and his precise English tinged with the slightest trace of old German.

"The file," Aaron would say, illustrating as he spoke, "must only be pushed forward, across the metal; never draw the file backwards over the surface. Slow, steady strokes," he would caution. "Take off too much metal and the piece is lost. Now, you try." Files for steel, files for iron, files for brass. Tools to maintain the tools. Soft brushes and hard, coarse, and fine whetstones. Oils on this part and grease on that one. From early in the morning to sunset every evening the lessons continued. Every instruction was accompanied by a lesson within a lesson. "When a man buys one of my rifles, it is an expression of trust," he would say. "He trusts that rifle for his survival, to feed himself with the game he shoots, to defend his home and family against intruders and oppressors. Trust cannot be bought, my sons; it is given freely only after you have earned it. No rifle leaves my shop that I would not trust myself. There are many kinds of trust which you will learn and grow to accept in life. There is the trust that a man and woman share when they become husband and wife, like your mother and me. In that trust we have grown stronger together. And although you are just a boy, the day will come when you too will find a woman, and fall in love. Don't wrinkle your nose at me; the day will come, and then you will learn to savor that trust, for there is no other like it. There are times that you may be betrayed by a trust that you have given. Then you must be strong and allow yourself to trust again, no matter the pain, for to do otherwise will make you weak. Remember this: to love and trust makes you strong while hate and unfaithfulness are weaknesses. I see that you are too young to understand these things, or perhaps it is I who cannot explain them. If God had wanted me to shape ideas, he would have made me a carpenter instead of a gunsmith."

Sadly, while John excelled at his father's craft, Travis and Squib only showed the most elementary talent or desire to learn gunsmithing. The joy of rifles for Travis and Squib lay not in the building, but in the weapons use. They were fueled by stories of frontier adventures — heroes like Daniel Boone and Simon Kenton, the callous villain Simon Girty, long hunts and exploration, men known and experiences shared — recited by their uncle Wes Drury. Boys of the wilderness they became, yearning for the forest trails, rifle and tomahawk in hand, hunting for game to fill the larder, furs which could be exchanged for provisions, and hard cash. Here the brothers excelled. Through this Aaron remained patient, giving advice and counsel, but never scolding or criticizing. Instead, he chose to support their wildness and by so doing gave them direction. It was Aaron who first suggested that Travis and Squib travel to visit their uncle Wes in St. Louis and accompany him on one of his long hunts on the western plains. This suggestion was eagerly accepted by the young brothers, who announced much to their mother's dismay that they would leave early the next morning. No, Aaron diplomatically cautioned, it was the wrong season for a journey across the continent. Such an expedition required preparation and training. Aaron reminded his sons that the famous Lewis and Clark expedition had required almost three years of planning before the explorers had embarked into the wilderness. The first step, Aaron said, was for the boys to write to their uncle Wes and request his permission to accompany him on one of his hunting expeditions. The boys had stayed awake all that night, sitting huddled together at the table, composing in their very best handwriting a long essay, clearly and with no modesty whatsoever explaining how advantageous their presence would be should they encounter wild savages, vicious beasts, or, accounting for Wes' age and all, hard physical labor. There was considerable hot discussion whether they should mention anything related to work, knowing how consumed adults became at the mention of the work.

The next morning Aaron woke to find the boys standing beside the bed, the completed letter held in their outstretched hands ready for his approval. "May I have my morning tea before I undertake to read this let… this omnibus," he asked, moaning inwardly as he realized that the boys must have used every sheet of his precious and expensive paper. The boys resolutely shook their heads. "No, somehow that doesn't surprise me," he said, and he sat up and begun to read. Rachel cuddled closer to him and read over his shoulder, jabbing him playfully in the ribs to remind him of the boy's somber presence when he started to laugh at their eager entreaties to their uncle. Solemnly he pronounced the letter a masterpiece, with a few spelling errors, which would no doubt be corrected very quickly, and he gravely returned the document to the boys, who scampered off to complete the corrections while their parents hid under the covers convulsing in laughter.

The letter had been only the first of many steps that Aaron had instigated leading up to the day when the boys would be prepared for the long journey west. In the ensuing years, the boys, under the tutelage of their father and elder brother, would learn and practice the many skills necessary for them to undertake, as Travis chose to call it, "their grand adventure." Now, after those years of preparation, after successful long hunts on their own in the mountains of Western Pennsylvania, they were on the verge of their grand adventure. Only now there was no glory, no excitement, and only a lonely sadness which they all felt as they stood silently and maybe for the last time together as a family.

John walked to the back of the shop and returned a few moments later with two long buckskin-wrapped objects. Curious, Travis with Squib following, stepped forward.

"Pa," the word stuck in John's throat. "Pa knew that one day you boys would want to head west. So, we put our heads together and decided to build you both a traveling gift."

John gave one rifle to Travis, the other to Squib. Dropping the buckskin wrappings to the floor, Travis marveled at the long rifle in his hands. A Lancaster style stock of dark hewed and richly polished curly maple, incised with intricate inlays and scroll work, gleamed and spoke of endless hours of labor with oil and bare hands. Set in the wood was a finely wrought brass patch box, its elaborate design incorporating numerous overlays mixed into a beautiful mosaic of brass and wood. The brass thimbles, ramrod pipes, nose caps, and trigger guard enclosing two set triggers were all engraved with a simple yet striking pattern of flowers and leaves. Travis recognized the lock as one of several expensive English waterproof flint locks specifically built for their reliability and almost exclusively used for matching sets of dueling pistols Aaron occasionally built to custom order. Travis turned the rifle slowly in his hands and saw, inlaid on the cheek piece and surrounded by a complex blend of relief carving with inlaid wire, an engraved eagle of bright German silver. With wings proudly spread, the eagle held in its beak the small end of a gonfalon unfurled, entwined by both talons, and streaming below like a battle guidon. Engraved on the pennon in script letters was the word LIBERTY.

Travis turned and saw that Squib held an exact replica of his new rifle. Holding his rifle up so Squib could read the inscription, Travis read the guidon on his brother's rifle: FREEDOM.

The boys continued to caress their rifles, commenting to each other and complimenting John and their father for their skills as John described the technical aspects of the rifles.

"Those barrels are a little heavier than we usually build, but Pa and me thought you might be needing a heavier caliber out west so that they will take about forty balls for the pound. Both barrels are sixty inches in length to give you a good sight bead. In your patch box you will find two extra mainsprings wrapped in oiled leather. If you break one, which you're sure to do some time, you can replace it. All your parts are completely interchangeable between rifles. Pa thought if you break or lose a part then you can craft a replacement from the working one. See how the rear sight has a larger leaf in the front which lies flat against the barrel? That can be lifted and you will be sighted in for twice the distance of the regular sight, with a double charge."

From the workbench behind him, John picked up two bullet molds and handed them to Squib and Travis. "See how these molds have two cavities?" John pointed. "The front cavity is slightly bigger than the rear one so when the barrels start to wear out and lose accuracy, you can cast a bigger ball and still keep accuracy. When the barrels are shot out you come home again and I can fit new ones."

Overwhelmed, Travis said, "John, this is too much. These rifles are worth a king's ransom; they must have taken months for you and Pa to build. They..."

John silenced him by holding up his hand and raising his eyebrows. "Wait, there's more." John nodded towards Beth, who walked to his side. In her hands, she held two large shooting bags made of soft buckskin. Suspended from the wide shoulder straps of each were two amber-colored Buffalo powder horns: one large horn and one much smaller priming horn. Etched on the large horn was a map of the Susquehanna River Valley.

Superimposed in the center was an exact miniature rendition of the Tanner homestead with an eagle flying overhead trailing a long banner, on which was engraved TANNER. The horns sat above the ornamented shooting bags that were inlaid on the flaps with garlands of tiny fleur-de-lis and bleeding hearts all in red and blue that emanated from the mouth of a fierce dragon wrought of silver and brass that acted as a closer for the bag. The edges of the flap and strap were stitched in a bright leather wrapped in fine copper wire.

From inside the bag, she pulled out a tin. "There's one of these in each bag," Beth said as she handed the tin to Squib. Unsure of the contents, Squib slowly pried open the lid of the tin. Inside there were ten paper cartridges.

"Why these, Beth?" he asked. "We don't use paper cartridges in our rifles."

"Ah," John replied, "You probably don't remember Uncle Wes' stories of when he fought up north in the Indian wars. Often," he continued, "many frontiersmen would get caught out alone on the trail where the Indians would try in a variety of ways to get the frontiersman to fire his single shot. Knowing it would take a few minutes for the frontiersman to reload, they would rush him before they could load again. Uncle Wes and your Pa would make up paper cartridges so they could reload quicker, often surprising the onrushing attacker with a quick shot."

Still not convinced, Squib asked, "Rifles don't shoot accurately with no patch down the bore; that's well known."

"That's the trick, then," John laughed. "Indians think the same thing. Not as accurate is true, but at fifty to sixty paces still good enough to hit a man easily. Pa said they saved their hides several times by shooting and reloading quickly with cartridges alternating one firing and one reloading. Enough so to discourage an attack."

Beth smiled and placed the tin back in the bag. "You can be sure if your pa and Wes believed in them, so should you." Then, passing a bag to Travis, she said, "For you. And you," she said as she gave the other to Squib.

"Beth," Squib blurted out, "these are beautiful."

Beth blushed. Travis, too overcome to speak, kissed her softly on the cheek. Not to be outdone, Squib tickled her other cheek with a hairy kiss that made her giggle.

"See here." In mock jealousy, John growled, "Find your own pretty girl; this one's mine." Wrapping his arms protectively around Beth, he gave the boys a hairy raised eyeball.

Feigning terror, Squib and Travis backed towards the door, stopping when John said, smiling, "Hold it, you scoundrels. You're not going anywhere till you make the bird sing."

"Yes," Beth repeated, "make the bird sing."

They all stepped outside, and the boys charged their rifles. Beth watched incredulously at the speed and dexterity with which they both loaded. Using the carved powder measure attached to his shooting bag, they measured and poured the powder down the bore, slapping the side of the barrel to settle the charge in the breech. Over the muzzle went a linen patch greased with a mixture of beeswax and mutton tallow, pressed into the patch was a round lead bullet; both were rammed smoothly down the barrel by the ramrod. After drawing the flint back to half-cock, they lifted the frizzen, blowing on it more from habit then a need to remove any dust, and poured the small priming charge directly into the pan from the smaller of the two horns. The frizzen snapped down, completing the loading.

"I've never been able to load that fast," Beth said, wide-eyed.

Squib winked and said, "Pa taught us. The trick is to start slow so you can do it in the dark without thinking; the speed comes by itself."

"Go ahead, Squib," Travis said, pointing to a life-sized iron rooster sitting on a post in a field a hundred paces from the shop. The rooster had been designed by Aaron years before to enable customers to test rifles they considered purchasing in an entertaining yet realistic manner. While the rooster's body represented a challenging target and rewarded the shooter with a loud gong for success, the real test was the cock's head, a target of but a few inches in diameter. When struck it would spin, ringing a small bell that hung suspended and protected behind the bird.

In the manner of many experienced frontiersmen, Squib cocked the hammer, set the trigger in one motion, and, bringing the rifle to his shoulder, fired immediately. The rifle cracked and bucked belching fire and smoke followed by a loud clang which testified to the accuracy of the shot.

"Good shot," Travis said. Then, duplicating Squib, he brought his rifle up and fired. They all listened for a gong. None came.

Suddenly, they heard a ting-a-ling, like distant sleigh bells on a frozen lake, as the rooster's head spun and rung the bell.

"Hurrah!" Squib cried, slapping Travis on the back. "Hurrah, for Liberty!"

Chapter 4

Wrapping his blanket tightly around him, Chester got up from his bed and shuffled across the darkened cabin to the fireplace. Taking a handful of kindling from beside the hearth, he stirred the ashes and looked for a hot coal still lingering from the previous night. Finding one, he placed a sliver of wood on top and blew on the ember till the wood flared into flame. Then he continued to add kindling. Each caught fire as he added larger and bigger pieces, which, entrapped by the building flames, snapped and hissed like a scalded cat. The fire burst with a roar, brightness and heat driving away the cold before them and enveloping the room in warmth. Chester dropped his blanket to the floor, picked up a clay pipe with a long yellowed stem, and slowly stuffed a wad of tobacco into the blackened bowl with his equally blackened thumb. Clenching the stem between teeth so grimed and tarnished that they appeared an extension of the pipe, he lit the bowl with a burning straw, puffing and sucking in slippery slurps till the pipe exuded a chimney of putrid smoke.

Stumbling back to his bed, Chester grasped the rifle he had left leaning against the wall. Lazily dragging the butt behind him, he crossed to the cabin door which lay partially open on one rotted leather hinge. Kicking the door open, he leaned against the door jamb, the rifle propped muzzle up under one arm, and puffed his pipe. Squinting into the blackness, McKay chuckled to himself, speaking aloud between long draws on his pipe. "No Injun's going to get ole Chester McKay," he mused to himself. "Gotta to get up well fore sunrise, to catch the ole Chester sleeping." He laughed. "Too smart for you Injuns. Too smart for white folks. Ha! How smart are you, Aaron Tanner? Who's dead now. Ha. You wait, them Injuns will be back. Ole Chester be killing Injuns while all you fancy folks be running away. Come on you red devils — cat lead."

Framed in the doorway and silhouetted by the bright fire behind, Chester's long shadow danced with the firelight across the ground in the front of the cabin. In concealment on a wooded ridge above, two men watched in amazement. Chester waved his rifle at arm's length, lunging and parrying at the darkness beyond and his own greater darkness within, engaging an unseen enemy in silent combat.

The morning sun broke on the eastern horizon while Chester continued to wage his silent war well into the dawn. Past the time more industrious men would have begun their day's work, Chester's only industry was in his mind. Indian battles were being fought in the swirling shadows cast from a dying fire and the deeper recesses of his imagination. Chester McKay — Indian fighter, self-claimed champion of mankind, hero extraordinaire — had never seen a wild Indian, much less fought one.

Succumbing finally to the advent of the day, Chester threw his rifle across his shoulder and strode purposefully towards the shed where he kept his mule locked for the night. Better to lock an animal away for the night than risk its loss to Indians, was Chester's belief. Opening the door, he seized the mule's bit, twisting it cruelly till the animal reluctantly stepped from the shed. Throwing a leg over the mule's backside, Chester pulled himself laboriously up and perched himself precariously on the mule's bare back.

Drawing the ramrod from the rifle, he had begun to raise it to strike the mule when a shot rang out, and a hot cloud of red and gray sticky matter splashed into his face. Stunned, Chester fell backwards, landing hard on the ground as the dead mule fell across his legs, crushing them. His rifle hit the ground discharging with a loud report, the bullet buzzing just inches from Chester's ear. Wiping the gore from his gunpowder-blackened face and eyes, Chester stared incredulously at the ragged bloody hole where the top of the mule's head had been. Shocked, he came to the only conclusion his mind was prepared to accept. "Injuns," he gasped. "Injuns!" his panicked mind screamed at him. Overcome by fear, trapped beneath the dead mule, Chester clawed frenziedly at the dead carcass, tearing shards of hide and flesh from the mule's back with his bare hands as panic yielded to terror, screams turned to shrieks. "Injuns. Injuns."

"You missed," Squib scoffed, as they crawled back away from the rocks behind the ridge.

"Did not," Travis snapped. "I was shooting at the mule," he said, as he eased himself away from the sight of the farm below. Safely out of sight, they both stood as Travis recharged his rifle.

"You — missed!" Squib laughed.

"I shot the mule," Travis retorted brusquely. "If we killed McKay — people would be calling us murderers and maybe making trouble for John and Beth. Now, let's get away before someone hears all that screaming and comes looking."

"Best we run," Squib agreed, chuckling, "wouldn't want people to know you missed."

Leaving the sounds of Chester's screams behind, they ran cautiously through the forest, found their horses, mounted, and began to ride away, Squib reined short, looking around anxiously.

"Where's Fidious?" he called to Travis.

"Probably chasing rabbits; he'll catch up. Always does," Travis called back as he spurred his mount down the trace.

Fidious sat on the ridge; head cocked to one side, watching the scene below. Only the upper portion of Chester's torso was visible as he fluttered and thrashed frenetically about, his arms flailing around and his head out of control. Suddenly he went rigid and rose slowly forward, his mouth opened as if he had exhaled a demon. Then he collapsed limply to the ground. The dog lost interest now that the movement stopped. Standing, he shook off the morning dew and bounded away. Some days later a local woodcutter came upon Chester's body and after summoning neighbors who all concluded from the evidence at the scene that while mounting his mule, McKay's rifle had discharged, killing the animal. The mule had fallen on Chester, trapping him till he died from exposure. Such was the folly of carrying a rifle continually cocked, they would say.

Chapter 5

Where the Allegheny River meets the Monongahela and the two become one greater river called the Ohio, lay the soon to be incorporated city of Pittsburg. Situated at the headwaters of the immense westward migration, Pittsburg was the supply house for every pioneer, settler, soldier, merchant, thief, and rogue, who, unlike their oppidan brothers, shared one common goal: to go West where free land was for the taking and become rich. Towards that dream, there also came the boat-builders, storekeepers, blacksmiths, coopers, merchants, tavern keepers, farriers, all who, while they listened to the pioneer's talk of wealth and fortune in the West, worked, built, sold, and serviced, supplied with hopes of securing their fortunes without the dangers of traveling further into the wilderness.

The smoke of countless wood and coal fires carried upriver for several miles from the bustling metropolis and lay in a thick haze across the river valley, tainting the forest with its smoky miasma.

Travis wrinkled his nose at the stink. Looking to Squib, he announced, "Must be Pittsburg."

"Sure do smell like it," Squib huffed in disgust. "Do all cities stink like that?"

"Most likely. But we ain't going there to live, thank God. Let's hurry; race you to town," Travis said, kicking his horse into a gallop. Squib spurred his horse and the brothers galloped into town.

As they reached the city limits, the brothers reined in their horses to a walk. Travis and Squib gasped and pointed in wonderment at the brisk activity about them. Winding their way slowly through the city, they looked for the boatyards. Being in no hurry to find them, they stopped at a tavern along the way.

The tavern keeper watched warily as the boys entered. The frontier attracted many types of men. Almost all carried guns; not all used them for good purposes. Most wore the long hunter's universal uniform of a greasy buckskin wamus worn over a linen shirt, buckskin leggings and moccasins stitched together by hand with leather and sinew, and tomahawks and long knives stuck in their belts ready for instant use, but it was the eyes the tavern keeper looked to for signs of trouble. He looked closely as the boys approached the bar. He smiled to himself. No trouble here, he thought. A couple of hunters, boys, the first time in the city from the looks of their wide-eyed stares. Out of the corner of his eye, he spotted Fidious as he slunk through the partially open door.

"No hounds in my tavern," he shouted. "You," he pointed at Travis, "get that dog out of here."

"He ain't my dog," Travis replied.

"Then," pointing at Squib, he said, "you get him out of here."

"Not mine," Squib smirked.

Frustrated, the barkeep asked, "Well, then whose dog is he?"

Laughing, Squib replied, "Well, we're with him, but he ain't with us!"

Now totally confused, the barkeep looked at Travis, who shrugged and said, "He's just his own. We kinda think he's not with us, but not against us either. Being half-wolf and half-dog."

"Or maybe half-demon," Squib cut in. "We think he gets a mite confused about who's following who."

"Yep, that's about the right of it," Travis laughed.

"You don't like him, you can tell Fidious to get out," Travis said, ambling to the counter.

"Fidious," the barman laughed, "what kind of name is that?" Suddenly, the huge wolf-dog jumped up with his forepaws on the bar and bared his drooling fangs inches away from the barman's face. The barman concluded very quickly that this was not a happy animal, and he backed slowly away from the bar.

"That's an unusual name," he whispered, his back against the wall.

"He doesn't like it much," Squib said, pointing with his thumb. "Get down, you big bear."

Fidious gave Squib a quick look of disdain, growled once more at the barman, and sank to the floor where he curled up and fell asleep.

With obvious relief in his voice, the barman asked, "What would you boys like?"

"Ale," Travis replied quickly.

"Milk," Squib said. "I'd like some milk, please."

"Milk?" The barkeep laughed. "I like you boys. Ale and milk it is." He turned away, his great sides rippling in laughter.

"Squib," Travis whispered out of the side of his mouth, "you're embarrassing me." He looked over his shoulder surreptitiously. "What will all these men think about you drinking milk. Men come here to drink ale and whisky."

"I don't like ale or whisky. I like milk," Squib replied calmly. "Besides it looks to me like the only other men in the place couldn't tell if we were drinking whisky or panther piss."

Travis looked carefully around. Except for themselves, the only other occupants of the tavern appeared to be either asleep or passed out dead drunk.

The barman returned and slammed two large tankards down in front of the boys. "Ale and milk," he said a little too loudly for Travis. "Headed for St. Louis, are you?"

"Yes," Travis stammered, "how did you know?"

"You boys ain't settlers or preachers, and if you ever lived on a farm you didn't stay there long, so it's St. Louis and the trapping country farther west."

"Our uncle Wes is in St. Charles. We hope to join up with him and try our hand at trapping, that's true," Squib replied honestly.

The barkeeper leaned forward, lowering his voice, "Boys, out here it's not a good idea to be giving too honest an answer when folks are asking you questions. We've got robbers and bandits here about that be more than happy to lift your top knots just for them pretty rifles you're carrying. It's getting so a man that asks you where you're going or where you come from is considered rude if not damn near hostile by some folks."

Following the barman's example, Travis lowered his voice and asked, "We want to sell our horses for boat fare downriver; can you direct us to an honest horse trader?"

"An honest horse trader?" the barman howled and fell back laughing. "Why don't you ask me for a skinny tavern keeper?" He patted his huge belly with both hands. "Or maybe an honest politician or a truly pious preacher or a repentant sinner." He shook his head. "Boys, ain't no such thing. But I'll tell you don't matter none anyway; every settler heading down the Ohio is trying to sell his horses beforehand, so there's no shortage of horse flesh hereabouts. A good saddle horse will sell for twenty dollars, and that's the best price you'll get, honest horse trader or not.

"Now if you want my advice, you take the twenty dollars, and you forget about trying to buy passage on one of them flatboats headed downriver. Half them fools drown before the river pirates get to them. Here, you buy one of my five-dollar jugs of whiskey, and take it down to the lower landing below the docks. There are trappers and woodsmen coming in every evening right about this time from upriver. You trade your keg for a good canoe from them, but be sure you're long gone by the time they sober up or you'll find your trade forgot and the canoe gone. Drink up, boys; you don't want to be hanging around this town longer than need be."

"Thank you for the advice," Travis said, lifting his tankard in salute.

"The drinks are on me, boys. You Tanners are welcome in my bar anytime."

"How did you—"

Travis was cut off when the barman pointed to their rifles leaning against the bar. "You boys ain't rich enough to be buying rifles the likes of those. An' only Aaron could make a rifle that pretty. Your Pa sold me a rifle back in seventy-six. I've had three wives since then who all turned mean and nasty on me, but that rifle still as sweet as the day I first laid my hands on her. I heard about your Pa a few days ago; I'm really sorry. He was a fine man." The barman extended his hand. "Ben Thompson."

They shook hands and exchanged greetings. "Travis and this here's my brother Squib. But I expect you to know that too," Travis said a little too sarcastically for Squib.

"The first drink and advice always be free for you boys. Been where you stand myself many a year ago. Had the adventure-lust myself. Born under a wandering star, my pa said. Been to the Mississippi and back many a time and the scars to prove it. Got more stories than fleas on your dog's back. Now best you get up to the docks if you want to find a canoe," Ben said, waving the boys towards the door. The boys were about to step outside when Ben called, "Wait," and he ran into the back, returning a second later with a large bone which he tossed to Squib. "For that wolf-dog of yours. Best you keep that animal happy."

True to Ben's advice, the boys found every stable and corral in the town crowded with horses of every description; however, after much haggling, they were able to sell their mounts for twenty dollars each. They gained an additional five dollars for their tack, but only after threatening to throw the equipment into the river rather than part with it for less. With more hard cash than they had ever held before, the boys eagerly sought out the docks so they could continue their journey. Distaste rapidly overtook curiosity and excitement as they wormed through the seething crowds that thronged about the waterfront. Along the beach, workmen hurried back and forth carrying lumber and tools to the carpenters whose steady staccato hammering beat permeated through the continual thunderous din of the mob. Children ran underfoot while laughing, teasing, and playing amongst the laborers and boatmen. Their parents stood sober-eyed and contemplatively waited to load their few treasured possessions on the completed flatboats. Others, their vessels loaded, joyously fired their guns in the air signaling their departure as the current dragged the heavily laden flatboats away from the beach accompanied by the cheers of relatives, friends, and spectators on shore.

Farther back, sedate groups of frontiersmen watched. Sternly silent and disgusted, they shook their heads and spat on the ground as each boat departed. Every vessel was another fissure into their life, another farm cutting into their trapping grounds, more hungry mouths destroying the forest and the game from which their living depended. Angrily they denounced the farmers, who flocked in every increasing number down the Ohio to the rich and fertile lands beyond. Lands pioneered by long hunters, who with little more than a rifle and tomahawk had taken to the wilderness, singly or in pairs, and wrestled Indians and nature alike into submission. At the forefront they alone had suffered, fought, and died only to lose it again to men they considered meek and selfish. What they had won by blood and force would be lost to forces they could not understand and to men more mendacious than themselves who inveigled the powers of commerce and law to their will. Resigned to the inevitability of settlement, the long hunters argued amongst themselves. The more optimistic sang the praises of the country west and north, citing the return of Lewis and Clark's great westward expedition and the uncharted lands beyond to be their salvation. Others who were more bellicose and impetuous watched the departing flatboats with hungry eyes, silently and surely selecting their victims by counting the number of competent riflemen on board, the victim's wealth, or for no other capricious reason than a comely girl whose charms had attracted their attention.

Leaving the crowds behind, Travis and Squib reached the lower docks. Quickly and with little searching they concluded the trade of their recently purchased jug of whisky with a French-Canadian voyageur who was more than anxious to be rid of his sturdy bark craft. No doubt he had stolen the canoe himself and was more than glad to profit from its sale.

The canoe, fashioned from birch bark and sewn together with strips of spruce root called watap stretched over a strong yet pliable framework of split saplings then waterproofed with boiled pine tar on the seams, was ideal in size for their journey. In addition to being light and fast, the canoe could be readily repaired and maintained from raw materials abundantly available in the forest. The canoe was a vessel the brothers were vastly comfortable and proficient in, as they had spent their early childhood plying the channels and backwaters of the Susquehanna River behind Aaron's smithy. Satisfied with the purchase, the boys loaded their possessions and pushed off quietly, their paddles propelling them soundlessly out into the current and downriver. Few people noticed their departure and those that did gave them little thought. Yet to the Tanners, it was a monumental moment for they had finally left the known bounds of their previous life. Now they were free of the constraints of their fellow man as each paddle stroke drove them towards the unknown west with no goal to urge them onward other than a trust that whatever lay ahead held the promise of adventure.

Chapter 6

L ate summer lay over the river like a wet woolen blanket: hot, steamy, and itchy. The broad, murky river swollen with heavy summer rains flooded the adjoining forest beyond intervening shoreline or beach, as it swirled and washed about the submerged trunks of the great oaks and hemlocks that bordered the banks. Pressing against an oak cautiously with his paddle lest the tree damage the fragile hull of their craft, Travis pushed the canoe through the trees. The bow slid through a thicket of drowned willows and came to rest on a patch of dry beach. Rifle in hand, he jumped from the canoe and cautiously peered into the surrounding woods before he turned and held the canoe steady between his knees while Fidious and Squib disembarked. Squib stood guard while Travis carefully moved the canoe further onto the bank but still partially in the water should a quick getaway be needed. Then, in a long-practiced ritual, the brothers separated, each scouting the shore. One went upstream, the other went down. Fidious ignored Squib's whispered commands and began his own patrol by leaping ahead and disappearing into the forest.

Circling away from the river into the thick woods beyond, they searched carefully, looking for a sign of game but more specifically predators, both animal and human. Later, their survey completed, they returned to the canoe. With a silent nod, they acknowledged the acceptability of the campsite and began to prepare for their evening encampment.

Travis leaned over the canoe and picked up two large catfish they had caught earlier that were lying on the bottom of the canoe wrapped in wet grass to keep them fresh. Tossing them on the ground along the water, he took the long knife from his belt and began gutting the fish. Now, with the scouting done, Squib pulled the canoe completely out of the water and hid it amongst the willows along the shore. He covered the paddles in the stern to hide them from porcupines and other critters who would chew them to pieces to get at the salt embedded in the shafts from sweat on the paddler's hands. Finished hiding the canoe, Squib carried the bedding and gear farther into the forest to an area above the high-water mark with a bed of broken rock and sand which he had selected for their campsite. Placing the equipment on the rocks, he carefully laid his rifle on top, picked up a large stick, and proceeded to beat the bushes in an effort to drive off any snakes which might be hiding there. Satisfied the site was clear of reptiles, he picked up pieces of driftwood and dry wood which littered the forest floor and tossed them on the sand. He continued till enough wood was collected for tonight's and tomorrow morning's fire. Reaching into the lower branches of the trees, he pulled down handfuls of wispy dry Spanish moss together with some of the smaller dry branches that were always found just under the greater living limbs of the trees until he had several large handfuls of the dry tinder. With the kindling at hand, he began to fashion a small fire pit in the sand. On a bed of the collected fire moss, he placed another small tuft of seasoned fire moss which he kept in the small horn in his shooting bag and drew out his fire steel and flint. By striking the flint on the steel, a shower of sparks flew over the moss that lay smoldering on the tinder. Quickly Squib blew softly over the sparks, coaxing them into flame before adding smaller branches which ignited with a hot smokeless flame.

Travis returned from the shore and gave the fish, now spread open and impaled on a grill of peeled willow branches, to

Squib who propped the fish beside the fire to bake. Then, Squib continued to feed the blaze while turning the fish slowly so that they baked evenly. Travis finished spreading their bedrolls in the sand. Reaching into a leather sack, Travis withdrew a stick of jerky and threw it to Squib. Taking one for himself, he clamped it in the corner of his mouth and, with a twisting motion, yanked a mouthful of the sinewy dried meat and sat back contentedly against a rock to chew.

"Squib. Do you ever wish you lived in another time?"

"You mean," Squib asked, looking up, "when there were knights in armor, and castles, and dragons like Ma used to read to us?"

"No. Years ago, when Pa and Uncle Wes first came west and settled on the Moshannon River. When all this country down past the Ohio," waving his arm, "was wilderness full of game and Indians."

"Can't say I ever have. Why?" Squib replied.

"Well, this land is so crowded now, with people coming down the rivers and building cabins and farms everywhere. You can't go ten miles without seeing one. We must have passed a half-dozen flatboats today on the river. Did you look at all them people? Ugh! Farmers. Farmers all of them. We're too late, I'm telling you; the wild country will be gone before we ever get a chance to hunt it. Roads," Travis spit out in distaste, "did you hear when we stopped at Wheeling, they have a road almost built from there all the way back to Cumberland." Squib shook his head; he could see Travis was really starting to get himself worked up. "Oh, you don't believe me," Travis said. "Well, they call it the National Road and they say it will eventually reach all the way to St. Louis. And towns. Why, Pittsburg has over five thousand people living there now. Five thousand," he spat the words out in disgust. "When Pa first came here, there weren't five hundred people in all of Western Pennsylvania. Uncle Wes said you could shoot elk and buffalo all along the Susquehanna.

All the years we been hunting this country, how many elk have we seen?"

"Two. And you missed them both," Squib chuckled, ducking deftley as Travis winged a rock at him.

"See, that's what I mean. Two elk, and I've never seen a buffalo. Uncle Wes said this country was so thick with game a man could shoot twenty deer a day, every day. But now, now we got to walk ten or fifteen miles to shoot three, maybe four on a good day."

"So, what's the point?" Squib asked, passing a skewer with one of the cooked bass to Travis.

"I just wish we could have lived here in the old days when the hunting was good, and there weren't so many people, excepting Indians. Then maybe we could have fought Indians; that would have been fun."

"Don't seem like killing people sounds like much fun to me," Squib replied thoughtfully, plucking a piece of fish from beside the fire and throwing it into his mouth.

"They are just Indians — they're not people like us," Travis replied indignantly, sitting upright and wagging the piece of fish at Squib.

Squib wagged his fish at Travis, mocking his behavior. "Seems to me last time I have seen an Indian he had two legs and two arms and a head just like you and me," Squib said, "and they eat and talk and walk; sure do look like people to me."

"But they're not educated and civilized like us," Travis contested hotly. "They are savages with ungodly ways. Always torturing and killing each other, and us too, when they have a mind. Remember the stories Uncle Wes told us about how them Shawnees tortured their prisoners? People, civilized people, don't go about ripping men's guts out and building fires in their bellies."

"Since when did you begin hating Indians so much?" Squib asked.

Surprised, Travis said, "Hate? I don't hate them."

"Sure sounds like hate-talk to me," Squib replied. "Ma or Pa heard you talking that way, your butt be so sore you couldn't sit for a week. Pa always said hate was the ugliest word in the English language. Every sin, wrongdoing, and cruelty starts with hate. You," Squib pointed accusingly at Travis, "can stop that hate-talk right now as I'm feeling very contented; we are having our great adventure like we always talked about."

"You're right, I suppose," Travis agreed reluctantly. "I just thought we might have had a fight with them, or exchanged some shots as they done in the old days."

Squib laughed. "Old days? Harrison done killed Tecumseh up there at Thames River not even that long ago. Could be some of them wild Shawnees still lurking around these here woods. Just waiting for us to turn our backs so they could come sneaking in here and slip a knife under our topknots. Maybe hiding in them bushes right behind you." Squib pointed into the darkness behind Travis just as a loud crash sounded from the darkened woods. Travis jumped up, grasping his rifle tightly to his chest as Fidious charged out of the bushes. He stopped and stared quizzically at Travis' rifle leveled at him as Squib convulsed with laughter on the sand. Indignantly, Travis pointed towards Fidious as the wolf-dog walked away and curled up in the sand.

"A fine lot a good that dog would do us if Indians attacked us. Look at him: come night he always moves off away from us and hides in the bushes. A good watch dog would sleep by the camp to warn us if we were in danger."

"Travis, if you were looking, you would see that dog is smarter than both of us. He always sleeps upwind of us. That way he'll smell anything approaching from the windward side and be between us and any danger from the upwind side while he can hear anything moving below us. Sounds pretty smart to me."

"Oh," Travis said, looking at Fidious with newfound respect. "Well, I noticed that," Travis replied defensively. "I'm not complaining or anything, but I thought we would have a few more escapades and adventures by now. Maybe when we get farther downriver, away from all this civilization, we will have more excitement."

"You go ahead and give that some thought," Squib replied. "Me, I'm ready for some shut-eye."

Tossing the last of their supper bones into the dwindling fire, the brothers lay their rifles by their beds and pulled their blankets over their shoulders.

"Your turn to read tonight," Travis said with a yawn.

"I'm too tired," Squib replied, pulling the blankets closer around him. "And the fire's too low; it needs building."

"That *Gulliver's Travels* is sure some book. Do you think Daniel Boone always read from it as Beth said?"

"She heard that from Uncle Wes. So, I suspect she's right. Don't matter none; she was real nice giving us that book to read. John said books cost near the same as a rifle. Goodnight."

"Squib, I have been thinking maybe that dog is smarter than us. If there were Indians about, we'd probably be dead by now. Or worse, captured. Maybe we should start pretending like there was Indians around and take more care in camp so that when we get west, we'll be ready."

"How do mean pretending?" Squib asked, looking at Travis from the corner of his eye. "You mean play-acting?"

"No," Travis said thoughtfully, "Just being more vigilant as we would be if there were Indians still about. Remember, Uncle Wes told us they always make a fire to eat, then move their camp just before dark to another location they had scouted out beforehand. One that was easier to defend and escape from if need be. And they would always hide their gear so they could backtrack to it if they were attacked. We should make-believe, 'cause one day it might be real and we'll be ready."

"Alright," Squib replied, "we'll start tomorrow. Goodnight."

"I sure hope we get west 'fore it's all gone," Travis lamented. "It's been awful tame so far, with settlers and immigrants everywhere. No adventure or scrapes to tell stories about. We was born too late."

"Goodnight!" Squib barked, throwing his blanket over his head.

Squib woke famished. Squib always woke hungry; the weeks on the river had left him ravenous for a change from catfish, corn cakes, and cold jerky. He remembered those mornings back home when he was a boy, and he would tiptoe barefoot, still wrapped in his blanket, into the kitchen. He would sit beside the fire roaring in the hearth while his mother slathered butter on a thick slice of freshly baked bread still warm from the ashes. He smiled at the memory. No matter what time he awoke, Rachel would be there, the smell of bread mingling with wood smoke. "A little something to warm you," she'd say, giving him the bread. Her dark eyes would flash in the firelight, the tiny lines around her eyes all smiling. While he savored the warm bread, he would watch his mother prepare the morning breakfast consisting of slabs of bacon and ham sputtering in the huge fry pan, and hotcakes filled with dried apple slices soaked in sugar water swimming in melted butter and warm maple syrup. When he had finished the bread, she would bring him a mug of milk, warmed by the fire, and tousle his hair while he gulped it down. His stomach growled at the memory and brought him back to reality. Reluctantly, he opened one eye, gritty and sticky from sleep, and peered around the campsite. Tiny tendrils of smoke from the previous night's fire stirred from a few hot embers and mixed with the morning mist off the river, turning everything into shades of gray. Travis lay asleep on the other side of the fire, Fidious curled up against his back with just his nose and one open eye sticking out of the mass of gray hair. One-eyed they stared at each other, silently daring each other to blink first. Squib lost as usual, blinking his eye clear so when he looked at Fidious again the eye had disappeared and only his nose remained visible above the fur, turned upward in a slightly disdaining, you-lose pose.

Suddenly, Squib tensed as a cold wave of fear washed over him. Something cold and sinuously alive slithered against his legs under the blanket. Involuntarily, his whole body shook and brought the presence to life; coiling up in reptilian menace, it rattled a sudden warning.

Squib froze and looked with one pleading eye towards Travis, who had been woken by the rattle; and the other toward Fidious. The great dog was instantly alert, his paws on Travis' chest as they both stared back wide-eyed at Squib who silently mouthed "SNAKE."

Travis rose quietly. With one hand on Fidious' collar, he gave him the quiet hiss sound they used when hunting to still the dog, then he pushed him giving him the "stay" command with his hand. With his rifle in hand, Travis stepped cautiously towards Squib. As he approached, the snake felt the motion and rattled its annoyance, moving suddenly under the blankets. Travis stopped.

A cold sweat broke out on Squib's forehead, the salty beads running into and stinging his eye. The itch was becoming more maddening each passing second, but he dared not move to scratch. Travis squatted and watched. Holding his rifle, he pantomimed shooting the snake. Squib moved his eye back and forth, no. Travis seemed to understand. Pressing his forefinger between his eyes, he indicated he would have to shoot the snake in the head to kill it, which was impossible since it was hidden under the blanket. Travis lay his rifle on the ground and mouthed for Squib to lie very still and that he would return in a few minutes. Squib glared at him. Tell me something I don't know, he thought, as his brother scrambled into the forest. He glimpsed Travis scrambling around on all fours through the willows along the riverbank as if digging for clams. Travis kept a cautious eye on Fidious, repeating the stay command several times as he scrambled about.

Several minutes later he returned, clutching something hidden in his hands. He stopped by their packs and dropped the wiggling object into the front of his wamus, where it squirmed and bounced against his chest. Next, he removed their fishing lines and hooks. With the line coiled in his teeth, Travis crawled cautiously on his belly across the ground and stopped when he reached the edge of the blanket. With one hand he reached into his hunting shirt, playing cat and mouse with his reluctant captive. He smiled and gave Squib a reassuring wink as he withdrew a large bullfrog from his shirt. Holding the frog with one hand, he fashioned a harness from the fishing line and wrapped it around one of the frog's legs while leaving one end free. He then gently placed the frog by the open end of the blanket.

Free the frog jumped under the blanket, hopping blindly forward and seeking the security of the warm darkness beyond when it suddenly stopped, sensing the snake. Momentarily snake and frog sat still, eyeing each other in the semi-darkness like two duelists awaiting the order to fire. In a flash the snake struck, burying its fangs into the frog's head. Travis saw the sudden movement under the blanket and yanked hard on the line. Propelled by the cord, the frog with the snake still attached flew into the air and landed some feet away. Travis jumped up, grabbed a piece of firewood, and beat the squirming snake while Fidious, who had sat quietly by and watched the entire proceedings, pranced about them barking and growling. Beat to a twitching mass of red pulp, Travis gave the snake a final smack which crushed the snake's head and bullfrog into a mushy mess.

Travis stood and turned to grin towards Squib, but his blanket lay empty. Walking to the riverbank, he found Squib sitting naked from the waist down in the icy river water, rinsing out his buckskin breeches.

"Well, aren't you going to thank me for saving your life?" Travis asked with a self-satisfied smirk, as he squatted on the bank.

"You're my brother; you're supposed to save my life," Squib growled back.

"Now, where have your manners gone?" Travis said, finally aware of Squibs ablutions. "This is not the time for a bath; what are... Oh!" Embarrassed, he stood and started back to the campsite. "I'll make breakfast; how's roast snake sound?" Travis laughed. Squib's sopping wet britches hit him behind the head which just made him laugh louder.

Minutes later, Travis had a small fire roaring. Several corn cakes were frying in bear grease as Squib returned and sat by the flames. "The cornmeal and grease are getting low," Travis said.

"Gawd, I'm hungry," Squib replied as he watched the corn cakes crisp up. Taking his long knife, he speared a cake, lifted it into the air, sniffed it carefully, and wrinkled his nose.

"Travis," he asked, "when are you going to learn that black is not cooked; it's burnt. Coffee is roasted dark brown; johnnycake is golden brown, bacon is crispy brown."

Travis shook his head and laughed. "It's all the same," he replied, holding up another burnt piece at the end of his knife. "Dip it in honey, sugar, or maple syrup, and it all tastes just fine."

Squib scowled in disgust, and changed the conversation. "I think we should stop farther downriver and do some hunting this afternoon. Some venison would taste good about now. We made good time in the last few weeks we can spare the—" Squib started at the sudden whirring chatter of a rattlesnake coming from behind them. The boys jumped to their feet, rifles in hand. Cautiously they followed the sound behind some bushes and found Fidious on his back kicking back and forth, his paws curled to his chest as he rolled spasmodically about. Protruding from his teeth, as he shook his head like a puppy with a ball of yarn, was the tail of the rattler. Fidious jumped up and dropped the rattle at Travis' feet, daring him to pick it up so they could play catch, but Travis was not in the mood.

He remarked with a glower, "No one taught this dog not to play with his food."

"His food?" Squib countered. "Corn cakes and snake were starting to sound really good a few moments ago."

Breakfast completed and the gear packed in the canoe, they set off down the river. Fidious sat contently in the center playing with his rattle and shaking it back and forth. He was delighted in his own dog way at the racket he was making until suddenly, in a fit of over exuberance, the rattle slipped from his mouth and flew into the air, traveling up in a great arc before landing the water where it vanished beneath the waves. With a sigh of disappointment, Fidious put his head over the gunnel and watched dejectedly, whining quietly to himself as the canoe rapidly drew away from his lost toy.

CHAPTER 7

Travis saw the deer first. He signaled silently to Squib by holding his paddle and pointing with his knuckles towards the buck standing on the point of land of what appeared to be a large island downstream. With hand signs, he signaled that they should continue past the point without frightening the deer, land downstream, and be downwind so they could hunt back up the island, thereby keeping the deer trapped between them and the water. Squib nodded in agreement; it was a good plan. A quarter mile downstream, they drew the canoe onto a small beach and noiselessly carried it into the trees. Travis pointed across the island, indicating they should walk inland together then split up and work parallel to each other back towards the deer. It was a tactic they had used successfully many times before. Travis pulled Fidious close to his leg and patted behind his knee to give him the follow sign as indication he should stay near to his heels. Moving slowly forward, one brother watched motionless while the other stalked a few paces ahead and then they alternated. Three times the area could be covered this way. Their only limitation was the thickness of the forest, but they moved closer and farther apart as the terrain allowed.

Travis took the lead. They had long ago agreed that the one who saw game first should lead the hunt. Their decision was based on the simple belief that the hunter who saw an animal first would likely have the best memory of where he had seen it and could best, therefore, control the hunt. What they would not acknowledge, however, was how their innate competitiveness made them more eager to be the first, in the process honing their senses to a keen edge as each sought to better the other. Hunting was as natural to the brothers as it would be in a wolf pack, and with the same cohesiveness of the pack, they intuitively responded to each other and the conditions around them without conscious thought. With a discipline that would make a drill sergeant proud, they ran through a mental checklist of factors which they altered and responded to constantly as they hunted. First, they had looked to their rifles. Quickly they cleaned the flints, tightened the thumb screw holding the flint, then ran a fingernail across the edge to freshen it. The frizzen was pulled open and the old priming charge blown out; the pan was brushed clean and a new charge poured. Finally, the sights were checked and dusted with a quick wipe from a moistened thumb. As they moved forward all their other skills came to full alert. The wind was tested with a moistened finger and would be continually verified as they advanced. Every sense hummed with activity, observing and accessing their surroundings.

Squib watched while Travis slid ahead. He looked for movement. Movement leapt at the eye, drawing it naturally to its every twitch. He meticulously looked at every slight variation in color or shadow that might reveal a clue about an animal's hiding place. He focused in on the unusual and unnatural signs: the horizontal line of a deer's back, which stood out from the vertical lines of the trees; ears or legs that become conspicuously alien shapes when exposed away from the sheltering foliage; a dark sparkling eye or wet glistening nose betraying the prey to the hunter and predator alike. Like predators, the brothers melted into the forest, imperceptibly gliding through the foliage with a feline gracefulness. Every instinct was keen and activated. Their rifles were leveled and instantly ready. Phantom hunters on the prowl.

Travis stopped. Squib watched for a moment. Then, slowly and painstakingly, he stepped ahead a few paces, drew behind a tree, and waited, poised, as Travis moved cautiously on his flank. Fidious, yielding his independence to his master's will and the necessities of the hunt, trailed closely behind him, as he had been taught. Travis paused. Squib watched and waited. Travis remained transfixed, frozen, almost invisible amongst the trees. Anticipating his brother had walked on to a deer, Squib cautiously raised his rifle slightly and pointed it ahead. Several long minutes passed. Anticipation began to yield to curiosity, for Travis had not moved. Squib looked more closely at his brother and saw him signaling by opening and closing his fist behind his back. This was the sign for come to me. Surprised, Squib moved cautiously to his brother's side, diligently keeping his eyes focused on the woods ahead as he did so. He could see nothing unusual. Even Fidious seemed transfixed to the spot, staring intently into the woods. This was too much for Squib and he gave into his curiosity. He leaned over slowly and whispered close to Travis' ear, "What do you see?"

Travis, seemingly in a trance, whispered back, "I saw a unicorn."

"What?" Squib said out loud, breaking the silence.

"I saw a unicorn," Travis said and pointed to a small clearing in the trees.

There are no unicorns in Ohio," Squib said, scowling back.

"Yes, there was," Travis contested, looking to Fidious for confirmation, but the wolf-dog had disappeared.

"LOOK!" he gestured with his rifle towards the clearing, as a mule-like creature, gray-white overlain with thick black stripes, stepped into the open, oblivious to their presence.

Stunned, Squib retorted back in a whisper, "That's not a unicorn. That's a zebra."

"There are no zebras in Ohio," Travis shot back.

Shocked into silence, the brothers gazed open-mouthed in fascination as the zebra grazed in the meadow.

"Pretty, ain't she?" a voice boomed behind them.

Startled, Travis and Squib scrambled about. Before them stood a small man dressed in ragged homespun clothes, leaning on his trade-style musket, his dark weathered features creased in a huge toothless grin. Travis looked around for Fidious, angry the dog had allowed a stranger to sneak up on them from behind, but the wolf-dog was sitting out of harm's way behind Squib. Even he looked surprised.

"That's the last one," the little man thundered, his voice giving a lie to its diminutive speaker. "Got to watch him; some Indian or one of them damn fool farmers will shoot him for that pretty striped hide of his. Stripes. That's what I call him. Stripes, good name. Gave him that name myself. Pretty good," he repeated, chuckling to himself at his own humor.

"Who are you?" Squib asked cautiously.

"Ken Woody," he replied, "but folks just call me Woody." He looked up at Squib. "Gawd, boy, your ma get poked by a bear? Your pa must be a bull. If you ain't the biggest man I ever seen, you're surely the hairiest. And who's this wildcat? You look like you got a sliver up your ass, boy." He gestured at Travis, who bristled with anger at Woody's reference to his parents. "Don't get mad, boys, no harm done, just talk, I talk too much. Can't help it. I been living alone on this here island too long by myself."

Turning to the zebra, Squib pointed and asked, "Where that come from?"

"Harman Blennerhassett brought them zebras here about ten years ago. That ain't all. He brung zebras, gazelles, antelopes, and some say, but I ain't ever seen one so I can't say for sure, but they say he brung a lion too. Only that one zebra left. Just Stripes and me now. All the way from Africa, he brung them. Ain't that something. Come on, boys, I'll show you his old plantation; it's something you'll want to tell your grandchildren about." Woody waved for them to follow him and bounded away towards the center of the island.

Squib looked at Travis and shrugged his shoulders. "We wanted adventure," he said, and then he ran after Woody into the trees. Travis hung back a moment, hoping to give an angry look at Fidious, but the hound had sneaked around him and was prancing merrily away at Squib's heels as they disappeared into the timber.

Travis ran and caught up with the group standing on the edge of what had obviously once been a large cultivated field, but now was covered with waist-high saplings and grass. Woody was pointing into the field. "This was all green meadow with the finest horse flesh on the Ohio. Ole Harman sure did love them fancy fillies," Woody said, winking. "Married his niece, they say. A real pretty thing too, from I what I hear. But folks run them out of town. An Irish lord, they said, real royalty right here in Ohio. Here! Come to the house. You ain't going to believe your eyes." Woody took off again, springing ahead silently, almost in a deerlike manner. No wonder he was able to sneak up on us so easily, Travis thought. Disturbed by the implications of anyone who could move so quietly, he caught his brother's eye and pointed silently.

"I noticed," Squib replied. They resumed their chase, running after Woody across the field. They followed him to a small hillock, where they stopped again.

Below them, partially hidden within a cordon of stately oaks standing like silent sentinels, its once brilliant white facade now reduced to a weathered gray, was the dilapidated palatial mansion of Harman Blennerhassett. Partially burned crumbled ruins had been abandoned to nature; what remained of the once majestic Corinthian columns was now blackened stumps swaddled by an advancing army of creepers and vines. The empty and smashed windows, as if dark portals to some horrific secret hidden within, stared forlornly from the front of the old mansion. Squib shivered as a feeling of foreboding fluttered through him; the house grinned at him, like a huge skull with evil blackened teeth.

Subdued by the scene, Woody said quietly, "Night's coming. Ain't much, but you boys is welcome to share my fire. If you want to explore around, that's alright too." Travis and Squib looked at each other, unsure if they should accept.

"Killed a fat cow this morning; be a shame to make jerky out of all them fine backstraps." Any reluctance disappeared as Squib's stomach replied to them with a loud growl. They all laughed. "Bring your canoe down to the landing over there." Woody pointed to worn partially collapsed dock by the water. "Bring your gear up to the cabin; just follow the trail. I'll get the fire built up," Woody said, taking off in his high-stepped lope down the hill.

After taking the canoe to the landing and hiding it amongst some underbrush, the brothers hoisted their traveling gear over one shoulder. Then, trailing their rifles in the other hand, they walked together up the path towards Woody's cabin. They reached a branch in the trail forking to the right towards the ruins of the mansion. Travis waved his brother on ahead and took the right fork. Yielding to his still growling stomach, Squib forged ahead, following his nose to the savory aroma of roasting beef drifting from the dilapidated log cabin that was barely visible in the sheltering woods. Fidious bounded ahead of him.

Travis dug the toe of his moccasin into the dirt beneath his feet and unearthed a bare flagstone. The trail from the river landing now encrusted with weeds and dirt had once been a broad laid path with a paved stone road winding gracefully through the extensive gardens to the mansion. Now overgrown by saplings and willows, the remains of the precisely manicured gardens still stood in contrast to the wild randomness of the dense woods beyond. Peeking out from the enshrouding wildness, the last few surviving flowers and shrubs sprouted last defiant petals and buds towards the life-giving sunshine. Their last stand for life gave silent witness to nature's first law, that the weak must yield to the strong and the survival of the hardy. Travis wandered about aimlessly, enthralled by the size of the now overgrown estate and the once lush gardens. Broken and shattered statuary bodies and limbs frozen in rigor mortis bobbed about like drowning sailors on a green sea. The trail wound its way to the front of the mansion. Travis found himself standing before the huge double doors, lying broken and shattered before the entrance as if a battering ram had smashed them down. After laying his gear down on the stoop, with his rifle leveled cautiously ahead he entered the murky anteroom. Standing for a moment in the gloom, he waited until his eyes grew accustomed to the dim interior. Slowly the closer items became visible and he was able to see deeper into the room. The vast anteroom opened left and right to what appeared to be a banquet hall and ballrooms given their size. In the center, the gaunt remains of an elegant curved staircase with marble stairs and heavy mahogany bannisters now smashed and broken wound up to an open balconied second floor. Winds blowing through the many shattered doors, windows, and burnt collapsed walls had built up piles of dust in the surviving corners of the mansion. A thick layer of dirt carpeted the heavy wood floors. The many tracks in the dust silently testified to the curiosity of other travelers. Travis wondered cautiously at the number of moccasin tracks, which far outnumbered the boot prints. The house was invisible from the river, yet from the tracks around the building there appeared to have been numerous curious visitors. Travis knelt down, mulling over in his mind why this bothered him. He knew most settlers moored their flatboats in sheltered coves and forted up for the night, almost universally refusing to step onto shore except at established settlements and towns. Vicious attacks by Indians and white renegades kept even the foolhardiest or most daring settlers from wandering ashore. Travis decided he would have to ask Woody where all these people were coming from.

His vision improved as he walked into the ballroom. The room was immense, larger than anything he had ever seen before. His father's home and workshop would have easily fit between its walls and still have room to drive a team of horses through the center. Holding Liberty by the butt and standing on his toes, he could not touch the ceiling with the rifle muzzle. At first, he thought the discolored walls had once been painted in a pattern consisting of many small now faded flowers and vines, but when he looked closer, he saw that the walls were papered. Painted paper, now that's something, he thought as he shook his head. He knew so little of the outside world. Little that had not come from conversations with his parents, Uncle Wes, and the few books he had read. But books and stories are only as powerful as the reader's or the listener's imagination. While he knew what a ballroom was, he could not imagine anyone dancing nor why they would want to dance. Although he had on occasion watched Beth in a moment of merry abandonment pirouette about, silently pantomiming a dance by holding her skirt in one hand, he had thought it looked silly and frivolous. The thought of dozens of people spinning about in this huge room seemed sillier. Beth had told him dancing was a natural response to music, as men and women enjoyed the rhythm and beat of the tune. Now there's something else he did not understand, music. He had heard music played only once before when a traveling fiddler passed by the house and paid for his supper with a few tunes. Squib and Travis had laughed themselves silly when John said it sounded like the time Pa slammed the barn door on a cat's tail.

He abandoned the thought, deciding that music and dancing were too ridiculous and confusing an image to pursue. The many moccasin tracks led across the ballroom to the back wall, and he began to follow them. Suddenly, a gust of wind rattled a dried leaf in the corner. Travis started at the rattlesnake-like sound. A cold chill crept up his spine. Curiosity forgotten, he slowly backed out of the house, turned, and ran down the trail to the cabin.

Woody's loud laughter and the warm aroma of roasting meat wafted from the open cabin door. Travis stepped into the brightly lit interior. He had expected rough plank tables and bunks. He found another mystery instead.

The interior of the cabin was illuminated by dozens of tapers set into several finely wrought and ornate brass candelabra sitting on a heavy oak dining table. The table was centered before a lofty walk-in fireplace set into the back wall. Woody lounged in a velvet armchair, one leg over the armrest, his other moccasin-covered foot on the table. Against one wall a cherry wood china cabinet overflowed with porcelain plates and silver cutlery. Three oak chests were placed randomly by the wall. Piled against the other wall were stacks of furs, feather quilts, and kegs of assorted sizes. A spinning wheel lay overturned in the corner. The walls were hung with oil paintings, tapestries, brass plates, and deer antlers. A tomahawk, buried to the haft, was embedded into the rough timber wall. Woody's shooting bag, powder horn, and tricorn hat hung from the tomahawk. Several carpets of different sizes and contrasting colors were scattered on the bare dirt floors. Squib sat to one side of the fireplace in another richly adorned armchair. Waving Travis over, he kept one hungry eye on a roast bubbling over the coals. A large kettle bubbled happily next to it.

"Come on in," Woody added his wave for Travis to come in. Travis joined his brother by the fire. He placed his broad-brimmed hat over the muzzle of his rifle and leaned it against the wall behind him. He sat down within easy reach of the rifle, snuggling his back against the comforting warm stones of the fireplace.

Woody pointed to Squib. "Yes, sir. Just telling your brother here this Ohio river has been awfully good to ole Woody. Them damn fool settlers are sinking and drowning every day on this river. Plunder drifts downriver faster than I can collect it. Them fools set out from Pittsburg every spring during high water with them boats overloaded with things no man needs or wants except to keep himself fed and dry. Come late summer the river starts to go down. Before long, every sandbank and river bar got more flatboats stuck on them than flies on shit. Ain't long before them folks getting tired unloading and loading all that plunder. Right soon, some bright feller with a mind stronger than his back starts leaving more in the mud than he unloads every time he gets stuck. Out comes the furniture into the mud for ole Woody to pick up at his leisure. Yes, sir. The Ohio is my corn-u-cop-i-a." He stretched the word as if he could only remember it in pieces. "You boys know what a corn-u-cop-i-a is?" Before either brother could answer, Woody pointed to the roast on the spit. "Say, boy. Better turn that roast 'fore she burns up on you."

Travis turned the roast a quarter turn on the spit. The roast was a round tender muscle that lay along a cow's spine, commonly called a backstrap. Although tasty and tender, the meat lacked any ingrained fat. A thick layer of belly fat had been wrapped around the roast, held in place with hickory slivers. The fat crisped and crackled, turning golden brown as tiny rivers of juice dribbled down onto the hot coals. Travis took a blackened ladle hanging from the mantle and gave the kettle a quick stir. A rich brown stew made of game and beef, wild onions, the tender shoots of bulrushes, and small sweet potatoes filled the cauldron to its brim. There was enough stew to feed a dozen hungry men. Travis turned quizzically to Woody. Woody read his look and laughed, flapping his toothless gums at him.

"Got no teeth. Can't eat anything that ain't boiled to soup first. I just keep that there pot full by adding to her every day and keep her cooking. Hell, there are parts of that there soup that's older than you, boy." Woody laughed. Travis wrinkled his nose in distaste.

Woody ignored the look and went on, "You just leave that soup to me. There's plenty of roast for you boys; shame to make soup from that good meat."

Squib pointed to the roast. "Cattle from a flatboat that sank upstream. Woody says happens so often he hasn't tasted venison in a year."

"Seems like you do pretty well from the suffering of others," Travis cut in sourly.

"Hell boy, don't go and get uppity on me. This here plunder was found all fair and legal-like. Folks that lost it is welcome to come to a claim it back anytime they get to wanting. Makes no difference to me. Weren't for ole Woody, this here plunder be furniture for the fishes."

Unsatisfied with the answer, Travis remembered the tracks. "Seen plenty of signs down by the house of people moving through the house. Maybe folks have been looking for their property."

Woody sat up. He glared at Travis; his voice grew hard and cold. "Watch your mouth, you little woodrat."

Abruptly, he relaxed again and resumed speaking in his usual loud, brassy manner, his scowl buried in a wrinkled grin. "Damn boy, you're sharper than puppy teeth. Plenty of folks coming and going; this here island is famous for those that know about her. You boys ever hear of Aaron Burr?"

Squib shook his head and leaned forward in anticipation of a story. Travis tried to sound knowledgeable and spurted out, "My pa's name was Aaron."

Woody nodded condescendingly to him in reply. "Ole Aaron — not your Pa — was once the Vice-President of these here United States. But Aaron, like all them tidewater politicians, he had a hungry eye. A keen one too, 'cause he shot Alexander Hamilton, another bigwig politician from New Jersey, in a duel and killed him. Well, them politicians don't much care for dueling; they'd rather talk your head off than shoot it off. So, Aaron, he tucks his tail between his legs and comes down here to visit his old friend, Harman Blennerhassett. Boys, this here island was sure something back then. Wait, that there haunch of meat looks about done. Dig in boys, while I finish this here story." Squib carved off a large slice of beef and passed it to Travis on the point of his long knife. Taking a slice for himself Squib leaned back, idly chewing the meat from the point of his knife while Woody continued his tale. Like all great storytellers, Woody began to punctuate his tale with expansive hand signs, pointing and gesturing about as he spoke. "Well, over there by the landing Harman built a dock for all the flatboats coming down the river loaded with supplies and workman to build his estate. He built a road with stones all laid side by side so close you couldn't slip a knife between them. The road wound real casual like he was in no rush to get to the house at the end. Course you seen the house, but back then she was something to see. All shiny white like fresh snow on a sunny morning. Real glass windows too, all the way from a glass factory up there in Pittsburg. Around the house, he built gardens full of flowers and bushes like you never seen before. Planted them, so there were flowers blooming almost all summer long, not just in the spring like most wild ones. Real pretty they were too, all red, white, blue, and yellow. Well, you can't eat flowers, so Harman built a farm on the other side of the island. Corn, wheat, and more kinds of fruit trees you ever did see. Those trees be so heavy with fruit that come fall, the bears would just lie underneath and let the fruit fall right into their mouths. Course,

Ole Harman had them bears killed, seeing as that there young wife of his liked to ride around them orchards so much. The prettiest damn woman anyone in these parts ever saw. Always wore red riding clothes. Red dress, red cape, and this here tiny white hat on her head. Just like a tiny red bird she were. But, Ole Harman he had no time for riding or that pretty wife of his and spent most of his day in his lab-or-a-tory," he stretched the word out as if he could only remember it in pieces. "You boys know what a lab-or-a-tory is?" Squib and Travis shook their heads. Woody sighed and continued, "No, me neither. They say Harman brewed up all kinds of potions and elixirs in there, stank the whole island up, smelled of fire and brimstone like hell's own kitchen. Now, I don't know what else he cooked up in that lab-or-a-tory of his, but I do know what Ole Aaron and Harman simmered up between them." Woody stopped to let the statement sink in, then picked up before the boys were tempted to interrupt. "Treason — High Treason. Yes, sir. As dangerous as a two-headed snake them two scoundrels were, and right here in this garden of Eden, with that pretty little wife an' all, them rogues was planning and scheming. And do you know what they were plotting?" He waited again to let the question sink in.

Squib, remembering his experience that morning asked, "Snakes got two heads?" Travis laughed at his brother, then looked at Woody for confirmation he had only been exaggerating. Woody ignored them both and said in his most serious manner, "Conquest of Louisiana. Yes, sir. Them snakes built a fleet of boats right over there by the landing — a fleet large enough to carry over a thousand men down the Ohio into the Mississippi and conquer all of Louisiana. Well, before Aaron and Harman could carry out their fiendish plans, our president, Ole Thomas Jefferson himself, heard of the plot. Well, that was the end of Aaron and Harman and the end of this here estate of his. Once folks heard there was treason and scheming going on, and God only knows what else with the likes of them two scoundrels, that were the end." Woody stopped and left the end tangling like bait for a fish to nibble at.

"What happened to the estate?" Travis asked.

"Folks come down from Marietta. Smashed and destroyed everything they couldn't carry off. Hunted down most of his fancy animals from Africa, except ole Stripes and that there lion. They tried to burn the house down, but every time they got a fire going, the rain would come down so hard it would douse the fire. Soon folks got a little scared like the devil wanted to stop them and they all ran back upriver."

"Did they hang the traitors?" Squib asked.

"No," Woody replied. "Them tidewater plotters went to trial up there in Virginia. Got off slick as can be. Them tidewater folks stick together." Woody stopped as Squib popped the last piece of roast meat into his mouth. He smacked his lips; the lack of teeth didn't stop his mouth from watering at the thought of roast backstraps.

"Boys, help yourself to the quilts and furs over there and roll under for the night. I just have one favor to ask. Ole Stripes is my only companion on this here island, and I don't want that hound worrying him during the night." Woody gestured towards Fidious curled up outside the door. "Tie your hound up in the shed."

"He won't like that," Travis said. "Squib, best you take him in the woodshed."

"Me?" Squib cried. "I'd rather curl back up with that rattler."

Woody stood and took a small pail which he filled with stew. He handed the pot to Squib, instructing him, "You just put that pot in the shed, and your dog will follow you. Don't worry none; he'll be so full, he'll never notice he's locked in."

Squib carried the pot to the shed. Fidious trotted in behind him and buried his head into the steaming pot. Softly, Squib backed out of the shed, closed the door, and slid the large bar into place to lock it. Squib scratched his head, wondering the purpose of a bar to lock a woodshed from the outside. Then he remembered the story of the lion, and quickly assumed that the hut had at one time been used to hold the lion or one of the other wild animals that once populated the estate. He returned to the cabin. Woody was already asleep, curled up in a quilt in front of the fire. His stentorian snore had driven Travis to seek refuge as far away as possible in the far corner. Travis cocked his head to one side as if in pain and plugged his ears with his fingers. Squib laughed. Pointing with his thumb, he whispered, "Now, that doesn't surprise me at all." He took a quilt from the pile, spread it out in the opposite corner, and lay down with his rifle at his side. Squib looked over his shoulder at Woody, thinking that while small in size, the old man was big on talk. Yet despite all the stories and talk, he had never once asked their names, where their home was, or their destination. Except for the dramatic gestures and pointed commands, it was almost as if they did not exist. He could well have been talking to his zebra for all the interest he showed in his guests. Time enough for questions tomorrow, he thought. Comforted for the first time in weeks by a warm bed and full stomach, he fell into a deep sleep.

A sharp stab of pain pierced Travis' belly, and he sat up with a start. Groaning, he bent over, holding his stomach and cursing himself for eating so much. He waited for the pain to subside and lay down again, rolling on his side to ease the pain. Only half-awake, he reached out to pull his rifle closer to him. He reached and reached, then jerked awake with a start. Liberty was gone. He leapt to his feet and looked around.

Squib and Woody were still wrapped up in their blankets. Travis leapt to his brother's side and began to wake him with a shake. Squib sat up alert, reaching automatically for his rifle. His hand came away empty as well.

Travis whispered, "Mine too, and all my kit."

Then he noticed the silence. Woody had stopped snoring. Travis jumped across the room and tore at Woody's blankets, revealing the bedding was piled to look like a sleeping person. Woody was gone.

Squib came to his side and asked, "What's happening?"

"We been robbed," Travis cried out.

Suddenly he remembered the canoe. "Maybe it's not too late; come on."

Grabbing Squib by the arm he pulled his brother out the door and together they raced towards the landing. Travis pushed his way into the lead. His lighter weight and leaner build gave him the speed advantage as he sprinted ahead. He ignored the winding footpath, instead choosing the more direct route through the trees straight towards the riverbank. Bounding through the trees like a frightened deer, he recklessly bore into the willows. Heedless of the risk, he jumped over the deadfalls. Squib quickly fell behind, only catching sight of Travis sporadically when he cleared an open space ahead. He lost him again as Travis leapt into the blackness.

The forest started to thin. Travis, ahead of his brother, could see the river. Something was moving on the water's edge.

Woody and the canoe.

Travis cleared the forest and bounded off the riverbank onto the gravel beach below in a clatter of flying pebbles.

Woody was just sliding the canoe into the current when he heard the crash behind him. He whirled about and yanked a rifle from the boat. Fanning the lock back, he lifted the rifle up and brought it to bear towards Travis who was charging at him from just yards away. His finger started the barest squeeze of the trigger as he tried to level the sights on Travis. Surprisingly, the hair trigger let go. The rifle fired. Travis crashed into the rocks.

Blinded by the bright flash of the powder in the pan, Woody reached into the canoe, fumbling madly about for the other rifle. Finding it, he fanned the hammer and spun about.

The rifle was yanked painfully from his hands and a huge fist slammed into his face, sending him staggering. Squib stepped forward. He held the rifle in one hand by the muzzle. With his other hand, he backhanded Woody to the ground. Woody sprang up. Unsheathing his knife, he swung a vicious backhand stroke that sliced through Squib's wamus. Rather than jumping back, Squib pushed forward. Getting inside Woody's reach, he seized his knife hand in an iron-hard grip; then, swinging the rifle in his other hand, he smashed down across Woody's imprisoned arm. Woody's forearm shattered with a fierce crack. Woody grunted in pain as his disabled hand lost its grip on the knife and it fell to the ground. Squib released the limp arm and stepped back, expecting his adversary to collapse. Woody surprised him and jumped for the fallen knife with his other hand. Too late he realized he was diving into a rising knee. Squib's knee caught him full in the face and crushed his nose flat onto his cheeks. Woody flew backward, falling spread-eagled into the water. Cautiously, Squib stepped forward, expecting no more fight from the procumbent Woody as he crawled on all fours. Emerging from the streambed, Woody suddenly picked up an apple-sized stone and smashed it down on Squib's foot. Squib howled. Staggering back, the rifle slipped from his grasp as he gamboled about. Woody leapt for the gun. He grasped the rifle and brought it up to aim when he felt two huge paws grab his shoulders and lift him into the air. Squib lifted Woody above his head and threw him with all his strength against a boulder. Woody smacked into the rocks with a sound like breaking billiard balls. Squib grabbed Woody by the hair, aiming a smashing blow to his skull. Suddenly, someone grabbed his arms, pinning them. "Stop."

Travis held Squib back and yelled again, "Squib, stop. You done enough. Let go."

Squib released Woody's hair, allowing his head to hit the rocks with a sickening crack like a dropped egg.

"God, Travis, I thought he killed you," Squib cried out, holding his brother in his arms. "Are you hurt?"

"No, I dove into the rocks when he aimed at me," Travis lied, afraid to admit that when he saw the rifle coming towards him his legs had turned to butter and he had fallen. Squib pulled him closer and gave him a bear hug.

"Put me down, you damn bear," Travis laughed. He stood back so his brother couldn't pick him up again. Suddenly he felt a blow behind his knee, and he fell backward as Woody crawled towards him with a rock raised in his hand. Squib wrenched the rock away and brought it down, crushing Woody's shoulder.

Squib stooped down and helped Travis to his feet.

"Damn, he doesn't know when to quit." Suddenly Squib fell back when Woody hit him with another rock in the leg. Travis and Squib fell on Woody and pounded him with their fists, raining blow after blow till their arms ached. They pushed themselves to their feet, staggering slightly from exhaustion. They watched incredulously as Woody rolled over and aimed a weak kick at them.

"Leave him," Squib snorted in disgust. "He's too broke up to do any harm."

"Damn, he should be dead but he keeps trying to fight. Ain't natural," Travis replied.

They left Woody on the beach and carried the canoe back into the trees. Satisfied no damage had been done to the fragile craft, they recharged their rifles before returning to the beach.

Woody was gone. Travis cocked his rifle and pointed towards the house, saying, "Get Fidious. He'll find him."

"No," a weak voice cried from behind them. "Don't send your dog. He'll kill me for sure." Travis stared into the water. A ghostly head emerged from behind a boulder. Painfully, leaning against the boulder with his shattered shoulder, Woody stood, teetering almost drunkenly back to the beach. Stumbling, he lurched forward, almost falling on his face. Squib lunged to catch him when suddenly Woody aimed a feeble kick between his legs. Squib easily sidestepped the kick and flattened Woody with a vicious swing of his rifle butt. The blow caught him in the face, his cheek crepitated with a loud pop, and he fell limply to the ground.

"Damn, Squib; you killed him."

"No," Squib replied, bending down to examine the body, "he's still breathing. Let's get him back to the cabin before I do kill him." With one hand, Squib grasped Woody's belt, lifted him, and, as if setting off on a picnic with a lunch hamper in hand, headed up the bank. Travis followed closely behind, scanning the dark woods around them with his rifle cocked and ready. Some things were starting to add up, and he didn't like the sums.

Squib forged ahead into the cabin while Travis went to the woodshed to free Fidious. Expecting the wolf-dog to come flying at his throat, he cautiously opened the door, keeping it between him and the dog. Fidious pranced out, completely ignored Travis cowering behind the door, ran to the nearest tree, and lifted his hind leg. Travis slammed the shed door and stomped off, mumbling to himself, "Damn dog, never know what he's going to do." Still fuming to himself, he stormed through the door and confronted Squib standing over Woody's recumbent form. His rifle muzzle was pressed tightly against the back of Woody's neck.

Turning to Travis, Squib pointed to a small knife on the floor and said in a shocked voice, "He tried to kill me again."

"Hold him there," Travis said, and he trussed Woody's hands behind his back and lashed them to his upturned ankles. Woody remained stoically quiet, not making a sound as Travis bound his torn shoulder and broken arm together.

Squib collapsed into an armchair, the rifle across his knee pointed at Woody's face. "What do we do with him?" he asked.

"We leave him and get out of here fast," Travis said, bundling up their blankets.

"He's not going anywhere," Squib replied. "Why not leave in the morning? I'm done in."

"You'll be done in all right. When his partners return, we'll all be done in."

Squib sat up with a start. "Partners?"

Travis squatted before Woody and poked him with his rifle. "How many partners you got, you ole bandit? How many people you kill using the zebra as bait to bring them curious folks in here for killing?" Travis gestured to Squib. "Folks going downriver see that zebra and come ashore for a look just like we have. Then ole Woody here arrives and gives them the same story he gave us except there's more of his partners waiting in the woods. Come night they sneak in here, and slash our throats are cut."

"You think they are waiting for us out there now?" Squib asked apprehensively as he peered cautiously towards the cabin door.

"I don't know," Travis replied. "The rifle fire will bring them if they're close; let's get out of here."

Moving one at a time, leapfrog style, each with his rifle at the ready while the other dashed to the nearest cover, they moved out of the cabin into the sheltering darkness of the woods. Then, abandoning caution, they ran madly to the canoe, jumped in with Fidious on their heels, and pushed off to the safety of the river.

Travis began to paddle furiously away from the shore when he suddenly stopped, catching Squib by surprise.

"Why did you stop?" Squib asked, looking back over his shoulder towards the burnt mansion.

"Look," Travis whispered and pointed ahead to the shoreline. "It's that zebra. Stripes. Standing in the water. But he ain't no zebra."

Squib stared at the creature silhouetted by the moonlight reflecting off the water behind.

"His stripes," Squib stammered. "His stripes are gone from his belly and legs. He's just a mule. A painted mule."

"A ruse," Travis retorted vehemently. "A mule painted like a zebra to lure unsuspecting settlers to shore so Woody can ambush them. That's what he is. We ought to go back and shoot that bandit before he attacks more settlers."

"What we ought to do is get out of here before someone shoots us," Squib answered. He drove his paddle powerfully into the water, pushing the canoe farther away from the shore.

The brothers paddled hard and fast, staying in the center of the broad river through the night until the early morning hours when Travis pointed at a small island and said softly, "There, the head of that island."

"It looks too small," Squib whispered back.

"Too small for anyone to live on," Travis replied, "and too little for anyone to land on without one of us hearing."

Squib nodded approval of the plan and they turned the canoe towards the bank. After a quick scout, they judged the island perfect for hiding and resting. Travis slid the canoe ashore, hiding it out of sight beneath the trees. As he removed their gear, he found two heavy sacks no doubt left by Woody. Too tired to investigate, Travis left them. He would take a look later. Squib swept their tracks from the soft sand with a large branch, settled himself under a large fallen tree, and was quickly sound asleep.

"I will watch while you sleep," Travis said, looking about for Fidious to accompany him. But the big dog was already curled up and asleep in the warm sandy hollow next to Squib. Travis had eyed the spot for himself and shook his head in disgust. Instead, he lay against the tree trunk and prepared to keep watch and wait the night out.

Chapter 8

An intense wave of sudden burning pain in Woody's broken arm jolted him from his sleep. He opened his eyes to the grinning demonic face of Major Torrens just inches away from his own. Sitting back his heels, the major prodded Woody by holding his tomahawk like a pistol by the head and poking him with the end of the handle.

"Have a nice nap, Mr. Woody?" the major asked sarcastically. Still bound up, Woody pulled himself slowly to his good elbow and looked past the still grinning officer to the grim faces of his soldiers standing behind. The toughened soldiers looked the hardened veterans they were; men who had spent a lifetime on the battlefield. Rigorous lives further evidenced by their well-oiled and carefully maintained weapons and the easy manner in which the arms were carried. Woody knew there would be no rescue or compassion from these men on this night. Nodding to one of the men, the major said, "Cut our friend here loose."

Woody was cut free by one of the soldiers who pushed him roughly to the floor with his foot. Woody slowly pulled himself to a sitting position with his good arm fighting the pain to keep upright.

"Fall out of your comfy armchair, did we?" the major asked, smashing savagely across Woody's broken arm with the handle of the tomahawk. Woody grimaced silently and fell back, clutching his arm to his chest. The major looked down in disgust, and then slowly rose to his feet. Turning to the men behind him, he pointed towards the mansion. He spoke quietly, "Sergeant, take two men and check our article hidden in the ballroom.. Best you leave the corporal, he can take the rest of the men and form a perimeter around the estate while I find out what's been going on here."

The men nodded and silently left the cabin. Looking both right and left as they passed the door, they held their muskets at the ready with the trained efficiency of well practiced soldiers. Each went to his assigned task without being told where or how.

The major turned to Woody and sat back down again on his heels. "Let's have a little chat, shall we?" the major asked quite pleasantly, emphasizing the word chat with another sharp rap of the tomahawk handle to Woody's broken limb. Another flash of pain coursed through Woody's arm. This time Woody responded with a cold shiver of fear, sensing the major's enjoyment of inflicting pain on him.

"What happened here?" the major asked, smiling.

"Bandits!" Woody blurted out. "Bandits done this to me. Snuck up on me like Indians and jumped me 'fore I could raise my gun. Beat me good and left me for dead. Had I been just a little younger they would never have snuck—" The handle of the tomahawk crashed down on Woody's broken nose, silencing him.

"Now, let's limit ourselves to the truth, shall we, Mr. Woody?" the major asked quietly. "Who were they and what was their number?"

Woody tried to think, but then he saw the handle of the tomahawk start to rise and blurted out quickly, "Two. Two young long hunters going downriver to St. Louis. They came and took my hospitality and when I wasn't looking jumped me and tried to—" Again, the tomahawk descended, smashing this time against Woody's broken cheek and driving the words from his lips. Giving in to the pain Woody whimpered and tried to pull away from the major. The pain was becoming unbearable now. Woody knew the signs; he could not take much more.

"Rifles," Woody said slowly. "Them boys had real pretty rifles. I tried to steal them but they caught me. I figured they were easy pickings, but they had that big dog an' I couldn't fight all three."

"That's better," the major smiled. "Did these boys have names, Mr. Woody?"

"Travis. And the big one with all the hair was Squib," Woody replied. "The dog's name was Fidious," he added as an afterthought.

"The dog?" the major laughed sarcastically "You say the dog's name was Fidious?" The major laughed louder and wagged the tomahawk handle like a scolding finger while he smiled coldly at Woody.

"Now, that must be the truth, Mr. Woody. Even your old twisted mind would never come up with a name like that." Slapping his knee and chuckling to himself, the major rose and turned to face the sergeant who had just returned to the cabin.

"It's gone," the sergeant reported, stepping back. He anticipated a sudden outburst of anger from the officer. The major's smile slowly dissolved in a red tide that flushed up from his neck as anger welled up and distorted his face.

"Wait outside," the major growled through clenched teeth. The sergeant backed quickly out of the cabin, shutting the door behind him. He knew that look. Someone was going to get hurt.

"No, Major. Please no," Woody pleaded as he tried to pull himself away. Aiming the toe of his boot at Woody's broken arm, the major unleashed a swift and quick kick that lifted Woody from the floor and sent him into a heap by the fireplace. The major walked slowly to his side.

"That, Mr. Woody, is for calling me major. My name is Washington Davis. What a fine American-sounding name that is, don't you think?"

"Yes, Mr. Davis," Woody replied between sobs. "It's very American." The major pulled an armchair close to the fire and sat down. Leaning back, he placed one foot on Woody's chest and threw the other leg over the arm of the chair. Then, ominously and slowly he turned the tomahawk around and held it correctly by the handle. "Now, Mr. Woody. I think we will begin with you telling me the whole truth concerning tonight's affair."

Outside the cabin, Sergeant White moved quietly to each of his men and sent them silently to new positions out of earshot from the cabin. Long association had taught him the importance of keeping the major's activities as far as possible from his men. The men knew if they were captured by the Americans, they would most likely be hanged as spies, but there was no need for them to know any more than the sergeant did, which was exactly nothing. Safer for all from both the Americans and the major.

Chapter 9

Travis saw them first. Two large freighter canoes rounded the bend of the river, then shot past the lower rapids out into the center of the river propelled by the steady rhythmic strokes of the paddlers straight towards the island.

Careful not to make any eye-attracting fast movements, Travis pulled himself slowly into the deep shadows of the underbrush. Once he was completely hidden, he tapped Squib on the back of the heel with his rifle. Conditioned to a hunter's life in the wilderness, Squib remained motionless, looking about slowly and moving only his eyes. Silently, he drew his rifle closer ever so carefully. With the other hand he grabbed Fidious by the collar and whispered for him to stay. Then he eased himself on his side, turned, and looked up the river. The canoes had reached the part of the river below the bend where the river widened and slowed. Here, the canoes drew apart and moved to take parallel positions within easy musket shot of both shores. Laying their paddles over the gunnels the paddlers let the river draw the canoes slowly downstream, closer to the brothers' island hideaway. Still too far away and partially hidden by the long shadows of morning, the men and their purpose were indistinct except they were now no longer in a hurry. There was no mistaking the large freighter canoes used by traders, merchants, and Indian war parties to move up and down the river. Squib and Travis had seen their like many times before. Those canoes were crewed predominantly by French Canadians known as coureaur de bois, men legendary on the frontier for their stamina, courage, and physical strength. Loading two hundred pounds of freight on their backs in crude packsacks held by a top strap to their foreheads, they would run back and forth between portages, moving tons of freight and canoes in what would take a normal man days they would move in a few hours. The ability to do the job faster than the competitor kept these voyagers constantly moving. Many times in the past, Squib and Travis had been caught by the surprising appearance behind them of the swift canoes which quickly overtook them. Each stroke of the paddle was accompanied with and in rhythm to many lively paddling songs, known simply on the waterways of the Northwest as the song of the paddle.

These canoes were different. No song of the paddle came from them. The slow, measured pace of the paddle strokes spoke of hunters. Hunters of what? was the question. The canoes drew closer. Shadow yielded to bright morning light. Five men filled each canoe. Four paddlers with muskets close at hand watched, while in the bow of the lead canoe a fifth man knelt alone. Musket cradled at the ready, he scanned the shore intently. Occasionally raising a telescope, he would look to one spot or another along the shore. The paddlers resumed a slow even pace just sufficient to maintain steerage; the paddlers too were concentrating on watching the banks of the river. Every few moments one or another would point silently to something that had drawn his attention and the others would stare at that spot. Ominously, one paddler would drop his paddle, raise his musket, and follow the location through his sights. The rough homespun clothes and sun-darkened complexions suggested settlers headed downriver. The tomahawks, knives, and pistols stuck about their belts did not. Their precise, deliberate, and practiced manner with their Brown Bess muskets spoke of soldiers or raiders, men used to the ways of weaponry and combat.

Coming abreast of the island and now two hundred yards from their position, Squib silently thanked Travis for choosing the island. Except for the odd glance, the men concentrated their attention on the far shores. The brothers remained still and silent for several long tense moments while the canoes passed down the river and disappeared around another bend. More from relief than exhaustion, the brothers lay quiet for several minutes more before Travis began to rise. Suddenly, Fidious growled from his bed in the tree hollow. Travis froze. Upriver, within a pistol shot of the island, a third canoe had unexpectedly appeared. Four grim-faced men with muskets aimed outboard occupied the canoe. The canoe drifted, silently bearing down on the island.

Fight or run. Travis glanced quickly at Squib, looking for guidance or a suggestion. Squib was flat on his belly, completely motionless. Keep perfectly still, that is the strategy, Travis thought quickly. The early day shadows are still dark and long, movement is the enemy, he reasoned. Every hunter knew that motion betrayed the prey before all else.

The canoe was closer now. Travis imagined every grim eye on him as cold sweat dripped from the tip of his nose and splashed off Liberty's stock. It took every bit of inner strength not to move. His feet screamed, run! Suddenly, one of the men jumped to his knees and aimed his musket into the center of the island. Travis was so shocked he couldn't move. Time stopped as he waited for the gun sights to aim at the center of his forehead and the deadly cloud of white smoke that would signal his ride into oblivion. The shooter's gaze down the barrel was so intense Travis could feel it bore into him like a knife. He slowly closed his eyes, afraid this was his end. It felt like an eternity and when no shot nor shout of warning came, he opened his eyes again.

The man had lowered his weapon and had sat down again. Obviously, the maneuver was planned to break any prey who could be watching by startling them into moving or running.

As the third canoe passed out of sight down the river, Travis felt lightheaded, then he realized he had been holding his breath since the man had leapt up. He exhaled loudly. Squib flinched violently at the sound and turned from looking down the river. He gave Travis a dirty look. This time they waited several minutes longer before starting to move. They were reluctant, until Fidious rose and started to nose about their small island signaling no need for further caution.

Keeping a watchful eye upriver, Squib slid carefully next to his brother and asked quietly, "Them men looking for us?"

"They were looking for somebody," Travis replied slowly. "If it was us then I'm sure glad we didn't meet. Those were no traders I ever saw."

"Soldiers," Squib volunteered after what appeared to be considerable thought.

"Why would soldiers be looking for us?" Travis scoffed. "Them was Woody's pals. Looking for us, for what we did to that thieving skunk."

"I was afraid you was going to shoot," Squib said after a moment.

"We can't just shoot people because we think they are after us," Travis replied sourly. "That would be murder; we would be hanged for sure."

"How are we going to know who to trust and who not to?" Squib asked.

"We don't trust anyone unless we know them," Travis thought out loud. "Remember what Uncle Wes said about being smart and know what's going on around you all the time. We have to be deer in the forest, aware of everything around us. Like hunting, excepting we are the hunted and the deer all the time. We know how to do that."

"And we watch each other's back like deer do in a herd," Squib interjected quickly. "And we have signs like when a lead doe raises her tail to signal danger or bobs her head up and down to get your attention away from the herd," Squib said excitedly.

"We need more signals so we always know what each other is thinking if we get into a scrape," Travis shot back.

"Right," Squib said. "If we had a signal and we needed to shoot we could have done it together."

"And," Travis interrupted, "we could have shot two of them and evened the odds better."

"But," Squib cut in again, "we need to know who to shoot so we don't hit the same one."

"How we gonna know that?" Travis asked, puzzled by the problem.

"Easy," Squib replied. As he leaned back, he started to stare off into the sky like he was thinking. "Since you're a better shot than me and faster too, you always take the most dangerous or harder shot and I'll go for the other."

Travis wasn't sure this was going the way he liked, and he said, "Squib, you're just as good a shot as me."

"No. No," Squib replied, trying to be humble, "you're much cooler and calmer than me on the trigger."

"So," Travis asked, "if we get attacked by two tigers..."

"Ain't no tigers in America!" Squib interjected.

"Ok, if we get attacked by two bears," Travis corrected, "I shoot the front one and you shoot the back one."

"Yep," Squib answered.

"And back a while ago I would have shot the man with the rifle in the canoe?" Travis asked.

"Yep," Squib replied, "and I would have shot the steersman."

Warming to the subject while the danger of the morning still stirred their imaginations, the brothers created and exchanged ideas on a variety of hand and eye signals. They lounged in the morning sun, safe and secure on their island hideaway. From simple winks to elaborate hand movements, they agreed on their signals that could be used for everyday hunting situations to the more dangerous shooting scrapes their imaginations could come up with.

The excitement soon started to wane and hunger intruded on their revelry with Squib professing, in his usual manner, that if he didn't eat something soon, they would most likely fall from exhaustion. He proceeded to dig into their provisions. It was then that Travis remembered the extra gear found in the canoe. He grabbed the two bags and gave one to Squib. He proceeded to open the heavier but smaller of the travel sacks. Squib, squealing like a hog in the feed trough, pulled from the larger sack bags of jerky and corn cakes together with jars of honey, maple syrup, brown sugar, cornmeal, and, much to Squib's delight, a large jar still warm from the night before of beef stew. Travis laughed as his brother, in an almost childlike manner, began portioning the stew equally and with precise care into their trenchers. The portions of stew were accompanied by corn cakes onto which he had generously poured honey.

Travis found treasure of greater worth as he pulled powder horns of fine black powder, lead bars, and flints. Next came a wooden box of hand-polished walnut that Travis identified immediately as the type used to protect dueling pistols. Gently, he opened the clasp of the box. Squib leaned over eagerly as the box revealed two finely made and presented dueling pistols. While the pistols had seen some wear and several of the indentations that would have held extra parts or tools were empty, the weapons themselves had been well-maintained. Squib reached over, grabbed one of the pistols, and proceeded to sight down the barrel. Aiming it left and right, he gauged the feel of the weapon in his hand.

"Well made," he pronounced knowledgably.

"Are these why those men are following us?" Travis asked.

"We don't know for sure they are after us," Squib replied. "There are plenty of renegades and thieves on this river already."

"True enough," Travis answered. "Could be they think we are partners with Woody back there," he said, pointing upriver with his thumb. "But it just strikes me that's not right."

"Best we use caution and treat them as dangerous till we know for sure then," Squib replied. "What about these pistols; do we keep them?"

"I didn't see Woody in any of those canoes, so unless we take them pistols back to him upriver, it's either throw them into the river or keep them."

"And have to fight Woody all over again?" Squib replied, shaking his head. "No, we keep them. Won't hurt any if those yahoos are after us to have a couple of pistols handy."

"I agree," Travis replied. "Let's get some sleep and then head down the river after dark. It will be safer till we find where those characters have gone."

Chapter 10

Morning came gradually to the river as the rains of the night before left a heavy fog that swirled slowly in eddies over the river, laying thick, dark, and impenetrable along the shore into the forest beyond. The muted sounds of the river rushing by enveloped the sergeant in a shadowy silence as he stood on the beach. He felt a deep chill from the wetness of the night's rain.

Sergeant White dreaded the thought of giving his morning report to Major Smith-Torrens after his return from the outlying pickets along the river. For the third night, they had camped on a vantage point on the river where sentries stationed along the shores would have a good chance of seeing their quarry if they passed. None had reported a sighting; they had seen nothing but heavy rain and fog.

And now the night patrol sent up the river in their canoe to scout any apparent campsites for the long-missing hunters had failed to return by their appointed time of dawn. They were no doubt lost in the fog or traveling slow for safety. Not that having a good reason for their tardiness will appease Major Smith-Torrens this morning, Sergeant White thought as he made his way towards their camp that was sheltered deeper in the woods. Indeed, the major was in one of his foulest moods yet, what with no sightings of the two frontiersmen they were seeking; further delays in recovering the "article," as the major called it; and now a lost patrol. Were it not for the need to keep their mission secret and their disguises as American backwoods men, the major would give some poor soldier the lash. Might as well fly the Union Jack from the canoes if the men were subjected to corporal punishment or military justice while trying to hide amongst Americans in their backwoods costumes. Or worse, if the men were pushed too cruelly, then desertion or mutiny would be the death of them all. The sergeant shuddered at the thought.

The officers who ordered this mission had done some right sneaky thinking before they embarked, Sergeant White mused. He would give them credit for that, alright. Picking the men with strong Irish, Scottish, and Welsh accents suited the multinational makeup of his command by matching those of many Americans they had encountered thus far on their mission. But for the major, they all passed very well as Americans. Oh, no. Not the major, the sergeant laughed to himself. Pompous, arrogant, overbearing, nose up in the air — he was truly a haughty aristocrat in buckskin. The major's arrogant attitude made him stand out from his soldiers and the many travelers they met along the way. On previous days when they approached settlers on shore or on their flatboats to ask if anyone had seen the fugitives pass in their canoe, they would not direct their replies to the sergeant, not even when it was him asking. No, they would direct their reluctant, sometimes hostile replies to the major.

Pausing briefly, the sergeant listened carefully to the sound of a small splash out in the river. He waited momentarily, and when no further splashes or sounds followed, he passed it off as probably a fish or some waterfowl and resumed his return to camp.

"About time, Sergeant," the major stormed on Sergeant White's return. "Report."

"No sightings or unusual activity sighted by the pickets, Mr. Davis," the sergeant replied, using the major's American alias.

The major bristled at the sergeant's use of his alias. Then, with a sarcastic sneer, he continued, "And what of the river patrol, Jacob?" He had used the sergeant's alias.

"No sign of them, probably delayed in the fog," the sergeant replied.

"Probably is not an answer; it is a guess." Torrens' face turned red as the anger in his voice intensified. "Probably could mean they deserted. Probably could mean they were captured and turned over to the Americans." Warming to his anger, the major was about to lash out at the sergeant again when the muted sound of paddles was faintly heard coming from the river. A ghostly canoe pulled slowly into sight, closing to the shore.

The major and the sergeant hurried to the water's edge. "Any sign?" the major asked.

Quiet shrugs and shakes of the head signaled a no.

"Campfires and campsites?" the sergeant asked.

"Some," the corporal in charge of the patrol replied. "All settlers with flatboats."

"And how closely did you search?" the major asked in a doubtful voice.

"We scouted them all from the river as well as close from the shore," the corporal replied. "No sign of their canoe, men like those described, or the wolf-dog."

Major Torrens released a loud, frustrated sigh as the soldiers waited quietly in their canoe for the usual anticipated outburst of anger and blame. Then, slapping his fist into his hand, the major turned to Sergeant White. "Enough of this game!" he barked. "They have slipped by us and are ahead of us somewhere downriver. We will assume they have passed by us and pursue based on that assumption. Bring in the sentries and prepare to embark." Turning on his heel, the major stomped towards camp. He commanded loudly over his shoulder, "Now, Sergeant!"

Out across the great river, sitting and back-paddling slowly in the dense fog, the brothers listened quietly. After the initial discovery of the patrolling canoe working its way along the riverbank, during a brief moment when the occupants had been backlit by a campfire on the shore they were able to confirm these were of the party they had seen on the river some days before. A long night of shadowing the patrol canoe by hanging back in the darkness and the rain followed later by a heavy fog, they had maintained a safe distance, hoping to find out more about their pursuers. While the brothers had followed invisible in the fog, the sound of their pursuers' voices carried across the water clearly enough for the them to know they were being chased by these men. Now arriving at the party's camp, they sat and listened through the fog to the muffled voices that drifted from the shore.

The final loud command of "Now, Sergeant!" surprised Travis and he turned over his shoulder and silently mouthed "Sergeant?" Squib replied with a brief shake of his head and shrug of his shoulders, wondering why soldiers would pursue them.

Allowing the current to pull the canoe quietly down the river out of earshot of the camp, the brothers waited patiently until they thought they were safe from discovery. They commenced to paddle quickly down the river. One thing they had learned from the patrol craft the night before was that its occupants were not efficient or competent paddlers, unlike the brothers who had spent their early years on the Susquehanna River where paddling a canoe was as natural as walking. The men in the pursuing canoes showed little in the ways of river craft or paddling skills, often splashing noisily about with wasted effort and clumsy movement. With powerful, rhythmic strokes, the brothers pushed the canoe swiftly down the river to the point they felt they could talk safely.

"Soldiers?" Squib asked.

"Must be so," Travis replied, then added, "No other reason for a sergeant, and that voice doing the ordering sure sounded like an officer." He added knowingly, "Like to tell people what to do, those officers do."

"What do they want with us?" Squib replied, ignoring Travis' sarcasm. "And why don't they have uniforms? I've never seen soldiers in canoes before; they always travel on flatboats or rowboats?" "All this sneaking around looking for us, why that?" Squib asked, confused by all the unanswered questions.

"Don't know," Travis replied. "But we know from watching that they are poor boatmen. Have you ever heard such noisy paddling?" Travis chuckled. "And those big freighter canoes of theirs are slow, with too much gear and too few paddlers in each. Maybe they're deserters. Been lots of those since the war began."

"Don't know," Squib replied. "Let's keep to our plan, push down the river, and keep a good lead ahead of them. And eat, I'm near starved."

With that, the brothers fell silent, putting their backs into the long, powerful, rhythmic strokes which drove them quickly down the river.

Chapter 11

Ensign Keen was not happy. For six days he and his detachment of eight soldiers of the 39th Infantry Regiment had been left alone in this bug-infested campsite at the junction of Turtle Creek and the Ohio River, waiting for Captain Johnson and the small party of government surveyors while they explored the upper creek. Pampering a bunch of government surveyors was not the kind of duty he had envisioned for himself upon his graduation from West Point Military Academy. Then the dispatch from the headquarters the day prior had put a complete damper on Keen's spirits when he had found out his regiment had been involved in a decisive action of the Creek war at the Battle of Horseshoe Bend in late March. The regiment had distinguished itself together with several officers, including Ensign Sam Houston whom Keen had met when first stationed with the regiment. The troops in his detachment, however, had taken the news of the victory with great joy and excitement. The men were especially pleased with the special sunset ceremony the ensign had put on the previous evening consisting of a triple musket salute followed by profuse spontaneous cheering and toasts, although Keen wasn't sure if the enthusiasm was for the victory or the double spirits rations that followed. The camp cook had even contributed several pies made with dried apples, raisins, together with cinnamon he had squirrelled away to the delight of everyone. Afterwards, the men concluded the evening of salutes, hurrahs, spirits, and pies around the fire with storytelling and songs.

As he now watched the camp detachment go about their morning duties, Ensign Keen mused to himself this was not how he imagined spending his time during this critical point during the war with Britain. Keen was anxious to get into the war that had been raging with Britain these last two years. Yet despite his best efforts to explain his desire for action with Colonel Williams, he found himself stuck on what he considered an undistinguished assignment. His protests were of no avail as Colonel Williams was quite adamant in his explanation that tradition has always been that less than plumb duties fell to the junior officers so senior officers could concentrate on greater responsibilities. Even old Captain Johnson, the officer in charge of this assignment who had fought Chief Tecumseh at the battle of Fallen Timbers and the later battles of Tippecanoe, said the same about his own junior officer assignments with a chuckle, going on at length about his own first undesirable commands. Captain Johnson was quick to point out he was getting too old for active frontline service, and would instead make room for aggressive young officers who turn in an excellent performance on these types of assignments. Hidden between the lines the message to Ensign Keen was be quiet, perform to my satisfaction, and get a good report. Captain Johnson was quite content to spend the last years of his enlistment shuttling back and forth escorting a bunch of map makers without further duty in more dangerous assignments on the front lines. His advice was of little consequence to Ensign Keen, for without combat duty, his opportunities for future promotions were significantly diminished while many of his fellow graduates were fighting in the North and farther South. Not here, he fumed; what experience or glory was he likely to carn here? Praise from an old captain was not likely to advance his career, and sitting around getting attacked by swarms of mosquitoes and gnats was not his idea of combat service. The constant, tedious routine of mounting guards, patrolling the pickets, and supervising the men was taking its toll on Ensign Keen's patience. And it is not doing my temperament much good either, he thought, with six new recruits who still struggled with the basics of the private soldier's life with its constant drilling and the multiple daily activities required to keep a safe, efficient, and orderly encampment. Ensign Keen deemed his troops so incompetent he had been forced to have the men carry their muskets unloaded due to several mishaps that almost caused casualties amongst themselves. Accidents of that nature could be highly detrimental to the officer in charge and his career, should he be convicted of lack of diligence by a military court. No, he sighed to himself, all muskets will be carried unloaded until the return of Captain Johnson's party from upriver. He was sure he could justify his decision to the captain by citing lack of any hostile activity in this part of Ohio and their distance from British attacks farther north. After all, he thought, instruction from the captain to keep muskets loaded at all times stemmed from his experiences at Tippecanoe where the captain claimed a massacre was prevented from a surprise night attack from Tecumseh's Shawnees by the men sleeping with loaded weapons. Tecumseh is dead, and no Shawnees remained hiding or lurking in the woods in this part of Ohio. In fact, there were no hostile natives anywhere in Ohio, except for Captain Johnson's Tuscarora guide and interpreter Ganiga, that is. Keen gave a brief shudder just thinking about Ganiga with his fierce perpetually painted war face, brusque mannerisms that bordered on threatening, and cold contemptuous stare. Only Captain Johnson appeared to have a close relationship and mutual understanding with Ganiga. The good captain, he thought, acted more Indian than army officer, even abandoning his military uniform to wear homespun linens, buckskin wamus, and Shawnee-style knee-high moccasins. His sword and pistol had also been abandoned, replaced by one of the newest Harpers Ferry rifles that had been issued to the few rifle regiments in the US Army. Not that Keen would complain about that as the captain's rifle and sharp eye accounted for a good supply of fresh meat during the expedition. The venison, turkey, and bear were welcome relief from tedious Army rations and contributed greatly to the men being in good spirits. The lesson of the importance of good rations was not lost on the young officer.

Well, at least the coffee is good, Keen sighed to himself as he finished the last gulp of his morning coffee. The crystal-clear water from Turtle Creek makes a fine pot of coffee, he thought while rising from the driftwood log where he had sat during his breakfast. Slowly looking around, he was pleased to see that the men had fallen into their new morning routines, and were now efficiently finishing their breakfast, cleaning up, and preparing for their morning inspection by attending to their gear and weapons. In Ensign Keen's view, ensuring their weapons were clean and spotless was an important daily ritual. The men were happy that they were now able to start the day in their linen summer roundabout uniforms since the change of orders from Washington had allowed the cooler uniforms to be worn in all commands during the summer months. Starting each day in a soldierly manner was a key part of a soldier's life, as far as Ensign Keen was concerned. A few hours each morning of drill together with dry fire practice with their new Springfield Muskets had been much more preferable to the men than the hours of physical toil that took over most of the rest of the day. Many changes had been made over the last few years to make the soldiers' lives more efficient and comfortable. The linen summer roundabouts were now authorized for northern detachments during the hotter summer months. The long hair queues of the past had been chopped to follow the European fashion of shorter neat haircuts that all ranks were now required to wear. Not everyone appreciated the new regulation. Many older officers were objecting to losing their long hair queues, but the war department had been very clear on that regulation. Cut or get out. And get out some did, but most accepted the regulations as part of growing a new modern army. Stubborn old fools, Keen laughed to himself, just more opportunities for the younger officers like myself with them gone. We are a new army now, like France with officers promoted in rank by their competence, experience, and boldness in action and not the archaic British system where rank was purchased by the aristocracy.

Looking up at the sentry post sitting on the bluff as a lookout to the encampment, the ensign saw the sentry being relieved and the new one taking his post. Expanding the game trail leading to the lookout had been the first of several projects the ensign had ordered the men to build. Using picks and shovels, he had ordered the expansion of the trail sufficient to move the men back and forth from the camp quickly and to better maintain a clear lookout on the river while doing so. At first, the men had grumbled about the work, but once the lookout was complete, they soon found that they all appreciated its advantageous location, not entirely for the military reasons Ensign Keen had ordered it built. Located one hundred feet above the river, a sentry could see not only the camp sitting below, but it also offered excellent views both up the river and down to the sentry assigned there. All the men were required to take a four-hour post each day. Most days the post experienced a steady cooling western breeze keeping the lookout virtually mosquito and pest-free. Sentry duty remained a boring yet greatly appreciated assignment for its salubrious ambiance and as a reprieve from fatigue duties.

Once again Keen smiled to himself, shaking off his earlier languor as he looked at the half-dozen large rocks perched on the edge of the post above camp. Three on the left and three on the right. If a warning must be sent to the troops in the camp below, the sentry only had to dislodge one of the stones with a push of his foot, sending the rock noisily crashing through the brush below as a signal someone was approaching the camp from upriver or down. One rock from the right would signal a small party was approaching from upriver. If threatened by a large party, then all three would be pushed off their precipice into the thickets below. While this was not a sentry tower like the ones the Romans would have built (for Keen was an ardent disciple of Roman history and military tactics and would have eagerly copied their tactics from one thousand years before), this sentry location would give adequate service for their short-term needs. Keen would much rather have built a walled encampment with a stockade and watch towers with clear fields of fire as the Romans would have built; however, eight men fell well short of the five thousand in a Roman legion.

Looking now to the river embankments, Keen decided today's project should be clearing some fields of fire around the water's edge of their encampment. The heavy growth of willows and reeds along the river would give good cover to any attacker while the encampment itself was completely open to fire from both the river and creek sides. Keen was startled from his thoughts when a rock tumbled noisily down the embankment behind him. Quickly spinning about, he looked up and saw the missing stone had come from the left side of the line of rocks, thereby signaling a small party from downriver approaching the camp. The sentry above held up two fingers, signaling that two people were approaching the camp.

Picking up his sword belt and pistol and throwing his telescope case over his shoulder, Keen turned to call to Corporal Davidson, "Corporal, muster the men and join me on the shore." He pointed to the small beach on the creek side of the encampment.

"Yes, sir," Corporal Davidson replied. "Should I order the men to load their muskets?"

The canoe just became visible around a bend in the creek, revealing the two young frontiersmen who were paddling towards the camp. They don't look likely to present much of a threat, Keen thought, and he shook his head. Patting his sword belt, he replied, "I think you and I can handle those two young fellows if we need to, don't you, Corporal?"

"Indeed, sir," Davidson answered with a grin, then he turned and began shouting to get the men formed up on the beach.

"Looks like our appearance has gathered a crowd," Travis smirked over his shoulder to Squib as they paddled toward the small beach.

"That's a good sign," Squib answered back. "If they were some of those yahoos we thought were chasing us, we would be dodging a few musket balls right now."

"We still don't know that," Travis answered, harking back to their last week of frenzied paddling downriver constantly watching over their shoulders for the pursuit of the unknown men. They had hid their presence by always cooking their meals at one place, then moving quickly to take a cold camp somewhere on the bluffs overlooking the river or deeper in the woods behind, keeping a distance from any other river travelers and homesteads along the way. Last evening, they had drifted slowly past this camp and watched silently from across the river. They saw that this smaller party than the one from a week ago was made up completely of soldiers. When they made their cold camp later that night, the brothers had talked about approaching the soldiers the next day and seeking advice or direction about being pursued by the ominous group up the river. It was not till the next morning when they saw the American flag flown from the camp that they finally decided to approach the soldiers, although they still had some apprehension.

Coming nearer to the camp, they saw an officer standing on the beach waiting for them. The troops on the beach hastened into a line behind him, shoved along by another soldier of some indeterminate rank.

"Hello, the camp," Travis called out. "May we land?"

"You may," Ensign Keen replied. Standing with his hands on his hips, he tried to assume a domineering stance in a posture similar to what he had seen from more senior officers when addressing civilians.

As the bow touched the beach, Fidious, who had been lying previously unseen on the canoe bottom, abruptly rose and jumped out onto the sand. With only a short sideward glance to the soldiers, he ran off into the woods.

"What is that?" Ensign Keen stammered out in surprise.

"Don't give him any worry," Squib laughed. "He's just big, but he hasn't eaten anyone."

"Not that we know of," Travis snickered. "I'm Travis Tanner, and that's my brother Squib," he said, pointing with his thumb.

"Welcome, I'm Ensign Keen, 39th Infantry Regiment at your service." Pointing to the large logs arranged around the fire pit, he offered, "Have a seat; join me for a coffee." Without waiting for a reply from the brothers, Keen turned to Corporal Davidson and said, "Corporal, have the men stack their arms and return to their duties, then have the cook bring us some coffee as well."

As they all sat on the logs, the brothers placed their rifles next to them within arm's reach while Ensign Keen without any delay launched into a description of the camp and their mission here. He only stopped when the cook brought them steaming mugs of coffee. Squib smiled when he tasted the coffee, finding it was heavily sweetened. They all sat quietly enjoying the coffee. Fidious returned and sat at Squib's side expectantly, watching for the presence of food. Breaking the silence, Keen asked, "What service can the US Army be to you both today?"

Travis looked to Squib who gave a brief nod, signaling him to begin to tell the story of their experience as they had agreed upon earlier. Still unsure of the officer's response and testing the waters of his story, Travis began slowly with their encounter with Woody on the island, their sudden discovery of the theft of their gear, and then the frantic fight on the beach. Finally, he told the officer about their flight down the river and their belief that they may be pursued by the threatening yet unknown men they had seen on the river.

"This Woody person," Keen asked, "was he killed in the fight?"

"No," Squib replied, "but he kept fighting like a devil; we had to beat him down good to stop him."

"But not dead?" Keen asked again.

"No, sir," Squib replied.

"The men who you think are chasing you," Keen asked, turning to Travis, "did they call out to you at any time? Did you see each other clearly? And did they attempt to harm you or threaten you in any way?"

"No," Travis replied, shaking his head. "Just the time one jumped up and aimed his musket at the riverbank while they passed, as I told you. A few nights ago, we followed one of their canoes," Travis added. "They couldn't see our canoe on account of the rain and morning fog. We thought they were searching for us along the shore and watching settlers' campsites very closely that night."

"We heard them talking in the morning," Squib jumped eagerly into the conversation. "We heard one of them called Sergeant, and they had un-American accents."

"How do you mean un-American?" Keen asked patiently.

"Un-American," Squib replied, feeling awkward at the direction of questioning. "Different from us," he said, pointing at Travis and to himself.

Ensign Keen chuckled knowingly. "Half my men here were not born in America. Scots, Dutch, French, and more from almost every country in the world. And as far as the one called Sergeant, it's not unusual for men from the military to be called by their military rank when they return to civilian life." Keen grew more serious and continued, "You don't know if they were chasing you or they were just extremely cautious and vigilant when you saw them. Sounds like a tactic; jumping up and aiming your gun at a suspected hiding place might shock an untrained assailant to reveal himself. Certainly, it is well known trick used by trained military officers like me."

Now feeling sheepish about their story, both brothers shook their heads. Travis replied, "No, not really, we can't claim for sure they were following us."

"Have you taken anything these men could have had or want to be returned, say something this Woody person stole from them?" Keen asked.

"We didn't steal anything," Squib answered, "but Woody did. We found them in a bag along with some provisions he had left in our canoe."

"Found what?" Keen asked.

"Food, provisions, and pistols," Travis replied.

"Dueling pistols," Squib interjected. "Good ones, in a fancy wooden case."

"Where are they now?" Keen asked. "Can you show them to me?"

"We have them," Travis replied. He went to the canoe and returned a few moments later. He passed the case to Keen.

Keen appraised the case quickly and noted it was of good quality, but not exceptional nor rare in a country where the gentry actively practiced dueling. The brothers watched keenly as the ensign showed a familiarity with the pistols. Keen opened the case. Inside, he found two well-mounted quality dueling pistols of a type commonly known as Dragoon style, as Keen remarked to the brothers while continuing his inspection. Also, the case with all the usual accessories of cast bullets, bullet molds, cleaning rods, bullet worms, along with spare parts again not untypical of the many held by gentlemen and military officers. But there was nothing exceptional with no extravagant carving or inlays nor mounted name plates with elaborate shields or banners as found on some of the very best dueling sets. The pistols looked very much like a set Keen's own father had possessed, of which he was very familiar, and others possessed by officers in his regiment as dueling was quite prevalent amongst the officer corps. Dueling was not an uncommon way for the gentry to settle differences when an individual's honor was besmirched or offensive conduct was implied.

"My father owned a set such as these," Keen remarked to the brothers. "These are very typical of the average pistols owned by most officers and gentlemen. They look to be new and little fired, if at all." Holding one of the pistols up in front of the brothers, Keen pointed out, "These are quality waterproof locks. The trigger will be quite crisp and quick in the release." As he pointed to the barrel, he said, "Many of the newer pistols have hidden rifling set back from the muzzle of the barrel, so they shoot much straighter than a smooth bore barrel. This is a practice found to be somewhat unscrupulous and ungentlemanly in some British circles, while the French believe shooting at each other with less accurate smoothbore pistols is cowardly since there is less chance of a fatal shot. Foolhardy behavior for both the former and latter," Keen remarked, shaking his head ever so slightly. Continuing, he tilted the pistol towards the brothers. "If you run your little finger in the bore like this," he demonstrated, "you can feel the rifling set back the bore." Surprised, Keen burst out, "What's this?" Pushing his finger deeper into the bore he could just feel with his fingertip some obstruction. Squib and Travis leaned closer to look as well while Keen passed them one pistol to see for themselves that something was lodged in the bore. Keen examined the other pistol and found its bore obstructed as well.

Travis retrieved a short cleaning rod from the case, and then he selected a bullet worm which he mounted to the end of the rod. He passed it to Keen. "Try this," he said.

Carefully, Keen placed the bullet remover in the bore and slowly twisted the ramrod so the prongs grabbed hold of the obstruction. He gradually pulled out a tightly wrapped document from the first pistol, then the one from the second pistol. Handing the pistols back to Squib he cautiously unrolled the first document. Keen was unable to read this document as it was written completely in French, but he recognized some of the names and the signature was well-known to him. Passing this one to Travis, he asked, "Do either of you read French?" Travis shook his head.

"No," Travis replied. "I speak some Shawnee."

Laughing under his breath, Keen replied politely, "No, not quite the same."

Repeating the effort, Keen unrolled the second document which was written in English. As Keen began to read, his hands began to shake; the color left his face as if he had looked upon the face of the devil himself.

"I cannot believe this; it cannot be true," he muttered, shaking his head and moaning as if suddenly struck ill. Holding the paper up, he began to read again, slowly mouthing the words while shaking his head in a confused manner.

"What does it say?" Squib asked. Keen remained quiet as he stared at the papers in his hand. Clouded by disbelief Keen sat still for the longest moment. Silent, he was unsure of what to say or what to do. Should he confide in the brothers what the documents revealed? Ensign Keen felt himself drowning in doubt, apprehension, and disbelief as he was faced with information beyond his experience or training.

As the brothers watched, Keen finally came to a decision. Moving cautiously, he pulled his telescope case from over his shoulder, removed the telescope carefully from its protective case, then carefully wrapped the documents around the telescope before placing them together in the case.

Holding the case aloft, he pronounced grimly, "These must be protected at all costs; the safety — indeed the future — of our nation depends upon it. You two will have to remain with me here until the captain returns and he can determine what our next course of action will be— " Keen stopped mid-sentence as Fidious jumped up and began furiously barking at something across the campsite. All activity in the encampment came to a halt as everyone looked first at Fidious as his barking and growling became even more frenzied and loud. Then, turning simultaneously towards a disturbance along the river, they saw men. Armed men were approaching through the underbrush towards the camp and had stepped into the open from the scrub while a large canoe loaded with more men came to the shore on the flank of the camp.

"It's them!" Travis cried. He jumped up, grabbing his rifle from beside him. "The ones who have been chasing us."

Turning to the brothers, Keen tossed the telescope case to Squib. Then, pushing Squib and Travis towards their canoe, he yelled loudly, "Take this and run. Deliver it to General Jackson. Do not fail." A sudden fusillade of gunfire from the far shore drowned any further words as Keen turned to face the invaders.

Chapter 12

Sergeant White threw himself headfirst into the shrubbery as the volley of musketry exploded in his direction, sending bits and pieces of branches, leaves, and debris to pelt down on him from above. Thinking he had been discovered, White pushed his musket forward in preparation to defend himself, then drew short when a series of hurrahs were heard from the camp some two dozen paces to his front. Slowly, White raised his head and looked through the undergrowth towards the bivouac only to have to duck his head a second time as another volley of gunfire erupted his way, sending more shattered branches on top of him, once again followed by more loud shouts. Now sure he was not purposely being fired upon, White watched as a third volley of flame and smoke was aimed just over his head, again a rain of fragments from above accompanied by a loud chorus of hurrahs accompanied by a series of cheers for the names of people that were not known to White. No doubt the sergeant thought the troops were cheering some local heroes or perhaps an American victory. The last and loudest cheers were attended by cries of "the pies" "the pies" accompanied by hilarious laughter and merriment much to White's bewilderment.

Moving slowly to the shadow of a large maple, White watched as the men in the camp stacked their arms. Oh, look at that, will you? White thought. They were stacking their arms without reloading them. Unaware they were under observation, the men formed up in a line with mugs in their hands while an officer passed from man to man, filling their outstretched mugs with what could only be spirits. The sergeant licked his lips at the thought of having a good drink; it had been some months since they started this mission without so much as a little taste. Quite aware of the enlisted men's penchant for strong drink, Major Torrens had warned that anyone apprehended drinking so much as a single drop would suffer severe consequences. Consequences or not, a few belts of that good colonial whiskey would taste awfully good. Best not report the spirits in the camp, White thought, as some thirsty soldier would risk himself and them with it for some strong drink.

White continued to watch, noting the numbers, placements, and layout of the camp. After giving it some thought, he decided to start back. He knew that the major may interpret the gunfire as some threat and come crashing through the forest, starting an action with no clear advantage to themselves. Just as he turned away, he stopped and cocked an ear to the camp. The men were singing. The tune was well known to White and popular in English regiments, as it would seem to be amongst the Americans as well.

"The dames of France are fond and free, and Flemish lips are willing,

And soft the maids of Italy and Spanish eyes are thrilling.

Still, though I bask beneath their smile, their charms fail to bind me.

And my heart falls back to Erin's Isle, to the girl I left behind me."

So much like us, White thought. But not. Not like the Frenchies who were so foreign themselves in their language, dress, and custom. These Americans were former British subjects with a commonality in language, culture, and indeed many were from the same families. Some officers had complained that the men when firing volleys would purposely aim high to ensure missing the American ranks ahead of them for these same reasons. Not my concern, White thought, I kill who I'm ordered to kill and that is the bottom of it. Although the French had much better loot and wine than these poorer Americans.

Moving slowly while looking around cautiously, White approached his camp, then, when close enough to be heard, he sank down to one knee and whispered the password... "Bulldog." Apprehensively, he waited, knowing a dozen loaded muskets were probably aimed his way and one incorrect motion could send him to the promised land.

"That you, Sergeant?" a voice called out quietly to his right. As he turned towards the sound, the dark cave of musket muzzle loomed at him just feet from his face.

Recognizing the broad Scottish accent of Private James Duncan, White replied, "Move that damn musket from my face or I'll make it your third leg."

"My, and a good evening to you too, Sergeant!" Duncan replied with a chuckle. "Better get back," Duncan said, pointing over his shoulder with his thumb to the camp along the river. "His nibs was in a right mood when he heard all that gunfire upriver. Thought you were a goner, that's for sure."

Just what I need, White thought as he searched for and found the major standing by a large tree.

Before White could speak, the major barked at him threateningly, "What have you done, Sergeant? You were ordered to reconnoiter, not start a battle."

Bridling at the accusation, White snapped back, "Not a fight, Major. The Americans were celebrating with a three-volley salute. Near took my head off, they did. They were cheering and giving hurrahs to the names being unknown to me."

"Do you remember the names?" Torrens asked.

"Yes, sir. Madison, Jackson, and Pies," White replied, hoping the darkness hid his smirk.

"The first two are known to me," Torrens replied haughtily, "but the third I'm not sure about, although it sounds familiar. What is the disposition of the camp, then?"

White completed his report, emphasizing his observation that the Americans had stacked their muskets without reloading together, adding his opinion the camp could be easily overwhelmed given their superiority of manpower. He shared his observation that the Americans appeared clumsy in reloading and handling their weapons, and concluded his report with, "The Americans look very vulnerable to a surprise attack." He quickly added, "Should that be your decision, sir?"

"Yes, it is, Sergeant. That will be my decision alone. For now, I believe our best plan will be to wait for a larger party of flatboats to approach and join them so we can pass unobserved from the camp. We passed one three days ago of suitable size. We will reconnoiter again in the morning to ensure you have not missed anything in your report." As Torrens turned to leave, he stopped and asked softly, "What songs were they singing?"

Caught by surprise, White hesitated before replying, "The girl I left behind me. Sir."

"Brighton camp, was it?" Torrens asked.

"No, sir, the Irish one."

"Irish. Well, they are all rebels, are they not?" The major replied with a huff, "That will be all, Sergeant."

Dawn arrived slowly on the river, heralded first by the songbirds as they darted through the trees with singing and cheerful chirping. The day creatures awoke and began their morning hunt for breakfast, the squirrels amongst the treetops, the otters scurrying along the shore, the bass leaping upon the river to catch the fresh hatch of insects off the surface. Human hunters, hidden amongst the willows, watched the American camp as it too awoke and the soldiers there commenced their morning activities of ablutions and breakfast.

Major Torrens nudged Sergeant White, who was lying next to him in the shrubbery, and pointed to the sentry climbing the knoll behind the camp. "You didn't report that," he sneered.

White silently cursed the major. He wanted to snap back, "No point putting sentries out in the dark, is there, sir." But White knew better and kept silent. The two watched while the camp finished their breakfasts, noting the soldiers made no attempt to reload their muskets from the previous evening's salutes.

"Should we need to attack this camp," Major Torrens began and pointed again to the sentry now ensconced upon the bluff, "he needs to be dealt with first or there would be no surprise possible. I would divide the men into two groups. The first one would take firing points along this side of the camp," he said while pointing to the edge of the brush close to the camp. "They would commence firing upon the camp, and draw the soldiers there to their stacked arms and equipment. While the Americans' attention is upon the attacking party to their front, another group in canoes will sweep around the camp and commence firing from their flank right there," he said, pointing now to the small beach where the Americans' flatboat was pulled up on shore. "With our superior strength and disciplined soldiers, the Americans should be easily eliminated, do you not agree, Sergeant?"

"Yes, sir," the sergeant replied. As good a tactical plan as any, he thought. On the battlefield, Major Torrens was a quick-thinking officer with a good deal of daring and boldness. These battlefield attributes no doubt earned him quite a few accolades in the officer's mess and from those in high command. The rankers, however, knew him to be a cruel officer with no concern for the well-being or the lives of those he commanded. Torrens had little pity for the poor soldier's plight on the battlefield or in the field. His nickname of Torrens the Terrible was well-suited.

Sergeant White was awakened from his reverie by another hard nudge from Major Torrens. This time he pointed to Private O'Hara, nestled in the bushes and guarding their flank.

"Have your man over there take up guard here and to stay until relieved. You and I need to have a little chat before we return to camp, Sergeant."

White inwardly cringed. A bloody chat, he thought. Now that cannot be good. Crouching over, he moved soundlessly to Private O'Hara's position.

"Paddy," he whispered when he drew near, "the major has put your first post here. Keep a sharp lookout; we want to know everything about these Americans — especially those frontiersmen and dog we were warned about. I'll have you relieved in four hours."

"I've had no breakfast yet today, Sergeant. I'll be gnawing on roots and leaves like the savages, if I go that long."

"Don't worry about your precious stomach, Paddy. I'll send someone with your ration when I get back."

"A nice hot cup of tea would be nice too, Sergeant," O'Hara laughed back.

"A cold boot in the arse is what you're going to get. Now take position over there and don't be seen," White replied, then he moved slowly, keeping himself hidden in the long morning shadows while he made his way back to the major's position.

"Done as ordered, sir," he reported as he approached Torrens who was still keeping a sharp eye to the American camp.

Nodding to O'Hara, Major Torrens asked, "That's O'Hara over there, isn't it?"

"Yes, sir," White replied, surprised Torrens remembered O'Hara's name.

"The poacher," Torrens continued, "the Irish poacher the colonel rescued from the gallows?"

"Yes, sir," White replied, not liking the direction the conversation was taking.

"Then he should be good at sneaking around the forest here. Best be him if we need to send someone to take out that sentry on the hill," he ordered with a smug smile.

"Yes, sir," White replied, relieved the conversation had not taken a more serious turn.

"Come then, Sergeant," the major ordered, and then the two of them worked their way quietly back towards their hidden campsite along the river.

Once safely out of sight and voice distance from the American camp the major slowed, turned to the sergeant, and said, "Sergeant, it's time we talked about this mission and our purpose here. As you know, from the beginning, I have held the true reason for our infiltration of this American wilderness a secret from you and the men. This was done for your and the men's safety should we be fallen upon by the Americans and taken prisoners. It was felt in high command better to do so since as an officer I would not be subjected to interrogation nor tortured to obtain information. But you and the men could most probably be made the subject of most cruel devices to give a word of our role here." Stopping, Torrens moved closer to the sergeant before continuing: "To protect this mission, you have been held apart from its true purpose. Since we now have lost the item critical to our mission, we must face the certainty we will not recover it. And so, we must discuss how we intend to carry on in its absence. Am I being clear to you here, Sergeant?" Torrens asked.

"Yes, sir," White replied. Inwardly his heart was crying out, "I don't want to know."

"Then, you must know now that the item lost to those backwoodsmen is critical to our mission and its success, but we must persevere and improvise a solution without it. While a vast fleet of ships together with a great invasion force makes way to the southernmost area of America, we have been ordered to make our way across the continent from the north as it was believed our approach would be less dangerous and less likely to be discovered than by approaching New Orleans from the far south to effect..." Just then the major was interrupted by the surprise appearance of O'Hara running rapidly upon them.

Out of breath, O'Hara burst out, "They are here, sir."

"Who is here?" the major asked in annoyance at O'Hara's return.

"The frontiersmen, sir. I saw them paddle their canoe into the camp. They had that big dog as we were told and they are talking to an officer as we speak... sir."

"You're absolutely sure it's them, Private?" Torrens asked, still skeptical of O'Hara's report.

"Yes, sir," O'Hara replied, then, seeing Sergeant White scowling from behind, the major added, "Two young-looking fellows dressed in homespun, big hats, long rifles, and a big wolf-like dog. Just as you described, sir."

Elated, Torrens turned to White, bursting out, "Then we have them. Sergeant, you know the plan. Return with O'Hara and verify the sighting. If they are the ones we are looking for, then send O'Hara to remove the sentry on the hill. I will send a detachment of five men to you. If these frontiersmen are indeed the ones we want, send one man back to me to confirm. Move your group into the position I pointed out earlier. Watch for the rest of the command; we will be coming in one canoe at speed. When we draw close and are about to become visible from the beach, you are to step out from cover and fire a volley into the camp. Order the men to double ball their muskets; that will increase the volume of our fire. Your diversion will distract them sufficiently so that we can land on the beach and fire another volley into their flanks. Then we all rush the camp and kill any still alive. I repeat, Sergeant, kill them, kill them all. Move, now Sergeant."

Looking at O'Hara with a cold stare, Torrens said, "You had better be right, Private." Without another word Torrens turned on his heel and ran towards the camp.

O'Hara used his years of experience hunting the king's deer to slowly ascend the hill where the sentry was perched. He cautiously chose his every step to remain silent. Stealth was paramount to speed. He picked the route where the underbrush would be thicker due to it receiving less sun and more shade with concealing cover. He knew that the morning's moisture would be retained longer from the early dew, making a wet but silent stalk. Long ago memories of his youth spent stalking, killing, and poaching the king's deer that inhabited the lush green forests of County Galway in Ireland had been both a way of life and joy for the young poacher. The poacher's life was free from the constraints of a life structured by the state, the church, and a culture of servitude. O'Hara was free, the freest he had ever felt wandering the woods with his long bow in hand and an arrow notched and waiting but for the quick draw and silent release with which he could take down the unwary prey. Silence was the key, a silent stalk and more so a silent kill were essential, for he seldom took a shot at running deer though he knew he was quite capable of a thirty-pace kill when needed. A surprised deer shot by an arrow can take time to bleed out, time enough to lose the trail in the underbrush, time enough for the forest wardens to stumble on the blood trail. Silent kills from the bow as opposed to the gun served as protection from the wardens who stalked the woods hunting the hunters. Indeed, it was a lucky poacher who escaped with his life if caught by the wardens, for all too often it was the hunter who ended up returning to the estate on a game pole. Even then the best a poacher could expect from a judge would be exile to North America or service to the king in one of his regiments. Either way could be death sentences; one was as difficult as the other.

Seems I've ended up with both, O'Hara thought as he spied the sentry ahead through the trees.

This stalk could be a death sentence if the sentry spots me, O'Hara thought, bitter at the major's constant belittling and giving him all the dirty details. Bugger has something in for me, he thought. Another dirty task, dangerous one at that. Not like stalking a deer.

As he reached the crest of the hill O'Hara crouched low. Carefully peeking over the edge, he saw the sentinel leaning casually, his chin resting over his musket. He was intently watching the camp when his attention was diverted by the appearance of the two long hunters now talking to the ensign below. The sentry then took a long, slow step back from the outpost, turned quickly, grabbed something from his shoulder bag, stuffed it in his mouth, and turned back to face down the hill.

Got you, Patrick thought. He's more concerned about sneaking his snacks and watching to see if he has been noticed eating while on sentry duty. Do that in the British Army and the sentry would be flayed by the lash, or worse, hanged as an example to others. Either way not a pleasant prospect. Next time the sentry scarfed down a snack and his attention was focused on whether his actions had been noticed down the hill would be the time to attack.

Placing his musket ever so softly on the ground, O'Hara silently drew his tomahawk from his belt. When hunting deer or men, he knew that speed with a sudden and quick attack was deadlier at close quarters. Timing was everything as he moved slowly to within striking distance and waited like a coiled snake hidden in the shadows of the heavy underbrush.

As O'Hara had anticipated the sentry took a slow step backwards, bent, and stuffed a treat into his mouth. Then he turned to face downhill again, searching to see if anyone had noticed.

Crouched low, Patrick extended his left hand to grasp the sentry while his right held the razor-sharp tomahawk ready to strike when he drew closer. Like an angered viper Patrick leapt forward to grab the sentry by his collar and throw him to the ground aiming to drive the tomahawk into his neck. The sun that had been low on the horizon unexpectedly broke through the morning mists, casting Patrick's dark shadow on the ground at the guard's feet. Immediately, Patrick saw his plan dissolve as the sentry with a young man's quick reaction spun on his heel to face him, bringing his musket up to aim directly at O'Hara's face.

Instinctivily Patrick grasped hold of the musket barrel and yanked it violently towards himself throwing the sentry off balance, forcing him to fall forward landing his knees. Stunned and off-balance, the sentry's surprise turned from fear to terror as the tomahawk descended, striking him violently above the left eye burying itself in his skull. Instantly dead, the limp sentry's body pulled Patrick down as he stumbled and fell over the dead man's body. Shocked and horrified, Patrick slowly rolled off the dead guard, winded by the quickness of the guard's response. For just a brief second O'Hara had looked down the bore of that musket. A seasoned, trained soldier would have pulled the trigger much faster, thereby ending the attack and Patrick's life.

Regaining his strength, Patrick grasped the dead sentry by his tunic and dragged the corpse back down out of sight from camp below before pushing the limp body over the edge of the escarpment into the brush. Returning to the outpost, O'Hara slowly peered over the rim just in time to see the major's canoe suddenly speeding around the riverbend, hitting the beach in front of the encampment to the accompaniment of a volley of muskets from the adjoining shrubbery. "Oh, that was a close one, Patrick," O'Hara muttered to himself.

Sergeant White waited until the canoe with the major and his detachment rounded the bend and drew level with the small beach before he gave the command "Fire!" The forest echoed the sound of the volley. The American camp erupted into chaos at the sudden appearance and attack of White's small command.

"Reload!" White commanded. Knowing he was breaking Major Torrens' specific command that his group immediately charge the encampment, White could see the Americans were little prepared as they rushed to their stacked arms, many without cartridge boxes or weapons. They milled around their stacked arms in confusion while an NCO kept up the cry of "To Arms! To Arms!" from the far side of the camp. Swiftly, with long-practiced speed and assurance, his men removed the cartridges from their cartridge boxes, reloaded them, and almost simultaneously assumed the ready position waiting for the fire command aimed towards the Americans now clumped together in the middle of the camp. White, with his own musket reloaded, watched the chaos in the camp and waited as the major's canoe landed and the soldiers scrambled out, immediately bringing up their muskets to fire. Torrens and White shouted "Fire!" The Americans were caught in a devastating crossfire from the double-charged muskets scything the Americans down like a hot knife through butter. Men screamed, bled, and died as Major Torrens' group swept into the camp attacking with clubbed muskets, tomahawks, and long knives at the few not injured in the opening volleys. Sergeant's White command sprinted into the camp and joined in the slaughter.

"Find the frontiersmen!" Torrens yelled as he pushed through his troops while they hacked and smashed down at any Americans remaining alive.

Sergeant White ran to join the major and stopped, suddenly pointing. He called to Torrens, "There, sir."

Torrens stopped and turned to look in the direction of White's pointed finger. Standing alone, with sword and pistol in his hands, was Ensign Keen. In the near distance behind the officer Torrens saw the frontiersman leap into their canoe, push off the beach, and begin furiously paddling down the river.

"On me," Torrens yelled.

He was followed by Sergeant White, who bellowed the command, "Join on the major!"

Not waiting for reinforcements, Torrens began running towards Ensign Keen, bringing up his musket the en garde position.

Keen lifted his pistol forward, aimed at the major who was running straight towards him, and pulled the trigger. Nothing happened. Keen realized suddenly he had not cocked the pistol. Keen threw the pistol at Torrens' head. Torrens laughed as he easily sidestepped the pistol and knocked it down with the end of his musket.

Keen swung his sword in a vicious slash at the major's face as he closed to engage the major only to have his sword blocked by Torrens' musket as he parried the blade to the side then followed up with a vicious blow to Keen's face. The butt of his musket smashed Keen's nose, knocking half a dozen teeth out with the power of the blow. Staggering backwards, Keen tried to bring his sword point up to engage the enraged major as he started another swing of the musket butt at Keen's face. Before he could do so, a intense burning pain pierced his chest accompanied by a sound like ripping cloth. Keen looked down the bloodied end of a long knife pushed through his breast. His scream drowned in blood and Keen fell face-first to the ground. Sergeant White stepped on Keen's back, tugged his knife loose, and wiped the blood off on Keen's shirt.

Major Torrens stepped forward over Keen's body and stopped on the sand of the beach. As troops arrived at his side, he ordered, "Load."

The soldiers quickly reloaded their muskets while Torrens gave instructions, "Aim high and ahead of that canoe by about its own length." The sound of ramrods being returned to the ferrules beneath the barrel signaled the guns were reloaded and ready to fire.

Torrens ordered, "Present." A dozen muskets came up.

"Fire." The volley came as one loud explosion smothering them in a cloud of sulphurous gun smoke and momentarily hiding their prey from sight.

Travis ducked his head down at the sound of musket balls whizzing and ricocheting off the water about them followed a second later by the clap of the shots and a sharp yelp of pain from Squib in the stern.

Turning anxiously to his brother, Travis asked, "Are you hit?"

"My ear!" Squib squealed. "They shot my ear off!" Squib held his hand over his ear as a copious flow of blood ran through his fingers and down his wrist.

"Remove your hand so I can see," Travis replied.

Squib withdrew his hand and looked at his blood-covered fingers. "Now that smarts some."

"Just took the bottom off," Travis said. "Luck was with you. Another inch over, and you'd be gone for sure," he added. "Keep paddling; we need to get out of range before they reload. We have to run as far down the river as we possible should if they decide to chase us."

Squib picked up his paddle and realized Fidious was staring intently at him with his head cocked to one side. "What's wrong?" Squib asked. "Never seen a man with one ear before?" He began to paddle in strong practiced rhythm to Travis' strokes.

On the lookout above, O'Hara watched the attack and slaughter playing out below. Sudden realization struck him that Torrens did not wait until the sentry was neutralized, instead he started towards the ambush site earlier then promised. Torrens planned to take advantage of the possible distraction of him tackling the sentry by drawing the soldiers away from watching the beach. "A sacrificial lamb," Patrick muttered to himself. "Dead or alive, that's what I am: a sacrificial lamb."

From his high position, Patrick watched the gathered soldiers shooting volleys at the fleeing canoe as scattered impacts from the musket balls slapped about and hit around or beyond the canoe. At first, he thought the rear paddler had been hit as he suddenly stopped paddling and grasped his head. But a moment later the man resumed paddling with no sign of weakness or impairment. Looking back down to the beach, he saw Sergeant White staring up at him. Fortunately, Major Torrens still had his eyes on the canoe as it vanished into a bend downriver and did not see him standing idle on the hill top. Running back, he grabbed his musket from where he had dropped it and ran down into the encampment straight into an angry Sergeant White waiting for him at the bottom of the trail.

"Damn you, Paddy," he said through clenched teeth. "Torrens would have both our hides, had he seen you standing about up there while we were fighting down here. Get to the canoe now; we have to chase down those two frontiersmen, so get moving."

White pushed O'Hara towards the waiting canoes and turned to gather the others as Torrens came running to him and stopped. "Sergeant, detail four men to destroy this campsite and dispose of the bodies. Pile everything into their flatboat there on the shore and burn it. They are to leave no trace of what happened here. Have them take the other canoe we left at our camp and follow us no later than tomorrow morning. Get moving, Sergeant; we can catch those rascals before nightfall if we move quickly. Now."

Turning quickly, White picked the four men standing closest to the canoe. "You heard the major: destroy everything." O'Hara, pretending he was part of the group, slipped behind the men hoping White would not see him. He stopped when White yelled, "Not you, O'Hara. You're our best shot. You get in the bow; we may have some target practice for you later. Move it, people."

O'Hara jumped into the bow of the canoe with his paddle at the ready as the rest of the men crowded into the canoe and pushed off.

The canoe had a full load with ten men paddling, but that also meant they should be faster than a canoe with only two like the one they were now pursuing. White turned to Torrens as he paddled and gave his opinion on their advantage in this case, but was brusquely cut off by the major. "I'm well aware of our present advantage, Sergeant. See to it we realize our advantage by pushing the men to capitalize on it. Have those front four paddlers behind O'Hara place their muskets close behind him so he will have loaded ones available when we draw within gunshot range."

Torrens stood against the stern of the canoe, watching for the brothers who had disappeared around a bend up the river only minutes before. The full force of the extra paddlers exerted itself as each man put his back into every stroke, pushing the canoe ahead and gaining speed faster and faster as the paddlers got their stride.

Squib looked over his shoulder and saw the fully manned canoe in pursuit behind them. He immediately realized they would be overtaken as Travis and he became more tired. "Travis," Squib called, "they are gaining on us."

Travis looked over his shoulder and was shocked to see how quickly their pursuers were catching up. Travis took another quick glance back as he tried to increase his strokes. "The front man has some extra muskets sitting behind him; they must intend to start shooting when they get into range."

"That's big trouble," Squib replied. "We can't shoot back and paddle. We could hit the shore fast and try and lose them in the woods or at least fight back from some cover."

"No good," Travis replied over his shoulder. "The woods in the river valley are too dense; we would lose any advantage our rifles give us while they could get closer and shoot quicker. You saw how they fired those volleys so quickly back at the camp. We would be goners for sure."

"Look over there," Travis cried out as he pointed to a channel where the river was drawn down through a narrow pass. "Paddle for that narrow neck where the rapids draw on the right. Maybe we can throw them off in that fast water. Draw to the right; we need to stay off the rocks."

The rapids approached quickly. The brothers' years of paddling experience allowed them to skillfully thread their smaller craft through a rock garden of boulders and debris. "Paddle hard on the right," Travis called out as they steered through a chute between the rocks. Paddling frantically, they skirted the obstructions until they were passing through into a large back eddy that pulled them gently towards the large beach behind.

"Look over there at the end of the pool," Travis called out. "See those big trees uprooted on the shore? Pull in behind them. Time for us to take a stand."

Pulling with all their strength, they paddled out of the back eddy, around the obstruction of trees and roots, then turned sharply, beaching their canoe on the sandy shore. Rifles in hand, they jumped onto the beach and rushed behind the barricade of debris. Squib called Fidious to his side, then they both joined Travis sprawled behind a large stump with his long rifle in the crook of a branch aimed up the river. Squib found a spot several feet away, then aimed up the river as well. "Here they come," Travis called out. "Shoot when I do. I'll aim for the lead paddler on the right; you try the one behind him."

Squib cocked his rifle, quickly checked that his powder in the frizzen was dry, then brought his rifle up and begin to draw a steady sight on the canoe as it speedily approached the rock-strewn rapids. Travis was gambling their pursuers would be so intent on their own efforts to navigate the same chute the brothers had just paddled successfully they would be unaware of the surprise waiting them. From their hidden lair one hundred yards downriver from the rapids, the brothers waited to spring their trap. Drawing a deep breath, Travis aligned his sight for a spot just below the coming canoe's bow as he waited for the canoe to draw into his point of aim. He pulled the rear set trigger, and it set with a firm "click." It was ready for the slightest touch on the front trigger to fire the rifle. Squib followed suit, setting his trigger within a second of Travis. Both waited nervously for the canoe to work its way into their ambush.

Caught in the vortex of the rushing river in the narrow chute of huge boulders, the soldiers desperately struggled to maintain control of their frail craft. They were almost overwhelmed by the sheer power of the roaring waters as they were sucked into the watery maelstrom. The paddlers struggled to keep their large heavy canoe upright as the weight shifted to the right from the force of the current that threatened to swamp the canoe. The paddlers on the left leaned awkwardly over the gunnels to retain balance while the bow paddlers fought to steer between the many dark brooding boulders and submerged obstacles looming from the depths.

Travis waited as the canoe reached the most perilous point of its passage between the rocks, suddenly shouting to Squib, "Now." His command was followed by the crack of his rifle as he fired. A fraction of a second later, Squib's rifle boomed out with a sharp bang.

O'Hara leaned into his paddle with all his weight, fighting the awesome push on the heavy canoe as the current sucked the vessel towards the rocky shore. Sergeant White, who was seated next to him on the bow, occupied the most critical paddle position in this maneuver as he grunted, paddling madly while trying to keep the bow aimed straight through the center of the boiling water in the chute.

"Almost there. Almost there!" O'Hara shouted. As they passed the midpoint, they were penned in by the huge rocks on either side. Free for a split second as the weight of the canoe fell to the right-side paddlers, O'Hara looked up quickly. The end of the chute was almost within reach, ending in a slow back eddy behind the rocks. O'Hara relaxed slightly and in the same instant saw the long hunters positioned in the debris on the far side of the pool. O'Hara screamed, "Duck!" and grabbing Sergeant White by the collar, yanking him sideways towards himself. At the same instant, he heard the crack of two shots followed by the gut-wrenching sound of two bullets striking flesh. The loud "Slap" was accompanied by grunts of pain and shock as two paddlers were knocked backwards. Instantly the bow of the canoe swung to the left. The huge weight of the overloaded canoe coupled with its great speed drove the canoe straight into a massive knife-edged rock. The stone sliced through the fragile bark canoe like a hammer through an egg, crumbling, smashing, carving, and exploding through the birch bark while scattering pieces of debris, baggage, and muskets into the air like a bomb burst in all directions as it passed through bow to stern of the canoe within seconds. The soldiers were totally unprepared for the devastation the rocks wrought by hurling them into the water as the frail wooden canoe was ripped apart. They were left to fight for their lives against the raging current that was swirling, smashing, scraping, and pounding men and limbs and bones against the rocks. The powerful undertow dragged the weakened and injured soldiers deep below the surface into a deadly vortex of rocks and rubble. Each soldier fought his own personal battle to survive against the cold, black, deadly water.

O'Hara hit the water headfirst and immediately sank. Held beneath the waves by the strong current he felt the air being squeezed painfully from his lungs by the tremendous force of the undertow. Helplessly he rolled over and over in the current until he smacked into an underwater stone shelf that trapped him in its icy grip. The relentless pressure from water in front pressed him to the rock behind. Frozen to the rock, he desperately tried to reach up with both arms to find a handhold to pull himself up from the water's murderous embrace. The slimy rock slipped from his fingertips as the relentless current drew him deeper, helplessly into the depths. Suddenly a heavy object crashed into him, knocking him away from the rock and huge pressure of the water on his chest eased slightly. Desperately pushing with all his strength, he rebounded away from the ledge. Lungs bursting, O'Hara frantically grabbed at the half-full water keg that had struck him and held tight as it pulled away and slowly lifted him from the grasp of the rock and current. As he swung into the back eddy, his head finally cleared the surface. He gasped for air, struggling to breath, he tried to back-paddle, but was too overcome by weakness. His grip on the keg loosened as he started to sink once again beneath the waves. Suddenly a hand caught him by the collar and slowly drew him into the side of a rock then into the shallows behind. Swinging into some logs, he wrapped his arms around them till he was swung up and clear of the current. Free now to turn his head, O'Hara came face-to-face with Sergeant White. Grinning like he just won a race, with one arm wrapped about another half-floating keg the sergeant laughed and said, "Now we're even, Paddy."

"Thank you, Sergeant; I thought I was a goner for sure," Patrick said, coughing up water as he did so. Slowly, using the keg as a float, they were pulled onto the sandy shore behind the eddy. They reached the shallows where they flopped down on the beach and lay unmoving, catching their breath. Sounds of coughing, groans, and calls for help brought them back to life. Turning over they sat up as others from their command dragged themselves onto the beach and lay in exhaustion on the sand.

White began counting the men on the beach. "There's Hawkins, Wood, Lewis, and looks like Jackson behind him. Oh, the major is here too."

"Pity," O'Hara said.

"None of that, Paddy," White growled back. "Who's missing?"

"Hughes and Billy James were behind me when the shooting started," O'Hara said, shaking his head slowly. "Shot or drowned, but missing for sure."

"Bloody Americans," White replied.

"There will be a lot less of us if them Americans over there start shooting again; they can't miss at this range," O'Hara said. White looked across the small bay, where the two frontiersmen remained with their rifles aimed at them, silently watching.

A few yards away, Major Torrens also saw the brothers watching with rifles at the ready. Torrens struggled unsteadily to his feet, standing tall and in full sight.

"Oh, look, the major is making a target of himself so we can run off and escape," O'Hara whispered to White.

"Enough, Patrick," White snapped back.

"Fine, but if those lads start shooting, I'm running for those trees behind us," O'Hara replied as he tensed, ready to sprint for cover.

"You will do no such thing," White commanded. "Unless I order it."

"Well, they have a bullet for the major standing over there for sure, so that leaves one for you or me," Patrick smiled, "and I'm faster I am."

White remained silent. As he glanced over his shoulder to the cover of the trees, he started to make sense of Patrick's argument. Drawing his legs slowly up, the sergeant tensed, ready to run at the first sign of movement from the brothers hidden in the driftwood pile across the water.

The devastation wrought by their two shots left the two brothers frozen. They watched the canoe crash into the rock, exploding like it was hit by a cannonball hurtling screaming men, equipment, and debris into the air as the disintegrated remains of the canoe were sucked into the depths below. Here and there, men's heads bobbed to the surface. The survivors struggled against the currents, the cold, and their injuries. Fewer men than went into the water fought to stay alive as they struggled towards the shore. Recovering from their shock, the brothers quickly reloaded, all the while watching the men gain onto the beach. Some crawled, then, staggering to their feet, they collapsed exhausted into the sand. Others pulled themselves to the beach and lay in the sand, too exhausted or injured to drag themselves farther.

One stood, staggered, then, remaining standing, turned and looked intently at the brothers, his gaze cold and unwavering as if challenging them to shoot. Even from this distance, the brothers recognized the leader of the ambushing soldiers at Turtle Creek.

"That's the leader from the ambush," Squib called over to his brother.

"I can see," Travis replied. "Load them two pistols; they might decide to attack us."

"What with sticks and stones?" Squib snorted in reply. "Looks like they have lost their guns and supplies, not much left of that bunch."

"Load them pistols anyway. Keep all the accessories from the case and bring it to me. Time we put an end to this chasing about. Keep hidden, so they can't see you," Travis said.

"Oh sure," Squib laughed back. "They may start stoning us otherwise." Staying out of sight, Squib ducked back to the canoe and tucked the pistols into his belt while he threw the bullets, molds, and tools in his shooting bag. Finished, he returned to the driftwood pile and passed the case to Travis.

Travis took the case, climbed up into the open, and stood on the top of the logs above the swirling river below. Silently, he stood, waiting until all the men on the beach saw him and had turned to watch him. Slowly he raised the case over his head so it was clear to all what he held in his hands, then he drew back and flung the case into the air with all his strength. It flew out, landed in the river with a splash, and sank, disappearing into the dark depths below. Without a backwards glance, Travis climbed back to their hide behind the logs, picked up his rifle, and started towards back to their canoe. He looked over his shoulder and nodded for Squib to join him while they pushed the canoe from its hiding place into the water. Travis whispered, "Don't look back; we need to show them we are not afraid."

"Well, speaking for myself," Squib replied, "I'm feeling a bit touchy on that right now. I haven't felt that way since that snake tried to sleep with me up the river. But I'm thinking them fellows are a mite more dangerous than that snake."

"I'm a little shaky myself," Travis replied, "but them bandits don't know that, and maybe they will abandon their chase of us now that they think we destroyed what they were chasing for."

Looking into the canoe, Squib was surprised to find Fidious curled up on the bottom. He slowly rose but remained quietly where he was.

Hurriedly the brothers climbed back into the canoe and turned down the river. Fidious curled up at Squib's legs as close as it was possible for him to get without climbing into Squib's lap.

"I think we are all a little shaky from what happened today," Squib remarked as he picked up his paddle, pushed the canoe off the sand, and began to paddle. Looking over his shoulder, Travis looked closely at Squib's tattered ear which was still weeping blood onto his shoulder. "Let's get down the river away. Then we can stop and get some honey on that ear of yours before it gets all festered."

Squib laughed aloud. "If there's any honey in that jar, it's going in my mouth, not my ear."

Travis laughed in return, commenting, "Squib, you're always hungry."

"That I am," Squib replied. "I was born hungry and will probably die hungry. Let's put some distance on from them yahoos up the river. Travis," Squib asked quietly as he continued to paddle, "did we do the right thing back there? I've, well, we have never shot anyone before."

Travis stopped paddling and turned to face his brother. "Squib, we saw the ambush back up there at Turtle Creek. Those fellows, whoever they are, didn't give us or them soldiers any chance. Had Fidious not given a warning, we would all have been dead up there."

Squib nodded and gave Fidious a scratch behind the ear. "That you did, dog."

Looking back to Travis, Squib replied, "Father never talked about anything like this happening to us that I can remember. He didn't tell us how doing the right thing may not feel right when it's done. I even have a hard time explaining it. Just that we were taught about good and evil and right and wrong. I always thought when I had to face a choice, it would be clear, and I would do the right thing. You would know what was right. You could act on what you knew it was what was needed or without argument what needed to be done without this doubt or apprehension it was wrong. What about you, Travis?"

Travis took a few seconds to think before speaking. "I feel the same way, brother. I have remorse for killing them fellows, but I know we had to do it or would probably die ourselves. I don't know, but maybe we will run into that again some time when doing the right thing seems so wrong. Maybe it's something those soldiers were taught that we were not. That officer, Ensign Keen, he saved us. And he died for it. I don't understand it all, that's for sure."

Squib shook his head and replied slowly, "Me neither, Travis; me neither." Then he added, "We wanted excitement and adventure. It seems to me we found it."

"Woeee!" Travis replied. "When those bullets were flying about our heads or skipping off the water beside the canoe, then ricocheting off the rocks in every direction… whoa. That was exciting all right."

"It seems to me," Squib replied, "that being shot at must be as exciting as it gets." Then, gently touching his shattered earlobe, he continued, "It stops being exciting when the bullets hit you, and you think one inch closer you'll be dead."

Travis remained silent. The truth of Squib's words weighed on him as he thought about how close to death they had come over the space of a few minutes.

Squib asked, "What about those messages hidden there in that telescope case? Should we read them? Maybe we will find some answers to our questions in them."

"I've thought on that too," Travis replied. "At first I felt they might have some answers. But I remember how Ensign Keen told us we have to get these papers to General Jackson as quick as we can. And he was killed trying to give us time to escape for us to do that. Then I thought what if the content of those papers is so important that we would still have no understanding of the situation here and blunder off course. Or so big. So momentous that we would be inhibited from following the ensign's orders and not fulfill the duty he gave to us to perform. Then he would have died for nothing. No Squib, this is big, and it's been dropped right into our laps whether we like it or not."

Squib sat quietly, thinking of what Travis had said. "All right, I agree with you, but we don't know anything about General Jackson; we don't even know where to find him. We could stop to ask folks along the river or at an outpost. That would be pretty slow in my way of thinking. Keen was clear we had to hurry and not be stumbling about. Not to mention what if those fellows have other spies along the way watching for us? They are not going to sit on that sandbar for long. They have two other canoes so they will be coming after us sure enough."

Travis smiled back at his brother, and said, "Yes, thought of that myself. Why, I decided our best plan is just keep headed the way we planned, and find Uncle Wes. Uncle Wes will know what to do."

Squib laughed back. "You're right, Uncle Wes will know what we should do. Pick up that paddle, Travis. We need to get some distance between them fellows back there and find Uncle Wes as soon as possible. That will end our troubles."

"Well, let's hope that's the end of it," Travis replied under his breath. Digging his paddle into the water with smooth, strong strokes he pointed the canoe down the river. Inside themselves neither brother was convinced this chase was yet concluded.

Chapter 13

"**W**ell, what was that all about, do you think?" O'Hara remarked to Sergeant White as they watched the case being flung into the river.

Some yards away, Major Torrens stood rock still, his fists clenched in silent rage and his face florid with burning hate as he watched till the canoe disappeared far down the river. Turning towards White and O'Hara still sitting on the beach, Torrens snapped angrily, "Sergeant White, bring O'Hara here, now!"

"Oh, now you done it, Paddy," White whispered under his breath as they both struggled to their feet and staggered closer to the major.

Ignoring Sergeant White, Torrens addressed O'Hara directly: "You're the woodsman, O'Hara. How far have we come from the campsite, and how long would it take us to walk back along the shore?"

"About six miles, sir. But with the injured and like we would not make the camp before darkness."

"And one man on his own?" the major asked.

"Oh, one man could be there well before dark, sir," O'Hara replied. Then he realized what he just said with a cringe. Now you've done it, Patrick, he thought. The smirk on Torrens' face turned into a grin. Here it comes, Patrick thought.

"Good," the major replied. "You're the man, O'Hara. You should make it in half the time if you run. And run you will, O'Hara. Have the men at the camp bring back both canoes and all our equipment, particularly any weapons from the Americans. Mount a lantern on the bow of the lead canoe so a sentry we have posted will see and warn them of the rapids. You will be the bowman of the lead canoe, O'Hara. You may go now." Looking at Sergeant White, the major pointed to the edge of the water before the rapids where the disaster with the rocks had occurred. "Sergeant, have that point manned in two hours to warn the canoes away from the danger when they arrive." Turning back to O'Hara, Torrens barked sharply, "I ordered you to run, O'Hara, now!"

Looking upriver, O'Hara spotted a small opening in the forest and began a slow, stumbling run towards the dark woods beyond the beach. With each step the exhaustion of minutes before was forgotten as O'Hara raged at Torrens' constant browbeating and oppressive depreciations. O'Hara's only escape turned his ambling pace into a head-on sprint. Jumping downed trees and debris on the shore, he leapt from the beach into the forest until he was lost from sight as he crashed through the thick underbrush. O'Hara continued running as the anger at the major's continued bullying filled his mind with thoughts of revenge. He smashed through the forest, ignorant of the scratches, rips, and cuts from his blind dash. Finally, overcome from the built-up fatigue of the day coupled with the danger, lack of food, and rest, he stumbled and fell to his knees. Exhausted, he sat back. Between ragged breaths, he cursed the major for his predicament and the unfair treatment that Torrens had wrought on him. Panting heavily, O'Hara stood, slowly looking around at the small glade in which he had stopped. Small birds were flitting from tree to tree above him, and the woods were filled with the soothing sounds that only the peacefulness of the woods can bring: the song of birds, the clatter of squirrels, the buzz of insects, the gurgle and splash of the river deeper off through the trees with the whisper of the wind through the canopy of branches above. O'Hara relaxed for a moment, enjoying his first time alone in the forest in many years. Soon, the anger wore off; he relaxed, calmer, more logical thinking took over as he realized with no one to order his every move, he could take his own dear time to return to the camp in a manner that suited him best. Smiling, he looked around again and whispered to himself, "Well, this isn't so bad, is it, Patrick? These woods are too dark and thick to pass through easily, but this side of the river faces south so there should be more open and drier ground farther up the escarpment above." Turning uphill, moving more slowly now O'Hara carefully chose his route through the scrub and brush climbing higher into more open ground above the river. His old skills at woodcraft spent stalking the game in the forests of Ireland came back, and before long he moved quietly amongst the trees looking left and right as he scouted for a game trail which he knew would probably run along the river. True to his experience, a large game trail came into view ahead of him: three feet wide, and well-trampled by the passing of countless numbers of wildlife. O'Hara stopped. Walking blindly into the open is as dangerous in the woods as it is on the battlefield, he thought. O'Hara waited, looking intensely up and down the trail, moving only his eyes so that no movement would betray his presence while he watched. He waited patiently for any motion from the surrounding forest or unusual scents coming from the slight breeze that blew from the valley below. Finally satisfied he was not under observation, he stepped out onto the path. Kneeling, he looked down and saw deer tracks predominating the sign in the dirt with deer scat spread about mixed with signs of smaller animals. More important, there were no human tracks.

Looking about he found a comfortable spot in the sun along the trail. Picking up a branch he poked about the soft moss for snakes then sat down comfortably to assess his situation. Taking time to check his equipment O'Hara he saw his boots were in decent condition despite the soaking in the river. This was no doubt due to the ample amounts of whale oil he conditioned them with every week. His soft buckskin leggings were scratched and torn in spots, but still serviceable. They were easily repairable with the needle and sinew thread he always carried.

His homespun linen shirt had more holes than he cared for, but nothing that couldn't be fixed. With the heat of summer, the rents and tears may provide a little fresh air, he mused to himself. He grinned with joy, noting that his long knife was still held in its scabbard by the leather cord he out of long habit had hooked it to was still attached. Flint and steel rested safely in the small buckskin bag he carried constantly around his neck as was the habit of the American woodsmen. He knew a knife and fire starter were key to his survival in this vast wilderness. Pulling his hunting bag and powder horn off his shoulder, he was pleased that the flap on the hunting bag had remained secure during the ordeal in the river. The bullet bag was wet but serviceable, and all the musket balls remained, including the small bag with its spare flints, clasp knife, and spare parts. Overjoyed, O'Hara removed several pieces of jerky he had hidden in his bag. The first food of the day had been softened from the dunk in the river, and now O'Hara savored the salty, rich flavor of each bite as he chewed slowly. He laughed and said out loud, "Major, I think I'll be late rather than early getting to the camp." As he chewed, O'Hara shook his powder horn. The soggy contents gurgled and sloshed about as he poured the black sulfurous liquid onto the ground. Shaking all the ruined powder out, he covered the spot with some rocks and moss. "No point letting any passerby know I've no dry powder," he said. "No musket either." But there were several spares back at camp, that is if the major allowed him to have one. Always and everything was at the major's discretion if you weren't in the major's disfavor, or Irish or a poacher or whatever foul mood or petty grudge he constantly maintained against someone or something. The thought left a sour taste in O'Hara's mouth.

Rising from his perch, he spotted a long straight branch lying on the forest floor that looked about musket length. He picked it up so he could carry it as he would a gun. Not that it would fool anyone from close up, but at a distance, in the right light, he could look like an armed man rather than an unarmed one and a few seconds of doubt could be a lifesaver if an enemy spotted him.

Enjoying his new found freedom in the forest, O'Hara dawdled along the path, judging he would arrive back at the camp an hour before sunset. Too late for a run down the river in the dark, he chuckled to himself. And if that didn't deter his comrades, then an exaggerated story of the disaster in the rapids should discourage any thought of a night river run. For the first time, O'Hara began to appreciate the vastness of the American wilderness consisting of great forests, teeming numbers of wildlife, and uncounted rivers and streams. Here the land was free for those who could survive and take it. No lords or royalty or king's troops to suppress the common folk. No game wardens with their cruel, arbitrary powers of arrest or unquestioned murder of those who looked to feed themselves with game from the forest. Here the wildlife was for anyone who had a gun, free for the taking. Freedom to roam a rich wilderness without fences or guarded gates, rivers without toll bridges or bailiffs or wardens or fat-bellied lords to tell a man that he has to starve when there was game for all and rivers full of fish for a man to catch where and when needed.

O'Hara sensed a subtle change in the wind direction from blowing into his face to now blowing towards the river side. The change could spook any game downwind of his position, alarming other wildlife or hunters who were keen watchers of sudden game movement. He slowed as the trail skirted a small cliff and across a clearing. He paused, looking downwind for any sign of game moving after getting his scent and saw farther down the river the bend where the ambush had taken place some hours earlier. Vague shapes moved about slowly by the water in the distance enough to know the men were starting to move around after their ordeal of earlier. Confidently, the deerstalker of the past resurrected, he moved across the opening of the trail to the woods beyond. He was bound for the ambush campsite and canoes.

The trail passed easily through the thinner forest above the river. As O'Hara walked along, he realized this trail must have been in use for hundreds of years, compacted by wildlife and native hunters or war parties traveling along the river. It was so clear that anyone traveling along the shores or in a vessel on the river would never know the path existed, hidden in the woods above them. Hundreds of ruffians could hide and move up and down the river without anyone being the wiser to its existence.

Torrens' order to run had been completely forgotten as O'Hara took his time along the trail. He stopped to pick the occasional berries to eat, or drink from one of the fresh springs he passed along the way, or simply watch the multitude of wildlife from the shadow behind a tree. O'Hara felt a new freedom he had never thought he would feel again, an absence of direction, censure, or orders from the life he had been living in the Army. He had freedom to make his own choice of what he was to do or where he could go. New energy lifted his feet along the trail and energized his gait while his body relaxed and his spirit soared.

Abruptly, that all ended with a crash when he passed around a bend in the trail and saw flames from the burning ambush site ahead. O'Hara stopped. Flames leapt high into the air from along the river, casting the trees about the clearing in the bright flickering light. O'Hara realized quickly he had delayed along the trail too long. The sun was now beginning to set in the West and darkness had began to blanket the river valley.

Bending low, he cautiously crept ahead, ever watchful for danger. No other sounds except the roar of the flames came from the encampment. Fearing ambush, O'Hara looked carefully about and saw the lookout point where he had killed the sentry on the bluff. He decided that was the best spot to scout the camp from afar. Moving into the deeper woods behind the point he climbed slowly up, watchful not to betray himself with sudden movements that could attract attention, until he reached the sentry point where he had begun this very day. Down on his belly, he crawled to the edge of the cliff. Below him, the American flatboat piled with castoff equipment was burning brightly in the darkening valley as night encroached on the day. Tents, equipment, and bodies still lay about the campsite where they had been discarded, leaving O'Hara confused. Had the detail left to burn the camp been attacked themselves? Several bodies not in American uniforms were strewn about the camp.

O'Hara drew back from the edge. What was he to do now? To go back the way he came was too dangerous if there were Americans on the river looking for his party. What if they were Indians? O'Hara dropped his stick musket on the ground. Not a lot of good that will do if there are armed men about, he thought. He needed a weapon. Whoa. Wait, he thought. He had dumped the sentry's body and musket behind the hill in the bushes; could they still be there?

Scuttling about on all fours, O'Hara searched about the bushes. The sentry's body was right where he left it, but the musket was not. The light had faded on the dark side of the lookout, leaving long murky shadows. Stopping to think, O'Hara visualized killing the sentry and flinging his musket into the woods. No, it had to be farther down the slope. Feeling around with his fingers, O'Hara felt in broad, slow circles around him, moving by inches down the slope. He stopped every few moments to listen to the sounds from the camp or the subtle sounds of ambushers moving towards him. Finally, he felt the cold metal of the musket barrel under his fingers and drew it close to himself.

"Ah, the saints are with me," O'Hara whispered and crossed himself for the first time in many years.

Picking up the musket, he checked the frizzen quickly to ensure the powder was still dry and came up in surprise. "No powder." Such carelessness would never have been tolerated in the English Army. Any sentry with a barren frizzen would be flogged for dereliction of duty.

Reaching down, he pulled the sentries cartridge box from the dead body and examined it carefully in the dimming light. Twenty-six rounds! A full box! The sentry had not loaded his weapon. O'Hara shook his head in amazement. What kind of soldiers are these Americans that the sentries have unloaded muskets? he wondered. "Dead soldiers," he whispered to himself. "That's what kind of soldiers you would have." The Frenchie would never make that mistake, you could be sure, he thought.

Picking a cartridge from the box, he quickly tore it open with his teeth and primed the frizzen with a small dab of powder, then he poured the rest down the barrel, stuffing the bullet and empty paper cartridge down the bore. Finally, he tamped the charge in place with the ramrod.

Armed with a loaded weapon, O'Hara felt new confidence he had not felt for a long time.. Slinging the cartridge box over his shoulder, he searched the dead sentry for anything else he could use pocketing a clasp knife, extra steel, and flints. From a small bag over the sentry's shoulder, he found a canteen, hardtack, and wrapped in the paper what appeared to be a piece of the pie. "Oh, the cook must have liked you," O'Hara spoke to the dead man, wagging his finger at him. "Thank you, my dead friend." Stuffing the savory apple pie into his mouth, he moaned softly as he wolfed it down, finishing it in two bites. Startled by a loud scream from the camp, he almost choked.

Falling to his belly, O'Hara crawled to the lip of the cliff again; with his musket aimed ahead of him, he peered over the ridge. Stunned, he saw a man staggering about the fire.

Patrick recognized the man immediately as Tobias Flint, one of the soldiers left to destroy the camp. Tobias was staggering about the fire, waving his burnt shirt in the air, and yelling incoherently above the roar of the flames. Sparks from the still burning fabric sprayed about in the air. In his other hand, Tobias waved a large jug as he wove about drunkenly, continually lifting the jug to his mouth he would attempt to pour the liquor down his throat. Satisfied, he wiped his lips with his bare arm and then fell flat on his butt, collapsing forward, he then dropped his cold drunk face into the dirt and passed out..

"What is this?" O'Hara asked himself. No Indian raid here. With musket cocked and aimed forward, O'Hara scampered down the path into the clearing. O'Hara soon found all the soldiers who had been left to destroy the camp lying passed out in drunken stupors on the ground. Each with a jug in one or both hands and a small cairn of empty bottles or jugs lying nearby. Tobias had obviously fallen too close to the flames. His burning shirt woke him from his drunken slumber to scamper about long enough to gulp down more liquor before succumbing and collapsing onto the ground again. O'Hara shook his head in distaste. He had seen this kind of behavior before. Soldiers without the officers present would drink themselves sick when they discovered or looted alcohol of any kind. Not that he was a teetotaler himself; sure, he enjoyed a tot here and there. The men had found the Americans' liquor supply and decided to make up for lost drinking time. Any question now of proceeding down the river this evening was out of the question. It would be late morning at best before any of them would be awake or useful enough to finish destroying the camp and evidence of the massacre here. Their late arrival downstream of the river ambush site was doomed to an angry and predictable response from Major Torrens. If he held true to the course of late, most if not all of his venom would be directed at O'Hara.

"I'm not going to take that anymore," O'Hara spoke aloud to himself. Startled by the loudness of his own voice, he looked about sheepishly. "No worry there," he chuckled. "No one here will be hearing anything but the snores of their drunken sleep."

The question, O'Hara thought, is what are you going to do, Patrick? Looking about he saw the cook tent was still standing; the large cooking pot remained over the now cold fire. Walking over, O'Hara dipped two fingers into the still warm stew and put them into his mouth. "Well now," he smiled "a man always thinks better on a full belly." Taking the ladle hanging from the cooking tripod, he sat down and ate quietly while giving thought to his situation. Right here, he thought, I have everything to get away from this life and start a new one in America. "There are provisions enough to supply my journey just lying about the partially destroyed camp, just waiting for my clean escape," he muttered, Quiet now, he thought, but where to go? Upriver towards the settlements, or downriver towards the wilder less settled regions. What he would do wasn't a question; he was a poacher, and a good one at that. Here in America, a man who can hunt or trap doesn't need anything but a good gun to survive, he thought. O'Hara smiled. Hunt and be free. Oh god, the thrill of that thought gave him goosebumps. I will just be another Irishman making America my new home. Can you do this, Patrick? he asked himself. "Ha ha," he laughed, waving salutes at the other men in their slumber. "Watch me, Tobias; watch me, Duncan; I'm free."

Still chuckling to himself, O'Hara began to gather everything that could be of use he could find. A new powder horn went over his shoulder and extra bullet bag with more spare flints went into his hunting bag. From the canoes, he found his French cowhide pack that Torrens had insisted they all use to hide their English origins further. There he found nothing in the way of personal effects so he emptied the pack on the ground and stuffed as many new provisions as the pack would hold. O'Hara stopped suddenly and thought, no, if I take my own pack, then Torrens or most likely Sergeant White (as he is the smarter of the two) would realize I had come back to camp and deserted. Better to just disappear, with no sign. Repacking his pack, he placed it back where it had been in the canoe. Looking about, he saw the major's effects in several large sacks wedged under the front thwart of the canoe. "What do we have here, Patrick?" he asked himself. Picking up the baggage, he opened them and dumped the contents on the ground. Something landed with a heavy thump and he heard the distinctive clink of metal against metal as dozens of gold and silver coins fell out onto the sand. Dropping to his knees, O'Hara scooped up the coins in his hands where they glittered and shone in the firelight. Bright shiny silver American eagles and gold Spanish reales — more money than he had ever held in his hands, indeed more than he ever seen in his entire life. Laughing at his good fortune, he said, "Oh no, Patrick. You'll not be a thief, will you?" Laughing to himself, he said, "Oh sure, Patrick, deserter, poacher, and now thief. No matter; if I'm ever caught, I'll dangle from a noose either way. Thank you, Major, I will name my first child after your great generosity." Laughing louder at his humor, he shook his head mockingly. "Now that will never happen." Patrick picked up the small bottle with a distinctive skull and crossbones symbol and the faded letters "ARSENIC" on the front. Patrick shook his head. Poison. Whatever does the major need with poison? he asked himself. "No matter, maybe he will poison himself; be no loss to any of us, will it, mates?" he asked his passed-out comrades lying about on the sand. Throwing all the gear back into the major's luggage except for the money which he put into his bullet bag, he scornfully dumped Torrens' pack into the canoe.

Returning to the firelight, O'Hara rummaged around the destroyed camp until he found an American pack and loaded his provisions into that together with a blanket which he rolled up and tied around the pack with a few extras: a shirt, a wool jacket, and socks. He hefted the pack with one hand. "Heavy," he pronounced, but not heavier than some he had worn on his back during the campaigns on the continent.

Sitting back on his haunches, O'Hara contemplated his next moves.

"If I take a canoe, for sure the major will believe it was me that took it. No, I want to just disappear like dust in the wind with not a trace of my coming. Of course, the missing money may be a problem and set the major into hunting down a culprit from the camp. No, not my problem," he decided.

Downstream or up? he wondered. Down increases my chance of running into Torrens and White. Upstream it has to be. Maybe I can join a group of settlers going down the river or inland. The wide trail by the river appeared to continue upstream, and we have passed some small settlements coming down the river that could not be more than a week of walking away. I'll take my time. I have plenty of powder and shot, as well as supplies. I could just disappear into the forest for a few months. Yes, O'Hara thought, there is that lovely stream we paddled by not three days ago. Clear, clean water, and a little valley all around with tall oaks, walnuts, and maples. A perfect place to camp and hunt.

Throwing his pack onto his back and with a musket in hand, O'Hara took a quick look about the desolated camp and drunken soldiers strewn about the fire. Throwing a mock salute, he said, "So long mates, see you all in hell!" Chuckling to himself, he slipped into the forest and quickly disappeared down the trail.

CHAPTER 14

Back at the ambush site, Major Torrens ordered the men to start searching for any useable debris while some others were sent to drag firewood for a fire that they would build once it became dark. The soldiers moved slowly, still winded and hungry after their ordeal. Private Hawkins, in particular, was staggering about as if in a daze or drunk; either way, he was earning scowls of anger from Torrens.

Looking up the river, the major saw in the far distance what looked like a man moving across a small sunlit opening along the escarpment.

"That's that lazy Irishman," Torrens said to himself. "Out for a Sunday stroll." Then he drew short in his comment. Years of combat on the continent he learned many skills to survive, including observation and appraisal of men and movement at long range. He could identify at a distance if a man was armed or not by his posture and his gait while walking. This man was one with a musket or rifle in one hand who was walking confidently through the woods. Looking about at his shattered command, Torrens immediately knew an armed man in the vicinity was not good news.

"Sergeant White," he barked. Then he pointed to an area of driftwood that formed a redoubt of logs by the river's edge. "Move the men over there and get a defensive position built by that driftwood. Leave the fire for later. Have the men lay into it now." Looking about, Torrens spotted Private Hawkins lying curled up by a rock, asleep.

"Sergeant. Put your boots into Hawkins there; no time for that slacker to be taking a nap."

At the shout, everyone stopped working and looked from the major to where he was pointing to Hawkins slumped down by the rock.

Sergeant White marched up and yelled into Hawkins' ear, "Get up, you lazy man, or I'll plant my boot up your arse till your nose bleeds." By then the other men had gathered around. Torrens stormed in beside White.

"Boot him. We have work to do!" Torrens screeched.

White ignored the major, bent down, and began to gently shake Hawkins by his collar. Hawkins' head rolled about, flopping like a rag doll as he was slipped over on his side. "Dead, he is," White said. Then, as if by command, Hawkins' mouth opened and erupted in a loud belch, spewing a vile gush of awful green liquid into the sand. Everyone leapt back in shock. Wild-eyed and stunned with horror at the hideous sight, they stared while holding their noses at the putrid stink of it.

"What the devil is this?" Torrens gasped, trying to cover the repugnant smell with his fingers over his mouth. Looking at the men's horrified expressions, he asked, "What happened here? Did any of you see anything?" The men shook their heads. They looked right and left to each other for someone to make a reply to the major's question.

"Well. Speak up!" Torrens barked angrily. "One of you must know what occurred to this man."

After a brief pause, Private Wood spoke up. "I think I know what happened here, sir." Wood turned to Sergeant White, waiting for the sergeant's permission to speak to his officer. White nodded and looked at the major.

"Speak, Private Wood. If you know something to explain this, then we will listen to what you have to say," Torrens snapped.

His face a mask of apprehension, Wood began, "It's the work of water demons, sir."

"Damn it, man," Torrens barked at Wood. "I don't want a story or silly superstition here. Did you see something or not?"

Wood stood silent. His hat now scrunched up in his trembling fists, he answered in a whisper, "I know some things. Things I heard in the Navy. Sir."

"The Navy?" Torrens sneered at Wood. "You were in the Navy? When were you in the Navy?"

Sergeant White looked about and saw the fear in the men's eyes. If Wood had an answer, then the men needed to hear it more than Torrens.

Nodding to Torrens, White said, "We have no answer here, sir; wouldn't hurt to hear what he has to say." After a moment to ponder Torrens simply nodded back with no reply.

"Tell your story, Wood. And no tall tales, just what you know or saw," White said.

Wood began again. Shaken by the major's outburst, he chose his words carefully, "I was a gunner's mate, sir. On the HMS Amethyst. A good ship she was too, sir. We were in a battle with a Frenchie frigate. We gave a good account of ourselves in that one we did. For me I got hit by a cannonball I was." Dramatically lifting his shirt, Wood turned slowly around, showing his brutally scarred chest for all to see. "Too injured to serve. That's what the surgeons said." Wood waited for some response, some acknowledgement or praise from his comrades. These were not raw recruits; they were veterans. No one was impressed by Wood's display; most of them bore wounds themselves, and in some cases multiple scars from years of fighting on the continent against Napoleon. Failing to get the desired reaction, Wood began again, "Invalided to land with no pension or thanks or future, I might add. But over time I healed, still sore but healed. Then one day, while I was begging on the street, this big Army sergeant comes up to me and says he would like to buy me a drink, being we all were serving the same king and country. Sure, that one drink turned into many and the next morning I was in the Army, being I'd taken the king's shilling while drunk all the night before. I've no regrets: better the Army than a beggar's life."

"Wood, what does that have to do with this here?" White asked, pointing to Hawkins' dead body.

"Ah, the point is, sir, in the Navy, I served with many men who had been in the big battles. Trafalgar, in particular, some years earlier. They had stories of what they had seen. Men blown apart, grievously wounded, and they saw many a sailor, ours and Frenchies' alike, that had been blown off their ships, thrown into the water and left to struggle or to drown in the cold sea. Those men that could be rescued were brought back onto the ships whether they were thought to be dead or alive. So, it was said, sir. Some of those men looked alive and acted alive when rescued. They were alive, walking about like they were living, but speaking all jumbled up like poor Hawkins here. These saved sailors were somewhat peculiar in their behavior as they recovered. Talking slowly or acting as if drunk they would. Oh, for a few hours for some, others for a maybe day or so, then those who saw said these drowned men would just lay down or collapsed, suddenly and completely dead. That's when the fowl demon water would rush out their mouths with a great roar and run across the deck back into the sea. Many stories of those I heard from men of their word. Drowned dead men who walked till the demons left them, they were. That's what I heard, sir. Just like poor Hawkins here, the water demons had taken him and returned from whence they came leaving him dead. That's what I know, sir."

Shaken into silence, no one spoke while staring fearfully at Hawkins corpse. Sergeant White spoke first. "Hawkins needs a grave on dry land, well away from the water." Pointing to a sand beach above the waterline, he said, "Bury him over there, we will give him a Christian burial." Anxious to get the burial done and over, the men crowded about, lifting Hawkins up by his arms and legs. They stepped cautiously as they carried him, trying to avoid the noxious green ooze still dribbling from his mouth onto the ground.

Noting the major had not joined them, Sergeant White stopped and looked back. White nodded to the beach behind, silently asking if the major was going to join them. Torrens responded with a quick head shake to the negative and turned his back to the sergeant.

"Bad form, that one," White mumbled under his breath as he turned to follow the men who had now reached the burial spot. Continuing speaking to himself, he added, "This command will fall apart if this continues. Hardship and danger these soldiers had learned to endure, but bad officers were another story altogether. Sloppy leadership and poor decisions got men killed."

White arrived at the makeshift gravesite as the men had just finished digging a shallow grave in the loose sand with their hands. No point digging deeper. Two feet by six feet of bank sand are no deterrent to the wild animals in this country, White thought.

The men now gathered around the grave. The few who had retained their hats from the recent dunking in the river now held them in their hands over their chests. Heads bowed, they looked to Sergeant White to speak. After a moment, Private Wood asked quietly, "Will you say a few words, Sergeant?"

Sergeant White nodded and for a moment stood silent, not knowing what to say. He was not a religious person, and by rights Torrens should be the one speaking. Thinking back, he remembered that in Spain, during their retreat from the French, there were too many dead to give a proper burial and the officers simply said a speedy Lord's prayer over the bodies before they were quickly buried along the roadside where they had fallen.

White took a deep breath, beginning, "Our Father, which art in heaven…"

The men joined in immediately, "hallowed be thy name."

By the river, Torrens watched and listened, only catching snatches of the prayer as the wind began to pick up across the river in brief but increasing gusts as a cool breeze started to blow down the Ohio.

O'Hara better be running, he thought, or we will have a cold camp if we spend the night here without our supplies from upriver. Inside Torrens knew O'Hara would not return with the rest of the command and a cold shiver shook up and down his spine. "Damn White," he snapped out loud. "He should have insisted on me sending someone more reliable than that Irishman. This will go in my report about him when this mission is completed."

Tobias woke with a start. The sudden movement smacked into his head like he had been clubbed. With a groan, the tree tops spun above him and he sank back onto the sand, covering his eyes with an outstretched hand. Even that small movement brought waves of pain mixed with nausea forcing him onto his side to vomit into the sand. After a few moments, he was able to stop heaving and dragged himself the few feet across the beach to the river. Plunging his head into the cold water, he drank until another bout of nausea forced him to heave that up as well. Rolling on his back, he slowly regained his senses. Abruptly he remembered where he was. Fighting the sickness in his belly, he staggered to his feet. Laid out before him was the demolished river camp from yesterday's battle. The huge fire they had built to burn the Americans' supplies and bodies still shot up flames, but it was now less vigorous than the night before. It was sending out a huge column of smoke into the morning sky. The camp they had been tasked to burn still lay in scattered piles across the clearing. Here and there his three companions lay in drunken stupors, dead to the world about them.

"Damn. It's morning," he said to himself. "Morning! Oh god, we are supposed to be on our way downriver to the major." Staggering about, he began to yell, "Get up. Get up!" Barely able to stay on his feet himself, he went to each of his companions and kicked them until they showed some semblance of life. Moving from one to another, he repeated the process of kicks and yells. Presently all were awake, attempting to rise from their sandy beds, and rubbing grit from their eyes in various stages of sickness and nausea.

"Get moving, you bastards!" Tobias yelled at them.

"Who put you in charge?" James Duncan asked. Grabbing the whisky jug that lay beside him, he lifted it. Giving the jug a quick shake, he could feel the weight of liquid still in it and raised it to his lips to have it brutally kicked from his hand by Tobias.

"Leave it, Duncan. We are in Torrens hellfire enough if we don't start to move," Tobias snapped at him. "All of you get over here now. We need all the gear in the canoes and move downstream. The major will be waiting for us, and the longer he waits the nastier he'll get."

"He was born nasty," Duncan said, then he groaned, bending over to throw up.

"Oi," Jacob Williams answered. "That American whiskey is nastier than him."

"Their whiskey will have us hanged if we don't get a move on," Tobias replied. "Leave off your yapping. Give yourselves a quick clean up. Sergeant White catches that whisky smell on you and we'll all be dead for sure. Get a move on."

As each gave themselves a quick head dunk in the river, the others began gathering the supplies lying about the ruined campsite and chucking them hurriedly into the canoes until they were ready to push off.

Tobias yelled at the men, "Grab any extra food and supplies as you go."

Fraser called out, "Tobias. Grab me an extra musket. The spring on my lock needs replacing."

Tobias nodded, answering, "Everyone pick up some extra muskets so we can scavenge parts for our own later."

Looking about a few moments later, Tobias asked, "Have we got everything? If we're ready, we better decide what our story will be when we find the others."

Not making eye contact with Tobias, the men looked sheepishly at their feet, shuffling about like lost children.

"Come on, then!" Tobias yelled at them. "How the hell are we going to explain to the major why we are so late and what happened here?"

"It's not the major," Fraser answered. "It's Sergeant White. You know what he's like. He will know we were up to something before we even get out of the canoes."

"Fraser is right," Williams agreed, shaking his head slowly. "That man knows what we are about to do before we do, and then all the saints in heaven won't save us from him."

"The more the reason," Tobias answered, "to have a good story we all agree on beforehand."

Speaking for the first time, Private Duncan spoke quietly, "If you ask me, we should quit this place before someone stumbles upon us standing here in the middle of all this ruination."

"Aye, you've got a point there, Duncan." Tobias then added, "We are already late leaving this place; the later we are, the more the major is going to jump down our throats."

"You mean before White skins us alive," Williams cut in.

"All ready, then, let us move out and speak about this as we paddle," Tobias agreed.

Without further discussion, the men took up positions in the canoes, secured the second canoe with a tether for towing, and pushed off into the river. They picked up some speed as they began to paddle.

CHAPTER 15

Captain Johnson enjoyed the rest of his morning coffee as the men, with their breakfasts complete, began to pull down their camp by the creek. Enjoyment turned to concern as he spotted his Tuscarora guide Ganiga running through the brush towards the camp some distance down the valley. Dropping his cup, Captain Johnson picked up his rifle. He called out to Corporal Wilson who was supervising the men behind him, "Corporal Wilson. Have the men stand to immediately."

"Yes, sir," Wilson replied and started yelling at the men, "Drop what you're doing now and fall in behind the barricade." Downriver, Wilson now saw Ganiga running along the path, leaping downed trees and bushes like a deer being chased by a wolf. "That could only mean trouble," Wilson thought out loud. Then he shouted, "Check your priming, flints, and steady, ready for my command."

The men quickly formed up behind the barricade built the night before. They checked the frizzens on their musket locks to see that the powder was dry. They lowered the flints back down to the half-cock safety position and assumed the ready stance with musket held forward, prepared for the command to follow.

Corporal Wilson, satisfied the men were organized, turned back to Captain Johnson and stated, "The men are ready, sir."

"Good work, Wilson," Johnson replied, nodding his approval towards the men for their quick and efficient response.

Just then, the two surveyors who were being escorted by Captain Johnson's command heard the ruckus and came running from up the creek where they were completing some survey along the shore.

"What's going on?" one asked as he drew up along with the soldiers standing behind the barricade.

With a quick glance, Wilson saw both men were unarmed and growled at them, "Arm yourselves and take your positions."

The surveyors quickly did as they were told. They returned a moment later with their muskets and began to clumsily load them.

"Why?" one cried out nervously.

Cutting the man off, Corporal Wilson calmly commanded, "Assume your positions as you've been taught, sirs. And kindly point your muskets away from my men and towards our flank. Thank you."

Captain Johnson smirked briefly to himself. Corporal Wilson was always the politest when he held people in contempt or disdain for their actions. This was a common enough situation with the two government surveyors.

By this point Ganiga reached the camp and stood still in front of the captain.

"What have you seen, Ganiga?" Johnson asked.

"No see," Ganiga replied. Touching his nose, then pointing downriver, he said, "Smell. Smell bad smoke."

"You smell bad smoke?" the captain asked patiently.

Ganiga nodded, waiting for the captain, but before he could say anything one of the surveyors called out angrily, "That's it. All this fuss because he…" pointing at Ganiga "he smells smoke."

"That will be quite enough, sir. Please step back into your position and be quiet, sir," Corporal Wilson chided the surveyor.

Without further words, Ganiga pointed at Captain Johnson signing for the captain to follow him upriver. Without further word he started back the way he had come.

"Wilson. You're in command. Defend this position until I return," Johnson said. Checking his cartridge box, accouterments, and rifle, the captain ran after Ganiga down the trail.

Ganiga kept a steady pace as they ran down the trail. No words were spoken as the men ran quietly through the woods. Before long Johnson became aware of the smell Ganiga had spoken of. The heavy scent of wood smoke. The normal sweet aroma of burning woods mixed with that of burnt meat. After several miles they approached their base campsite along the river, Ganiga slowed his pace. Cocking his weapon, he pointed the rifle ahead and began a steady stalk. He slowly looked left to right, up and then down, with no quick movements to give away his presence.

Johnson, knowing this routine well, followed behind Ganiga but slightly off to one side so that his view forward was not obstructed by the other. With practiced efficiency, when his guide looked left, the captain looked right; after up, he looked down and around at everything, seeing it all twice, and then they moved slowly ahead.

They approached a small trail joining the one they were on from upriver. Ganiga stopped crouching down. He looked at the tracks in the earth and spoke quietly to Johnson.

"One man," he said. "White man. Come from there." He pointed down the river. "Go there," he whispered, pointing towards their camp. By now the vile smell came on stronger as the morning shift of the wind brought the smoke in their direction.

They approached the camp, advancing more cautiously and stopping as Ganiga examined the sign on the path. They came to a fork in the trail. The right, Johnson knew from their time at the encampment, went around the bluff to the camp by the river. The trail on the left climbed the back of the knoll to the guard post at the top.

Silently Johnson pointed first to the right then to the left and made the sign with two fingers for Ganiga to lead the way. Moving to the left, Ganiga began a slow climb up the trail. Both men now concentrated on watching their right as the steep dark forest on their left was the least likely place for an ambush to come from. The lesser wooded forest at the right towards the top of the bluff gave ample opportunity for an ambusher to hide and attack them. Ganiga stopped staring quietly ahead through the bushes, and then he pointed ahead for the captain to see.

Lying partially hidden in the undergrowth was the body of a soldier. While his scout moved ahead to peer over the lookout, Johnson moved to the side of the dead soldier. Private Hughes' dead eyes stared up at the captain. He remembered the lad well. A good young soldier, friends with the cook whom he suspected had kept Hughes supplied with treats. Now dead. From the signs and lack of struggle, he assumed he had died while on guard with his body thrown down the hill by his assassin to hide it. Johnson looked about the body quickly. He had not been stripped or violated in any way except that his cartridge box, small possible bag, and musket were missing. Not the work of Indians, Johnson decided quickly. His reverie was interrupted by Ganiga's low hiss to pay attention. Ganiga beckoned from the ridge.

Joining the guide, Johnson was shocked by what he saw.

Below, a huge fire was sending a tall plume of black odiferous smoke into the air so great it blocked off the view of the far riverbank. On the creek's beach side, debris lay scattered about in small piles. Torn tenting, uniforms, boots, campaign hats, whiskey jugs, and several large pools of blood were scattered about, marking where bodies had lain. Drag marks across the sand from the blood pools led to the raging fire, giving evidence to the absence of bodies.

Ganiga hissed quietly to Johnson, pointing to the area of the river shore hidden by the smoke from the fire. Cupping his hand to his ear, he indicated he heard sounds and pointed to the camp. Johnson signed in return, touching his ear with his fist to ask "What do you hear?" Ganiga replied with two fingers pointing down, the man sign. Turning back to the shore, the scout pulled the hammer back on his rifle, cocking it ready to fire. Johnson did the same. Although he heard no sounds other than the crackle and snap of the fire, he was sure if the scout said he heard men, there were men by the river. No doubt armed men and the attackers of his camp. Angered by what he had seen, Johnson prodded Ganiga by making the number sign, displaying one, two, then three fingers in quick succession to signal "How many?" Ganiga signaled three or four.

Silently the two lay down, their rifles at the ready pointed towards the camp. They waited, watching intently for some sign of action from the men hidden by the screen of smoke whirling about the campsite. Johnson was familiar with the location the voices came from: a decent beach to land boats sheltered by bush on both sides. It would be very difficult to attack from their current position and an attack through the open beach areas below would be foolhardy. If the men would step out from behind the smoke, then the situation would be more favorable as Johnson and Ganiga could use the long-range accuracy of their rifles to pick off the attackers in the open.

Suddenly, Ganiga jumped up. "Canoes," he said sharply to the captain, then took off running down the trail across the embankment towards the creekside beach, with Captain Johnson hard on his heels. From the left they could see movement through the bushes to the river and two canoes heading both down and across the river, trying to make some distance from the shore.

An old tree, broken and bare of leaves or bark, hung over the water along the bank. Ganiga ran to it. Splashing waist-deep through the water, he reached a large branch over which he laid his rifle to take a steady aim towards where he expected the canoes to appear. Johnson joined him with his rifle laid on the tree as well; they both waited to open fire.

Fleeting movement through the bushes caught Johnson's eye as the canoes moved farther away from the shore. One canoe with men, and the other empty was all he could surmise from the brief glimpse as they passed. They disappeared momentarily, shielded by a huge tree blocking further vision from the shore, until abruptly the canoes burst from cover and became fully visible to Johnson and Ganiga as the four men in the lead canoe paddled furiously pushing to distance themselves obliquely away from the threat on the shore.

Johnson drew a steady bead on the paddler in the bow. "Front," he said loudly so Ganiga would know not to aim at the same target and shoot for one in the rear. Exhaling slowly, Johnson followed the bow paddler with his front sight. He then aimed an arm's length in front of the man holding the sight at head height to compensate for the distance and movement. Squeezing the trigger slowly, he continued to lead the man till unexpectedly the rifle barked. The rifle spewed forth a dense cloud of powder smoke that momentarily blocked a clear view of the man and canoe. Johnson ducked down past the gunsmoke just in time to see a man flung forward into the bow of the canoe. The plop of the bullet hitting home sounded like a good hit. Ganiga fired next; by then the other men in the canoe had begun to duck down. Ganiga's shot hit one of the paddlers in the shoulder, causing him to drop the paddle and fall face-first into the canoe.

Johnson and Ganiga reloaded quickly. By now, the canoe driven by the current had pushed them well over four hundred yards from shore, too far for a good shot. Ganiga and Johnson both held their fire.

Johnson stared angrily as the canoe disappeared from sight down the river and watched till they were completely out of sight. Turning, he realized Ganiga had moved back onto shore and was scouting the tracks and sign around the beach and fire. The captain began to exit the water when the scout held his hand up to stop, signaling he wanted Johnson not to ruin the sign from around the camp so he was not to step on shore just yet. Johnson pulled himself up on the tree and sat with his legs hanging down, like sitting in a saddle. He watched Ganiga in fascination as he meticulously searched the encampment. Ganiga was a master tracker. No detail was too small to avoid his attention from footprints, animal scat, scratches in the dirt, blood trails, or a bit of pocket lint. A good tracker can tell as much from what he doesn't see as that which he does, Johnson thought.

After some minutes, the scout returned and signed for the captain to come ashore. Cold and wet Johnson walked over and stood closer to the fire to warm his freezing legs. "Getting too old for this," he muttered to himself. The adrenaline high of the chase, the frigid waters, and then the high energy crashed, leaving him feeling worn and tired.

"Well, my friend," Johnson asked, "what story have you found for what happened here?"

Ganiga sat down on his haunches, thinking carefully. He pointed to the creek side. "Two men. Long knives." Ganiga always referred to American long hunters by the Indian term long knives for the big knives they all carried. "Come ashore there with a canoe. Big dog. Big dog like wolf come too." Shaking his head, Ganiga could not understand why white men kept dogs as pets.

Pointing further up the beach, he said, "Little Captain," (his name for Ensign Keen) "he go there. Sit with long knives."

Ganiga pointed to the logs around the fire pit. "Little Captain," he said again, now pointing at a pool of blood in the sand, "he die there."

"Killed?" Johnson asked. "Killed by the long knives?"

"No," Ganiga replied, "other long knives kill Little Captain. Dog long knives run to canoe and leave."

"You're sure, Ganiga?" Johnson asked apprehensively.

Ganiga nodded, annoyed at being questioned. "Me know; I see sign."

"Where did the other long knives come from?" Johnson asked.

"There." Ganiga pointed first to the far beach where they had seen the attackers running away from them. "They come in three canoes. One canoe with many men land there." He pointed to the bushes on the other far side of the beach. "More men hide there then shoot from trees."

Johnson looked about carefully. A perfect ambush. Caught by surprise in a crossfire, the men in the encampment were probably caught off guard, not expecting an attack.

"Who were those long knives?" Johnson asked.

"Not same dog long knives," Ganiga answered. "Those American long knives. Others soldier long knives."

Ganiga pointed at several clear tracks on the beach. Looking at them carefully, Johnson recognized immediately the footprints of men long accustomed to wearing boots, soldier boots. Their tracks always showed the foot landing heavy on the heel, whereas men who wore moccasins all their life would leave a footprint showing all their weight distributed evenly over the whole foot, not just the heel. Their print would be straight, while men used to wearing boots angled their feet left to right and had deep heel marks.

Ganiga walked over to the beach, beckoning Johnson to follow him now that his survey of the site had been completed.

Standing in the middle of the beach, just feet from the shore, Ganiga pointed down to where he was standing, then slowly spread his arms out to the side.

"Soldier long knives stand here," he said.

"How many?" Johnson asked.

Numbers meant little to Ganiga, so he held up one hand then four fingers.

"Nine," Johnson said.

Ganiga shrugged. Nine could be the same as thirty, as far as he was concerned. He pointed down to several tattered pieces of paper lying on the sand that Johnson recognized instantly. These were the tops of paper musket cartridges that soldiers would tear with their teeth before loading their guns.

"Soldier long knives, shoot all same time," Ganiga said. "Two times here." Then, pointing back towards the beach behind the campsite, he said, "One time there." He pointed again to the position in the bushes and said, "Two times there."

"Volleys. They fired volleys?" Johnson asked incredulously. Only trained soldiers would fire volleys. Frontiersmen lacked the training or the will to fire their rifles in that manner, preferring to take careful aim and only shoot when sure of hitting what they were aiming for.

Ganiga shrugged his shoulders again. The concept of massed volley fire was totally foreign to his way of both shooting and attacking an enemy. Stealth, shooting from cover, and quick, violent attacks was the Indian way of fighting.

"Who were they shooting at?" the captain asked.

"Dog long knives," Ganiga answered, pointing downriver.

"Long knives' dog piss in the soldier's coffee." Ganiga laughed at his own joke.

"Not funny, Ganiga." Johnson scowled back at him. "What happened to the rest of my command? Were they captured or all killed here?"

Ganiga's smile disappeared as he turned and pointed at the fire. Its flames were just beginning to die down to hot coals.

Johnson walked slowly to the edge of the huge burnt area, stopping when he could not take the heat any longer. In most places the wood had been totally consumed by the flames. Several skulls, their eyes vacant black holes and jagged jaws open in silent screams, showed through the smoldering embers and smoke. Johnson stared in horror and shock.

"Ganiga. Go back and tell Corporal Wilson what has happened here and bring the rest of the command as quickly as possible." Ganiga nodded wordlessly and turned, running back up the trail they had come from.

Johnson walked over to the logs where he and Ensign Keen liked to sit and have their morning coffee together. Whatever the story here, Johnson knew only one thing. As far has he was concerned, this was long from over and the hunt had just begun.

Chapter 16

Private Lewis was hungry. Not my dinner is late hungry or I haven't eaten all day, hungry. But two days without food your belly aches until that's all you can think of, hungry. Lewis looked from his perch on the riverbank back into the forest, thinking there must be something in those trees a man can eat. Tree bark, can a man eat tree bark? Give me another day, he thought, and I'm going to try bark. "Better keep your wits about you, Lewis," he said to himself. "The major has been sneaking up on sentries, trying to catch them not watching up the river for the rest of the command with supplies and food." Not much was visible on the river now. The sun had just set. The red-orange sunset was cooling to a dull gray and with it the visibility across the water was dropping from hundreds of yards to mere dozens as his eyes adjusted to the rapidly dimming light.

Trying to console himself for his misfortune to be stationed on this cold, rocky point, he reminded himself he had drawn first watch. No cold kick waking him from comforting sleep to take a post on the river in the middle of the night. Another two hours and he would be relieved with a full six hours of sleep till after his next shift. A small bonus for the hunger, but a bonus of sleep nonetheless.

Just then, out the corner of his eye, he saw a distant light on the river. It appeared to be moving slowly towards him. At first unsure of its source, he remained quiet, watching intently as it drew closer. Then, he recognized the lantern in the bow and vague movements of men behind paddling.

"It's them," he said quietly to himself. He stood up slowly. Then, as the truth dawned on him, he called over his shoulder to the others back on the beach.

"It's them!" he shouted. "Here we are here!" he began yelling at the canoes coming towards him. Jumping up and down, he waved his arms in the air over his head. "Here!" He laughed in relief. "Here. Over here!" he continued to yell.

"Stop that racket!" Sergeant White barked in his ear, surprising Lewis with his abrupt appearance. White grabbed the long branch they had whittled down earlier and laid out over the water to serve as a handhold for the paddlers. "Take hold, Lewis," he commanded. Lewis seized hold of the branch, then they swung it farther out over the water.

"Grab hold!" White yelled at the canoers as they were slow to respond, approaching the drop-off to the rapids. "Hold fast; we will swing you to shore. There are bad rapids just below us here, so be steady."

The lead paddler purposely dropped his paddle. Taking hold of the branch, he held on for dear life as the current sought to pull the vessel down into the rapids which had just come into view below the point.

"That's it; pull harder," White called out.

Several men from the camp arrived, jumping into the river and pulling the canoe onto shore where they wedged it into the embankment and tied it off safely. After smiling and laughing at their rescue, the men stopped, shocked into silence by the blood and gore splattered about the canoe. The canoe was in shambles, with packs, equipment, and supplies scattered about and covered in blood. James Duncan lay dead in the belly of the boat. Blood, water, and debris sloshed about him, his sightless eyes staring accusingly into the night sky above. Tobias Flint and William Fraser stumbled out of the canoe, flopping worn and exhausted onto the damp grass on shore.

"Where's Williams and O'Hara?" White asked.

Before anyone could speak, Major Torrens arrived and interrupted, "Never mind that now, Sergeant. Get these men and supplies back to the camp first, and we will find out the details after. We are not safe yet. Muskets, powder, and shot first." Pointing to the three men, he ordered, "Load now and take a position on our open flank there." Again, he pointed towards the edge of the foreshore.

Realizing the danger, the remaining men quickly emptied the canoes of stores and carried them back to the camp before returning to lift Duncan's body from the vessel and laying him haphazardly on the shore. That done, the canoes were turned over and carried across the point to the camp on the beach beyond where a large fire was burning behind a barricade of driftwood.

"You men get those supplies sorted out before getting into that food," White commanded. As the men began to work, White grasped Tobias by one elbow with Torrens on the other and pulled him aside, out of earshot of the men.

"Where are O'Hara and Williams?" Torrens asked.

Confused, Tobias said, "O'Hara was with your party, sir?"

"No," White replied, "we sent him back yesterday to bring you in last night."

"We never saw him," Tobias answered. "We destroyed the enemy camp, leaving this morning when you didn't return." He added quickly, "As we were ordered, sir."

White looked to Torrens, and remarked grimly, "O'Hara must have run into trouble."

"Or run off," Torrens snapped back, always looking for the worst in people and their outcomes.

White waved his hand in a circle, pointing to the forest beyond. "Not the place or time to run off with no supplies or weapons now, is it, sir."

Torrens frowned at the truth of White's comments. Then he turned his attention back again to Tobias. "What happened here, soldier?" Torrens demanded.

Tobias responded slowly, trying to keep to the script he and Fraser had decided upon on their float down the river. Keep it simple; mix the truth with the lie was the plan they had agreed upon.

"Sir, we burnt everything that you ordered us. We saved some extra American muskets for spares, some extra rations. Bacon, flour, beans, and coffee being as ours were getting a mite short. All the rest went up in flames."

"All the bodies?" Torrens asked.

"Yes, sir," Tobias answered. He waited apprehensively for Torrens to berate him for saving the extra muskets and supplies.

"Then what happened?" White asked before Torrens could respond.

"The next morning," Tobias continued, "we finished burning the rest of the camp, seeing as we wanted all the supplies destroyed. Some had not burned during the night. We delayed a bit picking things lying about an' all. Just as we finished loading the canoes, we were attacked by hostiles."

"Indians!" Torrens replied, shocked. "There have been no hostiles in this part of Ohio since last year, we had heard."

"Oh, indeed, sir, that they were." Tobias recounted how he had seen Ganiga running down the hill towards them with another hostile close in pursuit. Pushing off quickly from shore, they had paddled as fast as possible, seeking to reach the safety of distance from the Indians on the shore but to no avail. With their rifles they had shot Duncan, killing him almost instantly; and they seriously wounded Williams. Not stopping, they kept paddling until out of sight around a bend of the river. Then, they pulled to the other side of the river to stay as far as possible from the Indians following them.

"How many were there?" Torrens interrupted.

"Don't know, sir," Tobias responded. "We just paddled as fast as we could, keeping our heads down; it was not something I was pleased to be doing."

"Where's Williams, then?" White asked.

Tobias paused for a moment. "Williams was hurt grievously, sir. The bullet struck him in the upper chest and passed out his back through his shoulder blade. It were an awful wound, sir. Bloody bones sticking out his back. Blood all over. Seen the like before, all of us have, though not dead right away like Duncan there. Dead. Slow, long, and painful, but dead for sure. He thrashed about, screaming and kicking in the bottom of the boat. He kept yelling, 'I'm done. I'm done for!' Over and over, he wouldn't stop. We tried to calm him to keep him still and stop his shouting so as not to attract more hostiles. There was naught we could do for him being were not doctors, and we needed to get our boat away and join you here as fast as we could. Williams, he grows really quiet, like when all of a sudden, he stands up just as if he was on parade, he does. 'Sit down,' I tells him. 'You'll bring the savages down on our heads, you standing up there for all to see.' He just looks at me with that big grin he gets when he's been in the drink and spread his arms out like the padre giving a sermon. Then, still grinning, he leans back before we stop him and falls backward into the river."

"He fell?" Torrens asked, suspiciously. "Intentionally fell into the river?"

"Went of his own accord he did, sir. Almost swamped us, too, all that jumping around in a canoe carrying on and all."

Torrens frowned at Tobias, waiting for further response. None came. Torrens simply shrugged his shoulders. "Probably for the better. The wound would have killed him eventually.

We've no medical assistance of which to help him. He chose a quicker death. Nothing more can be done here."

Turning to White, Torrens carried on as if Williams' death meant nothing. "Sergeant, we have enough muskets for all of us; we are no longer helpless and stuck on this riverbank. You may compliment the men on their foresight to bring more weapons and supplies. Have the men fed after they remove all the blood from the supplies, and have the canoe cleaned up so we are ready to depart at daybreak tomorrow." Turning brusquely, Torrens headed back to the campsite, calling back over his shoulder, "Have Private Tobias take the next guard shift here."

Momentarily confused, Tobias asked Sergeant White, "Flint, I'm Private Flint. Just what am I guarding, Sergeant?"

"Us, the camp. From anything coming down the river," White replied.

"The hostiles don't attack at night, Sergeant. That's what we been told."

"And damn lucky for you, Tobias. From the stink of you, if they had attacked in the night you would all be dead. Found the Americans' whiskey and drank yourselves sick, is my guess. And don't be giving me that look, Tobias; I know when you've got yourself into the grog. Stay here and I'll send you up some food and arms and that's more then you deserve." Leaning closer to Tobias, he spoke quietly, "You could have brought us a jug, you selfish bastard. We all could use a good dram on this night."

Tobias watched White storm off and smiled to himself. "And damn good whiskey it was, Sergeant."

Later, after Private Fraser had taken a ration of bannock and bacon to Tobias, Fraser joined the soldiers now huddled around the fire. Looking about cautiously, he spoke softly to the other men as they lounged in the warmth of the blaze.

"Tobias said to me Torrens called him Private Tobias. The major had a strange look in his eyes as if he didn't know where he was. Looked a mite bizarre, he said."

"Bizarre?" Fraser replied. "What about White using our Christian names like were all chums and all? If you ask me that's odd, very strange indeed."

"Ha!" Lewis laughed. "The whole bloody country is strange, if you ask me. None of us knows where we are."

"Or where we're going," Fraser added. "Still, Tobias thinks the major is distracted."

"I agree," Wood said. He looked about guardedly for the sergeant and the major. Seeing they were still off by the river, he added, "White disagreed openly with Torrens several times of late. Questioning his orders right in front of all of us. Now that's not the way a good Sergeant is supposed to be acting, if you ask me. Nor will the major be forgetting."

"All I know is we went from a lovely little victory to defeat gone to hell all in one day," Lewis said with a frown. "I'm thinking we need to be watching our backs. Torrens is one for the lash, free to use it whenever he wants, so watch your backs and your tongues."

"Aye," they all agreed.

Fraser added with a yawn, "Aye, watch me wiggle my back into this nice warm sand. You can jabber on if you wish, but I'm betting Torrens will have us breaking our backs over a paddle before tomorrow."

CHAPTER 17

Captain Johnson sat quietly with his guide, Ganiga, waiting for Corporal Wilson to get the patrols' camp set up for the night and gather their remaining supplies together. Wilson soon joined them with steaming mugs of well-sweetened coffee in his hands. Passing them to Johnson and Ganiga, he sat down. They quietly drank the coffee. Johnson was the first to speak. "Where do we stand, for supplies corporal?"

"Better than we hoped, sir. Since we shortened our sortie upriver, we've brought back several days of rations. In addition, we salvaged some extra that were not burned, enough to last us about a week, not counting what you and Ganiga can bring us from hunting as well. We can thank all that good whiskey; our attackers didn't complete burning everything before they let the drink get the better of them. Why they burned the muskets and weapons is a mystery to me. We found all the muskets except for six burnt up in the fire. Lieutenant Keen's pistol was there as well. Looks like he never fired it, as the action was still in the half-cock safety position. Same with the burnt muskets: none of them looked to have been fired. The lieutenant's sword was located in the woods on the other side of the fire, almost like someone threw it at the fire but it passed all the way into the woods. Indians would never destroy good weapons, even the river pirates which we know haunt this river would not leave good weapons to be burnt. Nothing makes sense here."

"Ganiga," Johnson replied, "believes the attackers are in two or three canoes and may number eight to ten men. Maybe less, as we shot two in the last canoe. Also, there are two long hunters in another canoe who may have something to do with this attack or know why they were attacked."

"Dog," Ganiga said, shaking his head.

"Yes," Johnson agreed. "The frontiersmen had a big dog with them, which may help us identify them. An animal like that is rare in this country. Everything points to our party being caught in a devastating surprise attack. Yet we know there was a sentry up on the hill there." Johnson pointed to the bluff above. "The camp looked to be totally unaware of the danger till—" The captain stopped mid-sentence, and, jumping to his feet, pointed excitedly towards the bluff.

Thinking Johnson saw something suspicious, Corporal Wilson spun about, his musket in hand. "What is it, sir?"

Still staring at the sentry post intently, Johnson replied, "Look up there, Corporal. An answer and new questions appear."

Wilson followed the captain's gaze, at first scratching his head in confusion. His mouth dropped open in amazement. "The stones. One of the stones is gone."

"Yes," Johnson replied. "One from the left. If I remember correctly, Lieutenant Keen's system meant a small party coming up the river."

"I see it, sir," Wilson answered. "But nothing's missing from the right side where we know from the signs a large party appeared from."

"But no warning," the captain said with a confused look. "Did the sentry not see the large party, or assume for some reason no signal was needed and they looked completely safe?"

"I don't think so, sir," Wilson said. "Ganiga said the sentry was murdered at his post, so more than likely he was murdered to prevent him from warning the camp."

"Could that make the small party a diversion to keep the attention of the camp away from the attack?" Johnson asked.

The corporal scratched his hair under his shako, looking back and forth from the hill to the ambush site. "Then why did the big group fire at the smaller group, as Ganiga pointed out from the tracks and cartridges on the beach? Were they a diversion, or did they just happen to be here at the wrong time and caught in the ambush?"

"I have no answer," Johnson replied. "A revelation and with it a new question. What do you think, Ganiga?"

Ganiga stood up and began walking away. "Too much talk. Ganiga hungry. We eat."

"I agree, my friend," Johnson replied. "We hunt them all down and get them to answer our questions. We just don't know right now. We will assume until proven otherwise they are all guilty of this attack and treat them accordingly."

"Is he always like that?" Wilson asked, pointing at Ganiga. "So blunt?"

"It's just his way," Johnson replied. "Others of his tribe are the same. They don't waste words on the obvious, or overthink a problem worth bothering themselves with words such as could, would or should. If a thing needs to be done, they just do it. If they don't want to do something or think it need not be done, they will not bend your ear with long excuses or dialogue. They prefer a simple no, or else they just walk off and spare you the chatter. You will find it enlightening, Corporal, to spend time with the natives. They are fascinating people."

"You've known him some time then, I take it, sir?" Wilson asked.

"Not really," Johnson replied. "Since December last year was all. Ganiga's band of Tuscarora lived next to Lewistown in upper New York. When British launched a surprise attack on the town, Ganiga's tribe intervened, giving the townspeople time to safely escape. The British took revenge on the tribe, killing many of them in retaliation and they burned the town to the ground in the process. He has been with me since we hunted down the British who attacked his village and took our own revenge. He has no higher moral goals or political aspirations; he just wants to kill the people who burned his town and murdered his people."

"Do you have a plan, Captain, for where we go from here?" Wilson asked.

"Downriver," Johnson replied, pointing. "Ganiga and I will commandeer a river barge or whatever comes down the river and push for the Newport barracks in Cincinnati while we search for the men who attacked our comrades. You will be in charge here and continue with the surveyors. I will have you resupplied from Newport so you can continue with the mission."

Wilson frowned. "Must I stay with them?" he asked, pointing to the surveyors who were keeping themselves by the river beach as far from any work as possible.

"Yes, Corporal, you must. Look at it as an opportunity to prove yourself for that sergeant's promotion you so eagerly pursue."

"I had hoped to gain my promotion in battle, sir," Corporal Wilson replied while scowling at the surveyors.

Johnson laughed. "I'm sure you will have a fair amount of conflict in that regard, Corporal."

Chapter 18

Every bone and muscle in O'Hara's back and arms burned with fire in continuous pain as he struggled to keep paddling in time with the other paddlers. The pace was an unrelentingly fast fifty-five strokes a minute as the Coureur des bois drove the heavily laden freight canoe down the river. Stripped to the waist, his glistening back glowed crimson red while rivers of sweat poured over his sunburnt skin, drenching him right through to his leggings onto the canoe seat. The inexorable pace only yielded occasionally as the canoeists took advantage of the river's current to gain speed or push harder through back flows and slack water.

O'Hara had learned more about paddling and canoeing in these first two days with the voyageurs then the previous entire trip down the Ohio with the contingent of English soldiers. Where Major Torrens always sought the easier route through slower frog water along the shoreline or behind bends in the river, the Coureur des bois aimed for the fast water regardless of the hazards, almost flying like a toboggan downhill over the white water. When the water gave them speed that exceeded their paddling pace, the men would rest with a slightly slower stride, always accompanied by a more leisurely paddle song. They would sing a favorite that O'Hara was beginning to know: "Auprès de ma blonde."

Au jardin de mon père,
Les lauriers sont fleuris;

Au jardin de mon père,
Les lauriers sont fleuris;
Tous les oiseaux du monde
Vont y faire leurs nids.
Auprès de ma blonde,
Qu'il fait bon, fait bon, fait bon.
Auprès de ma blonde,
Qu'il fait bon dormir!

Cherishing the break, O'Hara feebly joined in the song with the good-natured encouragement of the voyageurs. He didn't understand one word; he just knew while the song lasted there was a short reprieve from the intense stroke of the paddles.

Looking about, he tried to measure how far they had paddled down the Ohio in the last few days. The distance was difficult to measure as the voyageurs had made a few extra stops by traveling upstream on several tributary rivers that joined the Ohio. On foot it had taken a couple of days of arduous travel through the forest upriver to cover the same distance. Enough time had passed on his march upstream to see his plan of going alone in a forest that he was unfamiliar with wasn't the best idea. His previous strategy quickly dissolved when he fell upon the voyageurs preparing their midday meal along the beach. After much discussion and bargaining on Patrick's part, he had convinced the sagely leader Jean-Paul to take him on for the trip to Cincinnati for two dollars. Passage only if O'Hara worked Jean-Paul demanded. Work meant paddling. Only once they resumed their journey had O'Hara realized he was taken on because the canoe was a man short; no reason was given for the shortage. This was paddling unlike that he had ever known. So speedily had they moved down the river they had passed the distance of his hike, the massacre site along the river, then the disastrous site of the ambush on the rapids in one day and beyond. Midway on the second day he had spotted the major and his party struggling downriver, warily sticking to the shore to avoid hazards. Keeping his head down, O'Hara counted the men and then again. "Three more gone," he muttered to himself as the voyageurs quickly passed, disappearing around another bend in the river.

More desertions besides myself, he wondered, or had they suffered another calamity, perhaps another attack or mishap?

Despite the backbreaking paddling, Patrick had found some entertainment from the inherent happiness of the voyageurs who cheerfully sang almost constantly. They jokingly changed the lyrics, to the amusement of their comrades who laughed or engaged in a cheery repartee with the singer. Paddling from before dawn to the edge of dusk with only one short break in the afternoon, the paddlers never complained, instead maintaining a spirit of joyfulness throughout the day into the evening at the nightly encampment. The nightly dinner of a robust rubbaboo of mashed peas, oatmeal, and copious pieces of bacon set the pace as the voyageurs kept up singing and dancing until they would collapse to smoke their pipes and engage in lighthearted conversation. Occasionally a few would speak to O'Hara in heavily accented English, asking about his origins, where he was going, and why he had been wandering alone by the river. They were always under the watchful eye of their leader, Jean-Paul, who would interrupt when Patrick's answer's required further explanation.

Not my concern now, O'Hara sighed. I'm free now and free I will stay. He realized that the hard pace of the coureur de bois should land them in Cincinnati a few days ahead of the major and his men. His joy was short-lived as the leader slapped his paddle on a thwart, the signal to pick up the pace; with military precision and without a missed beat they took up a faster beat of the paddles launching into another favorite song.

À la claire fontaine m'en allant promener
J'ai trouvé l'eau si belle que je m'y suis baignée.
Il y a longtemps que je t'aime, jamais je ne t'oublierai

Sous les feuilles d'un chêne, je me suis fait sécher.
Sur la plus haute branche, un rossignol chantait.
Chante, rossignol, chante, toi qui as le cœur gai.
Tu as le cœur à rire… moi je l'ai à pleurer.
J'ai perdu mon ami sans l'avoir mérité,
Pour un bouton de rose que je lui refusal…

"Oh, the saints preserve me," Patrick moaned. "I can do this," he said, as he began tapping his foot in an imaginary march to keep time. Only a few more days to a completely new life.

At the encampment that evening, Patrick lay exhausted on the beach with a full belly after eating a huge platter of pemmican stew. Jean-Paul approached Patrick and sat down next to him on the warm beach sand as he lit his pipe with a burning ember from the fire. They sat for a few moments quietly enjoying the smell of the native tobacco as it's aromatic scent drifted around them while they watched the sun set in the west.

"Those men," Jean-Paul asked, "in the two canoes we passed today. You are running from them eh?"

Shocked, Patrick blurted out a quick, "No, why?"

"Ha ha!" Jean-Paul laughed. "You stared at them as we approached from behind, then turned away, ducking your head down when we went by. I think you don't want them to see you. Maybe old friends?" He laughed again. Pointing around the campsite at the men now lounging by the fire, then to the river with his pipe, he said, "Many men come down this river. Some look for new lives. Some trying to escape old ones. Many more criminals run from the law, some deserters from the Army, and more broken men from the bailiffs and creditors. You Irish, you run too, eh?"

Apprehensively Patrick sighed, deciding to reveal some truth in hopes of hiding the damning reason of why he was here. "Aye, I'm a poacher."

"Poacher?" Jean-Paul asked. "I do not know this word."

"A poacher," Patrick replied, "is a man driven by hunger who cannot eat due to lack of work so he hunts the king's deer and small game. A crime that if caught results in being hanged or shot before reaching a judge."

Poking Patrick hard with his pipe, Jean-Paul replied with anger in his voice, "We have no king's deer here. All deer are for whoever hunts them, not owned by anyone. America has not a king. Are you Anglais?"

"Irish," O'Hara shot back. "Irish are like the French in America. Conquered and held as serfs to the English. No rights, no freedom, no ownership of our own country. Hounded and driven from our homes and sent thousands of miles across the sea to this wild, empty country."

"It is true," Jean-Paul replied. "We French have been held prisoners in our own country, much like you Irish. Many have stayed; others like me and my men have left New France and become paddlers with no country. Even in these lands where we had settlements like St. Louis and New Orleans, we are now the outcasts. Are you a criminal or indentured servant?"

"No. No," Patrick said. "Back in Ireland, I was wanted for poaching. To escape I joined those men we saw today. The leader, a man I learned to fear and hate because of his cruelty, offered me a chance to get away. Little did I know how dangerous he and his men were, realizing too late I may be in much more danger than back in Ireland. I decided to escape when I had an opportunity."

Patrick locked eyes with Jean-Paul, thinking that there was no need to say he was actually a deserter from the British Army on a spy mission. If the truth were revealed it could result in him being hanged or shot by a firing squad.

Jean-Paul thought for a moment. "A contract, did you have a contract to work with these men?"

"No," Patrick answered.

"Then a promise to serve until the end of the voyage, eh?"

"No," Patrick replied.

"Ah," Jean-Paul said with a smile. "Contracts and promises are very important to us who live on the rivers. We carry many valuable cargos to places along these waters for countless people. If we cannot be trusted, then no one will hire us and we too must poach to eat. There is more to your story than what you tell me, Irish; you tell me the truth without the pieces in between. Many men here are the same." Jean-Paul pointed around to the men who Patrick now saw had become quiet as they watched the two of them intently. In a flash, Patrick realized his life had hung in the moment. The wrong reply and one word from their leader, it would be all over for him.

"Henri!" Jean-Paul shouted to one of the boatmen. He punched Patrick playfully in the shoulder. "A song for our Irish friend here. A poacher song," he laughed.

"A poacher song?" Henri asked, confused. "Poached like the egg," he commented, much to the amusement of the men around him.

Jean-Paul looked at Patrick. "I think those friends of yours catch you, Irish, you will be like the cooked goose egg, eh!"

"Oui Henri," Jean-Paul answered, "just like the egg."

Chapter 19

Travis cut the bear backstraps into long, thin strips, carefully wrapping them around a green willow branch that he had stuck into the ground on the edge of the fire. The fatty meat started to crackle, crisping golden brown while throwing off the appetizing scent of roasted meat.

Squib, on the other side of the fire, slowly stirred pieces of bear fat in their cooking pot, rendering the fat into a clear liquid which they would use to bake cornbread, fry dough, lubricate the patches for their rifles, or rub on their skin to keep off biting insects, relieve sunburn, or soothe chapped skin.

"Mix some of that hot bear grease into the little bit of honey still in the jar," Travis said to Squib. "Your ear needs to be kept clean a little longer."

"I'd rather eat the honey," Squib replied, but he poured a few drops of the hot lard into the jar to mix the contents. Then he applied a small amount to his torn ear, rubbing it into the torn flesh gently.

The boys were feeling very relaxed after their successful hunt of the bear they had shot earlier. They planned that morning to take a long rest after the arduous push down the river to put some distance between themselves and their pursuers. While paddling up a small tributary river that emptied into the Ohio they spotted the fat black bear sunning himself contently on the hillside while munching the berries that grew in abundance there.

Having hidden their canoe in the underbrush, the brothers had taken a long, cautious stalk, taking advantage of the wind so as not to surprise the bear as he enjoyed the early season berries, unaware of the coming danger. Moving one at a time in a leapfrog manner, Travis and Squib had found a small defile to conceal themselves just below the feasting bear. Squib took a good shot from a hundred paces, striking the bear square in his chest knocking him flat to the ground. In an unexpected twist of fate, the totally limp bear tumbled down the hill head over heels, rolling down the damp morning grass like a giant black cannonball. He barely missed the brothers, who scarcely avoided being crushed by jumping out of the way. The bear came to a rest with a crash against an old tree stump. Not leaving anything to chance, Travis finished the bear with another shot. After the shock of dodging the rolling ball bear, the boys sat down and laughed together, joking at who was the nimblest in dodging the giant rolling furball.

Travis withdrew a small pot with a cork stopper from their travel pack, removed the lid, then carefully shook a small amount of coarse salt into his hand. He lightly sprinkled the salt on one of the branches of cooked meat.

"Almost out of salt," Travis said, as he passed the branch to Squib.

"Cornmeal, sugar, and coffee as well," Squib replied. He added, "We should stop at Cincinnati, it's not far downriver from here. We could resupply before pushing on again."

"I don't know if that's safe," Travis answered. "We don't know for sure we are still ahead of those pirates who are chasing us."

"Pirates? Is that what we're calling them now?" Squib asked.

"Better than yahoos, like you been calling them," Travis shot back. He added, "I don't recall yahoos running around ambushing and killing people for no reason at all."

"Pirates or yahoos," Squib replied, "I just want to be rid of them and continue on our adventure west. Seems to me we found a good deal more adventure than we bargained for. Cost me a good ear it has already."

"It's just an ear." Travis laughed at his brother. "Uncle Wes, he's got so many holes and scars on him it takes him a week to tell the story of them all."

"I never knew anyone with as many stories as Uncle Wes," Squib replied. "I remember Pa saying that Wes was the master of stories. That he could make a small story big just by the telling of it."

"I remember that," Travis laughed. "Wes, he just smiled and said, 'No point in having an exciting life if no one knows about it.'"

"Maybe it will be the same for us," Squib pondered aloud. "Famous frontiersman who explored previously unknown wilderness fighting off savages and wild animals. We could have rivers or mountains named after us."

"I don't know," Travis shot back with a gleam in his eye, "the state of one ear doesn't quite sound that exciting to me."

Squib laughed sarcastically, then he returned to the subject of stopping. "I think we can stop at Cincinnati to resupply. There's a fort with soldiers, so those pirates behind us won't be wanting to stick around. They aren't likely to cause trouble for us. What do you say, Fidious?"

Fidious slowly opened one eye to look at Squib, turned himself over, and went back to sleep, his belly full of fat bear meat.

"There you go," Squib pronounced. "Fidious agrees as well. He can barely contain his enthusiasm. Cincinnati it is."

Chapter 20

Captain Johnson and Ganiga arrived at Newport barracks early in the morning. They had flagged down a keelboat and requisitioned its use in the name of the war department several days earlier. The post lay wreathed in smoke carried across the river from the many fireplaces, open fires, and slash burns from Cincinnati which lay on the Northern Ohio shore. The barracks sat on the south shore at the juncture of the Licking and Ohio rivers. The smoke floated lazily, swirling about the river like a morning mist and offering fleeting glimpses of the buildings on both shores. Several boats crossed the river ahead of them, ferrying people and goods from Cincinnati to the fort and back. The docks on the Cincinnati side of the river thronged with people moving about randomly. A military band, their dark blue uniforms in contrast to the dull homespun clothes of the settlers, stood on a bandstand enthusiastically playing "Yankee Doodle." In the near distance, gunfire could be heard. This was not unusual, as most festive events featured a rifle frolic or the always popular turkey shoot.

"Looks like we arrived in time for some event," Johnson said to the keelboat owner standing next to him in the bow of the boat.

"Probably celebrating your arrival," the owner replied sarcastically. "I'll be more than happy to be rid of you and your jolly friend," he pointed back at Ganiga.

"The war department is paying you well for your trouble, citizen. Our presence hasn't slowed you down none," Johnson replied.

"A piece of paper is what I got," the owner shot back. "Given to me by a man who says he's an officer, but with no proof. His only soldier is that snarly old Indian there."

"That's quite enough," Captain Johnson snapped back. His dark scowl signaled the discussion was over.

"Pull up to the dock over there," the captain instructed, indicating the dock on the south side of the river where several new stone buildings were surrounded by multitudes of military tents all arranged precisely row upon row. In the background, a sturdy log palisade marked another compound behind the tented area. Johnson noted a battery of six-pounder field guns arrayed unusually, pointing towards the stockade. He also saw several swivel guns stationed on the verandas of the stone buildings facing out towards the parade area.

A squad of soldiers, smartly turned out in their blue dress uniforms, stood guard on the dock. They were led by a sergeant who was identifiable by the red sash around his waist. The sentries watched intently as the keelboat approached the dock. It was obvious to Johnson that whomever the commander was of Newport barracks, he set a high standard of deportment from his command. Most forts would have all troops dressed in their seasonal roundabout uniforms during the heat of the summer. As the boat moved closer, the sergeant hailed the boat in a stern voice:

"No civilian boats may approach this dock without written authority. If you don't have authorization, please pull away."

Standing tall and straight from long practice, Johnson took a prominent position on the boat and answered the sergeant's hail in an commanding voice:

"Captain Johnson. 39th Infantry Regiment requesting permission to land and report to your commanding officer, Sergeant."

Momentarily taken aback by Captain Johnson's rough backwoods attire, the sergeant fell on the tried and true practice of saluting everyone who looked, acted, and sounded like an officer. He quickly snapped off a smart salute. "Welcome to Newport barracks, sir."

"Thank you, Sergeant," Johnson replied, returning the salute.

Johnson and Ganiga picked up their rifles and packs and leapt from the keelboat to the dock. Johnson turned to the keelboat owner and thanked him for his hospitality, remarking to him loud enough for both him and the sergeant of the guard to hear, "Present the chit I gave you to this dock this afternoon. The sergeant will ensure you are paid as we agreed." Turning on his heel, he faced the sergeant again. He was ready to be escorted to the commanding officer.

"Standing orders, sir." The sergeant announced, "I will have to ask for your weapons until you have been presented to the adjutant. The commanding officer is away from the post presently."

Nodding to Ganiga to follow his example, Johnson opened the frizzen of his rifle and blew the priming powder from the pan, then handed the weapon to a private who stepped forward to take it from him. Ganiga reluctantly followed the captain's example.

"What's the special event?" Johnson asked the sergeant, nodding towards the far shore.

"The king's birthday," the sergeant answered with a grin. "The general thought a bit of merriment at the king's expense would cheer the locals up and entice more enlistments, sir."

"Which king would that be, Sergeant?" Johnson asked.

"The regent king. The old king is quite mad, or so we hear. Britain has a regent king now. And he is quite crazy himself. Or so the papers say, sir."

"Sounds lively enough," Johnson replied, "for this early in the morning."

"Indeed, sir, we've sent the regimental band as you can hear. The cooks have a buffalo on the fire and a tidy purse for the rifle shoot. Many of the local merchants are contributing food and treats. Folks for miles around have come to town for the day's frolics. This way, gentlemen," the sergeant commanded, leading Johnson and Ganiga with an escort of two soldiers on each side off the dock through the gate onto the base.

The road from the dock passed along a broad parade square occupied by formations of troops clad in their summer roundabout uniforms conducting drill maneuvers. The troops were accompanied by their watchful NCOs. Drummers wearing their dress red uniform jackets beat a steady march at the head of each group while the sergeants called the pace of "Left... Right... Left."

The large number of troops attracted Johnson's attention, and he remarked to the sergeant, "More troops than my last visit. Has this command been reinforced, Sergeant?"

"Yes, sir," the sergeant replied. "We are the training base for the Western command with stores for the entire West region as well. You see that stockade on the far side of the parade ground, sir?" The sergeant pointed. "That's a prison camp for British prisoners of war."

"It appears quite large; do you have many prisoners?" Johnson asked.

"Five hundred or so," the sergeant replied. "You will see, sir, we have more guards and guard patrols than most bases and very strict rules concerning entry, access to the prison, and possession of weapons as well." Johnson nodded. The number of guards patrolling the perimeters exceeded what one would find on a base this far from any hostilities.

As they reached a prominent stone building of obvious new construction, the detail halted at the entryway where they were met by another guard detail. The river guard sergeant explained his purpose to the sergeant of the headquarters detachment. After a few brief words, the escort sergeant turned to Johnson and said, "Sergeant McClure will escort you to the adjutant, sir." The sergeant ordered Johnson's and Ganiga's rifles to be given over to the new guards, then he executed a snappy salute, turned, and marched back to the river gate with his command.

Sergeant McClure stepped forward, saluted sharply, then escorted Johnson into the building, accompanied by the gate guard.

"Please wait here, sir. I'll announce you to the major."

The sergeant knocked on the door and passed inside closing the door behind him so he could speak quietly with his commander. Johnson stood at ease at the entrance while Ganiga found a comfortable spot against the wall to sit and fell asleep with loud snores, much to the chagrin of the guards.

After a few moments, Sergeant McClure opened the door and waved the captain to enter. Johnson marched into the office. The officer within sat behind his desk with the bright dawn sun shining through the window behind masking his face in dark shadows. Johnson marched to the front of the desk. He stopped and came to the military attention position, and threw up his arm in a precise salute and officially announcing himself.

"Captain Johnson, 39th Infantry—"

Abruptly Johnson was interrupted by a gruff voice saying, "Do you always report to a unit commander dressed in mufti, Captain?"

Surprised by the question, Johnson started to reply when the major interrupted again with a loud laugh. "Seems every time I see you, Captain, you're either out of uniform or in

mufti. Better do better than that if you want to be a general."
He laughed again.

In shock at the informal response from his commander sergeant, McClure was open-mouthed at what he was hearing. The major moved from behind his desk and extended his hand with a huge smile on his face. Johnson now recognized the major. They began warmly exchanging handshakes and slaps on the back.

Holding his hand on Johnson's shoulder, the major said, "It's been a long time, Martin."

"Too long, William," Johnson replied. "Much too long."

The major turned to the sergeant, smiling. "Sergeant, may I present my famous cousin: Captain Martin Johnson."

Officers customarily used each other's first name only when they were in their own company, but seldom when in the company of the ranks. The ease with which the major spoke to the sergeant revealed they probably also had a long relationship with each other.

"Pleased to meet you, sir; I've heard many stories from the major of your adventures on the frontier."

"Thank you, Sergeant," Johnson replied grimly. "Unfortunately, I do not come with good news to report."

Major Simmonds' smile vanished as quickly as it had appeared. "Sergeant, please bring us some coffee. Marty, have a seat. Tell me what brings you here."

Johnson sat and composed himself for a brief moment.

"Myself and a small unit from the 39th had been assigned to assist a party of government surveyors to map out some areas about a week upriver from this location. While on a scout up a small tributary stream to the Ohio, my base camp was ruthlessly attacked and all the men massacred."

"Indians?" Simmonds asked, surprised.

"That's the riddle," Johnson replied. Going over the details of the events, Johnson described his and Ganiga's appearance at the camp to find it entirely destroyed, the shooting of several attackers in the canoe, and the subsequent scout of the massacre site afterward.

As Johnson finished his report, Sergeant McClure arrived with coffee. The major summarized Johnson's story and asked him to stay after first requesting Johnson's approval of the sergeants presence which was immediately forthcoming.

"Sergeant McClure has been with me many years now," the major confided. "Since moving to Newport barracks, he has become a priceless source of local information on the population, settlers, and river traffic movements up and down the river. What you described is a mystery, Martin. Neither Indians nor pirates, of which there are a few along the river, would attack an army camp and destroy supplies or weapons. In fact, I cannot think of anyone who would commit such an act," the major said, shaking his head.

Martin replied, "We succeeded in shooting two men as they were escaping, but they were not natives. The empty paper cartridges along the river shore were suggestive of troops firing volleys into the encampment. Deserters possibly, but again, I've never known of deserters acting in concert or in those kinds of numbers. The burnt supplies defy any kind of logic I can think of as well. Then there's the mystery of the two men Ganiga believes were frontiersmen with a big dog who were being shot at downriver. Again, several volleys were fired, as shown by the cartridges on the ground."

"Perhaps those two had by chance come to the encampment and were surprised, but they escaped during the attack," Simmonds suggested. "Or there was some sort of disagreement with the larger party that broke down to shooting at each other."

"Sir," Sergeant McClure spoke up, "you say two men with a big dog in a canoe may be suspect in this attack?"

"Yes, Sergeant," Johnson replied. "Do you know anything about them?"

"Yes, sir," McClure replied. "Two such long hunters arrived in Cincinnati just yesterday morning by canoe. They had a large dog with them, which is unusual for these parts as hounds are the most common dog found about here and theirs looked to be more wolf. They stopped at our dock to ask for information from the guard post. Two young brothers on an adventure headed west to join their long hunter uncle on the upper Missouri."

"Did you get their names?" Johnson asked excitedly.

"Yes, sir; didn't have to ask. They introduced themselves quite proper like. Travis and Squib Tanner. Even introduced the dog, Fidious, which we thought a bit humorous."

"They hardly sound like ambushers or pirates to me. Criminals don't give their names at the drop of a hat," Simmonds asked. "Was there anything about them that struck you as unusual or that would make them stand out from the normal, Sergeant?"

"Not a great deal, sir," McClure replied. "Their rifles were high-quality Pennsylvania-style. They were well-armed with pistols, tomahawks, and long knives in their belts, but that's not uncommon in these parts. Dressed like any other long hunters, worn but well-cared-for buckskins and such."

"Nothing else you can remember, Sergeant?" Johnson asked.

"Now that you ask, sir, one had a leather telescope case over his shoulder. You don't see that, except on officers and government surveyors — too expensive for trappers and such."

Johnson jumped to his feet and yelled through the closed door, "Ganiga, come here now!"

Ganiga instantly appeared. He cautiously peered around the door, his hand on his knife in his belt, ready for trouble.

"Ganiga," Johnson asked, "did you find Ensign Keen's telescope back at the attack site?" Johnson knew Ganiga would remember the telescope as he would often ask to use it from the ensign whenever he could. He called it his Big Eye. On several occasions, he tried to barter for it with Keen, even promising to find Keen a good wife to trade for it. All to no avail as the telescope was a graduation gift from Keen's father and much valued by him.

Ganiga shook his head and replied, "No Big Eye."

"You're sure?" Johnson asked.

Offended at being asked twice, Ganiga simply shook his head and left the room.

Turning to Simmonds and the sergeant, Johnson shook his head in confusion before continuing, "We found the ensign's sword intact, his loaded pistol burnt in the fire along with his baldrick, but not the telescope."

The major ran his fingers through his graying hair, scratching the back of his head.

"Martin. What kind of men would in cold blood murder an entire squad of soldiers, burn their bodies and equipment, then calmly appear innocent as could be at our gate to ask for information while giving us their names and destination? What men would do that?"

"Very dangerous men," Martin replied. "Until we know differently, we must treat them as such."

"Agreed," the major replied. "Sergeant McClure, call out the post guard. I want increased sentries at all guard stations. Captain Johnson, my command is down to a few junior ensigns and one overloaded lieutenant right now, as the rest of the command officers are accompanying the general on a buffalo hunt. Captain Johnson, the defense of the base and the prisoners here must take priority, so I will ask you to take command of the mission to search out these frontiersmen. I apologize as the protocol is to obtain approval from your commander first; however, as you no doubt will agree, we do not have time for that, so I will take full responsibility for these orders, in writing of course. Take two squads to the merriments on the Cincinnati side; they may be present there or at one of the merchants. Find them and apprehend them. Bring them back dead or alive. Any additional thoughts, Captain?"

"Yes, sir," Johnson replied. "The other larger party may be here as well. We know less about their identity, or more critically their intentions, except that they are capable of brutal bloodshed done in military-like precision."

"Thank you, Captain," the major replied. "We have one squad under command of Sergeant Anderson on the city shore already tasked with putting on a musket drill with a live fire demonstration. They will act as your reserve. I will write orders up for them immediately." Turning to Sergeant McClure, Simmonds ordered, "Requisition ten rounds per man for your squads and an extra issue to Sergeant Anderson's group as they only carried enough cartridges for the firepower demonstration." Turning again to Johnson, Simmonds continued, "We have a large number of British prisoners here. Although they have been very peaceful, indeed cooperative, while in confinement, we cannot take any chances that these men you're describing may have some plan to liberate the prisoners. I will provide your command with all the support we have available, Captain. First, I will ensure we have taken additional measures here to protect our base and keep the confinement of the prisoners secure."

"Sir?" Sergeant McClure asked, "may I suggest we triple the guard on our storehouses and armory as well and issue an additional ten rounds per man on all guard posts together with loading our swivel guns and cannon?"

"Yes, Sergeant; that's a very good idea," Major Simmonds replied.

"Martin, you're in mufti, so it may be easier for you to mingle unnoticed amongst the people there. The festivities are just getting going. Find these pirates or whomever they are and exact some justice for our fallen soldiers."

"Thank you, sir," Captain Johnson replied. "I would like nothing better than to run down these men, whoever they are.

Sergeant, muster the squads behind the gatehouse so we don't garner too much attention from across the river; we may be watched. In ten minutes, if you please."

After Sergeant McClure had left the office, Major Simmonds sighed and a grim look settled on his face. "Marty, as you know, the war has not been going well for us. We have had some victories for sure, mostly against the natives who have allied themselves with the British. Your regiment's performance at the battle at Horseshoe Bend is a great triumph and has gone a long way to secure our frontier's borders. The general, however, received information from Washington just last week that Napoleon abdicated sometime in April and is now living in exile. With the French out of the war on the continent, Britain will be able to turn the full force of her huge navy our way together with tens of thousands of seasoned troops at her disposal. Ships and troops aimed at us. Our situation is grim. With our eastern seaboard effectively blockaded, England will be free to strike us where and whenever she pleases. Martin, this command has been recently ordered to prepare and ship large numbers of arms and supplies downriver to New Orleans together with recruiting local militias and volunteers. Our party across the river today was planned to try and draw volunteers to us so our recruiters could fill our training ranks. The communication from Washington speculated the British may send a large fleet south with the objective of seizing key cities to capture and secure for themselves on our southern flank, effectively sealing off the Mississippi. General Jackson has let it be known he believes New Orleans will be the target of the British attack. Martin, I don't have to describe to you what kind of mayhem five hundred trained soldiers could cause if let loose this far behind the lines. That kind of strike could cripple our supply and reinforcement and leave New Orleans in great peril of defeat, making it more important than ever to protect and supply our soft southern underbelly in New Orleans. This command, my command, has a key place in this defense. We cannot fail. If these men you are pursuing are the threat to this base, which we think they may be, then you are to destroy them completely. Totally. And to the last man. These are my orders to you; do you understand them and comply?"

"Yes, sir," Captain Johnson replied, saluting.

"Dismissed, Captain," the major commanded. As Johnson turned to leave the office, he added, "Marty, when this war is over and won, you and I are going on that great hunt to the West we have always talked about."

Captain Johnson smiled and replied before opening the door, "You can count on it, William."

Johnson and Ganiga gathered their rifles and joined the squads assembled behind the guard house, out of view from onlookers across the river. Sergeant McClure called the men to attention. "Ready for your inspection, sir."

"Thank you, Sergeant," Johnson replied. "Stand at ease."

The men stood at parade rest, eyes on Johnson and Ganiga as they waited for the captain to give them the necessary mission statement and orders.

Johnson stood quietly, gathering his thoughts. The importance of this moment was well known to him. A strange unknown officer from another regiment had just assumed command of their lives and their future. Experience dictated to Johnson that this moment and his next words could dictate the success or failure for these men.

"Gentlemen, I am Captain Johnson on detached duty from the 39th Infantry Regiment. I fought in my first fight as a young ensign at Fallen Timbers back in ninety-four." This drew several smiles from a few older soldiers.

"I see a few of you can do the math. Yes. I'm that old." This admittance gained a few more chuckles from the men.

"Fallen Timbers, Tippecanoe, Battle of the Thames, and a dozen more skirmishes in between." Smiles became admiration and a release as the soldiers recognized the unknown captain standing before them was a seasoned veteran.

Johnson knew that soldiers give trust grudgingly, without his actions seen or experienced directly they would be cautious in their acceptance of him. Satisfied his first part of the speech had gained him a little confidence, Johnson turned to the critical informative and inspiring segment of his speech.

"One week ago," Johnson began, "my command was engaged on a peaceful government survey mission up river from here. Myself and a small detachment accompanied the surveyors away from our main camp for several days. During our absence the encampment was attacked. The entire command, every soldier to the man, were slaughtered in a cruel brutal manner. There were no survivors. Without respect or due consideration, their bodies were burnt along with the supplies, leaving the camp devastated." Johnson paused for the weight of his words to inflame the emotions of the soldiers. "We do not have a clear picture of who these villains are but we know this they are vicious. They used military efficient tactics, shooting into the encampment in trained devastatingly bloody volleys and killing the wounded men with axes and knives without mercy. Two of the men we suspect are across the river in Cincinnati. We believe a major part of their group of anywhere up to ten men may be there as well. We do not know why. Our mission is to cross the river and seek out these villains whoever they are. These men must be captured and brought to justice. Let not one of them escape at any cost.. Any questions so far?"

A seasoned soldier spoke up first, asking the question each man wanted to know. "Dead or alive, sir?"

"Dead suits me fine, soldier. If we can capture the ringleaders for hanging, then all the better," Johnson replied, gaining grim nods from the soldiers. Turning to the sergeants, Johnson gave further commands so all could hear. "Sergeants, we will divide the command into two groups before we cross the river. The groups will land on opposite sides of the town so we will attract as little attention as possible. Sergeants, on landing divide your squads into two so we get more coverage while we search. Men, you will load your muskets with no bayonets affixed. Carry them at the trail or slung over your shoulder in a relaxed manner. Again, we don't want to scare the fox before we can entrap him. Keep within easy hailing distance of each other and if the suspects or anyone suspicious are seen, report to your sergeants immediately. Sergeants, unless fired upon, keep the culprits under observation and report to me."

"Where will you be, and how do we get you word quickly, sir?" Sergeant McClure asked.

Captain Johnson smiled and pointed up the road as two young drummer boys, now in casual dress, came running towards the gate. Stopping in front of Sergeant McClure, the boys stood at attention, announcing themselves in unison: "Reporting as ordered, sir."

McClure reached out with both hands and turned the boys around to face Captain Johnson. "That's your commander, boys. Report to Captain Johnson properly, if you please."

Surprised, the boys stammered out, "Reporting as ordered, sir." This drew smiles and quiet laughs from everyone.

"Gentlemen, here are your messengers. They are to be used to send messages between groups and to sound a warning when these villains are found. A couple of boys running back and forth through today's festivities will not be noticed by anyone. When you have found the suspects, you will send a runner to the town square where our band is entertaining the locals. Major Simmonds has sent instructions for the band leader to play a tune many will sing along to; that will be sure to get our attention and I will be there to meet any runner that is sent."

Sergeant McClure spoke up first, "What song, in particular, will that be, sir?"

Captain Johnson laughed. "Major Simmonds believes that with the large number of Irish and Scots in town for today's events, the familiar drinking song of "Garry Owen" should produce some noise we will be sure not to miss." His response drew smiles and a few laughs and whistles from all around.

Sergeant McClure responded in his broad Irish accent, "That it will, sir."

"Ganiga and I will take a canoe across the river and mix in with the crowd in the band area. Boys," he called to the drummers, "Take a good look at me. Now, my companion," he pointed to Ganiga. "Remember well what we look like."

The drummer boys looked sternly at Captain Johnson, trying not to laugh when he winked at them. Then they turned to look at Ganiga, who returned their stares stoically until breaking eye contact with a loud growl that sent the boys tripping and scurrying to the boats.

"Sergeants, you have your orders. We have some avenging to take," Johnson commanded, and then he watched the quiet efficiency with which his small mission embarked. Reflecting on his own experiences in the past, he thought, duty, patriotism, or family move men to accomplish many difficult and perilous deeds, but, in the end, revenge runs a darker deeper path.

Chapter 21

The cheerful sound of laughter from outside as the three guests finished their morning coffee brought a joy Mary Murphy had not felt for a long time. Her husband Colin had died late last year of the fever leaving her a lonely widow. Life was hard in this new land. Yet Mary had endured, for here in America she had hope. Hope for a new life. Hope for freedom and security. Hope that she did not have in Ireland. Hope that she thought she had by becoming an indentured servant when she boarded a ship for Nova Scotia and then lost when her new master proved as cruel as the one she had run away from in Ireland. Hope she found again when Colin found her, and together they smuggled themselves across the border into America to start a new life free from indenture and free from the king's bailiffs who hounded them to the border. Every evening Mary gave thanks during her prayers. She gave thanks for the roof over her head, the fertile land she and Colin had cleared, and the crops they had planted together giving them the wealth of food on the table.

This morning she was especially thankful. The previous day two young frontiersmen had arrived by canoe at the small beach where Colin's small punt was moored. They had respectfully approached the cabin to ask if Mary would allow them to camp on her property. Mary also agreed she would watch their canoe and supplies while they ventured into Cincinnati several miles downriver. Any reluctance Mary may have had to their requests disappeared when they offered a new bearskin in payment. They apologized, as they had as yet to finish tanning the hide, but the hide was in prime condition. Mary was delighted; the bear hide should sell easily in the open market in town and net her a good price in cash or barter.

At first, Mary was apprehensive of the boys' large dog, but a few soft words and some petting soon made them new best friends. She recalled laughing when the bigger brother said the dog's name was "Fidious." As she had never heard such a name or a word before, she questioned the meaning.

Squib replied the dog was named by their uncle Wes, who brought the young orphan pup to their home back in Pennsylvania and had called him Perfidious which the boys promptly shortened to Fidious. "Uncle Wes," Squib continued, "said Napoleon called Britain, Perfidious Albion, meaning they were not trustworthy."

"Well," Travis interrupted his brother, "it's not like he is untrustworthy, not unless he doesn't like you."

"Or you threaten myself or Travis," Squib added. "He just has his own way about things."

"That's about the only way we can describe him," Travis cut in. "He has saved our hides in the past."

"Several times," Squib added. "He seems to have taken a shine to you, Mrs. Murphy, and any friend of Fidious is a friend of ours."

Mary smiled at the memory. Sometime later, just before sunset last night, another stranger had arrived, walking along the river trail. He too had asked for shelter for the night, offering a silver dollar in payment. The tall Irishman had introduced himself quite properly as Patrick O'Hara. He had a relaxed demeanor about him that made it easy for Mary to offer him use of the horse's lean-to for the night. Easy decision, given a silver dollar would buy a week's room and board in town.

Mary had been busy that day baking trenchers and hasty pudding over the fireplace to sell at the festivities in town the next day. As tired as she was the prospect of companionship enticed her to invite the three visitors to join her for dinner. The men had all hit it off immediately upon meeting and spent the dinner period telling their adventures and stories of hunting here in America, for the brothers, and in Ireland, from Patrick. Squib's story of the rattlesnake that joined him for a night's sleep brought particular chills to both Patrick and Mary. The boys were amazed when they were told Ireland had no snakes because Saint Patrick had driven them all from the land.

To this, Squib had wistfully replied, "Wish that Saint Patrick fellow could come over here."

O'Hara, a gifted storyteller, made them all laugh with tales of the leprechauns and ghouls that were such a huge part of Irish folklore, along with other legends of his homeland.

The highlight of the evening for Mary had been twofold. First, Patrick had produced a partial bottle of whiskey, asking first for her permission to share with them all after apologizing it was not good Irish whiskey. Patrick and Mary were both surprised when Squib and Travis said they were not drinkers, though Travis did say he had tried some beers that were not so bad, and he agreed to try a drink. Squib, however, was adamant that milk and coffee were all he preferred in the evening. He disliked that "cursed English drink, tea." Mary then said she had something made with milk that Squib might like. She returned a few minutes later with a mug of milk mixed with rum and a good portion of maple syrup, which Squib found in his own words "very agreeable."

While they were enjoying their drinks together, Patrick asked her about the rifle hanging from the pegs over the fireplace.

"It's Colin's rifle," Mary spoke. "He was very fond of it. He was a good hunter keeping the household well supplied with turkey, deer, squirrels, and the occasional elk. It is of little use to me due to its weight and length," Mary continued. "I've shot the odd deer raiding my garden out back, but only when the rifle sits on the solid rest of the window sill can I hold it up to aim."

"Could I have your permission to look at it more closely?" Patrick asked.

"Be my guest," Mary replied.

Patrick took the rifle down from the pegs and looked it over carefully. After checking the lock and frizzen, he noted it was well taken care of and showed no sign of abuse or damage.

He asked Squib and Travis, "you both have fine rifles, being raised, as you said, in a gun-builder's home; do you have any opinion of this weapon?" He then passed the rifle to Travis and Squib for their examination. Both were of the opinion it was of the Kentucky style with simple ornamentation and a smaller bore size. The fittings and construction were sound, meaning it could be an accurate rifle.

"Mrs. Murphy," Patrick began, "I've been desirous of purchasing a rifle over the musket I now carry. Would you be willing to sell this rifle to me? I would pay fifteen dollars for it."

Mary gasped at the thought of fifteen dollars. She had never seen or possessed that much cash in her life. Mary thought for a moment, then replied, "Patrick, a generous offer it is. But I'm alone here on this land; without a weapon I would have no means to get meat or keep the predators away."

Patrick replied, "With this rifle, I would not need my musket so I would be happy to trade it to you for your use and protection and the fifteen dollars as well."

Mary thought some more. "Patrick, that's a very good price and I'm sure your musket is a very good deal, but it's even bigger than that rifle you're holding."

Travis interrupted, "Mary, not only were Squib and I were raised in a gunsmith's house, but our father tutored us on how to build and repair guns since we were small children. We can shorten Patrick's musket and trim a few pounds of weight as well, so you could have a carbine more easy to handle than both that rifle and musket. Don't you agree, Squib?"

Squib nodded, slurring his speech a little, "Easy peasy. In the morning, though, I'm a little..." Squib searched for words, "tired; I'm a little tired right now."

Mary laughed. "Then, Mr. O'Hara, we have a deal." She held out her hand and shook Patrick's in return. "And your cartridges as well?"

"Of course" Patrick replied. "And your mold and bullets in return?"

" Mr. O'Hara. Let's drink to our arrangement."

Lifting their noggins and tapping them together, they toasted one another: "SLAINTE."

Mary finished the last of her morning preparations for the celebrations being held in Cincinnati a few hours from now. On the table, she had piled several dozen small loaves of bread that would be cut in half and hollowed out to form trenchers that she would fill with her hasty pudding for sale to the spectators and participants of this morning's festivities. The week previous she had struck a deal with Caleb MacGregor, owner of MacGregor's General Store located on the edge of the grounds where the shooting match and festivities take place. Caleb had agreed to supply the ingredients for Mary's popular hasty pudding and the trenchers for the pudding at his cost. Mary would, in turn, pay him one cent for each trencher of pudding she sold at four cents each. Both were satisfied with their arrangement. Caleb's cost would be deferred by the one cent per trencher but more so by the spirits and store goods he would sell by hosting the celebrants in his backyard. Mary was a frugal woman, calculating that she could preserve some of the ingredients for her own use later and still make a minimum of three cents per trencher she sold. She knew from experience that many of the frontiersmen would want seconds if not thirds of her pudding, thereby leaving her a tidy profit for the day.

Mary jumped suddenly as a gun barked loudly just behind the house. Walking to the back door, she picked up her cup of coffee. She gulped down the last mouthful as she stepped outside to watch Patrick fire his newly purchased rifle. The brothers had set up a target of a hand-sized piece of driftwood dangling from a cord a hundred paces behind the house. The wooden piece now spun on its tether, showing a hit had occurred.

"Good shooting, Mr. O'Hara," she called to Patrick.

"Thank you, Mrs. Murphy. The boys have been very kind in showing me the ways of the rifle. I would be hard-pressed to hit a target like that at half the distance with a musket, that I would."

"Would you like another coffee, Mr. O'Hara?" Mary asked.

"No thank you," Patrick replied. "I'm happy you enjoyed it."

"Thank you for the coffee as well, Mr. O'Hara. You have been most generous to me; I feel I cannot repay your generosity in kind."

"It is your hospitality that I am in debt for, Mrs. Murphy. It's been many a year since I've spent such an enjoyable evening and morning with a lady such as yourself. An Irish lady, I might add."

"And I you as well, Mr. O'Hara. But you'll find many an Irish maiden in Cincinnati, we Irish have taken to the wilderness here about since driven from our home by those bloody British Redbacks. Now where are those boys? They were here just a minute ago."

Just then, Squib and Travis came from behind the cabin holding the now shortened musket.

"Mrs. Murphy," Squib announced proudly, "we have altered your musket as we promised; come try it out."

Squib held the musket out to Mary to take. She saw immediately the big changes the boys had made as she took it in her hands. "My. It's much shorter and weighs so much less than before."

"We cut the barrel back to twenty-six inches," Travis added and pointed to the buttstock. "We took off a few inches from the butt so it would fit your shoulder. Your aim will be better now as well. Squib cut the powder charge in the cartridges back to three drams and adjusted the powder measure to match. Those military cartridges had a heavy charge. Each cartridge has a ball and three buckshot in them so they will be quite effective out to fifty paces. It's a little unusual, as the military are the only ones who use ball and buck, but I think for your needs they will do fine."

Not wanting to lose any attention from Mary, Squib cut in and added, "I ground up a batch of powder to a finer grain for you to use in the frizzen." He handed Mary a small, finely made powder flask.

"That's a very fine flask, Mr. Squib. Are you sure you don't need it?"

"No, ma'am," Squib replied. "We had an extra one for our pistols that was of no use to us."

"You, all of you, have been so nice to me." Mary added, "I can hardly think of any words to describe your generosity. I feel very blessed to have met you. Thank you Squib, Travis, and you too, Patrick. These last two days are the best I have had for a very long time."

Taken back in their awkward way at the sincerity of Mary's words, the men remained silent. Then the boys' youthful exuberance kicked in as Travis said, "Shoot it, Mary. See how it feels."

"Yes, try it. Try it," Patrick and Squib echoed.

Mary tentatively lifted the musket to her shoulder and noticed right away how more comfortable it fit her shoulder with the loss in weight. Where before she could barely hold the musket up it now rested naturally.

Travis pointed at the lock. "We tuned the lock so it would fire more quickly and adjusted the mainspring to ease the trigger pull. It's loaded; fire it."

Both Patrick and Squib joined in chorus again, "Shoot it."

Mary looked at the wooden target across the yard, but before she could say anything Travis pointed at a closer tree about twenty-five paces away with a bigger piece of wood the size of a pie pan hanging from a piece of twine. "Over there, Mrs. Murphy; shoot at that one."

Pulling the hammer back all the way, Mary hefted the carbine to her shoulder and took a slow breath while she sighted down the barrel. A new large, bright front sight replaced the old bead. She held the sight on the center of the wood, slowly pulling the trigger as she had been taught by Colin. Suddenly the musket fired, knocking Mary back on her heels and hiding the target in a cloud of sulfurous gunsmoke. To her surprise, she saw the target swinging back and forth. Forgetting about the kick to her shoulder from the recoil, she excitedly turned to the men. "I hit it!" she cried out. "I hit it!"

They all laughed at her excitement. The brothers were pleased with the result of their handiwork, and Patrick was just enjoying the friendly warmth of the moment.

"If you will excuse me for a few minutes," Mary asked, "I would like to change for the event and will join you shortly." With that, she returned to the cabin and shut the door behind her. Some time later, Mary stepped from the cabin. The men stopped what they were doing to stare agog at Mary's transformation. Her thick black hair was combed behind her head so it flowed attractively over her shoulders. Gone was the worn once-white blouse, brown work garb and apron to be replaced by a dress of fine green wool with a golden wool mantle over the top. Mary held her wide-brimmed straw hat while she patted down her hair. Then she carefully placed the hat on her head, pulling the brim down slightly from the side to give it a jaunty look.

"Gentlemen. It's customary for men to compliment a lady when she puts on her finest clothes for a day's event."

Spurred from their stunned silence, the men answered in chorus:

"Beautiful."

"Pretty."

"Stunning."

"I would marry you myself," Squib blurted out, drawing guffaws from his companions.

"You will have to excuse Squib and I, Mrs. Murphy," Travis said, punching his wide-eyed brother in the shoulder. "We were raised with little contact with women, so we meant no insult."

"No," Squib stammered, "you're so beautiful my breath was taken away completely. I couldn't believe my eyes."

"Thank you, gentlemen. A lady doesn't want to be seen in her tatterdemalion work clothes and pampooties while attending such a public event like today."

"Pampa-what?" Squib asked.

"Irish work shoes," Patrick replied. "Similar to moccasins made of stitched rawhide."

Patrick stepped forward in front of Mary. After rummaging in his possible bag, he pulled out a small bundle of cloth in which he had wrapped a green ribbon. Carefully, he stretched the ribbon out and laid it across both of his outstretched hands.

"Mary, I've carried this ribbon in secret for many years, waiting for the day when I could once again wear the green without fear of bloody reprisal from those Redback British. At home, the wearing of the green is punishable by hanging, but here in America, we can wear the green again without fear, proudly, and with respect. Mary, I would be honored if you would wear it today while we accompany you to the festivities."

"Thank you, Mr. O'Hara. I would be proud to wear your ribbon," Mary replied. After taking the ribbon from his hands, she removed her hat and tied the ribbon around the crown with a small bow on the side. Then, with a cry of delight, she lifted her skirts to her ankles and ran into the small field next to the cabin. She hopped about like a rabbit, bending over several times till she found what she was looking for and returned.

"Your hat, if I may, Mr. O'Hara," Mary asked, holding out her hand. Patrick removed his hat, handed it to her, and she placed a green clover sprig into his hat-band. "Now, Mr. O'Hara. We will both be wearing the green."

"Thank you," Patrick replied, moved beyond words till Travis nudged him on the shoulder gently.

"You're wearing a piece of clover in your hat; why?" Travis asked.

"In Ireland, it's not clover," Patrick replied. "It's the shamrock. The sacred symbol of Ireland, the shamrock and green color of which is both banned and punishable by death if caught wearing by the British."

"There will be no trouble here, Mr. O'Hara; the British are a long way from here." Patrick flinched at the comment; if only the boys knew the truth of what was happening. Travis continued, "Anyone who stands against you or Mrs. Murphy stands against Squib and me as well."

"Thank you. Gentlemen, let's be off, shall we? I appreciate you helping me to carry this food and provisions for the big event today."

Chapter 22

The shooting ground set up on the village common behind MacGregor's store was starting to fill with both participants and spectators for the day's much awaited events, much to the satisfaction of Caleb MacGregor as he anticipated a tidy profit for the day. As people began to gather, there was already a brisk business in black powder sales, rifle parts, and assorted accessories together with sundry store items. Caleb happily noted Mrs. Murphy was having a good turnout at her stall selling her popular hasty pudding. Caleb chuckled to himself: not only had he received one cent for each trencher sold, the Army in sponsoring the event had provided the provisions for her puddings by paying him five dollars for Mary's efforts and supplies. Caleb chortled again; the Army was paying him a tidy profit for organizing and supplying the entire event. All he had to do now was watch and make sure there were no problems and he would be a happy man.

On the shooting grounds, Mary maintained a steady business of customers for her hasty pudding comprised of mainly rough frontiersmen, workers, with a few natives as well. From past experience Mary knew these men lived on a steady diet of roast, fried, or boiled game. Given the opportunity they hungrily craved the sugary sweetness of the hasty pudding with many slurping down repeatcd refills of the tasty delight in one sitting. Watching out of the corner of her eye, she enjoyed the sight of Patrick and Squib wolfing down their third trencher accompanied by Travis' humorous jabs and jokes on their frenzied eating manners. They howled with laughter when one or both of them choked on their food as they tried to swallow and laugh at the same time. Even Fidious was enjoying himself; hiding between the two brothers, he would watch for a trencher thrown on the ground by a satisfied customer and dart out to retrieve the prize. He would return to his lair where he would lick the inside of the hardened bread crust first, then, like he was chewing a bone, crunch his way through the loaf. When done, he would resume his vigil for discarded trenchers and dart out again when one was spotted, several times catching them before the bread even hit the ground or snatching it from the mouths of the other smaller dogs. Fidious earned himself angry looks from the meeker dogs' owners until they saw the brothers and Patrick watching, realizing this was not an argument worth engaging in. The young brothers had gained the hardened look of seasoned hunters. Though older than the brothers by ten years, Patrick's boyish antics and joking nature gave him a much younger appearance while maintaining a more seasoned if not life-toughened look. When one settler kicked out at Fidious for stealing a used trencher from his whiny little mutt, a dark hard look washed across Patrick's face that would make the devil himself think twice about crossing paths with the Irishman. With the little barking dog tucked under one arm, the settler quickly rushed away through the throng of onlookers, generating laughs and more teasing from Travis. For the first time since Colin's untimely death, Mary felt content and happy. The good-natured men's kindness and help were a welcome relief from the dreary loneliness of the last year. The sounds of drums marching towards the village common roused her from her reverie as a column of soldiers marched into sight. The soldiers were splendidly turned out in their dark blue jackets, bright red trim, freshly whitened webbing, shiny black boots, and brightly polished weapons.

They marched in perfect step to the rat-a-tat beaten out by two drummers in their crimson uniforms who led the way. Following behind them several men carried a large canvas-covered structure suspended from a pole over their shoulders, much the same way they would carry a dead deer. Knowing Caleb MacGregor's reputation for innovative and humorous targets from the many previous shooting competitions held behind his store, Mary suspected this was more of the same and she watched eagerly as the soldiers marched to the center of the common and halted at the shout of the senior NCO marching beside them. The two men carrying the canvas-covered item walked out into the shooting ground, stopping twenty yards from the soldiers. Sergeant Anderson turned to the gathered crowd and the drummers began a loud drum roll to bring the spectators to silence as they waited for the sergeant to speak.

"Ladies and gentlemen," Anderson called out in his loud, precise parade square voice, "on this day of celebration, the Army of the United States of America is proud to present to you a demonstration of the skill and expertise of the American Infantryman at musket shooting. You, sir," Anderson said, pointing to a young man standing in the front of the crowd, "how many aimed shots do you believe an infantry soldier can shoot in one minute?"

The embarrassed youth shyly blurted out a wild guess: "Two."

"Wrong!" Anderson boomed out. "A trained American soldier can fire five aimed shots in one minute." Anderson paused and looked about the audience sternly for someone to refute him. While several laughed or scoffed quietly, no one spoke up or argued with the towering and ominous sergeant.

Farther back in the crowd, Patrick knew from experience in the British Army that infantrymen were expected to fire four rounds per minute, but this number came after much training and drill. Five was a number that only well-disciplined, experienced troops were capable of. Seldom would it be called well-aimed musketry, but he kept his silence.

"Today," Anderson continued, "we will demonstrate for you several techniques that your country's soldiers will use in combat with our enemies, the British. First, a demonstration of aimed volley fire of five shots in one minute. Our drummers who stand here beside me will beat out a tattoo for one minute to mark the time to fire five aimed shots. Without a break, and I repeat, without a break, we will immediately start a rolling volley. For those of you unfamiliar with this military term, a rolling volley is practiced to keep a steady volume of fire upon the enemy by each soldier aiming and firing at the enemy in a precisely timed sequential manner for five shots each. Finally, we will order 'Fire at will' for one last one-minute period of time. Each soldier will be tasked to attain five aimed shots. They will drop to one knee when they have fired five shots. Ladies and gentlemen, may I present for your entertainment our target for today." Another drum roll followed and the two men standing next to the canvas they had been carrying now set it down upon a stand, holding onto both corners of the canvas. Sergeant Anderson announced in his best booming voice: "Ladies and gentlemen, this day we celebrate the birthday of the Regent King of England, I give you King George the fourth." At the command the canvas was removed, leaving a life-sized wooden and painted caricature of the king dressed in all his regal glory with a greatly exaggerated crown, mace, and ridiculously enlarged nose and ears, together with bulbous buttocks and a ponderous belly hanging over his belt.

The crowd immediately broke out into loud cheers interspersed with hoots and hollers and uncontrolled laughter.

Sergeant Anderson smiled and waited a few moments for the crowd to settle down.

"Ladies and gentlemen," Sergeant Anderson boomed out, "the firepower of the American Army!" Immediately the entire squad of men made a quick about-turn to face the lifelike caricature of the king. In a silent count they brought their muskets to the make-ready position with their weapons held perfectly vertical followed by drums beating a quick roll and ending with a quick double beat. The squad, in precise and practiced timing, brought their cocked muskets to the ready position. Another drum roll beat out and ended in another double beat. The muskets fired simultaneously in a huge flash of fire and white smoke. The drum roll commenced again as the soldiers reloaded and brought their muskets to the ready position while the roll ended with a double beat. The muskets fired in unison and the process replayed again. Five times the muskets belched fire, smoke, and destruction as the target of the king danced and lurched to the smash of the musket balls.

Again, the drums rolled. Now the troops began the rolling volley when the drum ended in the double beat. The first soldier fired his musket, followed two seconds later by another, and two seconds later another; every two seconds a gun sent musket balls crashing into the king's effigy. The steady barrage began to tear the king to pieces as shot after shot smashed into the target. The crowd that had sat silent in awe and silence of the power of the demonstration now began to cheer enthusiastically. Yells of delight, whistles, and cries of hurrah accompanied each shot that rang out in perfect unison over and over until each soldier had fired his five rounds. The final shot crashed out from the end soldier in line. Not missing a beat, Sergeant Anderson yelled out to the crowd's delight, "Every man who fires all five rounds in the allotted time wins a double whiskey ration for a week. Squad. Fire at will." The explosion of musketry that ensued was followed by a frenzy of quick loading and firing as the remains of the king target was blown apart. Pieces of shattered wood flew off in all directions as the first man to fire his five rounds dropped to one knee, with his musket held upright with the butt on the ground. The throng was screaming excitedly, totally caught up in the exhilaration of the moment, as each soldier finished firing and took a knee until the entire squad was finished. The crowd was ecstatic at the display of firepower and continued to cheer as the gunsmoke clouding over the range hiding the target slowly drifted off, revealing that not one portion of the target remained standing. Only a pile of smoking broken wood remained. The smoldering turned to flame, the flame to conflagration, and, in a bright flash of blue and yellow flames, consumed all that was left in ashes.

Patrick nodded in appreciation to Sergeant Anderson. Privately he thought that great musketry and a good deal of showman's magic had been thrown in as well. Patrick was familiar with the training a soldier underwent to become a competent soldier, but it was apparent to him these were the best of the best in the American command across the river. No doubt they had trained for weeks if not months beforehand to achieve the perfect split-second timing to fire at such a demanding rate of fire. Excellent musketry enhanced by the use of buck and ball cartridges added to the awesome destruction of the target. Nor did it escape Patrick's eye a ribbon was tied to a tree farther down the range so the soldiers knew where to maintain the point of aim when the target disappeared behind the clouds of gunsmoke. Counting silently, he noted that the drummers stretched the minutes to maintain the impression of five shots per minute, but it was an impressive show nonetheless.

The firing demonstration complete, Sergeant Anderson marched his squad off the common ground to the final enthusiastic applause and cheers of praise into the warehouse behind Caleb's store. The squad was pleased with their performance and they joked amongst themselves as they marched into the warehouse. They were looking forward to spending their day enjoying the festivities, complete with a promised ration of ale and freedom from duties for the rest for the day. Their smiles disappeared as they were met by a grim Sergeant McClure, along with his command of soldiers who began to hand out double packets of cartridges to the confused soldiers. After the last man entered the building, McClure assigned guards from his own troops to guard the windows and doors from any listeners. Beckoning Sergeant Anderson closer so he could speak quietly to him and the men, McClure solemnly announced, "Treachery is afoot here today." The stunned troops listened at first in disbelief and then with mounting anger as the sergeant recounted Captain Johnson's story. Finished, he turned to introduce Captain Johnson, who had been standing quietly with Ganiga in the shadows. Johnson stepped forward to address the troops.

"First, let me compliment you all on your impressive show of firepower here today. I will ensure both your commanding officer and general command will receive a favorable report of your great achievement here. You are now our reserve strike force. We will locate here and today these villains who attacked and ruthlessly killed my command in their murderous ambush. We will avenge our comrades on these villains in their own manner and with their blood." Johnson drew nods of approval and muttered words of affirmation from the assembled troops. "Prepare yourselves, clean your weapons and rearm, then you may rest till further called upon. Be ready. Be quick. And be ruthless when commanded to attack. Sergeant Anderson, Sergeant McClure will give you the details of our plan while I leave to intermingle with the crowds and ferret these weasels out."

On the village common the main event of the day was now well on its way. Many riflemen had gathered earlier in the morning to participate in some unofficial competition amongst themselves. Now, with the soldier's performance complete, the shooting field had been set up for the main event. At varying distances from the shooting line, numbered poles had been hammered into the earth for targets to be mounted upon. The first shoot was a popular, fun contest, the egg shoot or eat event. A raw egg was placed on the top of each post. The first dozen shooters waited for the shooting judge to give the command to fire. Behind the shooting line, a dozen excited women from the community waited with wooden buckets of cold water in their hands. The event judge summarized the event rules, much to the delight of the ladies, as they were commanded by the judge to douse any shooter who did not fire immediately when the order to fire was given. Further, any shooter who missed the egg must run as fast as he could to the egg, break it, and eat it before the frontier women following him on the run reached the shooter. If he failed to eat the egg immediately, or if in the judgment of the women the shooter exhibited tardiness in so doing, they were free to douse him with frigid water.

Travis waited on the shooting line. He nodded and smiled as Squib joined him. Travis laughed and said, "You're going to get wet."

"Not me. You," Squib replied, poking his brother with his finger. Travis noticed then that Squib had stripped off his extra weapons, shooting bags, and any added weight so he could run faster if he missed the egg. Too late for Travis to do the same, the judge raised his arm, and Squib and he brought their rifles up to aim.

The judge announced, "Ready." Barely a second later he dropped his arm and yelled, "Fire!"

The sudden command to fire caught several contestants unaware. Before they could draw a bead on the egg targets, they found themselves promptly doused with buckets of water by the enthusiastic ladies. The crowd jeered and laughed as the soaked competitors shook like wet hounds and soggily left the firing line. Two shooters had missed the target. Dropping their rifles, they sprinted towards their unbroken eggs with a crowd of howling women close on their heels. The slowest, an older man with jiggly hips and a ponderous belly, was quickly overtaken by several younger quick-footed women and received buckets of water for his lack of speed. The dousing stopped him in his tracks as he was drenched with cold water. The other more nimble shooter reached his unbroken egg before the woman bucket brigade could catch him. He grabbed the egg in one hand, broke it, and swallowed down the contents. Turning to face the women with his hands on his hips and a smug smile on his face, he laughed at the half-dozen women standing armed with buckets. Then the judge back at the shooting line announced in a loud voice, "Smugness in front of ladies is unacceptable behavior."

Before the shooter could move, six buckets of water splashed him in the face with a force that knocked him off his feet onto his butt. More laughs, hoots, and cheers from the spectators added to his embarrassment. The older wet shooter dragged himself back to the shooting line, relieved he at least didn't have to eat the raw egg, when the judge pointed at him and announced: "You didn't eat the egg." Immediately several women dumped more cold water on his head, much to the crowd's delight.

Patrick, standing amongst the spectators, laughed at the antics of the shooters and marveled at the spontaneity of the participants and audience. Mary, having sold her remaining hasty pudding, joined Patrick. "Not shooting today, Mr. O'Hara?"

Patrick smiled back and said, "I've never liked chickens, Mrs. Murphy."

"I see," she replied. "Maybe a little intimidated by the shooting you've seen today already?"

"Indeed, I am," Patrick answered. "Many more good shots here today than myself."

"An honest man," Mary replied over her shoulder as she turned and headed back to her hasty pudding stand. "And modest too. You're a rare one, Mr. O'Hara."

Patrick smiled, thinking that a smart man on the run doesn't attract attention to himself by participating in public events.

Just then Patrick felt a jab of cold sharp steel pressed against his ribs as a brittle unwelcome voice from his past whispered quietly, "Getting friendly with the enemy, Mr. O'Hara? Shame on you."

Patrick turned slowly and stared into the cold, emotionless eyes of Sergeant White as he pressed his dirk harder into Patrick's side.

"Why, if it isn't my friend Mr. White," Patrick replied, thinking quickly.

"Not so loud," White whispered back. "You will attract attention."

"That's the point," O'Hara shot back, nodding towards the shooters. "My friends over there have already noticed you."

White broke eye contact with Patrick and glanced quickly towards the shooting line. Caught off guard by Patrick's ruse, he stiffened when O'Hara suddenly stepped back, placing his own long knife on White's ribs.

"Patrick," White sneered, "you were always a wily one. Looks like we have a standoff. This cannot end well for the either of us."

"No, it cannot," Patrick replied. "A knife in the gut for one and a hanging for another. What's your choice, Mr. White?"

"Another day, O'Hara. It will be you hanging from a rope when this is all over."

Patrick smiled and answered, "And you will hang before it's all over if you don't back off now. Be gone with you. And give my regards to that lunatic Torrens." White held his tongue; already a few people were watching them as he turned to leave. He almost ran into Mary, who stood a few paces from them with one of Squib's pistols in her hands. White smiled and nodded to her, touching his hat as he pushed past into the spectators. He quickly disappeared into the crowd.

Patrick casually walked over to Mary and said, "And Mrs. Murphy. Are you thinking of joining the competition today?"

Mary was not amused. "What's going on, Patrick? Who was that man?"

"Just an old acquaintance," Patrick replied, trying to defuse Mary's obvious anger.

"An old friend, was he? And you just like to stick knives in each other's ribs to say hello?" Mary fired back angrily, pointing at White standing amongst the spectators.

Patrick turned and saw Sergeant White on the edge of the crowd, staring intently at Squib and Travis as they finished another round of shooting at eggs. Both hit their targets. White spoke quickly to a man standing close to him, dipping his head at the shooters as he did so. The man nodded in silent reply to something White said and started to move quickly through the crowd in the other direction. Patrick felt a knot of anxiety in his stomach as he recognized Tobias rushing away from the village common, no doubt headed to find reinforcements from Torrens and the rest of the men.

O'Hara gently took Mary's arm and spoke calmly to her, "Mary, I need you to trust me. Travis and Squib are in danger. We must get them away from here as soon as possible. Bring them over to that small shed behind your food stand."

Mary had watched White talking to the other man and recognized something was afoot in the way he ran off so urgently. What and why she did not know, but she realized immediately that her association with the brothers and Patrick meant they were all involved. Mary agreed, "I will; but you have some explaining to do, Mr. O'Hara." She moved to get the brothers.

Moments later the disgruntled brothers and Fidious arrived with Mary at the shed where they were shielded from the view of the spectators on the village common. Travis spoke first.

"This better be good, Patrick." Peeved at being pulled away from the shooting, he growled, "Squib and I were up to compete in the final round of the egg shoot."

"Aye. We are listening," Mary added.

Patrick remained silent as he mulled over his possible replies. He knew the three could shoot him on the spot if they didn't like what he had to say, or even turn him over to the Army to be hanged as a spy. There was no time for a long-drawn-out discussion as Torrens and the rest of the soldiers were no doubt on the way here if not already searching the crowds for them.

"I will ask you to listen to all I have to say before you take any action or judge me," Patrick finally began. "Time is very short, so please bear with me. Travis and Squib, you are in great danger. The men who have been hunting you are here looking for you in the crowd."

Squib drew his long knife from his belt, held it to Patrick's throat, and hissed, "How do you know about that? Who are you?"

Travis stepped forward, placed his hand on Squib's arm, and said, "Wait, he can't talk dead. Let's hear all he has to say before we kill him."

"I'm a deserter," Patrick began slowly. "I was part of that group chasing you since that incident with that character Woody upriver. After you shot us up at the river rapids, I snuck away and deserted."

"You're a pirate?" Squib asked, pressing his knife deeper into Patrick's throat and drawing a small drop of blood.

"No," Patrick replied, "I'm a deserter. That bunch are not pirates. They are all British soldiers, a group I deserted from a week ago."

"A bloody Redback!" Mary cried. Cocking Squib's pistol, she rammed the muzzle into Patrick's chest. "I should shoot you here and now."

"Wait," Patrick begged. "Hear my story first, then you can all shoot me if you wish, but Travis and Squib need to get away from here before those soldiers find them. The officer in charge is a cold-blooded killer. He will kill you. Kill us all if he finds us together. Squib. Travis. You possess something he desperately wants back. He will murder everyone in his path. You better run before he finds you."

Mary pressed the pistol harder into Patrick's chest. "Why should we believe you? What are you doing in the British Army?" Pushing Squib's knife away from Patrick's throat she struck Patrick across the face knocking him stunned against the back wall.

"Mr. O'Hara," Mary growled grimly, "you have till the count of ten to explain yourself or you will be telling your story to Saint Peter. One."

"Mary," Patrick began, "you left Ireland. You know how hard life was."

"Two," Mary counted.

"Life was tough. We had little or no food."

"Three," Mary counted. "You're telling me what I already know."

"Yes," Patrick snapped back, "I'm reminding you how difficult it was for us. All of us."

"Four. You're halfway to hell, Mr. O'Hara," Mary fumed.

"We were denied work," Patrick continued, "our land was taken away from us."

"Five," Mary announced and pressed her finger forward on the trigger so it set with a loud "click." Now the lightest touch would fire the gun.

"Mary. We were being hanged and left to rot on the gallows. Men and women just like you and me for wearing the green. Green like the ribbon I gave you and green like the shamrock you gave me."

"Six" Mary counted "your time is running out Mr. O'Hara"

"Mary, I told you the other night I was a poacher back in Ireland, but I failed to tell you that I was caught. I was given a choice. The noose or serve in the British Army. Not just myself but many more like me. We chose the Army. Judge me if you will, but that's the truth."

"Eight," Mary continued, unpersuaded by Patrick's answers.

"Eight!" Patrick yelped. "What happened to seven?"

"Time's up," Mary exclaimed. "I'm not convinced."

"Fine. Fine," Patrick replied, throwing his hands up in the air, then crossing his arms on his chest resolutely. "Shoot me. Let's get this over and done with. You," he pointed at Mary, "can explain why you murdered an innocent Irishman to Saint Peter."

"Aye, that I can, "Mary replied. Her tone softened slightly. "I've heard the stories. Many an Irishman came to America after deserting from the Redbacks' Army, looking to escape the noose."

Mary paused and asked, "That man I saw with his knife in your ribs, Patrick, was he your officer?"

"One of them," Patrick replied, sensing the softening in her voice as the pistol muzzle was lowered slightly from his chest. "That was Sergeant White, the second in command. He's the real dangerous one of that group. He's not the cold-blooded killer that Torrens is but he's smarter. He's been fighting the Frenchies for years and is still alive, so that tells you much about him. He's as British as you will find in the king's ranks, making him dangerous because he will follow orders from Torrens."

Travis turned to Mary, and said, "Those men chasing us have tried to kill us several times already; that's how Squib lost part of his ear. If they catch us here, many people could be hurt in the gun fight."

Mary lowered the pistol from Patrick's chest. "We can't wait any longer. You boys need to get out of here fast. Head towards the river and run back to my cabin. Patrick and I will watch your backs then join you when safe."

Patrick's jaw dropped like a rock. "Just like that you're in charge, are you?"

Mary smiled and pushed the pistol back into O'Hara's chest. "Aye. We need the boys to be safe from these soldier friends of yours, then I'll decide what happens to you after."

"Wait. Patrick. Did you shoot at us when the soldiers' camp was attacked?" Travis asked grimly.

Squib joined in tapping Patrick on the chest with his finger. "Maybe it was you that shot my ear off. I wouldn't take kindly knowing you had done that."

"No," Patrick replied calmly. "I was stationed at the lookout during the attack. I didn't shoot at anyone."

"How can we be sure about that?" Travis asked.

"If it was me shooting at you," Patrick replied with a straight face, "I wouldn't have missed."

"Sounds reasonable to me," Squib said after a little thought.

Mary rolled her eyes, shaking her head that the boys could be so naïve, though this only added to her fondness for the two brothers and her concerns for their safety. She dropped the pistol from Patrick's chest.

"Enough. You boys need to be going. I'll finish here with Patrick and meet you at the cabin later."

Squib wasn't sure. He asked, "What about you, Mary? I don't feel good about leaving you with this scoundrel." He pointed at Patrick. "You might not be safe."

"Oh, I will be safe enough," Mary replied and nodded towards Patrick's feet where Fidious sat next to him. Patrick idly scratched the dog behind the ear. "It was Fidious that attracted me to that sergeant fellow sticking his knife into Patrick's ribs. Fidious snuck up all silent, watching him closely the whole time, while I grabbed one of your pistols. Dogs know who to trust; that's good enough for me. Now, you boys git on out of here."

"Alright, Mary," Travis replied. "Keep that pistol." Looking directly at Patrick, he continued, "Use it if you need to."

"I will be alright," Mary replied again.

"I will watch your backs till you are in the woods," Patrick added. "Keep your wits. Whatever you do, don't let them get close to you. These are British regulars trained to fire four shots a minute like those American troops you saw earlier today. Speed and distance are your best defense; let them get close and you're both dead. So, move."

Ominously, a cannon boomed out across the river from the fort, followed closely by a second and third report that echoed off the hills behind. Musket fire rippled in the distance, crackling like a log in the fire.

"Prison break," Mary said, startled.

"What prison would that be?" Patrick asked.

"Newport Barracks is where they hold British prisoners of war," Mary replied. "In the stockade behind the barracks."

"How many prisoners?" Patrick asked, growing more concerned by the second.

"Hundreds, I've been told," Mary replied anxiously. "Is this the doing of that bunch you were tied up with, Patrick?"

"No," Patrick replied. "Not that I know of, but then we were never told what our mission was. It doesn't seem likely."

Grabbing the boys by the shoulders, Patrick pushed them towards the door.

"Whatever the story," Patrick implored impatiently, "hundreds of Redbacks on the loose puts us all in the pot." Giving the Tanners another push out the door, he said, "Move, boys, get out of here now. Hell is coming to Cincinnati."

CHAPTER 23

Captain Johnson was standing next to the firing line, sure that the two frontiersmen would be amongst the shooters at the rifle shoot unaware he had just missed them leaving, missing them by a few minutes. The menacing sound of cannon fire brought everyone on the common to a standstill as the spectators looked immediately across the river. At first, the crowd stood in shocked silence; then, sparked by the sound of musketry in the distance, the crowd en masse began a hurried movement in every direction as people ran for safety from the imagined danger. Johnson knew immediately that the cannon fire signified a prison break, and he pushed his way through the crowd to gather his command. Surprise turned to panic as people started running into each other, pushing and jostling in a frenzied effort to escape the village common. Mothers and fathers called out their children's names and looked frantically about. Husbands and wives searched, calling their spouse's name, trying to gather loved ones together to escape the perceived threat. Shocked spectators milled about, confused by those who, in a panic, were crying "Indian! Indian attack! Hostiles!" These cries escalated the crowd from panic to the edge of terror.

In the background, several cooler heads prevailed as a few Ohio militia officers tried to rally militiamen. "Men of Ohio, rally to your officers."

"Fall in on your officers," was heard as more men took up the cry and stood by their officers.

Captain Johnson had pushed his way through the crowd to the post band, and was now standing on the edge of the common. Approaching the drum sergeant, he coolly commanded him, "You may play the signal now, if you please, Sergeant Major." Johnson ordered, "'Garryowen,' make it lively and loud." Johnson's cold stare brought the band quickly to hand as they began to beat out the lively beat. "Louder!" Johnson shouted. The band responded immediately. The instrument men did not know who this rough backwoodsman was giving them orders, but the unmistakable voice of authority left no confusion about what their response should be and so they played as loudly as possible.

Satisfied, Johnson turned to a drummer boy standing open-mouthed with the band. "Boy," Johnson pointed at the young drummer so it was clear it was him being spoken to.

"Find Sergeant McClure and bring his troops there." Johnson pointed to the warehouses behind the village common and adjacent to the wharves, docks and other structures along the river.

"Repeat my command," Johnson spoke calmly to the still confused drummer boy.

"Get Sergeant McClure and his men," the boy stammered. "Bring them there," he said, pointing to the exact spot Johnson had.

"Good," Johnson replied. "Now move it like your pants are on fire."

"Yes, sir," the boy called out over his shoulder. He was already running to find McClure and his troops.

Johnson turned his back to the band, looked over the crowd milling about, and shook his head quietly. Not good, he thought. Too easy for innocents to get injured if shooting breaks out. Had he misjudged his prey? Had they used the Tanner boys as a diversion to distract attention from the prison to instigate the jailbreak? Were the men he sought here or over there across the river? Not the time to second-guess myself, Johnson thought. My duty is to reinforce the barracks, the prison, and the munitions across the river. As if to emphasize Johnson's thoughts, the cannons fired again, accompanied by a new flurry of musket fire.

Johnson thought quickly. Sergeant Anderson and his troops should move towards the sound of the guns and arrive amongst the buildings on his right towards the west side of the town. McClure should answer his summons with his troops arriving at his left by the warehouses on the east side. Looking over his shoulder, Johnson could see that several units of Ohio militiamen were moving into positions some distance away along the woods' edge outside the town square as their officers began to gain order and issue commands.

Johnson thought quickly, looking for the arrival of McClure's and Anderson's troops. "We need to sweep through the crowded docks and wharves to the river, then requisition boats from the many moored along the river and join the troops at Newport Barracks. The scattered sounds of musketry continued in the distance. Johnson weighed his choices quickly. Reinforce the fort or complete the mission?

Just as his decision was made, Johnson spotted the Tanners and Fidious running east towards the forest, dodging and weaving through the piles of crates, supplies, and merchandise that sat about waiting transit. At the same moment, Ganiga, standing quietly next to him, grunted "There!" Ganiga pointed to a group of heavily armed men running swiftly in pursuit of the boys from the west.

Ganiga cocked his rifle.

"Don't shoot yet!" Johnson barked. "There are too many civilians between us to shoot from here."

Johnson cocked his own rifle, but before he could take any action, a rifle cracked from behind a building to his left. The shooter, though hidden by the building, gave away his position by the cloud of gunsmoke along the corner.

Immediately one of the men pursuing the Tanners yelped in pain and fell, sliding to a stop along the dockage. Several men stopped, and began shooting at the gunman who by then had gone around the corner of the building. Pieces of wood splintered off the side of the structure and a window disappeared in the crash of fragmented, shattered glass from the gunfire. Two men who were obviously in command waved the other troops to not fire. They pointed vigorously at Squib and Travis, who had stopped at the gunfire, then resumed running as fast as they could away to the east.

This is getting out of hand, Johnson thought. We need to stop those men first. They are the real danger here; not the frontiersmen heading towards the forest.

Adding to the confusion, the band continued to play. Many of the Irish settlers who had helped themselves to Caleb's plentiful whisky earlier in the day begun to sing loudly the words to "Garryowen."

"Instead of spa we'll drink brown ale
And pay the reckoning on the nail
For debt no man shall go to jail
From Garryowen in glory."

"We'll break the windows, we'll break the doors
The watch knock down by threes and fours
Then let the doctors work their cures
And tinker up our bruised."

Sergeant McClure's men appeared between two buildings only a short distance from where the lone rifleman had first fired at Torrens' group. Spotting the gunsmoke drifting about Torrens' men, he stopped and ordered his soldiers to open fire upon the British who had finished reloading their muskets. Sergeant White saw the American regulars arrive and ordered his men to engage them as well. Simultaneously both groups opened fire on each other. With so many crates and dockage piled about, neither group had a clear shot at the other as they both sought better shooting positions firing as the opportunity presented itself. The British troops soon gained a slight advantage. Their superior firepower and numbers accounted for two wounded Americans who slumped to the ground and were now hidden by the stores and baggage. McClure sensed his danger immediately and pulled his men into cover. He ordered them to slow down their fire as each man only carried twenty rounds; it was not the time to run short of ammo.

Johnson and Ganiga worked their way cautiously to some crates to give them cover. Ganiga spotted another gunman firing from beside the injured soldier who had been shot by the mystery assailant a few minutes earlier. Both men had taken shelter behind a shipping crate. The unwounded soldier rose to fire on McClure's group, and ducked down behind his cover to reload, then popped up to take his next shot. Ganiga moved cautiously, keeping himself hidden while looking for a spot to take aim.. He found a crack between two bales and pushed his rifle through the opening. Kneeling on one knee, he carefully laid his sights where the soldier had fired before. Ganiga waited patiently.. The soldier rose to fire. Ganiga fired first. The bullet struck with a loud "slap" sound, hitting the soldier in the upper arm the bullet smashed through flesh and bone into his chest knocking him down to the ground. Unnoticed from Ganiga's position, two other soldiers rounded the side of several large barrels and took aim at Ganiga.

Captain Johnson saw the soldiers lift their muskets to engage Ganiga. Johnson yelled, "Ganiga, look out!"

Before his friend could respond, the two soldiers fired simultaneously. One bullet carved a furrow across the side of the crate, sending splinters flying in all directions. Several splinters pierced Ganiga's face like tiny arrows. The other shot struck

Ganiga, grazing him on the thigh before passing through the fleshy part of his hip with a loud slap. He was flung backwards, landing heavily on his side slamming his head violently against a a piling and rolled over limply on the dock.

Captain Johnson yelled, "No!" Leaping from his position while firing on the assailants from the hip he dropped to Ganiga's side and began to drag him back under cover.

Suddenly a loud voice yelled, "Captain Johnson, DOWN!"

Johnson threw himself over Ganiga to protect him. A second later a thunderous volley exploded from farther down the dock aimed at the British. The gunfire forced Torrens' group to the ground. Under fire from both fronts, the British huddled back under cover, reloaded, and waited for Torrens to order their next move. Johnson peeked from behind a hay bale and saw that the distance from which Anderson's group had arrived was too far to expect accurate fire. Fortunately they had drawn the attention away from Johnson and Ganiga who were out in the open and vulnerable to Torrens' soldiers' fire. Johnson jumped up and dragged his wounded companion back into the cover of the crates and out of sight from the British.

Johnson looked over his shoulder to see that Sergeant Anderson's group had taken cover behind some cotton bales and were reloading. Only their arms were visible with ramrods in hand rising behind the obstructions as they reloaded. Anderson ordered, "Fix bayonets," and a dozen bayonets flashed in the air visible above the bundles, followed by the distinct sound of metal on metal as the soldiers affixed their needle-shaped razor-sharp bayonets. Determined to keep pressure on the British and assist Johnson, who was still too close to his attackers, Sergeant Anderson rushed his troops from behind the bales and hurriedly formed them in line shoulder to shoulder.

"Squad, will present arms," Anderson ordered. "Fire."

The volley thundered out, driving the British soldiers further undercover as bullets passed about them, smashing through crates and dunnage before ricocheting in all directions around the dock.

Anderson raised his sword, pointed it at the British, and shouted, "Alright, lads; charge." Cheers went up from the soldiers as they screamed their war cries and charged forward with their bayonets glinting wickedly in the afternoon sun.

Sergeant White responded immediately with the only course available to him when faced with the charging Americans bayonets: "Retreat. Run for your lives back to our boat."

Major Torrens, in shock, stood glaring coldly at White. "That's not for you to command, Sergeant," he barked.

"It is, sir," White responded. "We're done here."

"Pull back," White cried out. "Pull back," he repeated, as he watched the Americans charging towards him.

"Then shoot those two wounded," Torrens commanded, pointing to Privates Jackson and Wood, who lay wounded on the dock while still vainly trying to reload and fight the rapidly approaching Americans. Shocked, both privates looked wide-eyed at Torrens then to Sergeant White in desperation.

"We can leave no witnesses alive here, Sergeant," Torrens growled, lifting his musket to aim at Jackson. Sergeant White grabbed the musket about the firelock with one hand as Torrens pulled the trigger. The hammer struck, cutting painfully into White's hand preventing the musket from firing. White yanked the weapon from Torrens' grip and pushed the major backward onto his heels.

"Move, Major, or you will be the one facing the firing squad," he said, then threw the musket at the major.

Turning to Jackson and Wood, Sergeant White spoke quickly, "Up with your hands, lads, your on your own now. Keep your hands up and surrender. Good luck to you."

He turned and ran after his retreating men, dragging the reluctant major behind him by the scruff of his collar off the dock into the forest beyond.

Wood immediately threw his musket down away from himself and reached over to tug Jackson's gun away from him and threw it aside. Jackson had fallen on his side, his wounds too grievous to allow him to raise his hands in surrender or to sit up. Wood crawled closer to cover his comrade and sat in front of him with both hands in the air.

The Americans were slowed by the massive amount of provisions scattered about on the docks as Sergeant Anderson tried to keep them in a cohesive line. Several charged around the dunnage and approached the surrendering Jackson and Wood. They were ready to bayonet them when Sergeant Anderson yelled, "Stop! They are surrendering; hold right there."

Looking at the British fugitives now disappearing into the forest beyond, Anderson ordered his men to halt and regroup as Sergeant McClure arrived with his few men with Captain Johnson hard on his heels.

"Your orders, sir?" Anderson asked, looking to the captain. Just as he began to answer, another volley of cannon fire sounded from the fort across the river..

Johnson paused for a second, looking down the river and across to the fort with the prison camp behind. His duty was clear. He sighed and reluctantly ordered, "Our duty must be to reinforce the fort. Gather our wounded with the two prisoners and move them to the boats as soon as possible. We're done here, for now."

"Your companion, sir?" McClure asked quietly.

"Wounded," Johnson replied, looking back to where Ganiga sat against a crate. A pool of blood from his horrendous-looking wound slowly spread about him. He had already begun to stuff herbs and moss from his medicine bag into the wound to staunch the bleeding. "He's been wounded worse. Now we will have to contend with an angry Tuscarora on our hands."

"The surgeon," McClure replied, "will not be too happy cleaning all that dirt and grass out of his wounds either, sir."

"Ganiga is a medicine man, the chief healer of his band some years ago. Any sawbones who tries to touch him will do so at his own risk," Johnson replied.

Johnson shook his head, trying to clear his ears that were still ringing from the fierce firefight on the dock. Slowly, as his hearing returned, he became aware that the band was still playing on the village common. Some spectators, oblivious to the battles and addled from the alcohol they had consumed, began to sing louder. The song "Wearing of the Green" boomed out across the docks.

"I've heard a whisper of a land that lies beyond the sea
Where rich and poor stand equal in the light of Freedom's day.
Ah, Erin, must we leave you, driven by a tyrant's hand
Must we seek a mother's blessing from a strange and distant land
Where the cruel cross of England shall never more be seen
And where, please God, we'll live and die, still Wearing of the Green.
She's the most distressful country that ever yet was seen
For their hanging men and women there for Wearing of the Green."

Johnson shook his head and turned to Sergeant McClure. "Have the band stop now, if you please, Sergeant."

Chapter 24

O'Hara watched the battle from a hidden doorway where he had taken cover after shooting at Torrens' group. He felt little remorse for injuring one of his previous comrades, but accepted it was necessary. Now was the time to leave, as many people were beginning to gather about, trying to see what was going on.

O'Hara walked quietly along the side of the building until he saw a group of militiamen heading down a parallel street. Pulling quickly back, he ducked into a doorway and leaned back as far as possible to hide. With a sigh of relief, he saw the men hurrying past to the woods' side of town. Patrick turned to spit out the rifle ball — he had put into his mouth for a quick reload — just then the door behind him opened and someone grabbed him by the back of his collar, throwing him hard upon his back to the floor. The impact drove the bullet he had in his mouth into the back of his throat and it wedged there. Patrick choked on the bullet. Rolling urgently onto his knees, He tried to cough the ball up, but it was too heavy. The more he tried to cough it up, the more it sank back in his throat. Patrick fought to breathe. Sweat beaded on his forehead as panic began to set in. As a last desperate effort he swallowed instead of coughing. Miraculously the bullet dislodged itself and plunged down into his gullet, settling in his stomach where it sat cold and hard. Sitting up slowly, he saw Mary sitting in a chair a few feet away, staring at him with emotionless, dispassionate eyes. His rifle was balanced across her knees and aimed at his belly.

Pushing himself back against the wall, he kicked the door which was still open hard till it slammed with a loud bang. Mary stared at him coldly and asked, "What makes you think I want to be alone with you, Mr. O'Hara?" Before he could answer, she pushed the barrel of the rifle towards him, almost touching his belly, and cocked it.

"My reputation, if not my very life, has been threatened already, Mr. O'Hara, by your actions. What makes you think I should be alone with you in this room?"

"I have a bullet in my guts," Patrick blurted out.

"What?" Mary replied, surprised by his answer. "What are you talking about?"

"I swallowed a bullet," Patrick replied again. He began to feel around his stomach, searching for the hardness of the lead in his gut.

"Mr. O'Hara, you're making no sense to me at all."

"I did," O'Hara answered. "I had a bullet in my mouth in case I had to reload quickly. And when you threw me on the floor, I swallowed it. I have a bullet in my guts. I could die."

Shaking her head, Mary laughed, and said, "You won't die."

"I could. Have you ever had a bullet in the guts?"

"No," Mary replied, feeling as if she were talking to a child. Laughing, she said, "But I'm sure it will pass."

Patrick laughed then bent over, clutching his stomach in pain. "Oh, don't make me laugh, Mary. It hurts when I laugh," he groaned.

"Here," she said, standing and sliding the chair towards him. "Sit. I'll get you some water."

Leaning the rifle against the wall she returned with a bucket of water and ladle and gave Patrick the dipper. "Drink."

Patrick gulped down the tepid water, then dipped it several more times till he had drunk half the bucket.

"Ah, that does feel better," he said. Suddenly he paled as the bullet moved about painfully in his stomach. Patrick jumped up from the chair and began to hop around, trying to drive the bullet down and out.

"Patrick, stop that. You will attract attention, and we don't want to be caught here together. There are soldiers all about, and we don't know who saw us enter. Be quiet now. We need to wait till dark to go back to my place. Come, let's sit in the corner over here where we can't be seen or heard." Mary lifted the chair, carried it into the darker part of the room, and sat down.

"Ah, you trust me now, do you, Mrs. Murphy?" Patrick pointed to the rifle still leaning against the wall.

"You made no attempt to grab your gun while I got you water," Mary replied. "So, let's leave it at that. Bring your rifle over here; we may need it before the night comes."

Patrick walked and retrieved his rifle, noticing for the first time the frizzen was open indicated there was probably no powder left in the pan. The weapon was harmless, which made him chuckle. He immediately regretted the laugh as the bullet dropped a few inches deeper in his guts to his instant discomfort.

"I think we have to talk, Mr. O'Hara."

"Oh no." Patrick laughed. "Not a serious talk so soon in our relationship."

"Sit," Mary commanded, not seeing any humor in Patrick's comment.

"You can start from the beginning, Mr. O'Hara. Where did you come from, how did you get here, and most importantly, what are you doing here?"

"It's a long story," Patrick sighed as he sat on the floor beside her.

"We have lots of time, Mr. O'Hara."

Chapter 25

Captain Johnson stood quietly, leaning against the door of the surgery. He watched the surgeon and his attendant work on the two wounded British soldiers after they had treated the wounded American troops first. In the corner, Ganiga sat on a cot. His favorite beverage, a cup of coffee sweetened with a handful of sugar, rested on his leg as he paid close attention to the surgeon's ministrations to his two patients. Between gulps of the heavily sweetened drink, he would shake his head and pull a sour face when the surgeon selected a tool from his medical kit. Several times he pinched his nose at the foul-smelling chemicals the surgeon applied to the wounds to clean them or staunch the flow of blood. He was particularly fascinated by the laudanum the doctor had administered to the patients as he observed the drug's almost immediate calming effect on the men. The surgeon finished dressing the men's wounds, withdrew a lancet from his medical kit, and begun to bleed his patient. Ganiga rolled his eyes in disgust, turning his head away so not to witness what he considered a barbaric practice.

The surgeon, having completed his attention to the soldiers, turned to Ganiga, but before he could move, Captain Johnson yelled across the room to the surprise of all, "NO. Don't touch Ganiga."

"See here, Captain," the surgeon replied, clearly put off by being yelled at by the officer, "I treat all wounded men — white, black, or red — equally."

"My apologies, Doctor," Johnson replied in a softer tone. "Ganiga is a medicine man, the doctor, if you will, of his tribe. He is here to observe you in your work, but I can tell you from my own experience and his own words he doesn't want you or any white doctor to touch him. His response to any attempt to do so on your part will result in three men being hanged tomorrow."

The British prisoners flinched at the captain's words and they exchanged fearful glances at each other.

"Hanged," the doctor replied angrily, his attention now returned to his patients. "These men are wounded soldiers. We do not hang wounded soldiers, Captain."

"Spies," Captain Johnson spit out. "Spies who murdered half of my command in cold blood while we were conducting a peaceful survey mission upriver. Burning their bodies without a Christian funeral or burial in the aftermath. They will hang, Doctor."

Turning on his heel, Johnson glanced out of the corner of his eye as Ganiga stared at the wounded soldiers with a wolfish grin of delight. Meanwhile, all the others in the room stood in shocked silence.

That will give them something to think about before we interrogate them, Johnson thought as he walked across the parade square and into the headquarters building. Sergeant McClure, who was waiting for him, quickly ushered the captain into Major Simmonds' office where they both stopped, saluted, and stood at attention.

"At ease," the major commanded with a wave of his hand. "It's been a hell of a day, gentleman. Martin, Sergeant McClure, and Anderson have given me their reports. I'll need your complete written one, but for now, fill me in on what happened today."

"I'm sure there's not much you sergeants have left out," Captain Johnson replied, "except my report will include their excellent and professional handling of themselves and their troops during today's mission and engagement." Nodding to Sergeant McClure, he continued, "Well done to you, Sergeant Anderson, and your men today."

"Thank you, sir," Sergeant McClure replied. "I'll convey your compliments to the men, sir."

Johnson turned back to Simmonds and said, "Bill, the men who attacked us today are trained British soldiers as evidenced by their skilled infantry tactics and musketry. Being out of uniform and dressed in homespun smocks and buckskins makes them spies by any definition of the word. They will hang for their actions upriver at my camp and here today. Their mission and reason for their presence here remains a mystery, although I'm confident the Tanner brothers are not part of this group. From our observations today, it appears they are being pursued by the British for some reason. I'm hoping our interrogation of the prisoners will reveal more information later this evening—"

Major Simmonds interrupted the captain, "I've already been visited by Colonel Seymour in that regard. The colonel is the senior officer of the prisoners being held here to inquire about the two British soldiers."

"How the—" Johnson blurted out and held himself as the major held up his hand.

"Martin, news goes through this camp faster than a bullet through a bag of feathers. The colonel requested he be allowed to interview the prisoners as is his right."

"Then we need to interrogate them before he does," Johnson replied. He continued, "I've put a bee in their bonnets that they will be hanged as spies. I intend to tell them if they cooperate, they will be shot instead of hanged."

"Not much at bargaining, are you, Martin. I can't see that will loosen their tongues in any way."

"Beg your pardon, sir," Sergeant McClure spoke up, "if I may offer my opinion?"

"Of course, Sergeant," the major replied.

"The men often talk amongst themselves and play a bit of 'What if you had a choice?' game, if you could choose being shot, hanged, stabbed, or blown to pieces by a cannonball sort of thing. It's been my experience, sir, that most favor being shot over all the rest. Hanging is not a favored way to go and many feel it's reserved for traitors and cowards. Most have seen hanging for the slow, painful demise it is. Giving the prisoners a chance to avoid the noose may well loosen their tongues."

"Thank you, Sergeant," Simmonds replied. "Useful advice as usual. Then I consent to the ruse to extract some information from the prisoners."

"It's no ruse, Bill. If they give us some information, then we put them in front of a firing squad," Johnson replied.

"Alright, Martin. A hanging is a nasty affair. Let's give it a try; at least they get to die honorably. Any information you can get out of them will help in your efforts. However, I can tell you that the prison break today had no evidence of outside influence or assistance."

"How so?" Johnson asked.

The major replied, "For some time now we have had conflict within the prison between the genuine prisoners of war captured in battle and the deserters we have apprehended away from the battlefield. The British officers have requested that we turn the deserters over to them so they could be tried and military justice applied. However, the general felt doing so would reflect badly upon ourselves or instigate reprisals against our own American prisoners in English prisons if the court-martial decided upon a mass hanging — which they would have every right to do according to law. The general advised Colonel Seymore the same, saying they could administer justice when they are released or exchanged. The rank and file have not been happy with that decision and taken the matter into their own hands and subjected the deserters to threats and physical abuse. When a rumor was spread we intended to change our policy and turn the deserters over to the prisoners for justice they staged a desperate mass escape to gain freedom. Forty-seven of them overpowered their guards and ran into the woods behind the post. When this occurred, a number of prisoners attempted to follow the deserters and either bring them back or administer the law themselves. Fortunately, there have been no serious injuries to our troops and most of the escapees have been apprehended. I will admit to having some concern for a time when the situation was extremely chaotic and given our talk the day before of probable plots and possible saboteurs. However, our strong show of force, including muskets and cannons fired over the prisoners' heads, finally brought back some order by day's end. The guard house is now crammed with forty-plus prisoners, and search patrols will look for the rest tomorrow morning. There is no evidence that the party you are pursuing is involved in the attempted prison break. However, I would like you to interrogate the prisoners before I have to allow Colonel Seymour to do so. Please report your results. Dismissed."

Yes, sir," Johnson and McClure answered in unison. They stood, saluted, and quickly left the major's office.

"Would you like my assistance in questioning the prisoners, sir?" the sergeant asked.

"Not presently," the captain replied. "I would appreciate some coffee supplied to us in the infirmary if you please."

"Yes, sir," McClure replied. He added, "I'll ensure there's an ample amount of sugar as well."

Laughing, Johnson replied, "Thanks. Hopefully Ganiga hasn't used up your entire supply."

Reaching the infirmary, Johnson encountered the surgeon as he was leaving the building.

"What is the condition of the prisoners?" he asked.

"I do not believe the seriously wounded soldier will survive, certainly not past a few days anyway." Then he added with a sneer, "The other one will mend quite nicely, certainly enough for you to hang him."

"If they cooperate with me, they won't hang. They will be shot by a firing squad," Johnson replied sharply.

Shaking his head, the doctor again began to renew his earlier protest. Unexpectedly, Johnson held up his hand and sharply ordered him to "Stop."

"This is not a discussion, Doctor. You will cooperate without protest from this point on or I will find you insubordinate and place you in irons. Is that clear, Doctor?"

Faced by the captain's sharp reprimand, the doctor simply bowed his head, replying meekly, "Yes, sir," and exited the room.

Johnson entered the infirmary and found two stern and heavily armed sergeants guarding the prisoners. The captain could see evidence of Sergeant McClure's thinking immediately. Placing senior NCOs as the guards would safeguard that no word of the events in the prisoners questioning would escape the room. The attendance of the sergeants would also make the prisoners more pliable.

Johnson nodded to Ganiga, who remained unmoved from his cot. His fresh cup of coffee was noticeable by the steam still rising from the cup.

The two prisoners lay on adjoining cots. The more severely wounded prisoner appeared to be asleep, rolled up on his side facing the wall. The other was sprawled out on his cot and engaged in a staring contest with Ganiga. He was obviously losing.

Johnson turned to one of the sergeants and asked, "Have they made any statements or requests?"

The sergeant laughed. "That one there, sir," he said, pointing to John Wood, " He is quite concerned about your scout here giving them the evil eye."

"You can talk to me directly you know," Wood spoke up. "I speak English".

"Who then might you be?" Johnson shot back.

"Private John Wood," he replied, pushing himself more erect on his cot. "A loyal soldier and Englishman. A veteran of the war against the great tyrant Napoleon. Wounded in battle both upon the land and at sea. I was a sailor serving upon the valiant ship HMS Amethyst in one of the most famous battles of the war at sea. Defeated the French ship Thetis. Sank her after a glorious six-hour bloody fight, we did."

"I thought you said you captured the ship?" the other prisoner asked over his shoulder.

"Sank after we captured her," Wood boasted, quickly backpedaling his story. "So damaged not a spar or deck was salvageable after being racked by our guns hour after hour."

Addressing the other prisoner, Johnson asked, "Who are you?"

"William Jackson, sir," the man replied without looking to see who he was speaking with. "And who might you be?"

"Captain Johnson," he began calmly, "39th Infantry Regiment. I was in command of the party of soldiers encamped on Turtle Creek upriver that you two and your party of spies attacked, viciously murdering them before desecrating their bodies by burning. For that heinous crime, you both will be hanged as spies at sunrise tomorrow."

"Spies!" Wood yelled. "We are British soldiers. Not spies."

"Soldiers?" Johnson snapped back. "Soldiers wear uniforms. Soldiers have discipline. Soldiers have honor. Soldiers do not attack innocent civilians."

Wood paled and slumped back onto his cot, lost for a reply to Johnson's accusations.

Silence fell upon the room as Johnson stared coldly at the prisoners, hoping the helplessness of their situation would break their resolve and spirits so further interrogation could proceed.

The sudden sound of metal scraping stone jarred the room as every head turned to Ganiga, who had taken his long knife from its sheath and was now slowly sharpening the blade on a wet stone. His grim expression and the slow grating of steel on stone cut the prisoners' spirits as surely as cuts to their own flesh. Wood began to shake in fear. Jackson, who was already resolved to his fate, simply shrugged his shoulders and sat up again, leaning painfully against the wall. He asked, "Is this where you offer us a deal for talking, or do you let the Indian there cut us up a bit first?"

A tiny gruesome smile lit Ganiga's face. He continued to stare at the prisoners while grinding his knife steadily on the stone.

Wood pulled as far back on his cot as possible, letting out a soft moan.

"You tell me," Johnson replied. "What do you have to offer that might interest me?"

"Not for me," Jackson replied. "I'm done. Been around too long and seen too many men die from less. My friend John here has been a good soldier and is a decent man who has survived too much to die here for naught but doing what he was ordered. I'll talk, if you spare hanging him."

Johnson nodded, replying, "Tell me everything you know and your companion here will go to a firing squad and die like a soldier instead of hanging."

"Oh God," Wood moaned. "It's a blessing to say the least you're giving me."

"Your choice," Johnson replied grimly.

"What do you want to know?" Jackson replied with a sigh.

"Why are you here? What was your mission?"

"We don't know," Jackson replied softly. "Tell him, John; I'm too tired."

"That's right, sir," John continued. "The major kept all the details of our mission secret. Even Sergeant White appeared to not know. We were all in prison and given the chance to be spared further punishment if we agreed to join the mission, except we were told it would be dangerous and we were not likely to return alive."

"So you're criminals then?" Johnson asked.

Jackson uttered a small laugh that was cut short by a painful moan.

"No, sir. Drinkers given to using our fists and O'Hara was a poacher. But no, sir, not criminals."

"Why were you selected over others, then?"

"The major, sir," Wood carried on. "He thought we looked more American than the others in prison, or so Sergeant White told us later."

Johnson stifled a chuckle and asked, "Did you receive special training?"

"No, sir. We are all infantry and spent a good deal of time fighting the frogs one place or another. Other than that, there's nothing special about us."

"Tell me about the two Americans you're chasing. What is their part of your story?" the captain asked, taking a different approach.

"We know no more about them," Wood replied. "They stole something from the major and he is determined to get it back."

"They didn't steal it," Jackson groaned from his bed. "That Woody character stole it when he also tried to steal their canoe."

"Wait," Johnson snapped, "who is Woody?"

"Woody was an American backwoodsman that the major hired to guide us down the river. The major hid something on a big island and left Woody to guard it while we went to meet a Frenchman who was ferrying supplies for us. While we were gone Woody tried to steal the item and the Americans' gear, but he was caught and they beat him up pretty bad for it and ran off with everything Woody had left in their canoe."

"Stop!" Johnson barked, holding up his hand. "Who was the Frenchman? What is his involvement in this plot?"

"Don't know," Wood replied.

"Could you or anyone else in your party recognize this Frenchman again?" Johnson asked.

"No, sir," Wood replied, starting to feel uneasy with his own lack of information. He added, "I didn't see the Frenchman. No one really did, as it was dark."

"What supplies was the Frenchman transporting?" Johnson asked, exasperated at all the negative answers.

"Don't know," Wood answered again.

"Do you know where the Frenchman was taking the supplies?" Johnson asked sarcastically.

"No, sir," Wood replied sheepishly.

"Where two rivers meet," Jackson spoke quietly from his cot. "I overheard them talking while on guard duty. Where the Ohio River meets another river."

"There are many rivers that empty into the Ohio," Johnson stated. "You heard no name?"

"No," Jackson answered. He continued, "The major wasn't pleased with the date as the Frenchman said the first week of October and the major said that was too early; it had to be by November. They argued. But the Frenchman wouldn't change his mind and they moved off so I couldn't hear any more. We left shortly after that and returned to the big island and found Woody lying in the cabin all beat up. That's when the major discovered his secret package was missing, and he tortured Woody to find out where it was."

"Wait," Johnson stopped Jackson, "did you see the major torture this Woody fellow?"

"No, sir," Wood replied and took up the story. "We were kept away from the cabin, but could still hear screams coming from inside. The men were shocked about what they heard and Sergeant White appeared upset. He ordered us to move farther away from the cabin. At that point many of us had some doubts about our leader. British officers do not torture prisoners. No, sir. It's just not done. From that point on the major became obsessed with catching the frontiersmen and finding his secret article."

"After that time you chased the frontiersmen down the river?" Johnson asked.

"Yes sir," Wood replied.

"If catching the frontiersmen was your objective, then why did you attack the encampment at Turtle Creek?" Johnson inquired.

"It was not the major's first intention, but then the frontiersmen showed up at the camp."

"They were in the camp?" Johnson asked.

"Came from upriver that morning and sat down for tea with the officer there nice and friendly and all. That's when the major decided to attack. We caught them in a vicious crossfire from our muskets, double-charged as they were. The Americans had no chance to fight back. We discovered after, that their weapons were unloaded."

"Unloaded?" Johnson barked at Wood in surprise.

"Yes, sir."

"You had no casualties?" Johnson asked.

"No, sir," Wood replied. "Not until the Indians attacked the next day and the frontiersmen caught us in a surprise ambush downriver. Then we lost four men in less than a day."

"Five," Jackson whispered from his cot.

"Yes, five," Wood corrected himself. "Five counting the disappearance of O'Hara. He was probably killed by the Indians."

Johnson sat in stunned silence as Wood continued to describe the events at the ambush on the lower river leading up to their arrival in Cincinnati. Mulling the information over, Johnson concluded he would not know the full story until he had found the Tanners, whom he now believed were innocent parties in the events on the river, or when he had captured the major and sergeant of the spies.

Johnson rose stiffly from where he was sitting, nodding to the two sergeant guards to follow him. They all left and walked down the hall until Johnson stopped and turned to the sergeants.

"I don't think there is any worry about either of those two escaping; they would not get far with Ganiga in the same room."

"There's a possibility they might try to overpower your native for his weapons, sir," Anderson spoke.

"Zero chance of that happening with Ganiga, Sergeant," Johnson replied. "Completely zero."

Just then, the surgeon entered the building with all his medical paraphernalia in his arms. He was followed by an orderly who carried a tray of coffee piled high with meat pies and sweet johnnycakes.

The surgeon pointed to the food-piled tray and said, "Major Simmonds thought you all might be hungry after your grueling day and had his cook prepare you some food."

Johnson nodded to the two sergeants and said, "Help yourselves."

He waited until they had filled their hands with pies and cakes and headed back to their barracks with a "By your leave, sir."

Johnson politely waved them to leave, adding "You did well today. My thanks to you both."

Johnson helped himself to a meat pie and sweet cake. Noting there was quite a bit of food still on the tray, he gave a quizzical look to the surgeon.

"I hear your native has quite the sweet tooth, sir," the surgeon replied politely. "I was hoping some pies and sweet cakes might encourage him to discuss some of his native remedies and potions with me." The surgeon finished with a smile. "I'm quite interested in native plants and herbs for medicinal purposes."

"Best of luck to you, Doctor. Ganiga is an amazing man. When you get past his grunted answers and tough exterior, you will find him to be both articulate and very knowledgeable about many subjects. It's in him to be the best of friends and the worst of enemies. I will tell you he will ask you two questions, and if you can answer them to his satisfaction, you may be rewarded by his sharing the many natural remedies and potions he uses."

"What are the questions?" the surgeon asked.

"One, why do doctors bleed a patient, even when they are already bleeding out from their wounds; and two, why you surgeons so quickly cut men's limbs off when they are wounded?"

"I don't understand the second question," the doctor replied, confused.

"Doctor," Johnson answered quietly, "have you ever seen a one-legged or one-armed native?"

The doctor's mouth dropped like he had been sucker-punched in the stomach. He stammered out, "No. No, I don't believe I have. I've never thought about it."

"Thank you, sir," the surgeon replied. Then he headed down the hall, with the orderly on his heels juggling the laden tray of drink and food precariously on his shoulder.

Johnson stepped out into the cool night air and sat on the steps of the building to eat his food while contemplating the information he had learned this evening. The prisoner's answers had simply brought more questions to his mind and added uncertainty about what his next steps should be. Sighing to himself, Johnson finished his meat pie and wiped his greasy fingers on his leggings. He stood up and began walking to the headquarters building while eating a sweet johnnycake. "Two heads are better than one," he said to himself. "Maybe Major Simmonds will have some thoughts on the matter."

Johnson found Sergeant McClure waiting for him at the door to Major Simmonds' door.

"A late night for you, Sergeant."

"Yes, sir," McClure replied. "All in a day's work for sergeants. The major is waiting for you, sir," he said, holding the door open for the captain.

"Have a seat, Marty," the major said as Johnson entered the office. "Well, it's been quite the day." Simmonds opened a drawer of his desk. He produced a bottle of whiskey and two tin mugs, then poured a dram in each. "Tell me what your interrogation produced."

"Thanks, William." Johnson took the mug, downed the whiskey in one quick gulp, and commenced to share the information he had learned from the two prisoners. Scant as it was about the British mission's goals and plans, he was able to surmise fairly clearly that the Tanner brothers were reluctant participants, and not part of the plot.

"We need to pursue these spies and, if possible, capture them alive to ascertain their plan," Simmonds concluded. "Are you up to the chase, Marty? I cannot spare any personnel to assist you as we still have escaped prisoners wandering about the countryside."

"Yes, Ganiga and I will continue to hunt them. He will need another day at least to heal, but I'm sure he will be ready if not eager to continue."

Just then, Sergeant McClure knocked on the door and entered when the major told him to come in.

"What is it, Sergeant?" Simmonds asked.

"I have some more information about the events this afternoon, sir," McClure replied. He continued, "Several people report seeing the Tanners and a stranger in the company of

Mary Murphy this afternoon. She disappeared shortly after the gun battle and hasn't been seen since."

"Is this Mary Murphy a suspect, Sergeant?" Johnson asked.

"No," Simmonds and McClure said collectively.

"Mary is a well-known favorite visitor, popular with all the officers' wives and families on the post," Simmonds said in a favorable tone. "A widow this year, she and her husband have been very active amongst our Irish and Scots community. You can be sure she has nothing to do with any British spies, soldiers, or anyone British."

"Well, I think I would like to visit her tomorrow; she may have some useful information."

"Yes," the major replied. "Take Sergeant McClure with you; he knows where to find her." In a grim voice he added, "After tomorrow's execution of the spies at dawn."

Recognizing an order when he heard it, Johnson simply nodded as he rose from his chair. "In the morning then, sir."

Chapter 26

Spurred by the vicious gunfight raging in the town behind them, Travis and Squib ran into the forest, dodging and weaving amongst the trees while constantly looking back over their shoulders for any sign of pursuit. Soon they found the side trail to Mary's cabin. With a cautious eye behind them, they continued up the main trail till they found a dry streambed. Leaping from rock to rock, they worked their way back through the woods, concealing their tracks until they rejoined the cabin trail some distance below the junction. Their passage was hidden to the untrained eye. Disdaining caution, Fidious bounded ahead to where the trail crossed a large clearing. He lay down, waiting. The brothers remained in the woods, skirting its edge so as not to be caught in the open until they found the cabin path again. They joined Fidious, who was lolling about in the grass. Travis raised his fist, calling a halt.

"Why are we stopping?" Squib asked, perplexed by the sudden halt. "Patrick said to stay out of a fight."

Travis ducked behind a large tree bordering the trail, pointing his rifle the way they had come. "I don't care what Patrick said," he replied angrily. "I'm tired of running. This is a good spot to ambush anyone following. The clearing is wide enough; we can get a couple of good shots at them and still speed-load a third each before they could get close enough to us," Travis added as he snuggled himself into the cover of the big tree's lower shrubbery. Once positioned, he rested his rifle across a large branch and aimed across the rapidly darkening stump-covered meadow.

Squib nodded in agreement. "I'm getting tired of being on the run as well. Your idea of attacking them back there on the river worked pretty well for us. But we should be cautious; they may not fall for an ambush twice. Let's do it." Squib looked back across the clearing and spotted a location a dozen paces to one side with good concealment. "That's a good spot for me over there," he pointed. "How will we know who is friendly and who's not?"

"Well," Travis replied, scrunching his face up in thought, "who might we expect to be on this trail going on into the evening as it is?"

"Mary and Patrick, for starters," Squib replied. "They will be fairly obvious even in the dark."

"And," Travis answered, "Fidious will know them so won't get alarmed."

Fidious perked up his ears at the sound of his name, giving them both his "Time to eat?" face, then he slumped back into rolling in the grass when no food was produced.

"Soldiers. Or them pirates," Squib thought out loud. "The soldiers will be easy to tell with all those fancy uniforms, hats, and equipment. They rattle like a stone in a tin pot everywhere they go. What do we do about them? We can't start a fight with the US Army."

"You're right, Squib." Travis replied. "If it's the soldiers, then we give up."

"No," Squib laughed. "First, we disappear into the forest and lose them in the woods. If we get separated, then we met at the canoe. Only if we get trapped do we give up. If it's those pirates, we shoot them up. I'm going back over to that brush pile, now; cover me. If those pirates show up, you wait for me to shoot first. They will probably duck behind some of those old stumps along the path, hopefully forgetting our rifles far outreach their muskets, and concentrate on me so you can get a few clean shots at them."

Travis agreed "Be careful; you're farther out from my help by being over there."

"I will," Squib replied. "Take Fidious with you. The cover is thinner where I am; he will be more in the open with me."

Travis called Fidious back when he started to trot after Squib. After some cajoling from both brothers, Fidious reluctantly joined Travis and lay down next to him as he had been trained for hunting.

Shortly after sunset, Patrick and Mary walked cautiously into the clearing. Patrick led the way as they moved slowly across the meadow. Squib stayed hidden until they approached his lair in the thicket. He called softly, "Patrick. Keep moving. We will watch your back trail till you're off the meadow."

Momentarily surprised, Patrick and Mary paused and then resumed walking off the trail into the dark woods behind, only stopping when Travis emerged from behind the tree. Fidious joined him then bounded over, looking for Patrick to give him a scratch. Squib, just behind them, stopped and resumed watching behind them.

Patrick smiled at Mary, giving Fidious a scratch behind the ear. "Fidious likes me."

"Doesn't know you," Mary replied coldly.

Suddenly Patrick bent over, clutching his stomach and grimacing in pain.

"Are you hurt?" Squib asked, anxious at Patrick's unexpected outburst in pain.

"I've got a bullet in the guts," Patrick moaned softly and was swiftly cut off by Mary.

"It's not a concern," she announced coolly. Upon seeing the stunned looks on the boys' faces, she added, "He wasn't shot.

He swallowed a bullet, that's all. Nothing some Glauber's Salt won't cure quickly."

"You're all heart, Mrs. Murphy," Patrick moaned, rubbing his belly.

"We can talk back at the cabin," Travis announced quickly. "You can fill us in on what happened in town then. Lead the way. Squib and I will watch our back trail and join you there."

Patrick and Mary silently nodded their heads in agreement and started ahead. Once out of earshot, Travis asked Squib, "What do you make of it? Is Mary still mad at Patrick? You think she's going to shoot him?"

"Beats me," Squib replied. "We'll find out back at the cabin."

The brothers approached the darkened cabin cautiously until Mary stepped out of the shadows to ask, "Anyone following?"

"None that we could see," Squib replied. They all stepped quietly into the cabin and waited without speaking while Mary closed all the shutters and lit a single candle.

"Where's Patrick?" Travis asked. Before Mary could reply, a loud groan sounded from the woods behind the cabin, followed by a louder laugh of elation from Patrick.

"I think Mr. O'Hara is rid of his ailment now," Mary announced.

A moment later, a pale and shaken Patrick joined them. Travis and Squib had a quiet chuckle together at Patrick's predicament. The seriousness of their situation quickly intervened on the humor of the moment.

"What happened in town then?" Travis asked.

"There was a big gun battle on the docks after you left," Patrick replied. "Several were wounded on both sides. Unfortunately, your pursuers escaped. The Army returned to the fort as there was lots of musketry and cannon fire from across the river. No doubt the Army deemed the defense of the fort to be the main duty and left off any chase of you two or your foes. You can hear it's all quiet now, so they will probably be back at first light to investigate what happened today and start after us all."

"Not all of us," Mary cut Patrick off sharply. "I'm innocent of any wrongdoing here and have nothing to fear."

"Which is why," Patrick interceded briskly, "you boys and I need to clear out as soon as possible so no blame can be laid upon Mary. Mary has suggested I be allowed to accompany you down the river."

"Why?" Squib cautiously asked.

"Patrick knows who these men are, Squib," Mary replied. "He can recognize them and help if you are attacked again, which he thinks you will be. Patrick says their leader is mean and ruthless; worse, he's cunning. Patrick believes he can help turn the odds in your favor if you run afoul of them—"

Travis cut off Mary's explanation. "Wait, Mary. Back in town, you were ready to shoot Patrick. Now you want us to take him with us?"

"How do we know he won't jump us and turn us over to those pirates?" Squib asked, growing more perplexed by this turn of events.

"I know this must be confusing," Mary replied. "Much of what has happened with Patrick was not of his choosing; he has had to do many things to stay alive. Things that I have much trouble understanding, but I believe he's a good man and will help protect you. We have little time to discuss this. You three must get down the river past town and the fort well before the sun rises. Do you accept his help?"

The brothers thought quietly for a few seconds. Squib relented first, giving a small nod to Travis, who replied, "Fidious seems to like him, so we accept."

"Good," Mary smiled, pleased at their decision. She gave first Travis and then Squib a gentle hug.

"All our gear is ready," Travis began. "We only need to load the canoe. Patrick, three in a canoe is an awkward number so you sit in the center. Time your paddle stroke with mine in the bow. Squib is the strongest so he is steersman, timing his strokes to ours on whatever side is needed. Are you clear on that?"

"Yes," Patrick replied. "I've been canoeing quite a bit lately; I know the routine."

Squib cut him off quickly. "We have seen how that group paddles, so pay attention. Travis and I have been in canoes since we were children."

Patrick bit off his reply and just nodded agreement. "Time to go," Mary urged and gave Squib and Travis another hug each.

Turning to Patrick, she held out her hand, which he took cautiously. "Good luck, Mr. O'Hara. May the saints give you peace and forgiveness in your future."

"Thank you, Mary," Patrick replied. He quickly followed the boys out of the cabin with Fidious running at his heels. Mary watched Patrick and Fidious disappear into the dark woods along the river where the boys had hidden their canoe. The brisk winds from the west of early evening had now become the heavier gusts of an approaching evening thunderstorm. The cool night air burdened with the scent of rain was accompanied by the flash and crash of lightning and thunder in the distance.

The first drops of rain spattered amongst the leaves overhead and plip plopped about the river as the three fugitives rushed to load and push the canoe into the water. Closer now, lightning exploded about the horizon in a cannonade of fire that ignited the night sky, signaling the storm's imminent arrival. The rain intensified, splashing harder with greater intensity about the canoe and its occupants.

The Tanners covered the frizzens of their rifles with leather coverings soaked in bear grease called "Cows Knees" to make them water resistant. They carefully tapped tight wood stoppers called "Tampons" (named by the French) into the bore of their rifles to keep the water out. Finally, they removed their broad-brimmed hats, wrapping them over the lock; and they tucked the rifles under their packs to further protect them from the increasing downpour. Patrick looked on in awe and shook his head as he had not planned nor taken any precautions to protect his new rifle. He simply covered the lock with his hat as best he could by placing his blanket roll on top with his pack to keep it from being blown away. He hoped the storm did not get worse. Worse came in full force.

Travis called softly from the bow of the canoe, "We are in for a lively ride tonight. I can see whitecaps on the water ahead. Those lightning flashes will make it more difficult to pass the fort unseen."

"Better for us then," Patrick responded, his voice barely loud enough to be heard over the rising fury of the storm. "Soldiers are the same everywhere. The sentries will have their heads down and backs to the storm behind any cover they can find. They won't be looking much at the river this night."

Squib grunted from behind Patrick, "We've been through worse. Keep your eye on Travis. Stop paddling if he does and keep still when he does. It's movement that gives you away at night."

Patrick, keep quiet, he thought. "Every soldier knows the best way to see movement is out of the corner of your eye, not by looking straight at it, and to keep one eye closed so as not to lose your night vision from a sudden flash of a gun, or on this night, a flash of lightning."

Any further thoughts were forgotten as the whitecaps coming across the water started to break over the bow of the canoe. Travis increased his pace as they all struggled to keep the bow into the wind, staying as close to the center of the river as the wind would allow while avoiding being sighted from the fort ahead. Brief sparkles of light from the fort appeared and disappeared in the distance as the lamps on the dock and the gatehouse behind bounced about with more lamps being blown out by the wind. The darkness about the fort increased.

The three paddled furiously now with no concern to the noise of their paddles as the wind howled about them, masking all sound from their passing with its screeching squalls. Paddling for their lives, the canoe slowly pushed ahead into the storm. Had they been paddling up the river, the storm would have been too powerful for them to resist, but with the added assistance of the current, they were slowly drawn downstream.

Cincinnati lay dark, hidden by the raging wind and rain. The occupants huddled in their homes, most seeking sleep or sitting behind closed storm shutters to keep the sight and sound of the furious storm hidden. The brothers and Patrick felt confident they would slip past the town and fort unseen. The danger now was that this part of the river was new and unknown to them with all the perils of unfamiliar waters compounded by the storm. The dangers were further exacerbated by the knowledge that Torrens' group had fled downriver and could be anywhere ahead — either hiding from the storm on the shore or paddling in flight. Torrens' group could even now be alongside them somewhere, invisible in the storm. Burdened by their weapons and soaked buckskins, the risk of being thrown into the river by crashing into another boat was extreme and would be the death of them all. Soon the small streams pouring into the river would be swollen from the runoff from the storm carrying logs and debris into the river. The flotsam of the storm created the potential for a collision that would rip through the fragile fabric of the bark canoe and sink them as sure as any cannon shot would.

Vaguely, Travis remembered Mary mentioning a large creek emptying into the Ohio below Cincinnati some miles from the town. The risk of passing the creek without damage was too great. Travis tapped his paddle twice on the canoe gunwale to signal to Squib, who was steering in the stern, that they were to head towards the south shore away from the creek ahead. Approaching the shore, Travis watched carefully to keep the canoe on the opposite shore from that of the creek entering the river on the other side while still fighting to maintain steerage and not get blown into rocks or trees along the shoreline.

The storm gradually withdrew to the east and the winds started to subside as a new danger presented itself: the current of the river, which was normally a steady flow, now gained strength and began to push them faster and harder towards the shore. Squib expertly held his paddle in the water, turning it so the flat side resisted the water's flow to slow the boat. Alternating the strokes, he could give the paddle a strong J stroke to push the bow left or right following Travis' hand signals. Long ago, they had agreed the bowman would silently signal the direction they would go by lifting one finger of the top hand on his paddle for right and two fingers for left. Many times, they had used hand signals to silently stalk game on the shore. Squib watched carefully now as the darkness was almost complete and Travis' signals needed his full attention. Along the shore the sounds of water splashing and rushing over the rocks and obstructions sounded warning. Time slowed as the occupants of the canoe constantly fought the raging currents and dodged drifting debris and rocks as the storm hurtled down the river. Finally, the night grew quieter as the storm disappeared into the distance with only the occasional lightning flash silently reflecting off the bottom of the clouds on the far horizon. The normal night sounds of the river returned. As the wind stilled, they heard the gentle lapping of waves on the shore and soothing sounds of water splashing and dashing about the canoe. After being carried a dozen miles down the river, Travis signaled a landfall ahead and softly braced his paddle against the gunwale to push them off the rocks. They finally pulled into a protected cove and drifted quietly onto a soft sand beach of a small island.

Travis leapt from the canoe and held it steady on the sand while Patrick staggered behind him, then Patrick took over holding the canoe while Travis drew the tomahawk from his belt and headed quietly into the trees to scout the island.

Finally, able to relax a bit, his arms aching from the force of their frantic paddling, Squib realized he was soaked from sweat and cold rain. Squib looked down at Fidious who had remained fast asleep at his feet through the entire trip, curled into a tight ball for warmth. Squib chuckled softly to himself. Not so bad, a dog's life, he thought. Squib held the paddle braced into the sandy bottom, ready to give the canoe a mighty thrust backward should Travis signal they needed to make a hasty exit back into the river.

Travis returned shortly, signaling it was safe to stay and disembark their gear. First came their rifles, which the brothers quickly and efficiently dried, cleaning the flints and frizzen of old priming and loading new dry powder ready for action should they require them. The canoe was pulled onto the edge of the forest and turned over to provide shelter for their gear from any further rain. Squib pointed at himself, then with two fingers at his eyes, signaled he would take the first watch while the other two rested.

Fidious had already begun to root around the island. He joined Squib later when his wandering about had proven their lair for the night was safe.

Dawn came slowly, the heavy rains and winds from the storm were replaced by a deep damp stillness broken only by the constant soft sounds of hundreds of drops of water splashing merrily off branches, leaves, and driftwood onto the forest floor. Patrick stirred from his short yet heavy sleep to the sight of heavy morning fog blanketing the landing in a thick haze, reducing the visibility to a few feet.

Travis appeared from the fog with an armload of dry kindling which he placed behind a pile of driftwood. Their campsite was a sheltered hollow out of sight from the river beyond. In the near distance the river made its presence known only by its gentle gurgling and the distant splashes of fish feeding along the shallow shoreline.

"This fog," Travis whispered, "is perfect for us to remain hidden while we have some breakfast before heading out." Travis began to dig a shallow hole in the sand, adding small pieces of dry kindling to build a fire.

"Won't the fire and smoke signal our position?" Patrick whispered to Travis.

"No, there's no wind," Travis replied. "Any smoke we make will be short-lived and disappear in the fog." Taking a powder horn from his pack, Travis carefully removed the large stopper and pulled out several long strands of dried Spanish Beard which he rolled into a small loose ball and placed amongst the smallest pieces of dry kindling. Using a piece of flint he kept in a small pouch around his neck, he struck it several times against the back of his long knife. This sent red burning sparks into the moss which smoldered then burst into tiny flames as Travis gently blew into it. Holding his hat cautiously over the flames to keep any drips from falling on the fire, Travis began to add to the pile of kindling in the hole. Slowly at first the wood caught the flame burst into a bright smokeless fire as Travis continued to add bigger kindling and branches. Squib joined him, holding in one hand their coffee pot and in the other a large roll of johnnycake dough on a piece of bark. Travis took the pot and placed it on the hotly burning flame as he continued to feed the fire now roaring in the hole. The pot quickly came to a boil. Squib poured a handful of coffee that he had just ground moments before into the pot, allowing it to settle into a vigorous boil for a minute before removing the blackened kettle from the fire where Travis stirred the coffee with a small branch. In the meantime, Squib had placed a spider skillet over the hot coals and thrown a dollop of bear lard on top to melt. The fat melted and sputtered as it grew hotter till Squib gauged the fat hot enough. He picked up the pieces of johnnycake dough to which he added a small amount of cinnamon and raisins, then flattened each piece with the palm of his hand and dropped them into the hot grease. When the dough turned golden, Squib expertly flipped each portion over with the edge of his tomahawk. He fried them further until deliciously golden brown all over. Placing several done cakes on a piece of bark, Squib handed the food to Patrick and began the process again with another batch. Meanwhile, Travis poured a cup of cold water into the coffee pot to make the grounds settle. After pouring a generous splash of maple syrup into three tin mugs, he added the hot coffee and passed around the mugs to Patrick and Squib.

Ravenously the three ate their sweetened johnnycakes, while holding the hot coffee mugs close to their chests allowing the warmth to penetrate their hands and bodies. The food and drinks soon drove away the damp chill from the previous night's adventures.

Squib fried up another batch of the succulent cakes for later in the day. He reserved one batch of the cornmeal mixture and formed it into a ball, rolling it around in the now cooled grease until it was absorbed into the mixture. He held this out for Fidious who gently took it into his mouth, moved away from the camp, lay in the damp grass, and ate.

"You're spoiling that dog," Travis grumbled to Squib.

"Ha," Squib replied. "I've seen you slipping bits and treats to him as much as me, except you're sneakier about it."

"Have to be," Travis laughed, "else he won't eat them knowing you cooked it. I don't understand why you like to cook so much in the first place."

"I don't," Squib replied. "I like to eat, not cook. With those burnt offerings you call cooking, I'd likely starve, so I have to do it myself."

Travis shook his head, finished his cake, then, holding his coffee in both hands, looked over the brim of the cup at Patrick and asked quietly, "What happened between you and Mary?"

Caught unawares, Patrick remained silent until Squib added, "You two were all best friends there one minute then — boom — strangers."

"We know about the British," Travis added. "Squib and I understand you had no choice and have done us right by your recent actions. But was there something bigger after that?"

"We had a falling out," Patrick replied reluctantly.

"About what?" Travis asked, his tone cold and unwavering. "We have agreed to take you with us. That gives us a right to know."

"I guess you do," Patrick replied. "As you know, Mary and I are both Irish. We lived through the same famines, cruelties and injustice that the British imposed on Ireland. Pushed to our limits Ireland rebelled. We tried to gain our freedom from the English and lost. We lost everything: our freedom, our culture, our language, and for many, their lives. The English passed the Penal Acts forbidding us from anything and everything that made us Irish. We were forbidden from owning land, forbidden from voting, forbidden from attending our church, forbidden from speaking our own language and forbidden from wearing the color green. If we were caught doing any of those things, the English soldiers would throw a rope around our necks and pull us up from the nearest tree. Men and women both.

"Mary indentured herself to escape not from Ireland as much as British rule. She met her husband and they escaped from Nova Scotia and came to America to escape the tyranny of British rule. To start life over in America. To be free. To experience liberty. I, however, did not. To sustain myself, I became a poacher, hunting the king's deer and game for my own food, and selling or trading it with others as impoverished as myself. Unfortunately, I was caught. Since the war with the

French had been going on for so long, recruits for the Army were getting to be few, and I was given a choice: I could go into the Army or I could hang. I chose life. And that's where Mary and I disagreed. She believed joining the English was akin to siding with the devil. She could not, in her heart, forgive me. She felt I had not done the right thing. 'The right thing,' she said. What is right for me, or anyone else for that matter, may not be right for all of us. Oh, sure, I could have refused to be recruited and been hanged on the spot. Would there be anyone who would say 'There hangs Patrick O'Hara; he did the right thing'? No. Would any of my kin, if they were still alive, have said, 'That's Patrick hanging there feeding the crows. He stood up to the English. He did the right thing'? No. If you two had not ambushed our party, driving the major to send me overland back to where we ambushed your soldiers, I would still be with them now. Now they can say I did the wrong thing, but for me, it is completely right. I'm for the first time in my life free. I'm at liberty to make my own decisions about what I do with my life. Right or wrong they are my right or my wrongs, but they are mine." He said, slamming his fist into his other hand, "for this liberty, for this freedom, I will fight. In Ireland to possess this fine rifle would be a death sentence. I see now why your father named your rifles Freedom and Liberty. He understood what those two words really mean." Patrick looked first to Travis and then Squib. "Hurrah for Liberty. Hurrah for Freedom!"

"Hurrah," Travis and Squib answered back quietly, surprised by the ferocity of Patrick's reply to their questions.

Travis spoke first, "We don't know what happened in Ireland, although we do know a few of your countrymen and the Scots who have come to America." Travis stopped speaking suddenly. Squib was silently reaching for his rifle while staring intently towards the other side of the island. Turning his head slowly in that direction, Travis saw Fidious was laid out flat on his belly, ears up, moving his nose up slightly left to right. He was trying to catch a better scent or sight of something in the distance.

Squib whispered to Patrick out of the side of his mouth without turning his head, "Move very slowly and get your rifle. Watch our backs while we investigate." Patrick could see Travis had taken a prone position and was belly-crawling through the underbrush away from the camp. Squib, on his belly, took a position farther to one side, with Travis in sight. Patrick pulled himself backward so his back was to the overturned canoe and he watched in the opposite direction with his rifle at the ready. The early morning fog was steadily being burnt off by the morning sun, with only a few wisps still clinging to the lower, wetter parts of the river valley.

Squib crawled to a small indentation on the forest floor and lay behind a tree trunk where he could see Travis out of the corner of his eye. Fidious held the scent of something and was moving slowly ahead, watching fixedly across the small waterway that separated this island from the mainland on the other side.

Travis came back on his belly, beckoning Squib and Patrick together while keeping his eyes on Fidious still in the woods.

"Something is going on across the channel from this island," Travis whispered. "I can see what looks like the remains of a smashed canoe on the rocks further down the beach. There are tracks and marks in the sand on the other shore that look like a keelboat had been dragged up on the beach. The boats now gone. There's some faint movement on the edge of the woods, but I can't make out what it is. I see some willows swaying and some are jerking back and forth."

"Can we make a run farther out on the river and pass by safely?" Squib asked.

"I don't think so," Travis answered. "The river narrows and turns a corner ahead; we would be in the open to anyone who wanted to ambush us by trying to force our way past."

"That would be a good ambush site for the major's party if it were them," Patrick suggested.

Squib looked back the way they had come earlier and pointed. "The forest at the head of the channel to this island is heavily forested. I could wade the channel, scout down, and see what lies over there."

"I'll go," Patrick said surprisingly.

"Why you?" Travis spoke. "Squib and I are better in the woods."

"Yes," Patrick answered, "but I'm still not inexperienced. Poachers learn very quickly how to move unseen through the forest. And you two are much better shots at a distance, so you could cover me should I need to make a run for it."

"True enough," Travis replied. "I'm for it."

"Me too," Squib added. "Give us a minute or two to find good shooting positions along the shore. If Travis and I see anything threatening to you, we will order Fidious to bark. This will warn you to get out of there fast. A dog's bark won't arouse as much suspicion as a shout, but if we start to shoot, you'll know the jig is up so head upstream and we will try and meet you. Good luck."

Patrick nodded acknowledgment. He checked his rifle to make sure that his powder was dry and his tomahawk and long knife were secure in his belt. Seconds later, he looked up to see that the Tanners had disappeared into the forest.

"Oh Patrick," he said softly to himself, "now what have you done?" Shaking his head at his own impulsiveness, he walked cautiously farther up the island until he found the narrow crossing that looked shallow enough to wade across and was sheltered by forest on both sides, out of view from any observers. Holding his rifle together with his hunting bag and powder horns above his head, he stepped into the cold water. The rushing water pushed against his legs, making the slippery rocks difficult to keep a foothold. After a few steps the bottom turned to sand and he was able to push strongly back against the current to maintain his balance. He crossed the side channel then vanished out of sight into the dark forest beyond.

Squib and Travis watched from their shoreline hideouts, but after seeing Patrick cross the river, they saw no further sign of him. As the minutes ticked slowly by with no further sighting of Patrick, both Squib and Travis began to worry what was taking him so long to move such short distance.

Becoming impatient at waiting any longer, Travis looked over his shoulder at Squib and hand-signaled by pointing across the river and holding his open palm up. Squib gave a small shrug to Travis who signaled back, "Wait." Out of the corner of his eye, Squib saw that Fidious had raised his head and was looking intently across the river. Travis saw it too. He grabbed hold of Fidious by collar to prevent any impulsive movement and gave him the shush command. At first, nothing was visible. Turning slightly away, Travis spotted a dark shape moving cautiously, stalking in the darker part of the woods. Nothing was clear, but there was definitely a possibility that Patrick was moving slowly towards the area where they had noticed the movement earlier that morning. Once again, Patrick disappeared from sight, then, after several long minutes, appeared again. This time he stepped into the open and waved the brothers to cross the water and join him. Travis called quietly to Squib, "Cover me. I'll go first." He started to rise and took his hand off of Fidious' collar to better steady his rifle. Before he could move to stop him, Fidious jumped up and into the river. He splashed and jumped across in great leaps to join Patrick's side. Squib laughed.

"There goes the element of surprise. Might as well be both of us now." Travis and Squib crossed the river together to join Patrick on the beach.

"What did you find?" Squib asked quietly.

Whispering, Patrick pointed to an area of the woods behind a pile of driftwood on the edge of the forest. "There are several people lying on the ground over there. They appear tied up and gagged but able to move some. I think they are still alive."

"An ambush?" Squib asked.

"No, not that I can see," Patrick replied, shaking his head, "But I'd rather have you cover my back while I go for a closer look."

"Alright, go ahead; we will guard here in the underbrush," Travis responded.

With a quick nod, Patrick turned while keeping his rifle aimed forward held at his hip, pointed towards the captives on the river. Travis and Squib watched intently from cover, their rifles cocked and ready for any possible attack.

A few minutes later, Patrick gave the all-clear. He bent down to lift a bound man from the ground into a sitting position before removing a gag from the stranger's mouth and cutting his bound hands and legs.

"Thank God!" the man cried. "Please help my wife and boys; they are tied up behind me over there." Running over to his family, the man began pulling off the ropes and gags while the Tanners and Patrick helped. Shortly everyone was safely untied and sitting in a sunny spot on the beach, trying to warm up after their night bound in the wet underbrush. While shaken and sore, no one was seriously hurt. Squib built a large fire to warm up the family. Travis and Patrick helped them towards the fire as the family stumbled about awkwardly on numb, cold legs. Around the warm fire, they masssaged their legs to regain circulation. Squib ran back to the camp and returned bringing water from the river as well as the johnnycake. The family gratefully gulped down the water and cakes. Soon the family all began to speak excitedly to one another in foreign language.

"You're not Americans?" Patrick asked the man.

"No," he replied. "We are from Denmark. I'm Lars Madsen and this is my wife Ella and sons Eric and Finn." Ella simply nodded at Patrick. It was obvious that she had not recovered from the fear and stress of the previous night. The two boys had their mouths full of johnnycake, so they just waved and tried to smile. "My family doesn't speak English good," Lars said. "But I'm teaching them. I was teacher in Denmark before war. But British come fight us and French come and we fight more. We grow tired of war and go away. Come to America for new life away from war."

"Looks like the war followed you," Patrick replied sarcastically. "What happened here, Lars?" he inquired.

"Last night, during big storm, men came in boat and smash on rocks there." The man pointed to the holed canoe lying on its side on the beach. "I think they see big fire and lose sight in their eyes and not see rocks and crash."

"They crashed into the rocks?" Patrick asked.

"Yes," the man continued. "They very angry at us. They grab us and tie us up. We very afraid. One man, maybe boss man, he say to others 'Kill them.' But another man, he say no. They argue and yell at each other. The boss man he yells that other man will hang. But other man says no again and tells men to leave us alone. He save us and they take our boat and supplies, leave us here to maybe die. But you save us. Thank you."

"Did the men use any names? Or could you describe them in any special way?"

"No," the man replied. "They look like Indians with guns and big knives. The boss man he call the other man who saves us, Sergeant. That only name I hear."

Patrick nodded silently.

"That's your old friends?" Travis asked. Surprised, Lars shrank back in shock and fear.

"Yes," Patrick replied. "That was obviously Sergeant White." Then, smiling kindly at Lars, he explained, "They are not my companions anymore. You're safe; they are gone now."

Just then, Squib returned from the smashed canoe where he had made a hurried inspection.

"We can patch the hole in the bow pretty easily and there are two paddles lying on the beach to use." Looking down at the family, he added, "We will get you fixed up so you can return upriver back to Cincinnati at least."

"We have no money. We have lost everything," the man exclaimed quietly.

"There is lots of work if you look," Travis replied. "It's not the new life you thought you would have, but you're alive and well, so that's a decent start. You will find Americans to be very generous and prepared to help you if you're industrious. Have no fear; your situation is not uncommon in these parts."

"Yes. Yes. Of course," Lars answered reluctantly. "Thank you again."

Leaving the man to explain their situation to his family, Squib and Patrick retrieved the damaged canoe. They pulled it up on the shore. Meanwhile, Travis rummaged around in their supplies until he came up with a pottery jar which he carried over to the fire and placed near the heat to warm up.

Squib called Lars over to his side, and said, "Watch what I'm doing here as you may need to repeat this if the patch starts to leak." The man nodded and watched intently as Squib began to stir the contents of the small pot.

"This is spruce gum. When we warm it, the gum becomes soft and very sticky. While I'm stirring this, grab some burnt wood from the fire and ash. Then grind it up between two rocks until you have a handful." While the man attended to the charcoal production, Squib took a small amount of bear fat from another jar and warmed this on a flat rock next to the spruce gum. He mixed the spruce gum, fat, and charcoal together into a sticky black tar.

Travis handed Squib a roll of birch bark. "There's more wrapped around a spare thwart under the stern. Just about everyone stores spare rolls of birch bark somewhere on a canoe for quick repairs." He probed the hole in the canoe, pulling as much of the old bark back into place while Squib spread the black gum around the edges and over the ripped pieces. Working quickly, a new piece of bark was applied over the hole and held in place till the gum hardened and set. Once the outside gum had set, Squib applied more gum to the inside, covering any loose spots and making the second layer of hardened gum as an inside seal. Finally, Squib applied a large glob of soft spruce gum mixture to a piece of bark and handed it to Lars.

"Here is some extra patching gum should you need any. Just warm it up first."

Travis pointed to the stern and said to Lars, "That's now the bow. Paddle into the current with that end as this end may reopen if pressured too hard. You will have to work to fight the current, but stick close to shore and you should get to Cincinnati later today. Sell the canoe and paddles when you get there and you can get some food with the money to tide you over until you can get some work."

Patrick reached into his bullet bag, pulled out a handful of gold and silver dollars, and gave a half-dozen silver dollars to Lars.

"That's a loan to get you started," Patrick said. "One day I may come back this way and need a grubstake myself." Laughing, Patrick added quietly, "Maybe with a wife and a boatload of children in need of a teacher."

"Thank you again," Lars replied gratefully.

Patrick, noticing the inquisitive looks from the brothers, commented casually, "I collected my back pay before leaving the Army."

"Soldiering pays pretty well, do it?" Travis asked with a sarcastic smile.

"Danger pay," Patrick laughed back.

Turning his attention back to a grinning Lars, Travis asked, "Did you have any weapons?"

"No, not like yours," Lars replied, pointing at Travis' rifle. "Only Amusette, the trader sell us."

"Amusette?" Squib asked inquisitively. "What is that?"

"Big like arm," Lars demonstrated, holding out his arm. "Big hole here," he said, wiggling his fingers. "Fill big hole with chopped up nails and light with flame here," he pointed at his upper arm. "Boom!" He smiled.

"It's a wall gun," Patrick interrupted. "Wall gun or a swivel gun. They came in many sizes and shoot a few handfuls of musket balls like a big shotgun."

"Chopped up nails," Squib grimaced. "That's just nasty."

"Deadly," Patrick replied. "At close range they can knock down a half-dozen men with one shot. Another reason for us to use the range of our rifles and avoid any close in shooting when we catch up to the British."

"Great," Travis replied sarcastically, shaking his head. "Outnumbered and now they have a small cannon. Our trip is being written by Jonathan Swift."

"Ah well, you know. He's a great Irish writer, he is," Patrick said with a smile, earning a sour look from both brothers.

Travis turned back to Lars and commented, "I would say your keelboat was smaller than most from the depth of those drag marks. Was anything about it different, other than having a cannon, so we can identify it over the others?"

"Not cabin, small covered area with roof and mast for sail," Lars replied. "Ella, she paint Danish flag on stern for good luck." Seeing the confused look from Travis he drew a rough outline in the sand and pointed with the stick. "Red there with white cross. You will know; we have seen none like it."

"All right," Travis replied. "You're on your own now. Rest up a bit and you should make it to Cincinnati before nightfall."

"Squib and Patrick," Travis said with determination, "It's time we took the fight to these bloody brutes. I am getting tired of running. Let's end it. Are you in?"

Without hesitation, Squib nodded and said, "Let's do it." Both brothers looked at Patrick.

"I don't want to live my new life running," Patrick replied. "I'm in."

Chapter 27

Captain Johnson stood on the dock and welcomed the morning fog, letting its cool damp crispness cling to him and cleanse him from the morning's events. The execution earlier had left him unexpectedly feeling violated and unclean, even though his only involvement had been to act as a witness. It wasn't the first execution he had seen, but he hoped it would be the last. The previous executions he had witnessed had been less personal and more detached, as they were not anyone he knew or had been involved with in any way. The memory sent cold chills up his spine. He thought of the brave acceptance of his fate by Private Wood who had woken that morning to the death of Jackson during the night from his wounds. Wood faced his fears alone while waiting for the final moment. His only request had been that he not be blindfolded; this request was denied firmly by Sergeant McClure. The sergeant had, in a kindly and almost fatherly way, explained to him that the members of the firing squad had never participated in an execution before. The sergeant believed if the squad was forced to stare into the eyes of the victim, they may be shocked and reluctant to pull the trigger or aim off which could account for a more slow and gruesome death for Wood. Few men can stare into the eyes of man and pull the trigger without compassion or grief over the cold-blooded killing of another human. McClure explained that the firing squad, which was now facing away from him, would be ordered to fire very quickly after the blindfold was put over his eyes.

True to his word, McClure tied the blindfold. While he marched towards the squad, he ordered them to about-turn. He called the orders, "Ready. Present." As he stopped beside the firing line, he called, "Fire." Before the smoke from the combined shooting could clear, he ordered an immediate "about-face" and marched the soldiers off the parade ground with Captain Johnson close on their heels, leaving it to the surgeon to examine the body for any signs of life.

Johnson was roused from his thoughts by Sergeant McClure's arrival along with several privates and a rowboat in tow.

"My apologies, Captain, for keeping you waiting. I thought an extra ration of spirits for the men in the firing squad after this morning's event was needed."

"That's fine, Sergeant," Johnson replied. "I would have thought, however, that they would have needed it before the shooting."

"That they did, sir," McClure replied. "Before and after."

Johnson smiled grimly. "Good work, Sergeant; wish we had the same."

"And myself, sir," McClure answered. "But we have a lovely morning to refresh our hearts and souls on the jaunt across the river."

"Wait!" Johnson cried out, looking around hurriedly. "Where's Ganiga?"

"Ah. Forgot to mention that," McClure responded guiltily. "Your native companion and the surgeon have struck up quite the relationship, it seems. When I went to fetch the good doctor for the execution this morning, he and Ganiga had the infirmary in complete disarray. Ganiga was at the time applying what looked like honey to his sutures."

"Whoa," Johnson interrupted in astonishment. "Ganiga had his wounds sutured by the doctor?"

"Yes, sir," McClure replied. "They were getting along quite famously, laughing and joking like a couple of kids they were."

"This I will have to see for myself when we return from across the river. Let's be off, then, Sergeant, and you can tell me what you know about Mrs. Murphy before I interrogate her."

Once settled in the boat, the crew began to row out into the current. McClure turned to Johnson and began to brief him about Mrs. Murphy.

"The Murphys have been in Cincinnati several years and own some property upriver aways. Mr. Murphy died a while ago from consumption and Mrs. Murphy has held on by gardening, acting as a guest house for travelers, and selling her much sought-after baking in town to travelers and during the many shooting events held locally.

"She is a lovely Irish lady with a ready wit, good humor, and smile to help anyone in need of assistance. She is well-liked by everyone who knows her and would make a very good wife to the right man for sure."

"Sergeant," Johnson replied, "is match-making now a duty of post sergeants, because that's what I think I'm hearing." The captain's comment drew some chuckles from the men manning the oars. In turn, this solicited a sharp rebuke from the sergeant.

"Put your ears to the front and your backs to the oars," McClure ordered.

"Yes, sir." Realizing his error, McClure quickly corrected himself. "No, sir. It's just she's very close to my wife Lizzy and my girls. Being I'm away quite often or kept on the run, they spend time together cooking, gardening, and organizing events about the post."

"Alright then, Sergeant," Johnson replied. "I take it you have a great deal of confidence she has nothing to do with the spies or recent events."

"I'm quite sure, sir. She hates the British, just as every other Irish or Scots person does in this country. She's no spy or sympathizer."

"We shall see, Sergeant," Johnson replied. "I think it best that you introduce us, then leave us alone while I question her."

"Yes, sir," McClure replied glumly.

Captain Johnson and Sergeant McClure walked the mile to Mary's cabin. The sergeant kept up a monologue of the events at Newport barracks in the last year until they arrived at the small meadow that surrounded the small log-built home. Mary was nowhere in sight, nor was there any recent sign of her when they arrived at the cabin door.

McClure knocked on the door, anxiously calling out, "Mary, it's Sergeant McClure. Are you home?"

A faint voice replied from behind the cabin, "I'm out back, Andrew. Come on around."

Captain Johnson said with a cocked eye and slight grin, "Andrew?"

McClure simply shrugged his shoulders, replying, "It's an Irish habit to be less formal with our countrymen." With McClure leading the way, they scurried behind the cabin.

Mary was bent over, facing away from the two soldiers and filling a sack with spotted brown pawpaw fruit. She called over her shoulder without looking, "I thought you might drop by today, Andrew, so I picked some pawpaw fruit for you and the girls to take back with you."

Mary turned and stopped suddenly as she saw Captain Johnson standing next to McClure.

McClure smiled a quick greeting, tipping his Tombstone hat in a polite manner. "Good morning to you, Mrs. Murphy. May I present Captain Johnson of the 39th Infantry at Newport barracks on detached duty here to ask you some questions about yesterday's events."

"Good morning, Mrs. Murphy," the captain said, removing his hat. He nodded politely while holding the hat at his side.

"Captain, is it?" Mary asked with a small smile. "Good morning to you, sir."

Johnson replied, "Excuse me being out of uniform, Mrs. Murphy. I would like some of your time if you please."

"Certainly," Mary replied. "Not often we see officers in Mufti at this base; the general prides himself as running a tight ship, he does. First, will you gentlemen give me a hand and haul these fruits into the shade over by the cabin? Pawpaw does not take the heat well once they have ripened and fallen to the ground. I'll put some coffee on for us."

"No need…" Johnson attempted, but was quickly cut off when Mary interrupted strongly,

"I get few visitors here, Captain; please allow me the pleasure of providing some refreshment while we talk. Andrew, please pull that bench beside the house over into the sun so we can enjoy the warmth after last night's storm. Thank you." Mary hurried off into the cabin, leaving the two soldiers slightly but pleasantly surprised at being on the receiving end of orders.

McClure pulled the bench over as asked then called after Mary in the cabin, "Mary, I have business to attend to in town. I will leave the good captain to ask his questions of you." With a nod and slight smile, the sergeant saluted the captain, adding, "I'll be off, sir, as you previously requested." He turned back towards town singing "Spanish Lady" to himself as he marched briskly away.

"In all my life I never did see
A maid so sweet about the soul
Whack for the toora loora lady
Whack for the toora loora lay."

Johnson shook his head in amusement, then he leaned his rifle against the cabin wall before moving the sack into the shade as asked. He took one of the dark spotted green fruit in his hand, feeling the slightly soft texture with his thumb, and then tested it for a sweet fragrant scent that signified ripeness. "Seems ripe," Johnson said to himself quietly.

"They are quite ripe," Mary said, surprising Johnson as she handed him a steaming mug of coffee and a spoon. "Have a seat, Captain; we don't dwell on formality here on the frontier." Johnson politely remained standing, waiting for Mary to sit first. Mary busily pulled another fruit from the sack, sat down on the bench, and drew a short dagger from her sock. She expertly cut the fruit in half lengthways. This released the sweet fruity scent further. She handed a half fruit to the still standing Johnson.

Surprised, he asked, "Do you always carry a knife in your sock, Mrs. Murphy?"

"Never hurts for a lady to be prepared," Mary replied, holding the knife in her palm for the captain to see clearly. "In Ireland, we call this a Scion. The Scottish call it a Sgian-Dubh or some just call it a Dirk or a dagger."

Johnson smiled. "Any other weapons I should know about, Mrs. Murphy?"

Mary smiled back, and said, "Just my Shillelagh behind the door and my musket over the fireplace."

"A Shillelagh?" Johnson inquired with a grin.

"My deceased husband Colin's, Captain. You need not worry; we are both Americans here and I'm no threat to you at all."

"No insult intended, Mrs. Murphy," Johnson replied politely "Just a soldier's habit to note and mark the presence of weapons."

"Please sit, Captain." Mary pointed to the bench beside her. "I won't bite. These pawpaw are just ripe, and at their best eating."

Johnson sat, placing the coffee down beside him, and he dug a large piece of the soft pulp from the fruit. He spooned it hungrily into his mouth, seed and pulp together. Johnson chewed and swallowed the fleshy sweetness and looked cautiously about where to spit the seed, not sure if that would be the gentlemanly thing to do. Mary noticed out of the corner of her eye his reluctance to spit the seed in her company. She drew back her head and spit a seed, hitting a bucket sitting several yards away.

"Your turn, Captain," she laughed. She took another spoonful of the syrupy pulp into her mouth. Reluctantly, but not wanting to be outdone, the captain took up the challenge and spit his seed at the bucket. He missed, falling far short of the target.

Mary laughed again and fired another well-aimed seed that bounced off the wooden bucket. "Two for me, Captain!" she cried out victoriously.

Johnson smiled politely back at her and fired his next seed harder this time, but it was too fast and cleared the bucket by a foot.

"Hah. You will need to do better than that to beat me!" Mary laughed, then spit another seed to bounce off the bucket.

Johnson let another seed fly and this time hit the bucket square on. "You're in trouble; I've got the range now." He laughed.

Mary shot another seed that ricocheted off the bucket. Johnson retorted with a grunt and his next seed hit just short of the bucket again, much to her merriment.

Laughing like kids, they wolfed down the sweet fruit and spat seeds at the bucket accompanied by catcalls and laughter for some minutes till they couldn't eat any more. Johnson and Mary leaned back against the warm walls of the cabin, enjoying the morning sun's heat and quietly drank their coffee. They listened to the chirp of songbirds, the scratch of crickets in the grass, and the distant gentle murmur of the Ohio tinkling through the forest from behind them.

"Would you like me to tell you about yesterday's events?" Mary asked after a few minutes.

"Please," Johnson replied. "From when you first met the Tanner brothers and this other fellow that was with them. Everything you can remember."

"Yes." Mary began, "The other fellow wasn't with them, but arrived at the same time. His name is Patrick O'Hara, and he is an Irishman who deserted the service of the King of England."

Mary began to slowly recount the events of the previous two days much as a storyteller would tell a tale of adventure. Johnson listened contently, relishing the story told in Mary's lovely Irish lilt. He enjoyed the way her eyes smiled at the gentle happier parts and the way she furrowed her brows when angry or recounting the more serious events. A sense of contentment and peacefulness fell over Johnson and left him not wanting to do more than sit back and listen to her lovely voice uninterrupted by questions from himself. Mary ended her version of the day before and asked Johnson if he had any questions.

"The questions that remain," Johnson replied, "are why these English soldiers here, where are they going, and what is their plan or objective? If this Patrick O'Hara is telling the truth, he doesn't have the answer to those questions either, so that further implies only the two officers have that information which under the circumstances make complete sense. As far as the Tanner brothers are concerned, you have confirmed what we suspected earlier that they are innocents caught up in some game of espionage or treachery, certainly not of their free will or knowledge."

"What will you do?" Mary asked.

"Find the spies before they reach their objective and eliminate them," Johnson replied.

Mary nodded her head sadly, and rose reluctantly to her feet. "The war. The war never ends; does it, Captain?"

"No, it doesn't seem so," Johnson replied quietly as Mary went into the cabin. Johnson sat back against the warm cabin wall and closed his eyes briefly to think if he had missed something or if some bit of information had slipped by him in his conversation with Mary.

The sweet scent of baked spicy apples roused Johnson from his thoughts. As he opened his eyes and looked up at the sun, he realized with a start that he had napped for a few hours.

Mary smiled sweetly and handed him a mug of cool switchel. She also gave him a large bowl containing a huge slice of apple cobbler made with generous portions of apples, raisins, and cinnamon topped with a surgery oatmeal maple syrup crust, all drowned in warm cream.

"You're too generous, Mrs. Murphy," Johnson smiled, accepting the food and drink.

"Not at all, Captain; it's my pleasure," Mary replied. "I've never known a man in this country without a healthy hunger and a sweet tooth."

Johnson took a sip of the switchel, followed by another. "This is quite refreshing. Mrs. Murphy. I don't think I've tasted a switchel like it."

"My own recipe, Captain. A little more honey and less molasses take the bitterness from it."

Hoping to stave off any further discussion of his plans, he pointed to a shed behind the cabin.

"I see some tack and bridles hanging in the back of that shed, Mary. Do you have horses?" Johnson inquired.

"No. Not now," Mary added sadly. "It was Colin's and my dream to raise horses on another piece of land we have ownership of further inland on the Kentucky side of the river. Not something so easy to do for a widow on her own in the backcountry. Are you good with horses, Captain?"

"Horses," Johnson said with a smile. He finished eating his cobbler and washed it down with a last gulp of the refreshing switchel. "Horses are my passion, Mrs. Murphy. My family raised horses on our farm in Virginia. I'd hoped to join my father in running the business. Regrettably, he came down with the fever and died suddenly. I am the youngest son; the farm went to my older brother so as to prevent any discontent amongst the family I was sent off to join the military."

Mary jumped up and clapped her hands in glee, then offered her hand for Johnson to take. "Let me show you the finest piece of Kentucky bluegrass you've ever seen where the strongest and fastest horses in America will one day be raised. We have to climb the hill behind, but we can see it from the knoll above the river. Come with me."

Sergeant McClure contemplated the events that took place on his visit to Cincinnati as he hurried anxiously down the path to Mary's cabin. The captain had asked him to ferret out any additional information from his many contacts pertaining to events the previous day, expecting not much new would be found. What he found instead was a mother lode of information from a Danish family who had been attacked just downriver from the town. The sergeant knew that this news would be both timely and important to the captain's quest, especially concerning the Tanner brothers.

McClure reached the edge of the meadow of Mary's farm. Stopping suddenly, he slid silently into the shade behind a large elm tree, drawing the pistol from his belt as he did so. Everything was quiet. Too quiet. McClure scanned slowly about the cabin area, noting the trenchers and mugs sitting on the bench with the sack of pawpaws still next to the building. The sergeant gaped in disbelief when he saw the captain's rifle leaning against the cabin, an action no woodsman nor seasoned soldier like Johnson would commit intentionally.

McClure carefully cocked his pistol, holding his hand over the frizzen to muffle the sound as it locked; then pointed the pistol in one hand ahead of him, and the other on the hilt of his sword. Remaining in the trees' shade, he slowly began his approach to the deserted-looking cabin. Mary and the captain were nowhere in sight, yet there were no signs of trouble or indications of a scuffle which would have been the case for the captain was not the kind of man to surrender without a fight. Nor Mary for that matter.

A cautious circuit of the cabin revealed no easily visible clues to the disappearance of the two of them. Out of the corner of his eye, he saw a slight trail leading off behind the tack shed into the forest. From the past he remembered Mary had spoken about a trail to a promontory further inland that looked over the river and the green hills on the Kentucky side of the river. Bending down to one knee, he looked close to the ground into the distance and could see a slight trail through the grass showing someone had passed through since last evening's rain.

McClure followed the trace to the shed, stopping every few yards to drop to one knee and peer ahead through the tree trunks. Unexpectedly, he spotted movement further into the woods — mere shadows flicking between the trees. Slowly, so as not to attract attention, he began to aim his pistol forward when he was surprised by Mary's laugh ringing through the woods followed by the deeper voice of Captain Johnson. McClure jumped to his feet and trotted back to the bench by the cabin. He uncocked his pistol and stuck it back in his belt, then assumed a relaxed pose, leaning back with his feet crossed in front of him as if he was sleeping.

No sooner had he become comfortable when Mary called to him excitedly, "Andrew. Andrew! I have the most wonderful news," she cried as she ran across the meadow. "Captain Johnson's family raises horses in Virginia and they may be interested in financing some new horse farms in Kentucky. They have heard Kentucky bluegrass-raised horses are some of the fastest and strongest in the country and want to introduce some new breeds here. I can start my horse farm we spoke about so many times."

Captain Johnson joined Mary, smiling happily. "Mary, as I cautioned, the war will have to end before we can put out a call for financing—" Johnson stopped himself abruptly. "Sergeant McClure and I will not be retired until the war ends as well, so we will have to be patient."

"Patience be damned," Mary retorted happily. "This dream is going to happen. I know it. For the first time in quite a while, I feel it in my bones."

"I hate to interrupt this good news with more somber war news, but I have some information about the town," McClure said. He nodded to the woods so he could speak with Johnson somewhere apart from Mary.

"Excuse me, Mrs. Murphy. The sergeant and I have to discuss his news." Johnson beckoned for McClure to follow him out of earshot. Once they were far enough away, he signaled McClure to begin his story.

Sergeant McClure quickly summarized. His visit to town had produced little new information to be learned, until just as he was about to head back to Mary's, a rider arrived from downriver with information about the attack on the Madsen family the night before. The family were encamped a mile out of town, too exhausted to continue any farther. Sergeant McClure had requisitioned a horse and rode to their encampment to get the details of the attack firsthand. While the Madsens were safe and not seriously injured, they were able to give a good accounting of the attack and their subsequent rescue by the Tanners.

"It would appear, Sergeant," Johnson replied after some thought, "the Tanners are once again innocently stumbling onto the path of these British spies."

"No longer, I think," McClure replied anxiously. "Mr. Madsen said the brothers and their Irish companion have had enough and are going to seek a more violent ending to the spies' progress down the river."

"That is not good, not one bit," Johnson replied grimly. "These spies are trained and experienced soldiers, and the outcome to the Tanners will not weigh to their advantage if they are caught unaware. Remain here while I say our goodbyes to Mrs. Murphy." Johnson turned quickly and returned to find Mary standing waiting for him where they had left her a few minutes earlier.

"The war calls, I take it?" Mary asked solemnly.

"Yes," Johnson replied succinctly, "but there is good news as well. The Tanners have rescued a family that were attacked downriver. They are all well, thanks to the boys helping them. I now believe there is no remaining doubt of any intentional involvement with these British scoundrels." Swiftly he recounted the story of the Madsen family as told to him by Sergeant McClure.

"Sounds like the family may need some assistance," Mary said thoughtfully. "I'll go into town and see if they would like to lodge here with me till they can get back on their feet."

"That would be very kind of you, Mary," Johnson replied warmly. "I'm sure Sergeant McClure will be happy to get the Army to assist you as well."

Mary nodded her thanks, adding, "Comes as no surprise to me about the brothers; they're young lads just out for some fun, exploration, and freedom. Will you be going to their assistance, Captain?"

"I will," Johnson answered. "Thank you, Mary; I had a wonderful time visiting with you today."

"I as well, Captain," Mary replied with a warm smile as she bent and picked up the sack of pawpaw fruit and handed it to Johnson.

Johnson turned to leave. After several steps he stopped and turned back to Mary.

"Mary, may I call on you upon my return to the post when this is all over?"

"I would like that, Martin. I would like that very much."

"Thank you, Mary; I look forward to seeing you again."

Johnson quickly marched over to Sergeant McClure, who waited patiently in the shade of the trees, and handed him the fruit sack. McClure thanked him and asked the captain, "And did she say yes, sir?"

"Yes to what question, Sergeant?" Johnson replied guardedly.

"Why, if you could call on her again, sir."

"Is this a sergeant skill you have or just the best hearing in the country?" Johnson replied, laughing.

"A bit of both, sir; it's why we become sergeants."

Johnson laughed "Well, you're correct, Sergeant. Now we have some spies to catch and justice to mete out so we can help end this war."

Chapter 28

Travis woke with a start. Something had stirred him from his sleep, but he did not know what. All about him seemed quiet. There were no signs of alarm from Squib, who lay just a few feet away; or from Patrick, who was on guard duty on the embankment behind the campsite. Maybe a gust of wind had blown a leaf or some debris on him; he could hear the wind low in the distance blowing through the trees. The wind. The wind woke me, he thought. Wait, there's no wind moving here, he realized. The air sat as still, stagnant, damp, and heavy upon the land with the morning dew as it had when he first lay down to sleep after his guard shift.

Travis turned his head slowly, cautious of sudden movements in the still dark before the dawn. He looked Squib's way. Squib was awake, frozen on one elbow and staring into the distance towards the sound of the wind in the distance as if he were trying to see the sound. Something is wrong, Travis thought.

The sound of the approaching wind increased yet was still faint in the distance. A storm approaching, Travis thought. Unfamiliar sounds came from the forest. At first faint, he could hear the scratching sound of branches rubbing slowly. Then he heard the rustle of leaves, and the crunch of objects landing on the ground. He perceived voices, sharp and keening like insects chirping in the distance. More sounds came now. Louder, more urgent. Shouts and screams like children. Children, hundreds of them their voices raised in terror and fear running through the woods blindly. Children bashing, battering and pounding themselves and the forest in every direction.

Rifle in hand, Travis scrambled next to Squib. Shoulder to shoulder, the brothers pointed their rifles into the dim woods, waiting for the unknown.

"Run. Run!" Patrick yelled as he scrambled down from his lookout on the embankment into the campsite and fell next to the brothers. His body shook; his face white, etched with fear as he grimaced in the dawn's early light. "They are coming for us," he yelled. "They're coming," he repeated frightfully.

"Who?" Squib asked as he pushed up on one knee to better aim his rifle at the crashing and smashing sounds that approached through the woods towards them.

The shrilling, chattering, and screeching grew louder and more intense, surrounding the camp like a ceiling of sound. Voices of fright screamed in the dark, the ground shook, and twigs and leaves began to rain down upon the camp.

"Who?" Squib barked at Patrick. "Who is coming?"

"Banshees!" Patrick cried out. "It's the end of us all. The end is here. The banshees will have us all!"

Suddenly Fidious came flying from the bush, shocking the brothers as he skidded on all fours and came to rest against Squib. His hair stood on end like a giant porcupine. He squirmed into Squib, cuddling under his arm. Whining and shaking in fear, he buried his head under his front paws.

"Patrick!" Travis yelled, grabbing the Irishman by the collar and shaking him. "Pick up your rifle. Guard the flank. No shooting till you have a target," Travis ordered, trying to remain calm.

"There will be no shooting that will kill them," Patrick moaned, but he assumed his position, grimly resolute of their fate.

A hurricane of sound roared around them surrounding the camp in a storm of frightened voices screaming in the dark.

"Banshees. Banshees," Patrick continued to mumble as they came in a tidal wave. From out of the darkness, hundreds of gray ghostly leaping, flying, and jumping shapes collided with the camp, scattering everything in their path. One dark shape hurtled through the air and drove into Patrick with enough force to knock him to the ground, leaving him stunned but unhurt. Dozens more gray shapes careened about the camp knocking gear about, smashing into Squib and Travis, then bounding past into the night towards the river behind.

Squib and Travis turned their backs to the onslaught of gray projectiles while Patrick whimpered, curled up behind a log frozen in fear. Fidious huddled closer to Squib, his whining lost in the roar of the gray shapes flying about them in the hundreds. Abruptly a gray flying shape slammed into Squib and fell stunned to the ground between Squib and Fidious. Instantly Fidious recognized the gray invader and his fear vanished in a twinkling. With a bark of joy, he snapped his jaws onto the creature and held it down with both front paws. Grasping the hide with his fangs he stripped back the skin to feast on the small animal by repeatedly tearing at it till he had greedily swallowed it whole, leaving only a long gray tail hanging from the corner of his mouth until it too disappeared.

"Squirrels!" Travis and Squib cried out simultaneously.

"Squirrels. They're squirrels!" They laughed together. "We're being attacked by squirrels!"

"What?" Patrick asked, still crouched behind his log sanctuary.

"Squirrels," Travis repeated. "Thousands of them. Look Patrick." Just then a squirrel jumped and skittered over Travis' back landing on the ground where it was immediately seized, chewed, and swallowed by Fidious. The hunted became the hunter, as the dog snapped at and missed his next quarry which flashed just inches short of his jaws.

"Fidious is having breakfast. Let's join him," Squib laughed, lunging at a passing squirrel and missing.

Travis jumped about, trying to catch the fast-moving gray speeders with his bare hands coming away empty-handed with each attempt. Together Squib and Travis jumped and scrambled, clawing about, but continually came away empty as the quicker and spry squirrels dodged from their grasp. No sooner did one squirrel dodge their feeble attempts at capture when another was presented and lost.

"We will starve," Squib laughed, "trying to catch one of this lot!" He dove into the dirt and came up empty-handed once more.

"Not to fear, my friends," Patrick proclaimed proudly, holding a canoe paddle in the air. "Remember my story about hurling, Ireland's national sport, and the use of a caman stick to hurl about a ball?"

"Patrick, you have so many stories it's hard to remember every one," Travis retorted as he lunged and missed another fast-flying squirrel. The squirrel leapt away and immediately ran into Patrick's paddle where it was batted unconscious through the air into Travis' hands. Fidious jumped up and snapped at the comatose squirrel, Travis snatched it away before Fidious could reach it. "Get your own," He admonished the dog. A sickening thud sounded as Patrick whacked another squirrel out of the air. Squib and Fidious raced to catch it.

Twirling about, Patrick backhanded another squirrel to Squib who caught it with one outstretched hand, then suddenly lost it as Fidious leapt and stole it from his grasp.

Several more squirrels had fallen to Patrick's skillful paddle technique when Travis announced, "Alright, enough, two each is plenty for us to eat."

"Where are all these squirrels coming from?" Patrick asked.

Travis shrugged his shoulders and replied, "Don't know; I've never seen anything like this before."

"Not where they are coming from that counts," Squib responded in a thoughtful manner, pointing towards the river. "Look, they are all headed south just like the ducks and geese when fall approaches. Maybe it's some kind of migration."

"Like the pigeons?" Travis questioned then answered his own query as he ducked a flying squirrel, knocking it sideways where it quickly dodged a wild swing by Patrick's paddle. "That makes some sense. The waterfowl, pigeons, and even deer move south when winter is on the way. Could be the same here. I'd say from the sounds around us we may be eating squirrels for quite some time. We have another foggy morning today; let's build a fire, Squib. While I dress these fellows out, Patrick, would you get water for coffee? Dawn is on us. Be careful; we have no idea who might be out an' about."

"Don't think anyone is going to hear us with all these squirrels crashing about," Squib retorted as he slapped at several gray rodents trying to crawl up his legs.

Patrick walked to the river accompanied by frenetic critters leaping about him into the water. Taking care to stay concealed in the bushes, Patrick cautiously filled the coffee pot by holding the brim just under the water so as not to draw in any sediment or debris. The river lay in a heavy blanket of fog. Here and there a small wisp of wind revealed squirrels swimming across the river towards the opposite shore accompanied by splashes as more continued to jump into the river. Patrick laughed quietly to himself. "And Patrick, here you have another story no one back in Ireland would ever believe if you told them." Banshees and the attack of the flying squirrels, he would call it. "Squirrels," he murmured with a chuckle, remembering Travis talking about pigeons that would blacken the skies for days and all a man had to do is shoot straight up in the air to knock down a handful. Pigeons and squirrels in numbers beyond counting, how many more wonders await me? America is truly amazing, he thought. Vast forests and waterways populated by animals of every description in numbers beyond counting. All there for the taking to anyone bold enough to take it. "Patrick, you have found paradise!"

Patrick prepared to get up when a dark, silent shape appeared out of the fog, drifting quietly downriver. A keelboat with a small red and white Danish flag painted on it drifted noiselessly within a rock-throw past Patrick heading down the river. In the stern, a steely-faced man with cold dark eyes stared silently at Patrick, his eyes riveted on the Irishman. Neither man moved. Frozen, Patrick kept his head down, counting on his hat to hide his face in dark shadow as he prayed White would not recognize him. Their silent eyes locked on each other as the boat passed slowly by and then disappeared once again into the misty fog.

Patrick let out his breath. Sergeant White, he thought. He had me. With my rifle in the camp he could have had me. Patrick cursed himself for being a damn fool venturing out unarmed.

Patrick started, surprised, as Travis whispered behind him. "Did he see you?"

"Saw me. Looked into my eyes and soul and said nothing," Patrick replied, shaking his head in disbelief. "My hat shaded my face; I don't think he made who I was. They were ahead of us. The ferryman at the falls said they were ahead of us; how did they get behind us?" Patrick asked.

"Don't know. Doesn't matter now," Travis answered flatly. "They're ahead again."

Travis and Patrick slunk back to the encampment where they were welcomed by the smell of three roasting squirrels on skewers over the small smokeless fire. The meat dripped fat and crisped over the hot coals.

Squib was happily feeding johnnycake crumbs by hand to a squirrel that was sitting on the log next to him.

"Taken to feeding the squirrels, have you, Squib?" Travis asked mockingly.

"You never know," Squib replied sheepishly. "We may be eating this little fellow's relative. Could be the compassionate thing to do. He's right friendly, this one."

Just then, Fidious' large black head reared up from behind the log and snatched the squirrel, his jaws firmly latched. He snapped the squirrel in half before he commenced to devour it with several huge crunchy swallows.

"So much for compassion," Travis quipped darkly. "We have bigger problems. The British just passed us on the river. They saw Patrick back there along the shore. Why didn't they do anything, Patrick?"

"I can't say," Patrick replied, shaking his head. "It was only Sergeant White who saw me. The two in the bow were watching the water ahead. I had my head bent down so he may not have been able to recognize me, and he's not likely to start a fight when he doesn't know the odds. Unlike the major, who has a major hate for me." Patrick laughed at his pun and then continued, "One thing that's been going through my head lately is the sergeant acting strangely. Twice I know he has argued openly and challenged Torrens in front of the men. Back up the river that incident when White refused to kill the Danish family is an act of mutiny in any soldier's army. In England, the sergeant would at best be given a few hundred lashes and busted back to private or at worse hanged. It's not proper behavior for loyal sergeants to argue with officers. Something is going on for sure, but I don't know what."

"What about the other men?" Squib asked.

"They are probably confused, scared, and wary," Patrick answered after a moment's thought. "Here," Patrick waved his arm to the forest, "anything is possible. Back in England or with the Army, the men will unquestionably follow the senior officer's orders. That's the way we have been trained. A thousand miles from British territory, with half the command dead or captured and on an unknown mission in hostile territory, well, your guess is as good as mine. The one thing you can be sure of is they are still very dangerous."

"Well, for now, they are ahead of us again, which is where we want them," Travis said, raising his hand and pointing. "The fast water below us in this camp makes it impossible for them to push back upriver to surprise us. The cliffs are a barrier for them to come overland, so we are probably safe from a surprise attack. We rest here and start downriver at nightfall. Agreed?"

Squib and Patrick nodded their heads in agreement.

Travis added, "Fidious will give us early warning if he scents anything." Looking around for Fidious, he spied him lying on his back, fast asleep, with his squirrel-stuffed belly resting against a log.

"Maybe not," Patrick laughed. "I'll take first watch. Owl hoots the warning signal?" he asked tentatively.

"No," Travis replied disgustedly. "Owls are night calls. What's the day call, Patrick?"

"Blue jay," Patrick answered, sounding the blue jay's distinctive warning squawk.

"That wouldn't fool a Shawnee raiding party, but a bunch of British soldiers don't know a squawk from a hoot," Squib replied sarcastically.

Squib waited a few moments while Patrick proceeded to the lookout up the hill. "Travis, I'm still conflicted if we're doing the right thing about that paper in the telescope case. We could have left it back at the fort and been done with it. Nor have we rushed ahead to get to Uncle Wes either. Have you thought about asking Patrick about it?"

Glancing towards the lookout, Travis replied quietly, "Patrick has said repeatedly he doesn't know the reason the British are here and I believe him. We promised to deliver the paper to that General Jackson fellow, but that was before we knew we were going to be hunted and shot at continually. I think our plan still makes the most sense right now. Those

British spies are not about to stop their plans because we have their paper; plus, we are behind them so maybe we can stop them if they try anything they shouldn't. Better yet, we ambush them and end this whole thing once and for all. Patrick is on the up giving us better odds in a fight. He's a good shot and competent woodsman. His help doesn't even the odds against them but we do better with him. We both like him, even though some of his stories seem pretty farfetched; he is fun to have around. I have had no second thoughts on our plan, but I'm feeling you don't like it."

"I'm not keen on killing," Squib replied sadly, "if that's what you mean. But I don't see we have any other means out of this situation. The river flows only one way. Like it not, we are all going the same direction."

CHAPTER 29

Ganiga removed the bandages the doctor had applied to his wounds. He grunted with satisfaction at the speed of which the wounds had begun to heal from the combination of the doctor's stitches, his herbal ointments, and clean bandages. The red swollen gashes were still tender, but showed no signs of putrefaction or worsening symptoms.

"The ferryman sold me some honey for your wounds," Captain Johnson announced as he returned from talking to the river pilot who guided boats past through the falls of the Ohio. "He has quite the collection of goods he has accumulated from keelboats smashed from going over the falls on their own. He's willing to sell for outrageous prices. I'm sure he will make a huge profit from the Army for that chit I gave him for the honey," Johnson laughed. Ganiga didn't share Johnson's humor. He stared back stoically.

"The Army will only pay him the fair market price, not his exaggerated price," Johnson continued, trying to prod Ganiga into seeing the humor of it. Ganiga remained unmoved. He took the honey from Johnson and began to apply it gently to his injuries. He rubbed slowly, letting his body heat melt it into his wounds.

"White man humor," Johnson shrugged, giving up.

"White man humor," Ganiga replied with a straight face.

"Ah, yes," Johnson retorted. "But you like white

man cooking well enough," he announced as he pulled a loaf of cheese bread from hiding behind his back, flashing it at Ganiga just out of his reach. "Freshly baked by the pilot's wife," Johnson teased. "Filled with bacon and cheese, two of your favorite foods."

Ganiga's eyes lit up as he looked hungrily at the golden-brown bread that sprouted bacon tags profusely from its crust. Food was a common topic between the two men as Ganiga believed the two best things the white man had brought to North America were food and guns. He was particularly fond of sugar and cheese, two items with nothing comparable in native foods.

Johnson broke the crispy bread in two and handed half of the still steaming hot loaf to his companion.

As they ate, Johnson continued to explain to Ganiga the purpose for the visit with the river man. "The river pilot saw both parties just a day ago. He guided the keelboat through the rapids and then saw the Tanners in their canoe portage around the falls sometime later in the day. He didn't know anything we don't already know. We are within a day of both, but I'm surprised the Tanners were still behind them. They should have easily outpaced them in their swifter canoe."

"No surprise," Ganiga muttered through a mouthful of the crunchy cheese bread. "Follow, wait for a place to attack."

"We have had this discussion," Johnson replied, tearing off a chunk of bread. "Three against five or six is not good odds. The British are trained soldiers so will put up a lively defense; they are not likely to be caught in the open."

Ganiga shook his head in disagreement. He paused from plucking pieces of bacon from the crust of his cheese bread, popping them in his mouth, and smacking his lips in delight. "Better to attack," Ganiga replied, "ambush, and pull back. Drive them like animals into traps, then destroy."

"You may be right. We don't have a better reason. In that case, we need to pick up our pace and join the Tanners so we can even the odds."

Johnson noticed Ganiga had strung his war bow and placed it in the bow of their canoe with a small quiver of five arrows together with a small clay bowl of freshly made war paint. Johnson looked at Ganiga and nodded towards the canoe, lifting his eyebrows in silent question.

Ganiga ignored the inquiry and stuffed the last piece of cheese bread in his mouth. He jumped up. "More bread first," he mumbled through a full mouth.

"No, you don't," Johnson replied as he stepped in his way. "You will scare that poor woman half to death. I'll do it."

"Get two. Use Army voucher. Cheat poor woman," Ganiga laughed, sitting down again to tend to his wounds.

Johnson stopped and looked back in the canoe. A cold chill shivered up his back as he realized that in the next few days, if not hours, he could be locked in battle with a superior number of proven deadly British soldiers. Ganiga was ready. Am I? he asked himself.

Sergeant White shook his head, mouthing a silent curse to himself. "Damn. That American on the shore resembled O'Hara. His body and clothes were familiar, but as his face was hidden in the shadow of his wide brimmed hat and so I can't be sure. This haze is playing havoc with my vision. If my left eye wasn't so weak, I would have used the sailor's trick John Wood taught us all of alternating between eyes when peering through the fog so as to leave one for when clearer vision was needed. It was probably just some frontiersman. Besides, he thought, O'Hara and his group were behind us, not ahead.

The major has given me the "O'Hara jitters," he thought, seeing Patrick responsible for all the ills that have plagued us of late — from his missing bag of money, the American ambush on the docks in Cincinnati, and anything else that struck the major's fancy that went wrong. His behavior has grown more isolated, angry, and illogical with each passing day. Yesterday's rant was one of the worst. The major suspected O'Hara revealed to the Americans the purpose and destination of our mission. Damn fool still hasn't revealed the particulars of our mission to me or anyone else, so how would O'Hara know? he wondered. The major had confided he couldn't trust anyone but himself to know the plans. it was all big secret for their own safety. To top that off, the major had whispered sotto voce to him the mission was more important than the men; the men were expendable. Expendable, White silently grimaced. The British Army is made up of two parts: the commissioned officers, and the men. Sergeants are part of the men.

White had wanted to yell into the major's face, "I'm one of the men; WE ARE NOT EXPENDABLE." He didn't. Nothing would be served by making the major more distrustful and withdrawn, not to mention endangering his own life in the process.

Look at that fool, White sneered. Sitting hunched over on the deck of the boat cutting up musket balls into quarters to use as grapeshot in their little cannon. He already had a tidy little pile of them set aside so he could pour them into cartridges he had fashioned last night from the pages of the Bible he had scavenged from Wood's abandoned pack. Defacing the Bible had not sat very well with the men or himself; whether devout Christian or superstitious, there were some things that were just wrong and invited trouble.

White snapped his attention to Smith. Stationed on the bow he had just raised his right hand to indicate fast water approaching, then swept it silently left, indicating White should steer away from the shore. The sergeant could see the fog thinning as the fast water created its own breeze that was partially clearing the view into the rapids. A bumpy ride awaited them ahead.

White kicked Tobias, who was sleeping curled up on the deck boards, and signaled him by nodding ahead that he should take a station on the oars. Tobias picked up an oar and nudged Fraser, who was asleep on the other side of him, to take his place opposite him. Within moments, the men were awake, ready to act. These are good men, White thought, smiling to himself. Napoleon was right about the British soldier when he said they were "Fearless warriors led by fools." And right now, the fool was fussing because his little pile of musket fragments was being scattered about as the boat bounced into the white water.

Chapter 30

Night approached, bringing with it a cold wind that blew down the river and signaled an early approach of winter. Orange, red, and yellow leaves blew in the wind and landed on the water resembling miniature boats floating downstream in flotillas of autumn colors. They were joined by the scores of still migrating squirrels jumping and splashing into the river in a torrent of rodents.

Patrick relieved Travis on guard watch by the river. "Squirrels are still coming," he said as he sat down.

"Numbers are dropping off," Travis replied. "Might be settling in for the night."

"The river seems quiet of late," Patrick remarked. "Less boats and people moving down the river."

"Fall is here now," Travis replied. "The rush of new settlers comes spring and summer so they can find land and build before winter. Just a few traders going downstream at this time of year. We have seen no boats at all today. Just us and the British spies and any river pirates."

"Do you think we will run into pirates?" Patrick asked.

"No," Travis replied. "The ferryman back at the falls said they only jump small parties of settlers and easy prey that are incapable of fighting back. They hide out back up the Wabash in caves and only sneak out when they spot easy pickings. Long hunters like us have nothing they want or are willing to die for.

We still need to be cautious, but I don't believe they are a big risk for us."

"Good," Patrick answered, pointing back to the camp with his thumb. "Squib has hot food ready for you back at camp."

"Let me guess," Travis said, "squirrel?"

Laughing, Patrick responded, "I think we will be eating squirrel for a while. He's made a stew with them in a rich, tasty brown gravy poured over cornbread. Has he always been a cook like that?"

"Pretty much," Travis answered. "Ma was a good cook. She could make shoe leather into a delicacy if she had to, and Squib, well, just kind of watched her to see how she did it. And I'm glad for it."

"Me too," Patrick replied. "Get back before your food gets cold. I'll join you when night falls."

Patrick returned to the camp just as Travis finished his last bite of food by wiping a piece of johnnycake with gravy from his trencher.

"I've been thinking," Patrick announced knowingly.

"Oh, that can't be good," Travis fired back sarcastically before Patrick could finish what he was about to say. Laughing, he added, "Alright, what's on your mind?"

"The moon is rising low to the south—" Patrick began, and again Travis cut him off.

"We should paddle on the south side of the river; stay in the shadow of the shoreline and not out in the open moonlit areas. Is that what you were going to say?" Travis smiled mischievously.

"Yes," Patrick conceded. "In addition, this could allow us to pass the British if we overtake them when the moon is low as they will travel closer to the opposite shore tonight."

"Why?" Squib asked.

"Because," Patrick replied, "they will want moonlight to employ their advantage of superior firepower. The major favors double shot muskets for the first volley, and let us not forget they have a cannon as well, giving them a tremendous advantage in a nighttime shootout. I think the reason they are ahead us is they are moored at night, hoping to catch us in an ambush."

"You know them better than we do," Squib replied. "It does explain why they are ahead us."

"Load up," Travis ordered as he began packing their equipment into the canoe. "Come on, Fidious, jump in."

They all laughed as Fidious staggered his way to the canoe and dragged his bloated belly over the gunnel, flopping down on the deck with a loud burp.

The miles passed quickly as the river was smooth and flat without riffles or rapids to impede their journey. Several times the frontiersman slowed cautiously as the river twisted this way and that, seeking to keep to the darkened shores.

The canoe rounded a wide bend in the river when Travis signaled Patrick and Squib to stop paddling. Drifting slowly down the river, they could see in the distance faint movement along the banks on the opposite side of the river. A keelboat appeared to be moored at the headland of a small island. Travis directed the canoe towards the shore and anchored the bow alongside a large log sticking out into the river where they could observe unseen.

Suddenly bright flashes of gunfire extended from the far shore lighting up the night, followed seconds later by the sharp bark of guns being fired one after another. A few seconds passed when a fiery volley of explosions cracked out from the moored keelboat aimed simultaneously towards the beach. The gunmen on the beach continued to shoot at the keelboat at a slow but random pace while the keelboat shooters commenced a steady paced stream of shots evenly spaced one after another at the beach shooters. The bright orange flashes reflected off the water, revealing a boat pulling away from the shore towards the anchored keelboat.

"That's the British in the keelboat," Patrick whispered to the brothers.

"How can you be sure?" Travis asked.

"Count the seconds between their shots," Patrick replied. "Four seconds from one shot to the next. Those are British soldiers firing, rolling volleys."

"Who are they shooting at?" Squib asked.

"Not soldiers," Patrick replied. "Those fellows are shooting too erratically with no unison to their shots."

"Pirates," Travis opinioned. He pointed and said, "that boat is almost halfway to the keelboat. They will be boarded soon."

Abruptly the river was lit up by a huge orange tongue of fiery destruction. The brief flash lit a scene of horror as bodies were thrown into the air, followed by a roar like thunder that rolled across the river echoing from the high banks beyond. Screams of panic and pain sounded from afar as the pirate boat disintegrated in an explosion of torn fragments and disappeared in an instant, leaving the few pathetic occupants floundering in the river.

"Cannon," Patrick said, looking at the brothers.

"Cannon," they both replied together in shock.

"We are not going by them." Patrick pointed at the British who were now shooting deliberately at the few remaining pirates. "That's a perfect ambush site to catch us going downstream. Now you have witnessed why we can't take them on at close range. The cannon gives them a huge advantage over us."

"What do you suggest?" Travis asked sheepishly, realizing his lack of military training. "You're the soldier."

"I think they will pull out before dawn," Patrick replied. "The pirates could spread themselves out in the underbrush during the daylight and then the advantage of the cannon and volley fire will be lost. We should tail them at a distance and look for an opportunity to take them out at our advantage."

Travis nodded his OK, looking to Squib for agreement.

"Agreed," Squib answered. "We pull back and camp on the other side of the river. There will be some angry pirates about on this side."

"Wake up," Squib shook his brother by the shoulder and nudged Patrick. "They're on the move. Just like you said they would be, Patrick."

In the distance, the sounds of pounding wood on rock carried across the river. "Their boat was pushed onto the shore by the current overnight. Half of them are in the water trying to get the boat afloat and back into the current." Squib laughed, pointing through the brush downriver. "Lots of cussing and angry shouting going on. Here's our breakfast while we wait."

Squib passed Travis and Patrick each a large piece of johnnycake with strips of venison jerky wedged between the slices. Patrick hungrily took a large bite of his johnnycake sandwich and smiled in surprise at the tender sweet-savory taste.

"What is this?" Patrick asked, smacking his lips in pleasure.

"I soaked the jerky in a bit of maple syrup and water last night to make it tender and chewy. The johnnycake is from the other day and softened from the maple water drippings," Squib replied, smiling.

"Travis," Patrick mumbled with his mouth full, "when this is over, I'm going to marry your brother."

"You'll have to fight Fidious for the pleasure first," Travis quipped back sarcastically as Squib fed some of their breakfast to the dog.

Squib ignored them both and patted Fidious on the head. "Just jealous," he said, then he turned and looked down the river again. "Finish up. The boat is turned around and they are pulling out. The fog is not so thick this morning. We will be able to see their big boat from a distance and with luck they shouldn't see us."

Morning fog led to blustery cold northern winds ripping autumn leaves from the trees to fly skipping across the river, covering the water in a blanket of multi-hued colors. A few squirrels still braved the cold waters to swim to the far shore. The masses of the previous days had dropped as had the interest of the many predators that now sat torpid with full bellies watching from shore and treetops, too satiated for further chase.

The Tanners and O'Hara easily kept pace with the British keelboat, taking advantage of the turmoil on the water to hide their presence while trailing behind them. Day turned to dusk and still the keelboat kept a steady pace without slowing or making for shore.

Travis turned from the bow of the canoe to speak with Patrick and Squib. "If they don't turn to shore soon, we will have to decide to follow or make for shore ourselves," he said.

"Going to be a dark night," Squib replied, "Cloudy, no moon, and a fickle wind. I venture they will go to shore."

"I agree," Patrick said, then he pointed ahead. "Look, they are making for shore. Paddle to that island on the opposite side of the river. We can camp there and watch them safely out of sight."

They leaned into their paddles, pushing across the current to draw their canoe onto the lee shore of an island. Along an embankment they found a hidden sandy beach shielded by huge piles of driftwood, safe from observation from the far shore. They pulled out of sight behind the debris, dragged the canoe under cover, then turned it over to act as a windbreak. Travis left Squib and Patrick to do a quick scout of the island and watch the British keelboat across the river. He returned to the camp a few minutes later. "They are digging in for the night. The boat is pulled up high on the beach and they have a big fire roaring on the shore already. We are safe building a fire invisible behind all this dead wood; the wind will blow any smoke into the trees. I'll take first watch. Patrick, you next. Squib—"

"Don't worry," Squib interrupted, "I'll get a fire going and some hot food."

Patrick laughed and said, "I think I can take to this frontier life. Lots of adventure, good food, and no one yelling down your neck to do this or that."

Squib laughed back, adding, "Well, since you're celebrating this great life, dig a hole over there and fill it with some small kindling for the fire."

Before sunrise, Patrick joined Squib as he held a lookout watching the far shore. Patrick observed that the British had maintained a large fire burning through the night. Squib whispered, "Cold must be getting to them."

"No." Patrick replied. "We never had a big fire like that. The major was too afraid of being seen. We could barely heat our evening meal and we had cold breakfasts every morning. There is something wrong, but I don't know what."

"Has it been burning that big since you arrived?" Patrick asked.

"No," Squib replied. "it was much bigger a while ago and burnt down somewhat since then. "Oh no!" Patrick moaned and spun around and grabbed Squib by the shoulder. "It's a ruse. Quick, we need to get back on the water; they have pulled up stakes in the night."

Squib and Patrick woke Travis with the news. They loaded their gear into the canoe and were soon paddling furiously towards the fire on the far shore. They slowed down, holding their vessel back from the light of the bonfire so they would not be visible from the shore. There was no sign of the keelboat anywhere on the beach or near it.

Travis shook his head in disbelief. "Do you think they saw us?" he asked.

Squib replied first. "No, our fire was totally hidden. We were too far away for them to hear or see us."

"Pirates?" Patrick asked. "Maybe they suspected the pirates were going to attack and moved before they could sneak up on them at dawn."

"Doesn't matter now," Travis announced with a scowl. "We need to follow them and be extra cautious they don't ambush us. We have to move downriver slower than before as we don't have them in sight to follow. Keep your eyes open for an ambush; they have the upper hand again."

The easy trailing of the keelboat from the day before became a slower stalk as the three of them paddled a zig-zag pattern down the river, trying to keep as far from any obvious ambush sites as possible.

Later that day, the Tanners and Patrick rounded a wide bend in the river. In the distance they could see a narrow channel to the left of a large island and on the right, an elongated sandy beach marking a small point jutting into the Ohio. A river of clear green water merged into the main river flowing downstream.

"That must be the Wabash," Travis said. "It's just as the ferryman described back at the falls."

"Which way did they go?" Patrick asked.

"Probably to the right where the two rivers merge," Squib ventured aloud. "The channel on the left could bottom out. Deeper water will be to the right, draw to that side. The beach will add distance if they are hidden in ambush and gives us room to pass."

Paddling ahead, they crossed the center of the river, leaving the island to their left. Coming around the bend, they caught the faster water in the seam of the river when Travis cried out, "Look out! There are men on the beach over on the Wabash side of the river. Pull left. Pull left." Too late the fast water had taken control over their craft, pulling it into the open water making them visible from the beach. Over a dozen men were arrayed around a beach fire and behind them sat a huge freighter canoe. Bales of supplies were scattered about. Surprised, some of the men turned to stare at the Tanners canoe as it drew closer to their position.

"If those are pirates," Travis announced apprehensively, "we're dead meat."

"Wait," Patrick said with a smile, "I know those men. They are the French-Canadian voyageurs I told you about. They can help us."

"You're sure?" Travis asked skeptically.

"Yes. Yes," Patrick replied as they could now hear some of the voyageurs singing about the fire in the distance. "Land over there along those trees," Patrick pointed excitedly.

Pulling their canoe up on the shore, the brothers and Patrick disembarked and secured the canoe to a tree. Several of the voyageurs left the fireside and walked over, calling, "Irish. Welcome back." Laughing, they waved the others over to join them and soon the brothers found themselves surrounded by a half-dozen of the paddlers all slapping Patrick on the back and jabbering away at him cheerfully in French.

"You speak French?" Squib asked, surprised.

"Not a word, "Patrick replied. "Come on, let's find Jean-Paul."

Surrounded by the laughing voyageurs, Patrick and the Tanners joined the rest of the Frenchmen around the campsite – only seeing at the last moment their grim, unfriendly faces with muskets held at waist height aimed towards them. Taken by surprise the brothers and Patrick found themselves encircled by a dozen men who grabbed them tightly and snatched the rifles from their hands.

"Do exactly as you're told and you will not be hurt," one of the men ordered.

Fidious snarled and barked, lunging at the surrounding Frenchman.

"Hold your dog," a deep, commanding voice ordered from behind the men who now parted to reveal Jean-Paul standing facing them. "Hold your dog, or we will shoot him. Now."

Squib reached over, clutching Fidious by his collar, and held him tight.

"Jean-Paul!" Patrick cried out in shock. "What's going on?"

"Irish," Jean-Paul replied with a thin smile, "this is not a good time for you to be here."

"Why?" Patrick replied, confused. "We are friends."

"It's not you, my friend," Jean-Paul answered with a shrug.

"It's me," a familiar, dreaded voice replied, stepping through the crowd of Frenchmen. "It's me, you traitor," Major Torrens spat out, his teeth clenched in rage as he approached the captives with Sergeant White close on his heels. "Time to pay for your treason, Poacher," Torrens scowled, pulling his long knife from his belt approaching Patrick.

"Stop," Jean-Paul ordered.

"Keep out of this," Torrens ordered. He kept his eyes locked on Patrick's as he drew closer.

"Stop!" Jean-Paul ordered again, waving his hand and pointing towards the major as the voyageurs cocked their muskets aiming in the major's direction. "My men will shoot. Put your knife back in your belt. Now."

Torrens looked about at the grim Frenchmen, and reluctantly put the knife away.

"You are making a big mistake taking this man's side," the major growled.

"I take no man's side but my own," Jean-Paul replied. "We are here to finish our business arrangement, nothing more. Your business with these Americans is yours to settle but not here, not on my beach, not now. When our business is concluded, then you do what you have to do. Not before."

Major Torrens scowled at Jean-Paul then turned to Sergeant White who was standing calmly behind him, leaning on his musket. Torrens nodded to him. White turned towards the river and gave a loud whistle.

"Let's conclude our business, then," the major replied with a sarcastic grin. "Give us our goods and we will be on our way." Just then, the keelboat, which had been hidden farther up the Wabash, drifted into sight propelled by the remaining soldiers who pushed the boat with poles into the shallows along the shore.

"But we will conclude this business on my terms, not yours," Torrens sneered as White gave another sharp whistle and the English boatmen drew their muskets from hiding and aimed them at the Frenchmen on the shore. Private Smith pulled loose a tarpaulin covering the swivel cannon, turning it towards the voyageurs. Its ominous black muzzle was aimed at Jean-Paul and his men.

"Check and checkmate," Torrens laughed haughtily. "You are outgunned. I am in charge here. Lower your weapons."

Jean-Paul nodded slowly, recognizing too many of his men would be killed or wounded in an exchange of gunfire with the determined British. Reluctantly he signaled his men, waving both arms towards the ground for his men to lower their musket barrels.

"Good," Torrens replied, "now we can conclude our business and you lot can be on your way. Bring the goods to me."

Jean-Paul signaled for several of his men to comply. They returned shortly with three large, tightly wrapped bales of material and placed them at the major's feet.

"All appears to be in order," Torrens announced after giving the bales a quick look over. He waved some of his men to come ashore to pick up the bundles.

"Not so fast," Jean-Paul snapped angrily. "There is the matter of the thirty gold reales promised in payment on delivery."

"Yes," the major hesitated awkwardly, "the gold. The gold was lost." Torrens pointed at the Tanners and Patrick. "Lost because of them. They ambushed us up the river and we lost the gold in the river."

"And some good men as well," Sergeant White added.

Trying to free himself, Travis struggled with his captors and yelled back, "You were trying to kill us. We were only defending ourselves."

"You stole from us," Torrens replied. "You are of no importance to us. You should have just surrendered."

"And be slaughtered like you massacred those soldiers in the encampment," Squib countered.

"That was you?" Jean-Paul asked, surprised.

"They were of no consequence as well. We are at war. Men die. Enough of this arguing. The gold was lost because of these hunters; however, we had a gentlemen's agreement and I will gladly give you a letter authorizing the payment of thirty Spanish pieces redeemable from the British Army."

"No," Jean-Paul barked at Torrens angrily. "Our agreement was gold, not a worthless piece of paper. Your goods stay with me till I receive the gold."

"You're in no position to argue!" Torrens laughed. "You give it up or we take it; your choice. Decide now or I end this here." Torrens nodded over his shoulder at Smith who immediately aimed the cannon directly at Jean-Paul. The Frenchman glowered back at Torrens in helpless fury.

"I will pay for the goods," Patrick cried out suddenly. He lifted the money bag from his belt. "I have thirty gold reales; give the cargo to me." Stepping forward, he held the money bag out towards Jean-Paul.

"Thief!" Torrens screamed at Patrick, throwing himself frantically into the Irishman with a sudden body slam throwing Patrick to the ground. Patrick rolled over quickly, catching the major's boot as he tried to stomp into his face, twisting it, and tipping the major off-balance onto his back. Patrick jumped to his feet. Torrens kicked out, catching him hard on the shin slamming Patrick down on his back, stunned, onto the sand. Torrens jumped up and aimed another hard kick at Patrick's face. The nimble Irishman skillfully dodged the kick and followed up with a hard punch into the major's groin, driving the officer to his knees in pain. Torrens lay bent over, clutching his groin. Unexpectedly he ordered, "Smith. Fire. Fire now."

Shocked, every head turned to face Smith in the keelboat as he raised his slow match to the cannon and steadied his aim at Jean-Paul and his men. The slow match was inches from the cannon's touch hole. Smith abruptly lurched once, twice, and a third time, then fell forward with three arrows buried in his side. The sizzling slow match fell from his dead hand into the river.

Patrick looked in surprise as Smith's dead body slipped into the water. Seeing him distracted, Torrens rose to one knee and drove his fist into Patrick's belly. Winded by the blow, Patrick stumbled back as Torrens followed up with two quick punches knocking him stunned to the ground. Torrens fell on Patrick and held him down with his knees while raining a hail of vicious punches to the Irishman's face. With a grotesque grin, Torrens pulled the knife from his belt and held it to Patrick's throat. "I win, Poacher," he gloated, pushing the blade slowly into his neck drawing a thin line of blood. Sergeant White's shadow alerted Torrens to look up. Shocked he watched helplessly as the sergeants tomahawk flashed in the bright sun and smashed into his forehead. The sun faded as the world turned black; Torrens' lifeless body fell back..

White stared down at the dead officer, spit into the sand, and growled, "Bastard."

As he bent down to retrieve his tomahawk, he heard from behind him, "Don't move."

Captain Johnson stepped from the brush along the shore, pointing his rifle at Sergeant White's belly. "Don't move," he ordered again.

Jean-Paul gasped, realizing he had been holding his breath the last few moments. "Welcome, Captain Johnson, my friend," he said sarcastically to Johnson. "Better late than never, eh?"

Johnson shook his head. "That cannon had to be taken out before we could do anything. We saw the result on some river pirates. Nasty business that."

"There was no cannon mentioned in your plan, Captain," Jean-Paul accused Johnson.

"We didn't know ourselves till we saw the carnage done to the pirates," Johnson replied.

"Hmm," Jean-Paul replied, not convinced he hadn't been taken advantage of.

"Who are you?" Travis asked, surprised by Johnson's arrival.

"Captain Johnson," the captain replied. "Those were my men these scoundrels murdered back at the Turtle Creek encampment."

"You knew about these spies and didn't try to stop us?" Travis asked incredulously.

"We have been following you since Cincinnati," the captain replied. "We didn't know why the British were chasing you or where you were going. Not till we ran into Jean-Paul below the falls were we able to intercept you and the spies."

Sergeant White shook his head at the exchange and began to walk towards the keelboat.

"Halt," Johnson ordered.

White stopped, looking at Johnson defiantly. "We still have a standoff here. My men still have their weapons aimed at you and your companions are still unarmed. We are leaving. We have had quite enough of this damned country and we are going home." The soldiers on the boat responded with an outburst of smiles.

Johnson looked to Jean-Paul but his resolute face showed he wanted no further involvement. "You soldiers want to kill each other, you go ahead. We are done here," Jean-Paul announced with a wave of his hand. He nodded to his voyageurs who were holding the brothers. They released the Tanners and returned the frontiersmen their rifles after quickly blowing the priming charge from the flintlocks. Squib still maintained a hard hold on Fidious as the dog tried a quick bite at the departing Frenchmen. As if nothing had happened, the voyageurs began chatting merrily to each other dragging their canoe down the beach to load their gear.

Ganiga arrived on the beach. His ferocious red and black painted face and profusion of weapons brought everyone to a complete standstill.

Jean-Paul looked calmly at Johnson and announced, "Not our business." He waved his voyageurs into the canoe and they pushed off into the river. The voyageurs picked up their paddles and struck up a fast-paced paddling song and soon disappeared down the river.

Sergeant White followed and waved his men to leave.

Johnson shook his head in frustration then capitulated, "Lower your rifle, Ganiga. Let them all go." Johnson pointed at White. "You go. Go back to British territory and don't let me ever catch any of you on American soil again."

Sergeant White chuckled saying, "Not a chance we will ever come back to this accursed country."

"Wait," Patrick called as he struggled to his feet, holding his hand over his bleeding throat. "Why," he asked, "why did you save me?" He pointed to the major's body.

All movement on the beach came to a stop as everyone turned to listen to the sergeant's answer. White froze for a moment then replied, "I'm just a soldier doing my duty. That man was a monster." He pointed to Torrens' lifeless body. "He said the men were expendable, as long as he was kept alive.

The men are never expendable, not the men in my command."
With that, he threw a leg over the gunnel of the boat and pulled
himself in. "Well, what are you all staring at?" he barked at
the soldiers standing open-mouthed in shock. "You want to go
home, or stand about all day? Move."

The soldiers lowered their muskets but kept them handy as
they began to push the keelboat back into the current. Sergeant
White picked up Torrens' pack from the bottom of the boat and
threw it to land next to the major's body.

"Maybe that will have some answers for you," White called
to Johnson.

Travis and Squib had enough. They started to prime their
rifles when Johnson saw what they were doing. He ordered,
"Let them go."

"They tried to kill us," Travis began to argue, but seeing
Johnson's cold hard stare thought better of it. "You're right,"
he replied reluctantly. "We have had enough of them as well."

Travis and Squib joined Patrick.

"Let's see the neck," Squib asked.

Patrick removed his hand and lifted his head. "Bad?" he
asked.

"No," Squib answered, "I've cut myself worse shaving."

"You haven't shaved in years," Travis pointed out.

"I know. My neck was getting so carved up I thought I
ought to quit before I really hurt myself."

Patrick shook his head. "I'm bleeding out and you two are
cracking humor like a Shakespeare comedy." He laughed as
Travis handed him a cloth to hold against his neck.

Travis and Patrick turned away to attend to the wound
while Squib watched the British boat be pushed off into the
current. Squib grabbed Patrick as he passed and asked, "What
does that mean?" He pointed to the departing boat.

"I don't see anything unusual," Patrick replied, confused.

"One of those soldiers was holding his hand out to me with his middle finger raised. Is that a sign?"

"Oh, that," Patrick laughed. "That's an old English sign meaning we are one with you. Whenever you see an Englishman, give him that sign and he will want to embrace you."

"That's rather nice of him," Squib replied naively.

Patrick, barely holding back his laughter, slapped Squib on the back. He pointed to Travis and Johnson who were standing around the bundles left on the shore.

"Are you going to stand there, staring, or are you going to open those bundles?" Patrick asked.

"You don't know what's in them?" Johnson asked skeptically. "You were part of that bunch at one time."

"Not a clue," Patrick replied. "None of us knew. The major never said what our mission was nor where we were going, only that we would find out at the proper time."

Tired of waiting, Ganiga drew his knife and began sawing through the ropes and canvas wrapping of the bundles. "Too much talk," he mumbled as he cut the material away, revealing several large packages wrapped in a layer of wax paper and string. Sliding his knife through the wrapping, he ripped the parcel open, revealing a blue uniform coat. An American soldiers coat.

"What the devil?" Johnson asked as he lifted the coat to examine it. "Current issue. Infantry."

Curious, they opened the bundles and were amazed by what they found. The contents included complete kits consisting of American infantry-issue uniforms with white belts, cartridge boxes, Tombstone shakos and boots.

"Fourteen," Johnson counted aloud.

"Fourteen," Patrick said, shaking his head. "That's how many of us started out on this mission."

"But why?" Johnson asked. "What could fourteen imposters do way out here, miles from the war?"

"Like I said, I don't know," Patrick replied. "It seems the more I know, the less I understand."

Squib and Travis looked at each other. "Now's the time," Squib said.

Travis nodded his agreement removing the telescope case from around his shoulders that he had carried and protected from the day of the ambush upriver.

"We may have an answer for you, Captain," he said, holding the telescope case out to Johnson.

"That's Ensign Keen's telescope," Johnson said curiously.

"It is," Travis replied. "Before giving his life to save ours he told us to deliver this to General Jackson in New Orleans. It's yours now. We had no intention of being involved in any of this. We had planned a canoe trip down the Ohio to do some hunting with maybe a little exploring thrown in, and to join our Uncle Wes in St. Charles."

"Tell them about that scoundrel Woody that started all this mess," Squib interrupted.

"Let me tell this story," Travis replied, peeved at his brother's interruption. "We landed on Blennerhassett Island with the intent to do some hunting and met an old hunter called Woody." Travis continued to recount their experiences of the attempted robbery, the attack on the American camp, the chase leading to the ambush on the river, and subsequent events leading to this day. Occasionally, Johnson and Patrick would stop him to ask questions until, finally, Travis finished. "Ensign Keen wanted us to deliver that case to General Jackson but he said to trust no one. We trust Uncle Wes, and so we sought to meet up with him and see what he thought we should do. We didn't mean to drag so many people into all this."

"That's quite the story," Johnson replied, shaking his head. "You wanted a little adventure, sounds like that's what you got. Let's see what this document tells us."

Carefully, Johnson opened the telescope case, drew out the documents inside, and began to read. Johnson's face showed astonishment and shock turned to anger as he read.

"What we have here," Johnson announced angrily, "looks to be a plot to disrupt the defenses of New Orleans with the murder of a prominent citizen by laying blame on President Madison. This document claims to be an order issued from the President in Washington. An order for the apprehension of two accused traitors, murderers, and pirates by the name of Pierre and Jean Lafitte. They are to be shot as traitors. All their properties and possessions are to be confiscated, and anyone associated with them to be declared enemies of the State and treated accordingly. The Lafitte brothers are very well known and popular members of the New Orleans French community, I have read of them in the recent news from New Orleans. This mission is a devious attempt to inspire a rebellion by the French in Louisiana. Possibly to hide a bigger plot or as a diversion to a large attack? I don't know; I suppose that's conceivable. Even if they could have captured Jean and his brother and shot them as this letter states, what then? The chances of them escaping are almost zero. If even one of them had of been captured and confessed he was an English soldier then the whole plot would have fallen apart. Maybe if everyone died before capture. However, you can lead men into battle, you can't order them to kill themselves."

"Let me look at the major's pack," Patrick suggested, not admitting he had gone through the pack before. "Maybe he left some other clues."

Patrick dumped the pack contents onto the sand and rummaged through them, but found nothing new or different from the last time he looked. "Nothing here," he pronounced after several moments. He then spied the bottle of arsenic and picked it up. "This is very unusual. A bottle of arsenic. Deadly poison. What do you suppose he intended to do with this?" he wondered. "Poison the Frenchman if he couldn't shoot him?"

"That doesn't sound likely," Johnson replied. "Maybe kill himself instead of being captured."

"I doubt that as well," Johnson continued. "He would have had to wait until you were all killed before giving up his own life. Suicide is not something an officer would plan."

Ganiga shook his head in disgust, pointing at Torrens' body. "Kill soldiers after killing Frenchmen. Americans believe Frenchmen kill American soldiers. French people believe Americans kill Frenchmen. Everyone fooled and all kill each other. Good plan."

"He's right!" Patrick yelled out. "Sergeant White said Torrens told him we were expendable. We shoot the Frenchmen, Torrens gives us a gill of happy grog each, and then sneaks away in the confusion. That's it, isn't it!" Patrick screamed at Torrens' lifeless body, kicking him and smashing his rifle butt into his back. "You vile blaggard!"

Squib grabbed Patrick by the back of his shirt and pulled him away, patting him on the back calmly. "Enough of that, Patrick," Squib ordered. "No need for such language or kicking the dead. It's done here."

Johnson sat down and held the paper at arm's length, looking at it sadly. "Ganiga. That's as good a story as I can think of. Looks like we're heading for New Orleans. We need to get there as soon as possible. Christmas in Cincinnati is not in the cards for us."

Ganiga laughed. "Irish woman will wait."

"Mary?" Squib, Travis, and Patrick all said at once in surprise.

Johnson rolled his eyes. "Never tell an Indian a secret," he moaned.

"White man talk too much. Indian listens," Ganiga replied mischievously.

Looking at the Tanners and Patrick, Johnson asked, "Care to join us?"

"No," they replied simultaneously.

"We are headed west," Travis replied solemnly "This country is getting over crowded with settlers and farms pushing out the wilderness and moving the game farther and farther back. We want to see the West while it's still wild and unexplored. We want adventure, not war and politics."

"You?" Johnson asked Patrick.

"No, I'm free. Free for the first time in my life. I'm with Travis and Squib here, going west. Need to keep them out of trouble, you know," he smiled, winking at the brothers.

Washington, April 1815
Octagon House, Temporary Residence
of President James Madison

resident Madison sat quietly and watched as the tall, lean major marched into his office, stopped three paces in front of his desk and executed a crisp salute. The officer's sun-bronzed face and hands bespoke an active field officer, unlike the many florid-faced dandies that frequented Washington since the war ended.

"Major Johnson, reporting as requested, Mr. President," Johnson announced respectfully.".

Madison rose, stepped to the side of his desk, and extended his hand to Johnson. "Thank you for coming, Major."

The two shook hands briefly. The president noted that the majors hand was cool, dry and callused, a far cry from the usual plump sweaty hands common in the halls of the capital.

"Please sit," the president instructed. "First, let me congratulate you on your promotion. General Jackson's report highly praises your efforts and contribution to his command during the engagement at New Orleans."

"Thank you, Mr. President," Johnson replied politely.

"I've requested your presence here today, Major, as I have some questions concerning the events preceding the battle involving the British spies and their mission. I have read your and the general's official reports, but I would like to hear about what happened in your own words. Please describe the events preceding and ending in the spy's elimination."

Johnson took a quick moment to gather his thoughts. He had repeated his report so many times he could speak it almost word for word. The President was looking for something beyond the official report; as yet Johnson did not know what that was.

He began with the attack on his encampment. "My command, stationed at Turtle Creek on the Ohio River, was viciously attacked and massacred in an act of cold-blooded murder by the British" Johnson began his story. For several minutes he continued to describe all the events leading up to the final confrontation and death of the British spy leader.

President Madison sat and listened intently until Johnson was finished. "You have repeated your written report perfectly. What I would like to hear now Major, are your personal thoughts about the events and the people involved. Start with the mission objective. Do you still believe the aim of the mission was the assassination of the Lafitte brothers?"

"Mr. President," Johnson replied, "I had some doubts originally about their mission goals as they sounded far-fetched and unrealistic in the extreme. However, while serving in New Orleans, I met with the Lafitte brothers and their supporters on several occasions and observed their charismatic leadership. The impact of their loss would have seriously jeopardized our efforts to defend New Orleans. More so, an implied American attack on the Lafitte brothers could have caused many of their supporters to turn against our troops and other Americans. Such an event would have been catastrophically detrimental to our defense." Johnson paused for a moment as he realized his comments could be interpreted as criticism of the official view from general command.

Madison nodded thoughtfully before answering, "There are others in the war department who share your opinion. Of greater concern currently, we believe releasing the details of this story now would create distrust of our intentions amongst the Cajuns in Louisiana. We are anxious to put the war behind us and resume our normal trade relations with both France and England. We must move cautiously on both those fronts so as not to be drawn into any further hostilities on the continent." Seeing the confused look on Johnson's face, Madison reached across his desk and tapped his forefinger on a piece of paper. "Just two days ago we learned that Napoleon has fled Elba, returned to France, and is gathering an army".

"I wasn't aware of this news," Johnson replied carefully, "but I'm not surprised. Indeed, many officers of my acquaintance have conjectured that his imprisonment on Elba would be short-lived."

Madison raised an eyebrow, asking inquisitively, "What is your basis for your argument?"

"Napoleon," Johnson replied, "conquered most of Eastern Europe; his armies were some of the most successful in military history — so much so he was able to crown himself Emperor of France. The crown once worn is seldom left to lie unworn."

"True enough," Madison replied, "and this is the reason we have decided that the details of this mission to murder the Lafitte brothers are to be kept a national secret. You and those involved will be credited with eliminating British spies. No mention will be made of the discovered letters and uniforms, or the suspected mission objectives. We believe the British will be content to speculate; we did not discover their intentions and raise no questions in this regard. That leaves yourself and the others named in your report. Can we count on their silence as well?"

"Speaking for myself, Mr. President, I can assure you no details of the assassination attempt will be spoken of by me. I believe the others — Ganiga, the Tanner brothers, and the Irishman O'Hara — have given very little credence to the suspected murder plan and will speak no further on the matter."

"The Frenchman Jean-Paul?" President Madison asked.

"Jean-Paul had left before we opened the bundles of uniforms, and he did not witness my possession of the letters."

"Excellent," the president replied. "I see in the report from General Jackson that you are retiring from the military. What are your plans?"

"I intend to return to Kentucky, Mr. President," Johnson smiled as he replied. "My wife-to-be and I are going to raise horses."

"Horses," Madison replied. "Our growing nation will require many horses as we expand to the West; you have picked a lucrative enterprise for yourselves." Madison stood, prompting Johnson to do the same, and extended his hand. "Thank you for your service, Major. The best of luck in your new endeavors."

Johnson saluted, did an about-turn, and approached the door to leave when he was halted by the President. "One more question if you please, Major."

Johnson turned to face the president who was now standing with his back to him looking out the window. "What about these Tanner lads. What are their plans? Have they headed west to seek their fortunes?"

"No, Mr. President," Johnson replied, smiling. "They seek something far greater than mere wealth and riches."

The President looked over his shoulder and asked, "What treasure would that be?"

"No treasure, Mr. President," Johnson replied. "Adventure. They seek adventure."

"Adventure!" Madison laughed, turning back to the window. Wistfully, he added, "Adventure. Now, that is a far greater treasure."

Author's Notes

Early America

Early settlers were drawn to America for many reasons, including freedom from religious persecution, to escape political oppression, and to avoid economic disasters and the constant war that characterized Europe in these years. Many were reluctant settlers. Slavery existed in many of its vile forms: captured slaves from Africa, convicts and indentured servants from Europe, and Indigenous natives enslaved in their own lands.

These early settlers arrived in a land rich beyond their belief and comprehension. Vast forests of trees of every description and of immense sizes covered the land as far as the eye could see. These seemingly endless woodlands were populated by game animals in a variety and numbers few could even imagine. The thousands of rivers and streams were clear and clean of human contamination with fish in such great numbers they could be harvested simply by dipping a hat into the water.

For the adventuresome, the destitute, and the refugee, the land was there for the taking.

Blennerhassett Island

The brief history of Blennerhassett Island and its notorious owner Harman Blennerhassett reads like a modern spy thriller novel.

The island, located several miles below the present city of Parkersburg, West Virginia, was purchased in 1796 by a wealthy Englishman named Harman Blennerhassett. Harman had fled to America when his involvement with the secret seditious group, the United Irishmen, had been revealed. Some sources claim his real reason was to hide an incestuous marriage to his sister's daughter.

Blennerhassett built an enormous mansion on the property, landscaping it with lavishly designed gardens and lawns. At the time their home was known as one of the largest and most beautiful in America. In addition to the manor house, it was said that several outbuildings contained laboratories where Harman conducted scientific experiments and a large menagerie of animals from Europe and Africa.

The Blennerhassetts stay on their island was short-lived when Harman became involved with the former Vice President of the United States, Aaron Burr, and consequently allowed his island to become the headquarters for a treasonous military force believed set to conquer Mexico and parts of Texas and claim the Louisiana purchase for themselves. President Thomas Jefferson heard of the plot and issued an arrest warrant for Burr, which resulted in the local militia occupying the island and plundering the estate. The conspirators Burr and Blennerhassett fled prior to the militia's arrival but were later captured and imprisoned. The convoluted legal proceedings after their capture are again the stuff of modern mystery novels.

The once magnificent mansion and grounds remained deserted for many years until it was rebuilt in 1984 to become Blennerhassett Island Historical State Park.

No record exists of the fate of the animals held in the island's menagerie, but it would not be surprising to find local legends of mysterious animals roaming the island.

North American Mass Squirrel Migrations

Were it not for the observations of noted early Americans Lewis and Clark, John Audubon, and many other wildlife observers, the casual reader would believe mass squirrel migrations to be fictional. Although the exact reasons for these migrations were not completely understood, researchers suspected squirrel numbers fluctuated significantly each year based upon the availability of food and increases in population. These fluctuations led to several years where food was overly abundant, resulting in higher birth rates amongst the animals until the environment reached a saturation point. When the food sources became insufficient to maintain the population of squirrels, or when severe growing conditions reached a peak, the squirrels would, en masse, migrate south in search of better food availability and less competition.

Records of the first mass migrations date back as far as 1749 when the state of Pennsylvania paid a bounty of three cents per squirrel resulting in 640,000 hides being collected in the first year.

Later, in 1803, Meriwether Lewis observed thousands of these animals swimming across the Ohio River for a period of over a week. His command availed themselves on the abundance of easily obtainable meat.

Later, in 1819, naturalist John James Audubon witnessed a mass migration in progress while floating down the Ohio River as well. He wrote: About one hundred miles below Cincinnati . . . we observed large numbers of squirrels swimming across the river, and we continued to see them at various places... At times they were strewed, as it were, over the surface of the water, and some of them being fatigued, sought a few moments' rest on our long 'steering oar,' which hung into the water... The boys, along the shores and in boats, were killing the squirrels with clubs in great numbers.

The quadrupeds of North America by John James Audubon and John Bachman, Volume 1

By John James Audubon Page 272

Biologists and wildlife managers have estimated that the numbers of animals taking part in these early mass events to be in the hundreds of millions, some researchers claimed numbers reaching over a billion. As America's vast forests were destroyed and turned into farm fields and small woodlots, these migrations diminished significantly and continued to weaken through the twentieth century.

Wamus (Wammus)

The wamus was a frontiersman's buckskin shirt worn long below the waist and cinched tight with a wide leather belt. Handmade, the style often reflected the owner's particular needs or available resources and time he was prepared to spend on the creation of the garment. Early frontiersmen favored a simple buckskin frock with no decoration, but in later generations long fringes (individual pieces were called wangs) were added to the sleeves and legs to assist quick drying of the wamus when it was wet. Elaborate decoration with colored beadwork became more common with the exposure to Indian beadwork as the mountain men moved west.

Dry Drowning or Secondary Drowning

Over recent years there are, on average, 3,500 drownings per year in the USA. Drowning is generally accounted as the second most common accidental death after auto accidents. In eighteenth-century America, drownings were no less common as early settlers and frontiersmen faced repeated dangers of crossing and traveling along the many rivers and water bodies.

Sailors were amongst the first to observe and comment on what is known now as dry drownings, secondary drownings, or the medical term post-immersion syndrome. Symptoms vary from short-term erratic behavior by a person recently rescued from drowning to longer-term unusual behavior culminating in the sudden death of the individual. Sailors have a long history as descriptive and superstitious storytellers whose accounts of these events would ascribe the causes to spirits, demons, or religious sources.

Hurling

Hurling is an ancient Gaelic team sport and the National Sport of Ireland. Play involves two teams of fifteen players each on a playing field similar in size to a rugby field with goal posts at both ends. Each player has a stick called a caman which is similar in appearance to a hockey stick. The caman is used to carry or knock a ball called a sliotar successfully through the opposing team's end zone and drive it to the shelter over the opposing team's goal post.

The game is rugged, some would say brutal, with injuries common as each team fights to gain control over the ball and run it to the opposing team's end zone.

The Importance of Song

The importance of song in life on the frontier is often ignored or given short mention in modern writings. In fact, music in the form of common song was a factor to everyday life in all areas of the colonies. Field workers, laborers, and boatmen would sing the traditional melodies while working, especially when doing so in groups. Many men who served in the military or in local militias would sing while marching in their encampments and hold musical events while on post. The diversity of the music was as great as the diversity of settlers, being common across many cultures and preserved through civilian life as well.

The Irish brought rowdy drinking songs to America such as "Garryowen"; rebel songs from the great rebellion such as "Wearing of the Green"; or more melancholy ballad songs such as

"The Girl I Left Behind Me" or the English version sang by British troops entitled "Brighton Camp".

The Scots brought with them more sorrowful ballads from their highland homes such as "Coming through the Rye", "Greensleeves", and "Barbara Allen".

French-Canadian voyageurs were well known for their talents for paddling the wilderness waters of North America to the accompaniment of songs. Well-known paddling songs include "A La Claire Fontaine", Alouette", and "Aupres de ma blonde".

In the deep South, Spanish colonies provided a mix of music with a Latin flavor reflecting their history that in itself was an exciting mix of the many cultures predating their arrival in America.

The Colonial Gourmet and Frontier Cooking

If we were to believe what we see on TV and in the movies, the American frontiersman could live by sharing a single rabbit spitted on a stick over a campfire. The colonial settler is portrayed as subsisting on a meager gruel of stew or beans spooned sparingly into a trencher with a crust of bread in accompaniment — hardly sufficient nutrition for an early American settler or long hunter spending long grueling days of physical toil and activity.

Nothing could be further from the truth, except under conditions of hardship or famine. A single rabbit would provide little nourishment to a person attempting to survive under the extreme surroundings of the frontier. Americans took advantage of the vast choice of foods available to them. The extensive forests were occupied by immense herds of buffalo, elk, deer, bear, dozens of fish species, and a multitude of water and wild fowl that lived in massive numbers throughout North America. In addition to game, native American foods included corn, potatoes, tomatoes, pawpaw fruit, blueberries, cranberries, and chocolate. Spices were readily available with pepper, ginger, and cinnamon being favored for their availability, abundance, and price.

This enormous abundance of food was cooked and eaten in just about as many ways. Colonists from every country and region in Europe brought their own culinary favorites to the dining table.

Colonists brought cookbooks from their native homes and adapted recipes to the abundance and huge variety of food choices available. The first American cookbook, written by Amelia Simmons in 1796, was the first to be published in all thirteen colonies by an American. The full title reads: *American Cookery, or the art of dressing viands, fish, poultry, and vegetables, and the best modes of making pastes, puffs, pies, tarts, puddings, custards, and preserves, and all kinds of cakes, from the imperial plum to plain cake: Adapted to this country, and all grades of life.*

Jean Lafitte

Jean Lafite and his brother Pierre, were French privateers and smugglers who became famous for joining with American forces during the battle of New Orleans in 1815. Jean and Pierre lived extraordinary lives filled with legendary adventures, escapades and intrigue. Much of their history is shrouded in mystery and intrigue synonymous with their activites living outside the law. When British forces arrived and laid siege to New Orleans in late 1814, they sent an emissary to negotiate an attempt to purchase Lafittes support prior to their attack on the American forces. The British offered the Lafitte's bribes consisting of large tracts land, pardons for all previous crimes, British citizenship, and 30,000 Pounds in cash. A vast sum equal to 2 million in today's dollars. Some sources have even suggested Jean was offered a Captinacy in the Royal Navy. It's not hard to imagine how that would have sat with the Admiralty. The size and scope of these bribes does indicate the degree of importance the British were prepared to commit in thwarting the pirates from aiding the Americans. It would not be difficult to speculate that if the British were prepared to entice the Lafitte's with such large sums of money for their assistance, they may have also planned more deadly countermeasures to keep the pirates out of the battle if the bribes failed. The chaos created by the assassination of the Lafitte brothers would have been tremendously damaging to the Americans defense. Adding the perception the murders were committed by American soldiers acting upon the Presidents specific orders would have been catastrophic to the American forces and ultimately the future of the entire Louisiana territory. Had the British captured New

Orleans on that day in January 1815 history may have taken a different turn from what we know today.

Why did Jean Lafitte ally himself and his crews with the American cause and not accept the rich bribes offered by the British? Given he returned to his previous plundering and smuggling career soon after the wars end he could have just accepted the British bribes and been that much richer. We will never clearly know why Lafitte joined the American forces as the past has proven Pirates like dead men tell no secrets.